I Knew You

Charity Massengale

For permission requests, email the publisher at
theromancebookerypub@gmail.com

Paperback ISBN: 979-8-9923472-0-3

First edition, September 2025

Edited by E&A Editing Services
Cover by Ever After Cover Design

The Romance Bookery Publishing
All rights reserved

For those who never give up hope.

PROLOGUE

Bram | *December 20, 2008*

"**D**racula, think fast!"

I turned at my best friend's voice behind me, just in time to catch the football he threw at my head.

"What the hell, Whit?"

I gripped the ball, my large fingers spreading over the pebbled leather, and threw it back to him from where I stood behind the porch railing. He caught it easily. Whitaker East was the star quarterback at the University of Alabama. Nobody expected anything less.

"Keeping you on your toes." His smile was bright against the darkness as he walked up the driveway full of parked cars. He was holding the hand of his new girlfriend, someone whose name I didn't bother to remember because the position changed so frequently.

Yet it wasn't just Whit and his girlfriend who had arrived at Bentley Clark's Christmas party. Whit's sister Julianna trailed behind the couple. I froze at the sight of her. Julianna never showed up at any parties. She was only a year younger than Whit and me, and a senior in high school, but she didn't have a social bone in her body. Her arms were crossed tightly over her torso, her gaze shifting everywhere, her expression dour. My whiskey-tinged breath came out in puffs around me. It was freezing, but she was only wearing a long-sleeved shirt. Where was her coat?

I'd spent half my life living at the East house with Whit, his grandmother, and Julianna. I was familiar with Julianna's mannerisms. I could tell she was uncomfortable.

"Why do they call you Dracula?" Whit's girlfriend asked me when they got closer.

I just stared at her, unamused. I'd come outside for a moment to catch my breath because inside was full of bodies writhing against each other, too-bright multi-colored Christmas lights, the stench of weed and alcohol, and so much noise I thought my ears would bleed. Even outside, I could hear the rock Christmas music echoing throughout the block.

"Because he's out for blood on the field," Whit quipped as they came up on the porch. "Ain't that right, Bram?"

I did not attempt to answer.

"Pretty sure it's because his name is *Bram* like Bram Stoker, the author of Dracula, but whatever." Julianna's mutter went unnoticed by her brother and his girlfriend, but I heard her. I smiled her way, but she averted her gaze, holding herself tighter and shivering.

I took off my jacket.

"Julianna, think fast."

Twill blue flew through the air, and she caught it. She looked from the jacket to me and back again. Whit glanced at the action, ready to say something, but the unnamed girlfriend tugged at his sleeve. "Come on, Whit! My friends are here, and I want you to meet them."

Julianna started to put on my jacket as Whit and the girl-friend walked in the front door. It was obviously smaller than what she needed, and a part of me wished I hadn't given it to her. I didn't want her to struggle with the size.

Alcohol clouding me, I walked up and took the half-on jacket off her completely. A blush swept over her cheeks. I wrapped the jacket around her shoulders, skipping the need for her to put her arms in the sleeves. I brought it together in the front and tugged to make sure she was sufficiently covered.

She looked up at me with her chocolate brown eyes sparkling in the porch light. I took in her heart-shaped face framed by her long, flowing chestnut hair, soft and glossy. Seeing her standing in the dark and cold with the strains of Korn's "Jingle Bells" pulsing in the background was so wrong, it was laughable.

Julianna was shy and quiet, usually hiding inside her books. Her intelligence and wit were unmatched. She was full of emotion, but she didn't let it show too readily, although I thought I was good at reading her. She did not belong at this party.

"Why are you here?"

"Under duress," she said, and her eyes flipped to my lips, and then back up to my eyes. "Whit promised a quick trip to get some pie, and here I am. I had no choice."

I took a deep breath, annoyed at Whit, but selfish enough to be glad Julianna had come. I'd had a secret thing for her for a while, even though I'd tried not to. I didn't want to complicate family dynamics. Yet she was everything I wanted in a girl. I couldn't stop thinking about her, even after Whit and I had left for college. We were home for holiday break, and I wanted to spend time with her. This was the perfect opportunity.

"Does he do this all the time?" she asked, pointing toward the door Whit had disappeared into. "At college? He's barely spoken to me all night. I wasn't trying to be a third wheel. We picked that girl up on the way to pie, which I didn't even get, by the way." She blew out a breath, a gray cloud releasing around her.

"He's figuring things out, I guess." I couldn't think of any other excuse to give for my best friend. "Want to go inside?"

"Not really, but I'm freezing, and I'm sure you are, too." Julianna looked at her feet.

Before I could stop myself, I walked up to her and threw my arms around her, pulling her tight to me. Even though I feigned nonchalance at her closeness, I was trembling inside.

"Better?" I asked.

"Um, what are you doing?" The words sounded curious, but she made no move to extract herself from me.

"Body heat," I replied plainly, as if my actions were natural. "I don't want to be here either. I only came because my dad was on a tangent, and I thought Whit might show up. Didn't know about the new girl, though."

"I don't even know how he met her," she grumbled.

I chuckled.

The door to the house opened, and out poured Whit, the girlfriend, and two other girls, laughing like something hysterical had just happened. Julianna and I split from each other, and Whit didn't seem to notice we'd been awkwardly embracing.

"Hey man, can you take Julianna home?"

I furrowed my brow at my friend. "Where are you going?"

The girls all laughed among themselves, their voices piercing my ears.

"Taking Amber's friend's home. But then I'll probably go to Amber's. Jules, is it okay if Bram takes you home?"

Julianna's mouth gaped slightly. When it came to girls, Whit did not have much of a brain, but Julianna had no way of knowing this was how he always acted at these parties.

"I've been drinking," I said, grabbing onto my best friend.

"Oh," he said, but was not deterred. "Can Julianna drive

your truck home then? I'll come back and get you in a bit. I don't want her hanging around all this. I don't think she wants to be here, and this is my fault."

He didn't stop to see if I would answer. He ran off with the giggling gaggle of females.

"I want to be shocked, but I'm not," Julianna said when they'd walked away, rolling her eyes. "You can drive me home."

"No, I can't. I've had a few shots, and I don't want to—"

"Are you really that drunk? You look fine," she said with a dismissive wave of her hand.

Was I able to drive? I thought so. If I were stopped, would I be tested? I had no way of knowing. But I knew an advantage when I saw one. She didn't want to be at the party. I wanted alone time with her. The house was close.

"I'm okay. Let's go."

"I'll tell you what happened, just drive around a little bit," Julianna said. She was giving a long tale of Grams' fight with the Christmas tree. I felt a little unsteady with my vision at times, but I was able to manage the drive. Plus, the roads were empty, given it was the dead of winter and late at night.

I forgot how much I missed being in Julianna's presence, and I wanted to keep her talking. So I did as she suggested and pulled the truck onto a back road. I watched her laugh and talk, her southern charm blooming. It was probably why I couldn't recall when a flash of fur jumped into my vision.

Tires screeched, and two hard objects collided.

The distinct smell of rubber filled the air.

A scream tore from Julianna as the truck swerved.

I held onto the steering wheel, trying to regain control.

Trees came straight for us. Flying empty soda cans, gym

shoes, and random small hand tools pelted my skin. Loose papers floated around me. The clear absence of gravity made my body fly uncontrollably, even though I was tethered to the leather seat by my seatbelt.

The belt held like a vise, and I held it out from my chest as much as I could. The truck rolled, seemingly never-ending.

Was this how I was going to die?

I let go of the belt in time for the airbags to deploy all around as the truck landed forcefully. I jolted back to earth as all four wheels met the ground.

We'd landed at the bottom of the steep hill, in a wide ravine. The road was above our heads and to the left. I heard my heartbeat in my ears first.

I reached to my right and felt the solidness of flesh beneath my fingers. It was Julianna, breathing heavily and alive. The moment I realized I was unharmed, I unbuckled my seat belt. "Are you hurt? Can you move?" I asked.

We looked at each other. Julianna was bleeding from her forehead, red rivulets trickling down her nose and chin. "Oh my God, your face."

I grabbed a random T-shirt and dabbed her chin, nose, and forehead, where the blood seemed to originate from.

"Is it bad?" she asked, her voice hoarse.

I leaned closer. It was dark, but a small bit of moonlight lit the truck cabin. I grabbed my phone from my pocket and held the tiny screen up to her face.

"Bram, it's—"

"I swear to God, if you say, 'it's okay,' I will lose it," I stated, my patience on a hairpin trigger.

She stayed quiet as I took in the gash. It needed stitches.

"It doesn't look too bad," I lied. "We gotta get out of here. I don't know what could happen since we hit the gas tank against that tree."

I felt for the lock of her seatbelt and undid it. She moved to open her door.

"Wait! Stay still," I insisted.

I exited the truck and ran to her side. The door was jammed. After a few hard pulls, I was able to force it open and look at Julianna up close. Nothing appeared askew. I gently helped her out of the vehicle, and she fell over onto me.

I pulled her close, taking her weight. "What's wrong?"

"My back. It's probably pulled muscles. I'm sure it's whiplash. I'm fine." Her teeth gritted, and I knew it was something more. We could reassess once we made it up the hill.

I put an arm around Julianna and led us, step by step, up the embankment. It felt like it took forever, but eventually, we came to the empty, dark road where there was no sign of the deer that had darted in front of us. I looked back down the hill we'd climbed up. The truck had cut a large swath through the saplings and underbrush. It was a random detail I'd remember for a long time.

"Should we call 911?" Julianna shook, and her words echoed in the silent darkness.

I looked toward the mangled truck and nodded. Calling for help meant welcoming the authorities. They'd find out I'd been drinking. I'd have a record. Then I'd lose my scholarship. My life was over.

But all of that paled in comparison to Julianna's injuries.

"Yeah. Of course." I took the phone out of my pocket where I had stashed it, and nearly fumbled it in my hands.

"What's wrong?" she asked, but then her eyes went wide as realization dawned.

"We have to call." I ignored her shock.

"Oh my God, Bram. I shouldn't have asked you to drive. I shouldn't have suggested we drive around." Her voice took on a desperate plea. "Isn't there someone we can get a hold of? Whit?"

"You're injured. You need medical attention now," I said, shaking my head. "I wouldn't have driven if I'd thought this would happen. I shouldn't have risked you."

Tears rolled down her cheeks. "There was no way to avoid the deer. It's not your fault."

I flipped the phone open, and Julianna grabbed my arm, but I wretched it away.

"I'm calling the ambulance," I stated definitively.

"Don't!" she cried, grabbing hold of my arm again. "You'll lose your scholarship. I can't live with that." She squeezed my forearm. "What about Whit? You can't leave him alone at college. He's already unhinged. He's not the same as he was. I can feel it, and—"

"Stop," I interrupted, my voice tight.

"Your father will murder you, Bram," she continued, as if I hadn't spoken. Her desperation bled into her tone. "What if he takes it out on you or your mother? Why would you risk that?"

I looked directly into her tear-filled eyes, flailing my arms out to the sides. "Because I'd do anything for you. Anything." My breath hitched, and she froze at my passionate admission.

She opened her mouth as if she were trying to find words, but they would not come.

Without preamble, I pressed my lips to hers. I couldn't think of any other way to show her how I felt and have her believe it. The kiss was anything but tender. When I pulled away, she was stunned, her eyes wide.

I took a deep breath and returned my attention to the phone in my hand. "I have to call."

Her face morphed from shock to anger.

"Then leave," she spat. "Go. Whit left me at the party. You gave me your truck. I lost control. Easy as that."

I shook my head. "That's not a solution," I replied. "How will you explain being out on this road in the middle of nowhere?"

"Leave that to me," she insisted. "I'll call 911. Call someone to get you, someone too stupid to ask questions. If it comes out, I'll say I made you drive and made you leave me."

I shook my head and flipped open my phone again.

"I'll never speak to you again," she seethed as my fingers hovered over the keys. "I'll hate you for the rest of my life if you do this to me, if you risk everything. It doesn't have to be this way."

"Julianna—"

"No! If you care for me, then go. Please go."

We stared at each other in the darkness. The only sounds were the forest rustles and our heavy breaths. Fear had a hold on my mind. Could I leave her? If I did as she said, I might have a chance to walk away unscathed.

"You have too much to lose, and I have nothing to gain. This way, we'll both be closer to winning," she said coaxingly, when she sensed I was internally debating.

I scoffed. "None of this is winning for me." A war played out in my mind, but I knew time was of the essence. Julianna needed help. She was still standing, but slightly slumped. I watched her grit her teeth in pain.

I dialed and handed the phone to her. Her voice sounded garbled in my ears as she talked to the operator. When help was dispatched and locations were given, the operator asked her not to hang up, but she did anyway. She handed the phone back to me.

"It's done. You don't have long." She signaled with her head for me to leave. I closed my eyes.

"I can't do this, Julianna. I can't leave you." It went against every instinct I had. I would face the music. Maybe my Dad would have a way to cover it all up.

"You can and you will."

"Whit will know I left you."

"Whit will know what I tell him," she said plainly.

I ran my hands through my hair, over and over, the tension so tight between us I thought it might snap. Without a word, I collided with her again, my mouth covering hers, my hand splaying across her back gently, holding her up. I funneled my frustration and grief into our kiss, a complex and passionate thing. She acquiesced, but just for a moment, before she pushed away from me.

"No, you need to go. You don't have long. Please."

"I can't." I reached for her again. "I'm crazy about you. And—"

She pushed me, her palms against my hard chest. "We'll talk about it later. Go!"

I knew we wouldn't talk about it later.

"Good girls like you don't end up with assholes like me," I scoffed, the other part of my thoughts unsaid.

Her eyes met mine. I couldn't stand the tears that began to fall down her cheeks. Shame poured over me like scalding water.

I turned into the night and ran down the dark highway. I did not stop or look back.

THE PUTRID SMELL OF WEED AND SWEAT PERMEATED MY SENSES AS I shoved my shivering body into the front seat of the tiny brown Cavalier.

"Shit, man." Billy looked at me from the driver's seat with his glassy eyes and snarling lip. "Looks like someone busted you up bad."

Billy wasn't a close friend. He was a groundskeeper at my parents' estate, someone I would sometimes shoot hoops with when I was home. He didn't ask questions when I asked him to come pick me up on the side of the road. He took my directions and found me.

My chest was tight from the running and the cold. I bet Julianna was more injured than she'd let on. The adrenaline had kept us at a peak, but mine was wearing off. I looked down at my lap, unable to unclench my fists.

"You okay?"

I was broken, but my fight wasn't physical. It was mental.

Julianna begged me to leave her. Threatened me, even. But I knew as sure as I was alive that no excuse would ever justify me abandoning her. I had left her alone. I chose myself over her. Nothing would ever change that.

I closed my eyes.

"I'm fine," I whispered. "Drive."

Billy turned on some hard rock I couldn't be bothered to identify and whipped the small car around multiple curves in the forest. He was moving so fast that it was making me sick.

"Dude, slow down," I demanded, knowing I was taking my anger and worry out on Billy unfairly. Yet, the last thing I needed was another impaired wreck.

"Geez, fine." Billy put on the brakes, and I lurched forward. He resumed at a more leisurely speed. "Grandma poke slow enough for you?"

"Perfect," I muttered and looked out the passenger window.

With every heartbeat, her name ran through my head, followed by definitive thoughts: *Why are you doing this? Why did you leave her?*

I could go back.

My father could disinherit me. Whit might hate me, at least for a while, and I would lose my scholarship. Yet all of it would be bearable if Julianna knew, truly knew, that I cared more about her than myself.

"Stop the car."

Billy slammed on the brakes, and the car halted in the middle of the road. He looked at me with bloodshot eyes.

"Listen, I don't know what's wrong with you, but you're totally killing my buzz."

"Take me back to where we came from. There's something I have to do. I'll make it worth your while." Cash, weed, booze—whatever Billy wanted, I'd find it for him.

He gave me a weird look, but he turned the car around and headed back from where we'd come. I held my breath as new fears assaulted my mind. Had Julianna been keeping the full extent of her pain from me? She had been limping while we argued, and she had let me bear her weight up the hill. How bad was the damage?

Soon enough, we came to the scene.

"Whoa, what's this?"

Billy slowed to a crawl as we approached the flashing lights on the road.

"Let me out here and then get out of here unless you want to be caught with all this smoke," I told him, and he stopped right in the road, some thousand feet or so from the nearest cop car. "And thanks for answering when I called. I owe you."

I didn't have time for a handshake or further words. I unraveled myself from the tiny vehicle and willed my feet to walk toward the lights. I felt the chill of the night in my bones.

There were four cop cars and a wrecker on the scene. A man was making his way down the hill toward the truck. There was no ambulance. No sign of Julianna.

I put my head in my hands, unable to stem the rising tide of emotions overwhelming me. I wanted her to be there still, so she would know I came back for her, but I was too late for all that.

I walked up to the first officer I found, a man in his mid-fifties with a thin mustache and even thinner, gray hair on his head.

"Sir? Where's the girl?" I asked in a rushed inquiry, tapping him on the shoulder.

He turned and looked me up and down, a grimace visible on his sagging face. "Who are you?"

Anger at myself rose inside me, and I tried to get it under control. I didn't want to appear rattled. I wanted to be calm. Resolute. But all I could think of was that they'd sped off with Julianna to who knows where, and I wasn't there with her. She was alone.

My faraway stare must have been alarming because the police officer grabbed my arm, stirring me out of shock. "You okay? Were you in this?" His head tilted toward the accident scene.

I felt exhausted, and my shoulders slumped. I hadn't answered him. His eyes narrowed on me. "Where were you?"

It must have been obvious I'd been in a wreck - my clothes were tattered in places, my appearance was disheveled, and I had Julianna's blood from her head wound on me.

She's gone. I should have been with her.

"I did this," I said, eyes whipping up to face the police officer. "I wrecked the truck. Julianna…"

"That's the girl?" he asked.

I nodded before continuing, "She wasn't driving, if that's what she said. There was a deer, but I was drinking earlier—"

The man's forehead scrunched up. "What? Why would you —if you'd just—are you of legal age?"

"Nineteen," I replied.

He shook his head, looking at the ground. "Dammit. You just outright confessed to a crime, young man. I'll have to take you in. You know that, right?"

"Yes, sir." My voice sounded steadier than I felt. "I'm not —I'm pretty sure I'm sober now. But I had to do the right thing."

The officer nodded, looking somber.

My thoughts and the officer's actions were temporarily halted when a car came around the curve, lights shining onto us. It stopped several hundred yards back, pulling over into the small sliver of grass on the side of the road.

It was my father's Mercedes. To make matters worse, he was driving. Not only was it out of character for him to drive himself anywhere, but he looked determined, too. I saw it in the way he stopped the car, got out of the driver's seat, and opened the door.

He pulled his sports jacket around him and buttoned it at the front before striding toward us. Many people in town said I was a miniature version of my father. He was handsome, to be sure, and that part of the equation felt good. But any other speck of my father that I inherited made me want to obliterate myself.

Even in that moment, when I should have feared his consequence, I hated him. I hated him for every insult he'd ever said to me. All the backhands and pushes into walls. The times I'd watched him hit my mother. Never enough to mar her beauty, but enough to make her feel like a bug under his shoe. I hated that he was never home, never a clear witness to what he did to his son and wife, as he treated us like objects he was forced to put up with.

He ran his hand through his slicked-back hair, and by the time he reached the officer and me, a couple of other nearby officers had made their way over to our huddle.

"Gentlemen. Chief McKay."

I stared at my father, my rage manifesting in a tick in my clenched jaw. He didn't even look my way. He kept his eyes on the chief.

"Ah, glad they were able to get a hold of you, Mr. Winchester. This is your truck?"

"Yes, it's mine. I'll assume all responsibilities and costs for the removal, of course. If you can instruct the wrecker to take it to whatever the nearest shop is, I'd appreciate it."

The chief's skepticism melted into thin air, making me huff

out an exasperated breath. The audacity of my father knew no bounds.

"Of course," the chief said, completely accepting the command, and instructed one of his underlings to make it so.

"Now, I'd like to take my wayward son home..." My father locked eyes with the chief as if telling him something without saying it out loud.

The chief swallowed.

"I can't do that, Mr. Winchester. Your boy here admitted he'd been drinking when they crashed."

"They?" My father's eyes narrowed.

"Yes. Your son was with a girl."

"Julianna East," another deputy volunteered, flipping through papers behind us.

"Yes, Miss East," the chief reiterated. "She was transported to the hospital. The EMT said she was stable."

My father's seething gaze turned onto me. I tried to keep my face neutral. I wanted nothing to bleed through so he could use it against me. The hardness in his expression told me everything I needed to know. This wasn't going to end well.

"We can resolve this amicably, right, Chief?" My father's voice was smooth.

The police chief's face paled. My father put his arm around the man, leading him away from me while talking in his ear. They spoke for what seemed like an eternity. Then they shook hands, hard and fast, like people in business, not like a deadbeat Dad and a sworn officer of law.

The moment my father turned away from the chief, his face transformed from that of a smooth businessman to a dangerous villain.

"Get in the car," he grumbled as he passed me. He would not dare to put a hand on me, knowing I'd fight back. Unable to do anything else, I followed him and got into his car's passenger seat.

He turned the key, starting the engine.

"What did you do?" I asked him sternly, crossing my arms.

"Don't take that fucking tone with me," my father spat as he drove in the direction of the house. "Your disappointments know no bounds, do they? Why did I have to be the one to spawn such an ignorant piece of trash?"

I winced but immediately felt anger tightening my chest. I wanted him to fear me for once rather than me fearing him, but I didn't know how to make that happen. I was at his mercy.

"Aren't you worried if I'm hurt? Or maybe about Julianna..."

"I couldn't give two shits about that girl. And you..." he pointed a finger at me while keeping his eyes ahead, "you deserve whatever injuries you have. So no, I'm not worried. What kind of stunt did you think you were pulling, anyway? Driving drunk?"

"That's awesome, coming from a man who just paid off the police." The words left my mouth before I could filter them.

"You should be thanking me," he said through clenched teeth. He was driving so fast that I closed my eyes to block out my inevitable demise once he lost control. "I should have had your ass thrown in jail. That little exchange cost me ten fucking grand. You left the scene, and then you came back? What the fuck?"

I swallowed, willing my voice to stay calm. Steady.

"Julianna begged me to drive. I was taking her home from a party."

"That's Leota East's granddaughter," my father snapped angrily.

"Yes, Julianna," I replied. "Leota is her Grams."

"Are you fucking around with her?"

"Not yet."

My Dad scoffed. "Well, you won't be. So get that shit out of your head."

"That's not your decision," I muttered, my blood pressure rising again.

"It is my decision, and I say you stay away from her and her grandmother. I don't know what you see in her anyway. She's got the body of a manatee —"

"Don't fucking talk about her like that." My voice was hardened steel, and I wanted to knock him out. But my father did not even flinch. Instead, he switched trajectories.

"Whit's going down a path to success, and I know you have to be around him, but those other Easts? Complete waste of time putting anything into them. I should have reined you in long ago. I let you be around them far too much and their fucking *Leave It to Beaver* life."

"You just hate them because of what you did," I snapped, my tone mocking. "Does the guilt gnaw at you? Do you ever think about how you sold that plant and threw a couple of hundred families in Mill Creek into poverty? Including Grams and Whit and Julianna? You don't like that little reminder of what a piece of shit you are, do you?" I watched as a vein in his forehead began to pulse. Yet I kept on. "Or is it because your only son chose them? Because I'll choose them every time."

He slammed on the brakes, and I lurched forward and to the right, my already tender head hitting the car window.

"Listen to me, and hear me well," he yelled, his voice ringing in my ears. "Get around that girl or her grandmother again, and I will see to it that you never play football again. You'll come back to Mill Creek and work for my businesses, and I will make your life a living hell."

It was my turn to scoff. "You can't revoke my scholarship. That's not up to you."

He laughed then, loud and boisterous. The blood in my veins turned to ice.

"You're so naïve, boy. The only reason you have a scholarship is because of me," he said smugly. "You think you earned that? Do you think you got first string as a freshman in the greatest high school football program because of your little record? No. The only reason you have a scholarship is because of me. I met with the chairman. I paid for the scholarship. I got you where you are. Not you. Me."

My heart plummeted to my feet as his words echoed in my ears, head, and bones. I couldn't feel, I couldn't think, I couldn't speak.

"So yes, you will stay away from Leota East. If I hear a single whisper of you messing around with the East girl, so help me God, I will take everything from you. You've seen what I'm capable of, and it can get so much worse. Don't fuck with me, son."

"Don't you call me that ever again." My booming voice echoed in the car cab. "You've never treated me like a father, and I want to be anything but your son."

His hands gripped the steering wheel, his jaw tight. "You were made from me, Bram Winchester. My blood runs through your veins. There's nothing you can do to change that." His voice quietened. "And don't say one word to anyone about what happened tonight. Julianna was driving. That's the beginning and end of the story."

My burning anger gave way to embarrassment and dejection as exhaustion swept over me. My father had paid for my scholarship. I didn't earn it. I thought I was free of him, but my whole future rested on his shoulders.

He was right. I was nothing. Blinded by the inexperience of youth.

Yet my father couldn't have been more wrong about Julianna. She wasn't a waste of time. She was sunshine, intelligence, and kindness—all things good and bright in the world.

But she was too good for me. She had always been and would always be.

CHAPTER ONE

Julianna | *September 17, 2024*

"Julianna East!" my neighbor's voice shrilled as soon as my tired feet hit the pavement.

I ignored her, heart pounding, letting the desire to flee propel me forward. The warmth of the late afternoon sunlight made it feel like a beautiful day, but it most decidedly was not. I swung my large canvas purse onto my shoulder. But I misjudged its weight, and the force of it made my back twinge. I lost my grip on the handles and could only watch helplessly as the contents of the open tote tumbled onto the ground.

Awesome.

After taking deep breaths and gently rubbing my lower back to ease the burning ache, I bent down and picked up the items. A headache bloomed behind my eyes as I hoisted the heavy box laden with personal effects from my back seat. I shut the car doors with my foot and shuffled toward my townhouse.

I was almost to the door when I heard the same voice behind me, following me. "Julianna! Did you hear me?"

I turned, put on my biggest smile, and met June Callahan's eyes. June was, without contest, the nosiest and most ill-tempered woman in the townhouse complex.

"Hi, Ms. Callahan." My voice was so saccharine, I almost didn't recognize it.

"My word, that's a lot of stuff you're carrying there." Her perfectly coiffed hair didn't move in the wind, a testament to her hairspray. Her fancy designer clothes were perfectly pressed, and her gold jewelry was blinding in the late afternoon sun. How could someone so put together be so sour?

I clutched the box. "It is." My biceps ached, and my nose itched from the dried tear on the tip of it. Not to mention my back was radiating pain the longer I stood and indulged her.

June's arms bent across her bony frame. Her lips pursed thin, and disdain darkened her eyes. "You parked in the wrong spot. I didn't know if you noticed."

I noticed. I didn't care because in a cruel twist of fate, my assigned parking spot was across the lot from the location of my townhouse. It wasn't typical of me to break the rules, but I'd chosen a closer parking spot so I could easily carry my stuff.

"Yes, Kare—June." I bit my lip at the slip-up.

Her eyes narrowed further as I continued. Had she meant for me to walk all my belongings across the lot for no reason?

By the look on her face, that answer was yes.

"I parked in Mr. Richardson's spot. He's on vacation with his daughter's family in Jamaica until Sunday. I'll be back in Siberia tomorrow, don't worry."

I turned and began walking again, effectively dismissing her.

She huffed. "It's against the rules. Just because someone is out of town doesn't mean..." The tip tap of her kitten heels followed me along the walkway. I swung around, maintaining my hold on the box.

She jumped.

"I'm well aware of the rules, June. I'll move from the spot tomorrow."

She crossed her arms tighter and pulled her face into a full pucker.

"Not good enough. You can't just do whatever you want."

I gritted my teeth. June had it out for me since I avoided the Fourth of July celebration that she coordinated for our complex over the summer. A few weeks ago, she'd left me notes about the dead flowers on my front stoop, which had withered in the North Carolina late summer sun. Then, last week, I had a note about how my trash leaked onto the walkway when I walked it to the dumpster.

Today, June didn't know she'd picked the wrong day to mess with me.

"Are you the parking patrol? Why have you been watching me so intently?" My voice sounded sharp and forceful, which was strange. I never spoke assertively outside of work. I continued anyway, "Did someone put you on security detail for the complex? Are you watching me for your entertainment or business? I need to know."

"Well, I've never!" She scoffed and placed a hand on her hip. "Somebody must watch this place. I don't want us to fall into anarchy like over at Summerhill."

I didn't know what fate had befallen Summerhill, but was it worse than June Callahan?

"I'm not moving my car until tomorrow. Now I have to get inside because this is heavy. Have a good evening." I walked away, balancing the load anew, feeling my grip on the box loosening. I hurried faster.

"This is not the end of this conversation, missy!" June shouted as I strained to put the combo into my keyless entry with one finger. She was still standing midway down the walkway when I closed the door with my foot.

I dropped the box on the kitchen bar and silently applauded myself. I'd made it through an unwarranted confrontation with the most annoying person I knew without letting my true emotions show. But the adrenaline and relief fell away, and the tears rose again.

Losing your job would do that to a person. And I was unfortunately that person.

I'd been a marketing specialist at Spalder & Spade Publishing Company for ten years. I'd worked my way up from a lowly part-time intern to the company's social media manager, and clearly, all that hard work meant nothing when a new management team swept in and began to clean house.

I was great at my job. I'd hoped that since they'd started canning people, my abilities would speak for themselves, and I wouldn't lose what I'd worked so hard for. It was the one thing in my life that I felt fully accomplished at. Yet, earlier that day, right when I was gathering my purse and laptop to leave, I was surprised by the sight of the newly hired HR manager getting off the elevator.

I'd never seen HR on our floor. When I spotted a yellow paper and a large envelope in her hands, I knew it was the end for me. My severance package included little compensation, an apology letter I didn't read entirely, and a cardboard box with the company's logo to pack my possessions into.

As I left, I eyed Brenda, the administrative assistant, across the open office. She would likely be replaced next. She was the last remaining employee on this floor from the original staff. I hoped they would spare her. She had four kids and a mortgage. I only had to worry about myself. I rented my townhouse and had no family or pets to support. I had no significant other to consider. All I had was my work, a writing obsession, a reading addiction, rage cleaning, and a bank of trashy television knowledge. It was a simple life, but it was all I needed.

I let loose a sob and bent over the countertop, letting my hot cheek fall onto the cool stone. I looked at the publishing logo on the box full of snacks, photographs, and awards I'd accumulated over my career. Everything I'd worked for was gone, and all that remained was one box of useless crap.

The sound of the code being put into my front door lock made me wipe away the tears falling down my cheeks. Only one other person knew the code to my door, and I couldn't let her see me looking like a wreck. This was not something even a best friend could fix.

As predicted, Kallie walked in without preamble, holding a cake box. She must have had a long day at her bakery because her black t-shirt and dark skinny jeans were covered in flour, and her blond hair was pulled into a bun atop her head, which had long lost its structural integrity. She looked through the open doorway, puzzled.

"Fight with the gigantic stand mixer again?" I asked.

She said nothing at my jab but stared out the open door. "Why is June Callahan standing on her stoop, watching me walk in here?"

I rolled my eyes. "Ignore her."

She closed the door. "What is her problem?"

"Not much has changed since you moved out, except now she's put me in her sights. She accosted me a minute ago about parking in Mr. Richardson's spot while he is on vacation this week. I was carrying this." I showcased the box in front of me like Vanna White.

Her face fell. "So, it's true? I hoped you were joking on the phone." She set her box on the countertop beside mine, walked around the kitchen island, and took me into her arms.

Our hug was awkward. We were very close, so it wasn't uncomfortable to hug, in theory, but we couldn't have been more physically opposite. Kallie was short, slender, and pixie-like. I was tall, curvy, and large. My frame all but swallowed her.

Despite our outward appearances, having someone in my corner who cared about me felt so good. Kallie had been that person for me since we became inseparable in college.

"I'm so sorry," Kallie soothed. I pulled back smiling slightly, but I was swallowing the lump in my throat and trying to keep my tears at bay.

This was another difference between us. Kallie was head-strong and opinionated—the epitome of a tough woman. I leaned heavily into empathy and thoughtfulness, typically only concerned with others. To have someone worry about me was the worst thing I could imagine.

I shrugged a little, softening the moment. "It is what it is."

Yet she saw right through me.

"You're allowed to grieve," Kallie scolded. "Quit acting like this isn't a big deal."

I leaned against the counter. "I don't have time to grieve. I have to scramble to find another job. I was too busy thinking they'd keep me around because of my success. And I did last longer than most."

"You did," she agreed with a nod. She didn't honestly know, though. I hadn't discussed my job much. I felt like a failure next to her, even though I was proud of her. It was a conundrum of emotions that was a hallmark of my personality.

Kallie wetted a dish rag and wiped the flour off her clothing. "How can we search for new leads on a job? This place isn't cheap, and your severance probably wasn't much."

I looked around the townhouse's open concept, recessed lighting, and granite countertops. It was a lovely place. Kallie and I had lived together there for five years, splitting the rent. When she'd decided a few months ago to move in with her new fiancé, Brandon, I stayed. I couldn't stomach moving.

"You would be correct on both accounts. This place is expensive, but also June is driving me insane, so maybe it would be worth a change?" I sighed. "I've got a little in savings. But I have to start searching for a job as soon as possible, and then maybe I can decide about the townhouse." I pointed at the cake, which had a clear plastic window at the top. "What is this?"

"It's my newest creation." Kallie put the rag down and lifted the lid. Staring back at me was the most decadently frosted cake I'd ever seen. My senses were overwhelmed by the scent of chocolate and caramel. "It's a triple-fudge-toffee truffle cake. Something I whipped up this morning. I brought it so you could try it and let me know if it's something I should sell."

I rolled my eyes. "You're the best baker in North Carolina, so of course it's going to be perfect," I mumbled, reaching into the silverware drawer beside me and pulling out a fork. "But I love you for bringing it here." I unfolded the box around the cake reverently. I went straight in with the fork, scooping up an undainty amount of cake and icing and shoveling it in.

Then another.

Then another.

"Verdict?" Kallie held out a glass of milk she'd poured while I'd been attacking the cake. My cheeks bulged, so I took a couple of gulps of milk before speaking.

"Would you be hurt if I admit I didn't taste it on the way down?"

"So hurt," she said sarcastically.

"It's delicious. The icing is creamy, and the sugar is perfectly balanced. Put it on the menu. I'll buy fifty of them right now."

Her smile grew wider. "Awesome. At fifty bucks a cake… you owe me $1,250 plus tax."

I drew my head back in mock surprise. "After I just lost my job?!"

"A girl has to make some money!" She laughed.

I quirked an eyebrow at her. "How did you come up with that figure so quickly, Miss I-didn't-pass-calculus?"

"Hey! College calculus is nothing to joke about." She pretended to shiver. "Gives me chills just thinking about being back there again." She took the empty milk glass from my hand and put it in the sink. "I gotta keep my basic math skills sharp. Those teenagers I hired aren't going to do it for me."

"Isn't that why you have a point of sales system?" I poked her with my elbow as she gave me a tiresome look.

"I know this has to bother you more than you're letting on. You know that if I had the revenue for an extra media person—"

"You aren't responsible for keeping me employed," I cut in, taking another small bite of cake. "I'm upset, but there isn't anything to do. I have to look forward, starting with building a resume, then putting in applications, and all that."

"I know, I know." Kallie grabbed a fork from the drawer to join me. "I wish you'd let me go give that ball-less group of corporate idiots a piece of my mind. They won't sell a thing without you."

I waved my fork dismissively. "I'm sure they've already replaced me with someone just as capable. I only wish I'd thought ahead and left before they canned me. I'm not prepared. I can't imagine how interviews have changed in ten years."

Kallie leaned over the counter, and we looked at each other, forks in the cake.

"You'll find something quick," she said. "But, if you don't, you can always come to the bakery and work with the teenagers. I always need someone to work the register. They draw straws on who will do it because they hate it so much."

"That's what you get for using child labor," I joked.

Kallie and I moved into the living room, away from the cake, and chatted about her employees. She wanted me to discuss my feelings about the job loss, but I declined to do so. I wanted to pretend that life was peaceful and normal for a few minutes. But when I sat on the couch, the muscles in my lower back spasmed.

"It's acting up?" she asked, alarmed.

I gritted my teeth and nodded.

"What can I do? Do you need medicine?" I rarely complained about my back, so the panic in her voice was as acute as my pain. I held up a hand for her to stop before she got up from her seat anyway.

"It's fine. I took some before I drove home. Give me a minute." I straightened out as much as I could and breathed my way through the tightness. "It's been getting worse lately." When the muscles loosened up, I lay back in relief.

"That was intense," she said, her voice laced with concern. "Tell me you have an appointment with your doctor."

"Tomorrow. Thankfully, my insurance stays active for two weeks."

Her mouth dropped open. "I didn't even think about the insurance. You will have to find something new quickly. You have to have insurance."

The health insurance was the first thing I'd thought of when I opened the company's apology letter, and my mind hadn't stopped turning since. It was essential for me. And if I did not find another job quickly, I could be in huge trouble.

Kallie's phone rang in her pocket. She fished it out, looked down at the screen, and back up at me. She pushed the button on the side, declining the call.

"Was that Brandon?" I asked. "You should get it."

"Yes, but I'm here with you." She smiled, and my heart sank a little, although I didn't let it show on my face. It had been hard to share my best friend with someone we met less than a year ago at a random restaurant. Brandon was a good guy. I liked him. But I sometimes wished he didn't exist, which wasn't fair to him or Kallie. It wasn't her fault that I didn't have a significant other or a social life.

"That's not going to work," I said. "You cleaned the flour off you for a reason, so where are you guys going?"

She sighed, placing her cheek in her hand where it was propped up on the arm of the couch. "We were supposed to meet up with Eloise and Peter, and some of Brandon's work friends at Portillo's. I was going to ask you to come with us before all this happened. Eloise would love to see you, and the work friends are a bunch of guys, and—"

My heart sank. Eloise and Peter had been good college friends of ours, and I hadn't seen them in forever. However, I couldn't wrap my mind around going out. "That's sweet," I cut in. "But it's been a devastating day, and I have to pass."

"I know, but I thought—"

"But you need to go."

She shook her head. "No, I need to be with you. I can't leave you after the day you've had. What if your back messes up again?"

I watched her expression and knew she was being truthful, but I wouldn't allow anyone I loved to sacrifice their time or attention on my behalf. I wasn't that important. Even though Kallie loved me, she also loved Brandon. She shouldn't have to choose.

"My back has been messed up since I was seventeen. This is nothing new. And do you think I want you to stay and wallow in self-pity with me? No thanks. I can sulk on my own," I quipped. "I will turn on some sad Taylor Swift and eat more cake. I will even try to taste it this time around."

She opened her mouth, and I guessed where she was going before she spoke.

"No more excuses." Her mouth closed. "Go! Have fun on my behalf. Give Eloise and Peter all my love. I want a nice night alone." My tongue was thick with every lie I said, but I was a master at masking my true feelings. She stared at me, trying to decipher what I was hiding.

"Okay, fine. But I'm coming back once it's over." She slowly got to her feet, and I mirrored her.

"Don't come all the way back here. Just call. I'll probably be asleep anyway."

I could tell she didn't agree with anything I was saying, but she held her tongue.

"Are you going to tell Whit you lost your job?"

My insides froze at her pointed question, but I didn't let it show.

"I'm not bothering him. I haven't talked to him since he went to training camp."

My older brother had been the starting quarterback for the Salt Lake Wolverines professional football team for the past thirteen years. He and I spoke, but we weren't as close as we were when we were kids. I told myself it was because we lived so far apart, and his football career kept him busy. But I knew the real reasons, and they threatened to overwhelm me with memories, and I couldn't let that happen. My day was shitty enough.

"You should tell him, but you already know that," Kallie said as we approached the door.

I waved, shaking my head. "Plenty of time to discuss that later. Go."

She hugged me again, causing my throat to clog with emotion. I did not want her to see it on my face, so I held onto the door as I playfully pushed her out.

"Okay, I'll go. But I'm having Chinese food delivered. You can't live off cake alone."

I leaned against the doorframe. "You're wrong, but I won't pass up orange chicken."

She turned and smiled back at me as she walked away. "Love you, bestie."

"Love you too, Kal."

Kallie's departure left the house without warmth or sparkle. I retrieved my fork from the sink, rinsed it off, and dug it back into the velvety chocolate cake. I ate, leaning over the counter, seeking the numbness I wished bingeing on the cake would give me.

When I came to my senses and my stomach started to protest, I wiped the fudge from around my mouth with my fingers and went to the fridge to retrieve the milk carton. I picked it up to find it almost empty, which triggered hot tears to fall down my cheeks.

I'd been so wrapped up in my quest for comfort via food coma that I didn't realize I'd still been holding back my emotions. My heart squeezed. My anxiety climbed.

I had to think of something besides food to calm my nerves. I was prone to panic attacks, and it had been one hell of a depressing day. Spiraling was imminent. I drank the last sip of milk straight from the carton, threw it in the trash, and washed the chocolate off my hands in the kitchen sink. Taking a deep breath, I blew my nose with a paper towel, grabbed a can of diet soda, and walked over to the small desk in the corner of the living area.

I was unsure if doing this would help or hurt, but I had to try.

I opened the lid of my laptop and exhaled slowly. The document of my newest project popped up on the screen. Although I may have worked in marketing for a book publishing company for years, I really wanted it to be my name on the front cover of the books.

I was halfway through my target word count, trying to figure out how to incorporate some new ideas I'd been carrying around. I strived not to dwell on my syntax's imperfection, even though "the imposter monster" threatened to rear its ugly head. Instead, I let my fingers strike the keys with abandon, words flowing better than I could imagine. My heroine schemed to take down evil bosses and fight corporate greed.

If I had nothing to help me process all the changes, memories, and pain, I always had writing. As complicated as it was to navigate, it had always been my greatest consolation.

I retreated into my pretend world and characters and felt my reality narrow into fantasy.

Chapter Two

Julianna | *September 18, 2024*

The next morning, I found myself sitting in a familiar patient room, my foot tapping nervously against the white-tiled floor. I stared blankly at faded paintings of birds on the wall opposite me.

"Julianna?" Dr. Billingsly poked his head through the door after a couple of courtesy knocks. I smiled as he entered. Dr. Billingsly's mustache and the thin glasses on his nose twitched as he cleared his throat. "How are you today?"

I shifted uncomfortably. "I'm doing okay. How are you?"

He and I had done this same song and dance since I'd moved to Charlotte more than a decade ago. I could read him well, so I knew something was off when his gaze averted.

"I'm fine." He rolled a small stool over and sat down right next to me with his tablet. Both things were new. "Let's talk about your MRI results."

A cold flush ran over me.

"Okay. What's wrong?"

"I will be frank with you. Your luck has run out. Your scan revealed that two discs have significantly shifted since last year. They have herniated and are pressing against the nerves in your spine."

I watched numbly as he brought up the recent images of my back on the tablet to explain where things were wrong. My increased pain hadn't been lying to me. Fear washed over me as the reality of what he was saying settled in.

"You will need surgery to remove the part of the discs pressing on the nerves. As the herniations worsen, they will press on the spinal cord nerve bundles more, which is going to cause either increased numbness or extreme pain, perhaps even immobility. It'll come upon you quickly." My breath hitched. These were facts I already knew, but knowing something and having it happen were two different occurrences.

He continued, "In your case, with the degeneration speed and the fusions you had done years ago at play, worsening could happen at any time. So your surgery needs to be a priority. Within the next couple of months."

I was wringing my hands in my lap as I spoke. "Are you sure? You're sure this can't …heal?"

"I am sure. You're welcome to seek a second opinion elsewhere, but the proof is right here in the scans. I am sorry, Julianna."

A lump formed in my throat.

How could this be happening just when I was about to lose my health insurance?

"Is there any way to get it done within the next two weeks?" I whispered, trying to keep the tears from spilling. He smiled slightly under his mustache as if I'd made a joke, his face full of empathy.

"Well, no, I'm afraid not." He dipped his head for a moment and then looked me in the eye once again. "There is another slight administrative issue with the surgery aspect of this. I am retiring at the end of this month. Your care will be transferred to Dr. Shaley.

"However, she will not begin until January 2, so there will be a gap. There are some legalities and such that won't allow us to schedule surgery with her until she's officially started. But I feel like that might be pushing it with the timeline. You need to be scheduled for surgery no later than November."

I'd never been without Dr. Billingsly's expertise. Panic settled in. I trusted him. November was so close. Tears sprang to my eyes, but I quickly blinked them away. I could not break down in the doctor's office.

"So what should I do?" I asked.

Dr. Billingsly took a deep breath and set down the tablet on the counter next to him.

"There are other orthopedic surgeons in the area who are undoubtedly able to do this procedure, and they might be willing to fit you in. But you're a special case for me, Julianna. We've been together since you came to Charlotte, and I want to see you with the best. I have someone I want to refer you to, but they aren't in the city."

"Okay..."

"Roanoke," he replied, clasping his hands together as he leaned his elbows on his knees. "Doctor Bahar Kaveh is an osteopathic surgeon at Carilion Roanoke Memorial, and she would be perfect for your situation. I don't want to take risks because of your previous work. And I have the utmost confidence in Dr. Kaveh. She'll know how to handle your procedure best since she is up to date on the latest techniques. I think you said you were from that area?"

I swallowed hard and nodded. Roanoke, Virginia, was only four hours from Charlotte, so distance-wise, it was doable. But Roanoke was also only thirty minutes from Mill Creek. The small town where I'd grown up. I hadn't been there since I left for college nearly fifteen years ago.

"Can I have some time to think before I decide?" My words came out shaky.

He nodded. "Of course." I saw the kindness and concern in his eyes.

It was then that I remembered that either way this went, I'd never see him again.

I got to my feet and offered my hand to shake, which he accepted. I instantly regretted that I hadn't hugged him, but I pushed the thought away. I didn't want to seem too forward.

"You've been so kind and helpful to me. I hope you enjoy your retirement. I will miss seeing you every year."

He smiled brightly. "Thank you. I will miss you as well. I hope you decide to pursue my suggestion. If you do, call. The front office has all the information for Dr. Kaveh and can schedule an intake appointment. Her office will schedule your surgery quickly. Sound good?"

"It does," I replied with a nod.

"Take care, Julianna."

After he left the room, I gathered my bag and began to process all he'd said.

There had never been a question of *if* I would need surgery again, but *when*. I had chosen not to think about it in favor of living without anxiety. While a worthy endeavor for my sanity, I was now faced with the reality of a necessary surgery, and there was no way I could pay for such a considerable procedure.

I sat behind the wheel of my old Subaru. Like me, the vehicle was on its last legs. The dashboard had been lit up like a Christmas tree for months, but I covered the lights with candid pictures of my Grams. There was an old snapshot of her, Whit, and me on a picnic at Mill Creek Park. All the photos were of her smile and fun times that I wanted to remember. I would only allow happy memories to cover my plethora of problems.

I felt the overwhelming urge to connect the moment I saw Grams' face, so I called Kallie and explained everything that had happened with Dr. Billingsly. She did not speak until I finished.

"How are you not crying?" she asked.

"I think I'm in shock. The results are terrible. Losing my doctor sucks. And I just lost my job and insurance. Maybe the universe is telling me another surgery is wrong for me."

"Um, no. You're smarter than that. MRIs don't lie." The bell for the bakery rang in the background, and I heard a door shut as Kallie moved into her office. "This is a rough spot, but that doesn't mean you don't need the surgery."

"I can't afford it," I said, picking at a loose leather spot on the steering wheel. "There is no way I can pay for something like this. I'll have to wait until I get another job and get onto their medical."

There was silence on the line. I knew what she would say even before the words tumbled from her lips.

"Call your brother."

I sighed. "Stop it."

"Call him, you stubborn woman!" Her voice was bordering on frantic. "I still can't believe your brother is a multi-million-dollar professional football player, and you can't bring yourself to ask him for one cent."

"I'm not calling Whit. It's not an option."

Whit and I hadn't had much of a relationship since Grams died, the same night Bram and I were in the vehicle accident. Neither of her grandchildren had been with her when she passed away. A neighbor had found her collapsed in the front yard while we were out at that Christmas party. It was a fact neither of us wanted to remember.

Without any remaining family, our whole lives were turned

upside down. We forgot how to communicate with each other as we coped with Grams' death. I withdrew and deflected while he sought destruction and distraction. I graduated from high school and moved to Charlotte for college. Whit went back to college in Alabama after I graduated and kept busy with women, football, and who knows what else. By the time the grief had become more manageable for me and Whit had his life back together, we had grown far apart. We made time to see each other every few years and texted or called each other every few weeks. He lived his life as a football celebrity in Utah, while I led a quiet existence in North Carolina. We never crossed paths.

"He's always sending extravagant gifts. Why not parlay that into paying for surgery?"

It was true. As far apart as we were, he always sent me expensive things, like all-expense-paid vacations and one of those huge bookcases with the rolling ladder that took up my whole living room.

"He's not even returned my last fifty calls."

"I have a hard time believing you've called fifty times, and he's never answered once."

I grumbled. "Okay, fine, I called maybe twice. But I'm just saying he probably wouldn't answer if I called right now."

"Okay…then text him."

I bit my lip as my back spasmed a little. "He has nothing to do with this. I won't drag him into my issues."

Kallie sighed.

"You two used to be super close—"

"We were. But that relationship doesn't exist without Grams. It doesn't feel right to ask him for money. I wish I could explain it better, but it feels wrong."

"He would give money to a stranger. He would help his sister. Hell, he might even rent you a private hospital. And a private doctor educated at whatever the best medical school is.

You know he would, and it probably wouldn't even dent his accounts."

I bit my lip, wanting so badly to bite through it so I could focus on anything except the solution Kallie wouldn't let go of. She continued, "Plus, if he pays for all this, you won't have to worry about money for a bit, and there won't be so much pressure to find a job. You can focus on your writing for a while, take a breather."

I rolled my eyes even though she couldn't see it. "I don't want Whit to think he has to rescue me, much less have me not working and mooching off his success."

She completely ignored my insistence. "That's rather presumptuous of you. He may not think that way at all. Sounds like you might be assigning people feelings when you don't know what they are thinking…"

"I don't need a psychology lecture. 'No' is my final answer."

I heard the distinct click of her nails on a keyboard. "Fine. I have to go. The kitchen is yelling at me." Her voice softened. "I am here for you. We will figure this out together. Go home, take a hot shower, eat some leftover Chinese—"

"Bold of you to assume there are leftovers," I muttered. "But okay. I'm gonna go home and get in an Epsom salt bath." I didn't know if it was a placebo effect because of the news I'd just gotten, but my back spasm wasn't letting up.

"Perfect. I'll come over as soon as we close, and we will talk about everything. We'll get through this together, Jules," she replied, her voice full of concern.

The nickname Kallie used for me was the nickname Whit always used, and it made my chest ache.

"I'll see you later. Love you." I quickly ended the call before she could respond and before I lost control and cried.

I didn't go straight home. Instead, I indulged in retail therapy. I didn't have a job, but I had a credit card with a decent limit.

I walked through the nearest shopping complex and entered every store, whether I was interested or not. I bought makeup and clothes—for what, I wasn't sure. I hadn't been on a date in months and rarely went out for fun. But the complexities behind why I was doing what I was doing were too much to unpack. I didn't think about facts. I let myself be numb. I didn't want to believe or ruminate about Whit or my job loss, so I threw all of it out of my mind.

Except for my back. It was definitely not numb.

I was limping by the end of my shopping, but I rounded out my spree with a large cinnamon sugar pretzel and a healthy dose of regret, which I chased with an iced espresso. As I hauled all of my wares across the townhouse complex's parking lot, the thoughts I'd pushed aside began to catch up with me, and the tears fell. I curled myself onto my couch with a blanket and fell asleep to get rid of the trouble that hung off me like lead weights.

That evening, Kallie found me clinging to my last shred of dignity, surrounded by new cartons of Chinese food on my living room coffee table.

"Oh, love," she cooed as she waltzed into the house, still in her baking garb, her long blonde hair piled on her head again. She let her purse fall to the ground, and she walked toward me like a specter. I didn't move to greet her.

I looked up at my best friend's slim face full of worry and concern. A few tears welled up in my eyes, but I cut them off.

"I'm fine," I countered, clearing my throat. "I'm braless and in sweats on my couch with Chinese food and wine coolers. How can life get any more comfortable than this?"

She chuckled and sat down beside me. She reached out and rubbed my back in loving strokes.

"I know it's a shit thing to say to all this, but I'm so sorry." Genuine sympathy reflected in her brown eyes.

I bit my lip and nodded. She grabbed some chopsticks and a carton of lo mein. I couldn't think of anything worth saying, and I could tell she didn't know what to say either. Neither of us could change my situation. Finally, she put down the noodles and fork rather forcefully. I looked over at her with a furrowed brow.

"What?" she asked, shrugging. "I've got something to say, but I wanted to get some food in my belly before you kick me out of the house."

My hackles rose.

"If this is about Whit, I swear…"

"It's not about your brother."

My eyes narrowed.

"But it *is* about a phone call you need to place to your brother."

I groaned and threw down my box of half-eaten food onto the coffee table.

"Hear me out, please. Even if you don't tell him you lost your job, you have to tell him you're having surgery. Text him. Smoke signal him. Something. He deserves to know."

"Why are you so insistent about this?" I asked. She sank into the couch.

"I can't understand how you two became so estranged," she said, her voice soft. "I would have given anything to have a sibling. And you've told me story after story about your childhood, and you guys were inseparable. Now you're willing to go in for a major surgery without telling him?"

I picked up my phone off the table and looked down at it.

"It's not like we're at odds," I said. "There just haven't been many reasons to come together anymore without Grams. I'm sure it doesn't help that we don't talk about any of it. We've never even talked about what happened the night she died." I

looked up at her through my lashes, watching her try to piece
things together.

"What does that matter?" she asked.

"He doesn't know Bram Winchester was with me the night
of the wreck. He thinks I took Bram's vehicle, and that I was
alone, that I was the driver."

Realization settled over Kallie's features, her eyes widening.
"Oh."

I clutched the phone harder. "Yeah. Oh."

"It was a million years ago, though, so why does it matter?
Are Whit and that asshole even still friends?"

"I-I don't know," I stuttered, ignoring her assessment of
Bram. "Whit never talks about him. The last I heard, Bram was
a forest ranger in Virginia. So it's not like they live in the same
place or do the same things. They may not even be friends
anymore." My heart dropped at the possibility. Whit and I had
been close, but so had Whit and Bram. Bram and I were never
truly close, but Whit was our bridge.

My best friend took the phone from me and placed it back
on the table, then grabbed my hands and turned us more fully
toward each other. Her face was brimming with nervous
energy, but she also had a determined glint in her eye.

"You can't let something like what happened a million years
ago keep you from knowing your brother again. Don't discuss
that night right now, you'll figure that out later. But you need
him through this. Not just for his money. Although that would
be quite the perk in this situation."

I swallowed the lump that formed in my throat. "You win.
I'll call him."

"Good." She squeezed my hands. "And one more thing. I
talked with my co-owner today. I'm going to take off for a
couple of weeks and come stay with you in Mill Creek and
attend to your every need after surgery."

Guilt settled heavily on my chest, and I shook my head.

"You can't do that. It's too far away. If something were to happen at the bakery or with Brandon..."

She shook her head fiercely. "No argument. Even if you tell me not to come, I will pitch a tent on your front lawn wherever you stay." She smiled, her dimples showing. "Why won't you let me love you?" She sang the last line, making me smile in return.

When our giggles subsided, I whispered, "This has been the weirdest forty-eight hours."

"I know," she said. "But no matter what weird gets thrown at you, you've got me. I will always sit with you in your weirdness." She picked up the phone and handed it to me. "I'm going to the bathroom. Call him."

When she'd left, I found Whit's name in the contacts and pressed the call button before I could change my mind.

It rang once. Twice. Three times. I was ready to hang up when the call connected.

"Julianna Joy East." Whit's deep voice echoed, tinted with a Southern lilt. A mixture of trepidation and relief washed over me.

"Whitaker Patrick East. My old, long-lost sibling."

"Old?"

"Yes, old. Did you misplace your hearing aid again?"

"Lost it when I tripped and broke a hip." I could feel him smiling through the phone. "But I probably shouldn't joke about that. That's the last thing I need, a career-ending injury." My back throbbed, and I thought about the irony of it as he continued, "How are you?"

It was the moment of truth. I closed my eyes. "I've got some news. I have to have surgery...again, on my back. I found out this morning. It's nothing major—"

"Back surgery is always major," Whit interrupted. "What happened?"

"Disc herniation. Happens all the time. In a strange turn of events, though, my doctor is retiring and wants to refer me to someone in Roanoke so that I can have the surgery in the next couple of months."

"That's so far. Are you sure you have to do that?" he asked, but then he gasped. "Wait, this couldn't be better timing. I need someone to move into Gram's house for a while. Bram moved out a couple of months ago."

My world stopped.

"Grams' house? You bought—"

"Yeah, sorry. I meant to tell you. It just never seemed like a good time. I bought Grams' house about fifteen months ago when it went back on the market. I wouldn't have known it was available, but Bram clued me in, so I snatched it up."

I could barely breathe.

Why didn't he tell me?

I called him to talk about my surgery, and he hadn't bothered to tell me he owned our childhood home. And he'd owned it for *fifteen months.* I tried to tamp down the sting of betrayal and focused on the second part of his statement.

"Bram Winchester was living in Gram's house?"

I closed my eyes. I could hear my heart beating in my ears as my blood pressure shot through the roof. Bram and Whit were still friends. I talked to Whit at least once every few months, and he'd never mentioned him to me. I never heard Bram's name. I could count on one hand the times I'd said it aloud. Yet I thought of him almost every day.

"Well, yeah. He moved in after I bought it. But he bought some land with a house out in the county, and he's moved out there now. It'll be good to have you in it for a couple of months until I find a renter or something."

Hundreds of questions swarmed through my mind, and maybe some should have been about the house and the logistics of Whit's omission of info, but instead, they were all related to Bram Winchester. Fleeting teenage memories of Bram's body pressing into mine that night of the Christmas party flooded my mind.

Was he married? He was thirty-four, so odds were that he was. But I was thirty-three and unmarried, unattached even, so maybe he was as well?

Oh my God, Julianna. It doesn't matter!

I'd searched for Bram on social media over the years, but I had never found him. Unlike Whit, I'd lost touch with the people and the news from Mill Creek years ago, and anything I'd gleaned was from context clues from Facebook friends who weren't friends. I had no way of knowing what Bram looked like, much less if he was attached. He had been intelligent and drop-dead gorgeous fifteen years ago. I doubted that had changed much. I was sure he was thriving.

I was about to bring it all up when Whit spoke again. "I want you to get the surgery in Roanoke. I want you to have the best of the best. I'll take care of everything. Who do I need to call? What do I need to pay for?"

"There's nothing for you to do." The lie felt sour on my tongue, but I pushed forward. "I just wanted you to know. If I decide to do the surgery in Roanoke, and I probably will, I would appreciate the use of the house. And I'll pay rent while I'm there."

"No, you won't."

I took a deep breath, overwhelmed.

"I can't live with myself otherwise, Whit."

He chuckled. "You always were the goody-two-shoes of this duo."

My cheeks heated as words from the past haunted me.

"Good girls like you don't belong with assholes like me." Why did those words, spoken by none other than Bram Winchester, still sting to the core?

"You have no idea what I've done," I replied, attempting to sound mysterious.

He made a derisive snort. "Like what? What's the last 'bad' thing you did?"

I couldn't come up with anything that wasn't a lie. I was a "good girl." I was quiet, low-key, a little withdrawn, and a whole lot bookish. I'd never so much as stolen a pen from the bank counter. But Whit didn't need to know that.

"If I told you my secrets, I'd have to kill you."

He laughed, loud and clear. "Don't make me fly to Charlotte and box your ears."

The euphemism conjured Grams in my mind. The saying was one of her favorites to use on us as kids.

"I won't argue with you on the phone. Let me kick your ass in person."

I could hear him still snickering. This was the most connected we'd been in so long.

"Well, the season is on, but I can fly out for a few days during bye week," he said. "Is it okay if I drop in then? It'll be early November."

"It's your house, so come anytime you want."

"I can hire you a caretaker for after the surgery."

I sniffed. "My best friend Kallie is coming for the aftercare."

"Oh. Okay, good. Bram will be in the area too, if you're in a pinch."

I would never find myself in that big of a pinch.

"I haven't seen or spoken to Bram since Grams died," I whispered.

"Then it would be good for you guys to catch up." Whit sounded as if it was the grandest of plans. "I don't get to see him much since we're both so busy. Maybe you can bring me up to speed."

I swallowed hard, choking the words out. "Yeah, maybe."

"It's been too long since I've seen your face. I miss you."

My heart pounded. Why didn't he call me back if he missed me so much? Why didn't he ever get on a plane to see me?

"You too," I replied.

"We might have to schedule some calls," he went on. "My time isn't my own again until next March."

I couldn't imagine his grueling schedule, the money, the social obligations—all the things that made him one of the most favored quarterbacks in football. Our lives were so different.

"I'll watch all your games, even if we can't talk."

I never missed a game. I loved seeing my brother succeed and exceed expectations.

"I know." I heard a high-pitched voice in the background call his name. "Sorry, I gotta go. My assistant is on my ass. I'll text you the code for the front door at Grams'. Keep me up to date, please."

"Sounds good. And thank you so much."

"Not another word."

We ended the call, but the weight I'd carried didn't release as I had expected. I couldn't shake the truth that my brother and I had a lot more to discuss later if we wanted a chance to feel like family again.

CHAPTER THREE

Bram | *September 23, 2024*

I clutched the large box in my arms against my chest. The street lamps of the small downtown square lit simultaneously, illuminating my way as I walked toward my truck parked behind Mill Creek's small Senior Citizens' Community Building. I wished I had a jacket to shield me from the cool fall breeze.

"Dracula! Hold up!" a familiar voice called out from behind me.

I looked back and saw Josiah Bell speedwalking in my direction. His steps were heavy on the gravel. Josiah was an old friend I'd played football with in high school, fifteen years ago. Our choices may have kept us in the same town, but our lives were vastly different. He was a science teacher and assistant high school football coach at Mill Creek High School, married with three young daughters. My life was more singular and quiet. It consisted of my job with the US Forest Service, a farmhouse with some land, and a beagle named Lakey.

"Hey there," I called out while setting the box on the open tailgate of my truck.

Josiah waited until he was closer to say, "Bram Winchester, you're a hard man to pin down. Always in the background at these shindigs." He smiled slightly. "Good turnout tonight, wasn't it?"

The weekly community dinners from Mill Creek Aid always drew a crowd of patrons and helpers. MCA was a local charity that served impoverished families in our area. I was heavily involved behind the scenes. Josiah, also a regular volunteer, always served in the main areas with the crowd while I stayed in the kitchen.

"Yeah," I concurred. "I'm glad people still come."

"It does a lot of good," Josiah replied. Then he stepped a little closer and, lowering his voice, said, "Did you happen to see the Douglas family? Dale's really struggling. His wife said the cancer has spread to his liver."

I hated hearing that. "I saw them come in. Terrible."

I knew all about Dale Douglas. Eighteen years ago, the man had been a low-level supervisor at Mill Creek's largest employer, Buncomb Industries. The owner of the factory had been my father, Vince Winchester. When the opportunity came around, my father sold the business for a substantial profit. Then the plant was shut down without warning, and the sudden job loss put over two hundred families into poverty. People moved away from Mill Creek to find other work closer to bigger cities. Those who stayed tried desperately to recover. Dale and his family remained in Mill Creek, and they were still struggling twenty-one years later.

I wished I could say I was surprised my father made the decisions he did, but I wasn't. He was the worst kind of man who sought power regardless of the cost to others. When I was old enough to realize I could make a difference, I made it a point to support those who'd been affected by him. Yet that didn't heal my reputation by association. I had to work behind the scenes most of the time because the town of Mill Creek at large didn't take kindly to me. Most saw me as an extension of my father. In reality, he and I hadn't spoken in over three years.

"I hope Dale's able to make it through the treatment. He's already so frail," Josiah lamented. He pointed to the truck bed, which was full of boxes. "You taking that food over to the shed? I'll follow you over there and help unload." MCA was an organization without an official headquarters, so extra supplies and nonperishable food were stored in a locked shipping container behind the police station. I'd brought a truck bed full of cutlery, napkins, catering equipment, and all the extra dry and canned goods for the dinner. There wasn't much left to take back.

The need to provide food to families seemed to grow every single year.

"No, I'm good. Get home to your family. I've got this." I smiled at him as I slammed the tailgate closed.

Josiah shook his head. "You're always doing so much, Bram."

"I've got time." I had the money as well, but I didn't want to say that. Flaunting wealth was not something I indulged in, and speaking of it reminded me of my father.

"The older folks don't appreciate you as much as they should, and it burns me up." Josiah spoke with feeling, but I adjusted the ball cap on my head and looked at the gravel. The number of times I'd heard, "the apple doesn't fall far from the tree," whispered when I walked by was innumerable. I hated it, but what could I do?

"That's kind of you, but they can believe what they want, as we all do." Their judgment stung, but I tried to see it from their side as much as I could. They'd been destroyed by my father's decision and needed someone to blame. Vince stayed away, while I stayed in the community. What else could I expect?

"But if they only knew what you do, all the people you help—"

"I hate to cut this short, but I've got a phone call I need to make before it gets too late." Something akin to panic washed over me. I knew compliments were going to fly, and I could not stand to listen to them. I moved toward the front door of the truck.

"Wait. Have you talked to Coach Mayfield lately?"

I stopped and looked back at Josiah.

"No, why?"

"No easy way to say this"—Josiah rubbed his hand over his face—"but he's retiring. Both the football coach and gym teacher positions. He and Betty are moving down to Florida to be closer to their kids."

Jim Mayfield had been a staple of Mill Creek High's successful football program long before Josiah and I came along. He meant a lot to me. He was a father figure during my teen years when my father was either absent or hostile.

"Well, that's sad, but I get it." It was well known that Betty had a stroke a few months ago and was still recovering. He was past retirement age and deserved to lay down those jobs after decades of shaping young people's lives.

"Yeah, me too," Josiah replied, putting his hands in his pockets and rocking back on his heels. "He's recommended you for the football coach position. He's already talked to the administration about it and everything. He wants you to come out this season and watch the games from the sidelines, get to know the players and the assistant coaches, so that you can be familiar with everything. He thinks they might go to State this year."

Not this again…

I hadn't played football since tearing my ACL in my junior

season at the University of Alabama. I'd told Coach Mayfield, more than once, that I had no interest in coaching, assisting, or anything of that nature. I didn't have the heart for it, and Coach knew that. Yet, instead of backing off, he did what he did best and kept pushing the issue. Now, he'd recruited others to join in the coaxing.

"I'm flattered, but as far as I'm concerned, it's a no. Tell him I said thanks. You'd be better suited for that, anyway."

"No way," he scoffed. "With Clara and the girls, I don't have time to be head coach, not if I want to do it right. You're the one with the plays and personality. You ever worked with teenagers?"

"Not really." I shrugged. "I encounter them at work sometimes, and here. But it's not why I'm declining. I don't play anymore. And just because I'm still close with Whit—"

"It's not that," Josiah interrupted with a chuckle. "We aren't that shallow. Whit might be a professional, but you were well on your way before…" His voice trailed off, seeming to know it wasn't my most pleasant topic.

I stuck the toe of my black boot into the loose gravel, doing whatever to avoid looking him in the eye.

"Either way, I'm not interested," I replied. "With my job, I don't think stretching myself further is a good idea." I was the superintendent for the US Forest Service at the Washington-Jefferson National Forest. It wasn't a difficult job overall, but Josiah didn't need to know that.

The anticipation in his expression fell away. "That sounds like a cop-out, but I'll take a man's word. You know Coach won't let this go."

"I know." I sighed and opened my driver's side door. "It's good to see you, man. Thanks for making time to come help."

"I'm always happy to. I'll never forget what MCA did for my mom and dad after the plant shut down. I'm sorry I haven't been able to help more in the last few months."

"Don't apologize. You do more than enough for everyone. Just glad to see you. Say hello to the family."

We shook hands, and I climbed into the truck. With a departing nod, he walked away, and I closed the door, exhaling loudly. The long day had stolen all my energy. I'd been in my uncomfortable ranger uniform all day, sweating. I couldn't wait to get home, take a hot shower, and lie down in my comfy bed.

First, I had some choice words for Whit.

He might have been a professional football player, and my best friend of over twenty years, but those facts didn't soften the blow of the text he'd sent earlier. I rechecked it to make sure I hadn't read it wrong.

> Whit: Julianna is coming back to Mill Creek for a while.

I had been pushing the words out of my mind as much as possible, keeping my focus on where I was and what I was doing all day. But now, it was time for the reckoning. I would have to call him right there in the parking lot, considering there was little to no cell phone signal on the way home, thanks to the adjacent mountains.

On the fourth ring, a frantic and loud "Yello!" sounded from the other end. Loud voices, rattling dishes, and footsteps filled the background. He was at a restaurant or bar.

"Why did you text me Julianna is coming back to Mill Creek on a random Friday and then not give me one fucking detail?"

There was a pause. "Huh? I told you what I know, dude. Jules is coming to town soon, and she'll be staying at Grams' house. What more do you want?"

The telltale lilt of Whit's voice and the inflections in his voice gave away his physical status.

"You're drunk." I put my hand to my brow, kneading the skin there, trying to will the headache that was forming to go away. Years of dealing with my Mom, who was constantly inebriated, gave me a radar for these things. My plans to talk this through tonight with Whit had little chance of happening.

"Meh, a little tipsy." There was more raucous conversation in the background. "I'm lettin' loose with the boys. Got a big game Sunday."

"That's great," I said, sarcastically, not caring one bit. "So when is she arriving?"

Bottles clinked in the background. "Uh…Sunday?"

My heart sped up in my chest.

"Sunday? As in the day after tomorrow?"

"No, next week, next Sunday. She's got an appointment with a surgeon on that Monday."

Now, my heart stopped altogether.

"Surgeon? What's going on? Is it her back?"

"Yeah, it's her back. She's going to a doctor in Roanoke for surgery. The details are fuzzy."

I shook my head and squeezed the phone tighter in my hand.

"Is she—"

"Listen, I'll talk to you later," Whit interrupted. "Too many people here. I can barely hear you."

His words were still trying to sink into my consciousness.

Had she been injured again?

"Whit! I need more details. Did she—"

"I'll talk to you tomorrow, promise." Then the line went dead.

I looked at my phone screen, mind whirling and insides tearing. Unchecked anger at Whit poured through me, and I tossed the phone into the passenger seat.

All I needed were details, and my best friend was too drunk to explain anything.

You don't have the right to know.

The sobering thought flashed through my awareness, and

my anger quieted, overtaken by a sadness that never really disappeared. I hadn't seen Julianna since New Year's Day, fifteen years ago. I could still see the silhouette of her broken body lying out in the hospital bed, the bruises peppering her face and arms, and the brightness of her smile at the sight of me, which had contrasted everything terrible that was going on at that moment. Then I remembered what came after that, and a lump formed in my throat.

I threw away the thoughts. Instead, I thought about Lakey and how she was probably wondering where I was now that darkness had fallen. It was enough to get me on the road and driving toward home.

I lived in a hollow thirty minutes from the town of Mill Creek. I had bought the large parcel of land a couple of years ago and put a lot of time and effort into reviving the old farmhouse that was the centerpiece. I'd finished the renovations a couple of months ago and moved in. It was perfect for Lakey and me. The house was nestled between three mountains, surrounded by sunlight and the natural beauty of Appalachia, a haven of solitude.

I wouldn't have known the piece of paradise existed if it hadn't been for Whit, who told me in passing years ago that it was Julianna's favorite place when they were kids. I couldn't get it off my mind after that.

I couldn't get her off my mind, either.

I'd spent my young life focusing on football and screwing around with every girl who would take my advances. Then, when I had Julianna in my hands, I broke her. It was enough to make me sick.

I had some casual hookups over the years, but nothing ever stuck. No girl was her. Whit had never suggested that she'd return to Mill Creek, so I couldn't pinpoint what kept me holding on to the idea of her. But she was always there, lingering in the corners of everything.

I frequently wondered where she was and what she was doing. Was she hurting? Was she packing for a trip to her hometown? Was she alone or with a friend? Or a boyfriend?

I was going down a dangerous path, but I let my mind imagine that I was helping her move back to Mill Creek. I thought having the right to touch her, to hold her, to help her, to know about what she was going through. In my alternate reality, she'd forgiven me a long time ago, and I'd spent every moment earning back her trust from the stupid decisions of my youth.

I was still crazy about her. But I'd have to count it a win if she ever spoke to me again.

SATURDAY MORNINGS WERE USUALLY RESERVED FOR SLEEPING IN, but I was awakened at sunrise by a distinct, piercing tone. Lakey's ears flopped as she ran with me to get the phone I'd left lying on the bathroom counter.

"You son of a bitch," I growled after I pushed the green button to answer the call.

"I know. Dude, I'm so sorry," Whit started. "I've got one hell of a headache, and I know I deserve everything you're going to say, but have a little mercy."

"You can start by explaining everything about Julianna. Now."

I could hear him gritting his teeth against the sickness and headache. We weren't young bucks anymore. Alcohol required a steep price.

"Julianna said she found out she needs surgery on her back, and soon. Something has happened with her doctor, so she's having the surgery in Roanoke. Weird choice of place, but apparently it's a doctor connection or something? Anyway, that's what's up. Herniated discs, she said. Nothing acute, but I don't know, sounds serious to me."

"Fuck." I expelled the curse with a breath, walked into my bedroom, and sat on the edge of the bed. Lakey lay at my feet and leaned her head against my bare foot. I ran my hand through my hair, nervous and scared, more emotional than I had a right to be over someone whom I didn't even communicate with anymore.

But she wasn't just anyone.

"Things still aren't comfortable between us, and I don't like it," he continued. "I've been a shitty brother to her since Grams died. But it's time that changes. I need to be there through this as much as I can."

I knew the relationship between Julianna and Whit was strained. From an outsider's perspective, it felt like a classic case of miscommunication. Maybe if they'd discuss the past or make more efforts in the present, things could be settled with them again.

Whit knew how I felt about Julianna. I'd told him about my crush on her one drunken night years ago when it was just him and me. I tacked on the addition that I knew she was too good for me and I'd never pursue her. He'd laughed it off and given me a long, inebriated speech about how I was Julianna's brother, too. It was a gross insinuation, and we'd never spoken of it again.

"I'm sure she'll appreciate anything you do for her, man," I replied, looking at the wood grain on the floor. "Julianna is the smartest woman I've ever known. She'll see you're making an effort."

He blew out a vast, elongated breath, sounding exasperated.

"What?"

"I can hear it in your voice," he said firmly. "You're still crushing on her, aren't you? You know how ridiculous that is, right? You're in love with the idea of her, not her. Neither one of us knows Jules anymore."

"She doesn't know us, either," I grumbled, not wanting to refute him. "She doesn't know how much we've changed."

"Look, I'm not trying to be a dick," Whit replied. "I know she meant a lot to you way back when. I know you still carry a torch for her, and that's why you've been jacking off for ten years instead of finding yourself a nice person to settle down with. But if you're gonna approach her once she's back in Mill Creek, you need to come from a 'let me help you without expectation' angle, not a 'get to know you and let me bone you' place. You get what I'm saying?"

"So she's single?" I asked, knowing it would inflame him.

"Don't even think about it, Bram."

I chuckled, but Whit was right. I could help her if she'd let me, but anything more could never happen. I wasn't the Bram of the past. But even at thirty-four, I lived under the weight of it, in a town that half hated me, struggling to do what I could to mend my reputation and be a good man. Regardless, Julianna would always need and deserve more than I could give.

"Noted. Is Grams' house ready to go?"

"It should be fine. She said something about driving a U-Haul to Mill Creek, so she must be bringing a lot of stuff."

"Oh, okay," I stumbled, thinking about how to phrase what I needed to ask. "Look, if you want me to—"

"Yeah, she's gonna need your help," Whit cut in. "She'll be alone, and with all that stuff with her back, we can't take chances. I'd be grateful if you could go over and give her a hand."

"Say less," I said, and I couldn't keep from smiling.

"Damn it. Are you smiling?" Whit chided, knowing instinctively how I was responding, and I grinned even bigger. "I mean it, Bram, don't fuck with her. Or fuck her or do *anything* but move boxes, got it?"

"Calm down," I said, standing. Lakey groaned at my movement. "I'll be a perfect gentleman. I want her to be comfortable. And safe. Just like you do, I'm sure."

"Damn straight." He cleared his throat, which meant he would get serious, and I braced for it. "You know, I still feel like a terrible brother for leaving her the night of the party." I froze, my heart in my throat. "She'd have been with me if I'd stayed away from Amber. Then she wouldn't have wrecked your truck and broken her back. If I'd—"

He still didn't know Julianna and I had been together the night of the wreck. The reality of what occurred was much worse than Whit leaving her alone to get off with an old fling.

"Can't look at it that way. Regrets don't change a thing. You can only move forward. You can show her you care. And I will show her a thing or two about how much I care." I couldn't resist chuckling and hung up the phone on his string of expletives.

I would respect Whit and maintain proper interactions with Julianna. But I would never not think about her in other terms. And I couldn't guarantee I wouldn't find appropriate, friendly ways to tell her how much I cared, even if romance between us was impossible.

CHAPTER FOUR

Julianna | *September 29, 2024*

I paid to break my lease at the townhouse and moved out. I no longer had the money for such an expensive place, and although it was a hard pill to swallow, I needed to come to terms with my circumstances.

I had hope. After recovering from surgery in Mill Creek, I would return to Charlotte, find a new place to live, and start a new job in social media marketing. I wove determination into my every thought for this plan.

I'd saved some money over the years, so I wasn't destitute. I even slipped Kallie a hundred-dollar bill to help me pack, although I found it in my purse at a gas station after I was on the road with the U-Haul. I left my Subaru with Brandon, who would take care of selling it for me. It had a slim chance of making it on any road trip. I resolved to rent a car in Mill Creek until I found a replacement I could afford. Focusing on what I could control, like the car and the townhouse, distracted me from the even scarier risk of surgery.

The drive to Mill Creek went smoothly, even in a moving truck that felt every little bump in the road. As landmarks began to become familiar, my nervous anticipation grew. Seeing the mountain town was like coming home and dying inside at the same time.

Nearly fifteen years had changed the landscape of the small town. The newness included a beautiful brick library, an Applebee's, and a new apartment complex. But so much had been taken away, like some old, twentieth-century houses that used to line Main Street downtown. Their lots were razed to make way for paved parking, banks, and small strip malls. No longer did anyone sell papers by the fountain at the town square. There were new lamp posts up and down the streets and what looked like a new sidewalk. I recognized no faces I saw along the way.

Not much had changed in my childhood neighborhood. I took the familiar turns and noted the old hangouts of my youth, places my friends and I had frequented, like the tiny park with the snow cone stand. Memories flooded me, warm and inviting.

Yet when I pulled into the short street that ended at Gram's house, I gasped, stopping the giant truck in the middle of the road.

The 1970s-style ranch house with dark brick had vanished. A highly updated brick structure was in its place. There was now a small porch, window boxes, a flagstone walkway, and a garage in the space that used to be a carport. The facade had been painted a crisp white, and the old burgundy shutters had been replaced with updated black ones. It was beautiful and modern, yet devastatingly foreign. It was as if the old had never existed.

A honk from a car behind me spurred me to move the truck

into the driveway. I parked and sat for a moment, gathering my will to go inside.

When I walked through the threshold, the inside was completely different. The walls had been torn down, transforming the main space into a single, large dining room, kitchen, and family room. The sunroom off the dining room, which had once served as Bram's makeshift bedroom, had been drywalled and converted into an office and library combo. All of the brown oak paneling throughout the house was removed, and smooth, off-white walls took their place. Features like LED lights and built-in luxury appliances adorned each space. It was excessive for the low to middle-class neighborhood. I did not doubt that Whit had made these decisions himself, considering the income level to which he was now accustomed.

In no way did it feel like the same place. The design and decor were so much colder than when Grams owned the space. I wanted a warm hug from the house, but all I felt was emptiness.

It had changed, and I hadn't been there to stop it.

I picked up things to move my body and use my hands. I could feel myself unraveling, alarm washing over me, and my extremities tingling. I was prone to intense anxiety and panic attacks, and I needed a plan, something to ground me.

There was still daylight left, so I began to carry in armloads of clothes, toiletries, and packed food. Everything else I'd leave in the truck overnight. I quickly realized I shouldn't have bothered bringing so many items from Charlotte. Every single cabinet and drawer was stocked with the best cookware and cutlery. I nearly fainted when I turned over the pots and pans to see Le Creuset stamps on the bottom. I'd never held such an expensive kitchen skillet.

I was unpacking personal items onto the bed in the primary bedroom when I heard a vehicle in the driveway. I ran to the bedroom across the hall and peeked through the wooden blinds. The view looked out onto the front lawn, and in the left corner, I saw part of a gleaming black truck beside the U-Haul.

I have a stranger in my driveway. Awesome.

I looked down at myself. I was sporting baggy, black fleece joggers that I'd dropped crumbs all over during the drive, along with a long-sleeved pink T-shirt that had "Nice Buns" and an illustration of Kallie's bakery on the front. My hair was in some knot on top of my head, and although I'd slapped some foundation on that morning, I had sweated off most of it by that point.

I went on guard, but I would not let fear dictate my actions. The millennial inside me reiterated that I wasn't required to open the door. Stranger danger was a thing. But they didn't knock. They rang the fancy doorbell.

I tiptoed to the front of the living room, amazed at how silent the floors were now that they'd been replaced. I did a little crouching sidestep to the window beside the front door, and ever so slightly moved the soft white curtain to look out. One glimpse at his profile and I knew exactly who it was.

Bram Winchester.

He wore a worn navy baseball hat, a camel-colored Carhartt vest over a white long-sleeved shirt, and relaxed, dark jeans with scuffed-up work boots.

My pulse thrummed frantically in my ears, and my palms broke out in a sticky sweat. I gasped as I re-realized my state. Fifteen years apart, and this was what Bram would see? Chip crumbs and haphazard hair with no makeup?

Absolutely not.

Whit hadn't contacted me since I texted him a few days ago. We'd had a pleasant text conversation, but he said nothing about Bram. Yet there Bram stood. Not a seventeen-year-old boy, but a man. A ridiculously attractive, full-grown man. One who hadn't spoken one word to me since he left my heart and pride in pieces on a dim hospital room floor. Yet he came to see me *now*? Alone?!

You're fifteen years too late, Bram Winchester.

"Open up, Julianna. I saw you look out. I know you're behind the door."

Shit!

The fleeting thought of pretending to be someone else fluttered through my mind. Not that the enormous moving truck in the driveway gave away my narrative. I rolled my eyes.

There was nothing left for me to do but face him.

I stood straighter and took a deep breath while shaking my hands out by my sides. Plastering on a huge smile, I opened the door.

"Dracula!" I exclaimed in a too-high-pitched voice, reaching for his old nickname, hoping it would show some familiarity without being too intimate. Intimacy was probably something he didn't want. He might have been there under duress for all I knew.

His face flashed a bit of shock before it mellowed into a delectable grin.

"You never called me that," he chided and then gave me a wink.

Time had been kind to him. He was even more handsome than he was so many years ago. He stood there confidently, his hands casually stuck in his pockets. I took in the short, trimmed beard along his angled jaw, his crinkled eyes, and his beautiful, welcoming smile. He'd aged like a fine wine and still had that cool casualty that made me want to melt down to my fuzzy socks.

Dear Lord, I'm wearing fuzzy socks.

My mouth gaped, not sure what to say next. I expected him to follow along in my artifice, say some polite greeting, and be a perfect Southern gentleman. But no, he had to come in with his honesty and charm, and I was very unarmed. I wasn't surprised, but I was shocked at the visceral way my body reacted to him, causing heat to rush to my cheeks.

A cold sweat broke out along my neck, and I willed my brain to form words.

"I thought I'd go for something you might not hear anymore, remind you of the old days." I bit my lip and leaned my face on the side of the door.

Then he did the singularly most attractive thing he could have done. He leaned his tall form against the doorframe and rested his arm on its top.

If he'd ripped off his clothing right there, I'm not sure I would have had a different reaction than I did at that moment. Heat flooded me from head to toe, and I began to feel that tell-tale tug toward him, the same one that I had felt as a head-over-heels teenager.

It was maddening.

I wanted to slap myself for having any reaction that wasn't indifference. I didn't want him ever to know how much I had cared for him and how much he'd hurt me. To think of him as anything other than a friend from my childhood wasn't an option.

I would never let myself go down that path again.

"You'd be surprised how long it takes for a nickname to die around here. I hear it all the time," he replied, that deep voice I loved so much washing over me. "Been here long?"

"No." I fiddled with my loose shirt, unwilling to meet his gaze. "I pulled in about an hour ago. This place, it's…beautiful. I can't believe this is the same house we grew up in. It doesn't feel the same at all."

He shuffled his feet a tad.

"I tried to get Whit not to do so much to it. It felt like erasing her," he said, his eyes wandering. "But I think he wanted you to have the best."

"Huh?" My head whipped up, and my eyes locked with his fully for the first time.

"The house. I remodeled it for Whit. Well, for you. It took me a couple of years because I could only work on it here and there, but I got it done."

I gasped. That was twice in less than two minutes that my mouth had dropped in shock.

"Since when have you known how to remodel anything?" I argued, feeling affronted by the shock. "Doesn't matter. I'm only staying here for a little while. I'm here for—"

"I know why you're here," he said, interrupting. "Listen, I think I'm stepping into things and making assumptions—"

"No. Let's circle back," I demanded. I stepped toward him, forcing him to look me in the eye. I would not let him charm his way out of explaining. "Whit bought this house for *me*? I thought he bought it for himself, so he'd have a place to stay when he was in town, or maybe because he couldn't forget our childhood. But for me? No way."

Bram shook his head. "I thought you knew. I shouldn't have said it."

I could tell he was shaken by the change in his eyes, but I wasn't worried about Bram or his loose lips. I couldn't believe my brother. For him to plan to give me a whole house, Grams' house, and in Mill Creek, no less? Why? What was he thinking?

"Ridiculous." I turned around and walked away from the door. "Why would he do it? He knows how I feel about him and his money."

Bram let himself inside since I had lost all sense of hospitality and hadn't invited him in. "I'm sure Whit has your best interests at heart. He thought if you ever wanted to come back to Mill Creek —"

I scoffed. "Come back to Mill Creek? For what? Why would I come back here?"

His brow furrowed. We hadn't been together for more than

five minutes after fifteen years, and I'd already made it awkward.

Our eyes met again. I could swim in their depths as he studied me underneath the brim of his cap.

He wasn't what I imagined. He was rugged and outdoorsy, and I didn't expect him to look like he'd been working outside with his hands. I'd expected him to look like he'd come from wealth. I expected him to dress like the last time I'd seen him, when he wore blue slacks and a white button-up, the day of Grams' funeral. He'd looked so grown up as he'd entered my hospital room. The memories sobered me.

"I've never had anything to return here for," I said, keeping my tone as even as possible.

Whit would never return to Mill Creek permanently, and Grams couldn't. Bram was here, but he was an enigma. Sometimes, as much as he was a part of my childhood, I thought maybe I'd made him up in my head.

Seconds that felt like minutes passed by.

"Everyone always comes home, eventually," he shrugged, as if what I had said held no weight. "Besides, you know the best dating pools exist in small towns. That's what I think, anyway."

He winked and took a few steps toward me. I took a few steps back, creating distance. I couldn't be too close to him.

Yet it was the closest to home I'd felt since driving into Mill Creek. I loathed it and loved it at the same time.

"Presumptuous much? How do you know I'm not taken or married?" I asked, a little breathless. How much did he know about me? How much *could* he know? Had he asked Whit?

"Honestly, I don't know, but my guess is you aren't." His eyes held a certain irresistible twinkle. Was he goading me? My face turned hard as steel with all trace of wonder gone.

"Why? Because I'm not relationship material, like you said before? Am I just a sister to every man I meet?" The ice in my tone could've frozen an ocean. From the narrowing of his eyes, I knew I'd struck something within him.

He remembered what he'd said that day at the hospital.

I hadn't meant to show my hand so readily, but I was feeling so much. Anger, resentment, disappointment, to name a few emotions. Remembering how he'd rejected me after declaring he cared for me was a wound that still bled.

"That was a low blow," he grumbled, his deep voice resonating. "That's not what I meant. You don't have a ring on. And Whit never said you were married or in a relationship. He and I still talk often. I have a feeling he might have told me something if it was significant."

"You think you're so smart," I muttered, but I knew he still heard me.

"Are you married?" he asked, point-blank.

I could lie to him. It's not like he or Whit knew me enough anymore to be sure.

"Maybe." I shrugged, and he frowned.

"Don't toy with me, Julianna East."

"If that's still my name…"

He rolled his eyes.

I rested a hand on my hip. "I'm assuming *you're* not married. I venture to say you're probably single." It was a wild shot in the dark, but he didn't need to know that.

He shrugged. "Maybe I am, maybe I'm not."

It was my turn to roll my eyes.

"Listen, Jules." I cringed at the ease with which he said my old nickname. "I didn't come here to disturb your peace. I didn't come to make you hate Whit, either. I'm making a mess of everything." His brow furrowed. "I came to help you unload your stuff. You don't need to carry anything with your back like it is now."

I tried to rein in my frustration and remain like stone, but it proved impossible.

I reached inwardly for resentment toward Bram and tried pulling it over me like a blanket to protect myself from the feelings of vulnerability he was pulling out of me. I didn't blame Bram for the wreck or my subsequent back surgery, but I needed to believe he was to blame so I could harden myself against him.

My complicated feelings weren't only about him, either. I was in a town I no longer identified with, far from Kallie and the familiarity of everyday life. This house, which was once filled with love and laughter I'd cherished, was not what I envisioned and had been wiped of the memories that held me together for many lonely days and nights in my adulthood. My brother had once again planned to buy my affection by gifting me our grandmother's house.

My chest tightened up, and I was unable to breathe easily. This was too difficult.

"I won't be carrying anything in here because I'm not staying here."

I walked over and grabbed all the snacks I'd unloaded and threw them into the box I'd moved them with.

"Whoa, what?" He marched over, grabbed the box of mini chocolate chip cookies from my hands, and put them on the counter with an audible *thwack*. "Whit may have changed his mind about the house. Hell, maybe he's looking to sell it after you go back to Charlotte. I don't know. But it's yours, for now at least, and you have to stay here until you get the surgery you need."

"No, I don't *have* to do anything!"

Bram jumped back slightly at my outburst. I know my attitude wasn't how he'd pictured me in his mind. I saw it in the way his eyes widened, startled.

"I won't let Whit gift me a house."

"He's your brother, Julianna. He has plenty of money to do whatever he wants."

"Exactly! He has his own life. He shouldn't be thinking about me at all!"

Bram huffed. His hands landed on his hips, and his stance became domineering. "Did you ever stop and think that Whit wants to be a part of your life?"

"If he wanted to be a part of my life, he would have returned my calls and texts."

Bram's eyes darted away, his shoulders rounded, and his hands went to his pockets. His annoyance moved to regret.

No, no, no.

I chanted the word over and over in my head as tears formed behind my eyelids. I would not cry in front of the only man I'd ever truly wanted. The man who'd crushed my will to be close to any partner into tiny fragments on a hospital floor.

The only man I'd ever loved, who never loved me back.

"I can't stay here," I heard myself whisper aloud. My hands shook. The dam of panic I'd been holding back broke. "This house…" I looked around. "I keep looking for her, and I can't… I can't find her." My voice cracked as grief overwhelmed me, and the tears began to flow.

He inched toward the end of the island, and his fingers twitched at his sides. But he never stepped into my space. Like with most situations with Bram, I wasn't sure whether to be grateful that he didn't make a move or regretful that I let myself believe, even for a moment, that he wanted to.

I shouldn't want him to. I couldn't look at him directly, afraid he'd see everything I was too scared to admit to myself.

"Then you're coming with me."

My heart stopped.

"What?" I asked. I used the back of my hand to catch the tears falling down my cheeks. "W-what do you mean?"

He moved to grab the box of snacks on the island. "You'll stay with me. No one lives with me, and I have plenty of room. At least for the night."

"No," I replied. The shock of what he'd said made the worst of the anxiety attack dissipate into thin air. "I can't do that." I grabbed his formidable arm and tried to stop his strides toward the front door with my snacks. "Stop. No. I can't stay with you."

"Why not? I've got two empty bedrooms." He dragged me along as I clung to him, only stopping when he got to the front door. "Can you get this for me?"

A headache was forming alongside my panic. "No, I can't 'get that for you' because I'm not going anywhere with you!"

"Give me one legitimate, good reason why you can't stay with me."

I shook my head, the whiplash of my motions and emotions making me dizzy. "Because...I can't!"

"That's not a reason. You don't want to stay here. You can't go back to Charlotte—"

"I can go back," I interrupted.

"Oh, so you still have a place there?" His eyebrow cocked, which of course affected me in all the wrong ways, but I continued, undeterred.

"My best friend will let me stay with her and her fiancé. She owns a bakery." I pointed at my shirt. "Brandon is nice, and they'll snatch me up in a second, no questions asked."

"Okay, well, at least the shirt makes sense now." He gestured with his head toward what I was wearing. I looked down at the words plastered over my breasts: "Nice Buns." I had forgotten. I gasped, crossing my arms across my chest to hide the graphic.

His eyes slowly paused on my covered breasts that were propped up for his viewing pleasure. I pretended not to notice that he was checking me out. But I did know, and I didn't appreciate how it made me feel a deeper flush of warmth.

"I'll stay here in this weird, haunted house. I will be fine.

Look, I'll even give you the keys to the U-Haul, and you can start unloading. That's what you came for, right?"

Bram wouldn't be swayed. "I just watched you burst out crying. I can't leave you like this. You're not ready to accept what happened here. I understand that. Remove yourself from the situation and come with me. You'll come back when you're ready to face it."

His irises were so warm. It was as if he were peering into my very being and could see all my thoughts, and perhaps even my desires.

That was a dangerous place for him to be.

"When did you grow up?" I asked, my tone sarcastic, but my question was asked in earnest.

"Therapy, about six years ago." He shrugged, and I marveled at how he didn't miss a beat. "You're not the only one with ghosts and regrets, Julianna." He swallowed hard and looked away from me toward the door, still holding that damn box. "Open the door. Let me load this stuff. Stay with me for a while, then come back here when you feel less fragile."

My mind grasped for words to hurl at him. I wanted to hurt him. I wanted to say something so scathing that he would break. I wanted to watch the pain work in his face and spread into the marrow of his bones.

But I couldn't, and I wouldn't. I was 'the good girl'.

"I don't even know you anymore," I said instead, but my words sounded hollow.

"That's fair. But I'm the same guy I was fifteen years ago in many ways. Different in other ways. Better, I think," he admitted. "I'm still your brother's best friend. I'm still me."

"Not a serial killer?"

And he laughed. A spark lit in his eyes.

"Not a serial killer. Come on, show me what you need for a short stay."

CHAPTER FIVE

Bram | *September 29, 2024*

O ne moment, I was driving into town alone to help my best friend's sister unpack her U-Haul. Next, I was navigating the back roads toward my house with Julianna sitting quietly beside me.

Having her within arm's length felt like a dream. I gripped the steering wheel tighter, knuckles white. If I reached out to touch her, would she disappear?

When Julianna opened the front door of Grams' house, she'd taken my breath away. She was the same tall beauty she had been fifteen years ago, but with more maturity. I'd seen snapshots of her on social media over the years using fake profiles I created so I could search for her. I avoided social media generally because I didn't find it a worthy use of my limited time. But for Julianna, I'd taken the time. The pictures had been gorgeous, but in person, she was a whole other level of beauty.

I noticed every slight wrinkle around her mouth and eyes, the subtle indicators of time. Even a little chaotic with her messy hair, she was the hottest woman I'd ever seen. Her attempts to shrink her presence by crossing her arms, standing close to objects, and wearing baggy clothes did not detract from her beauty.

I reached over and turned the radio down.

"So, you really don't have someone waiting on you in Charlotte?" I asked, trying to sound nonchalant.

She stared out at the darkness engulfing the mountains on the horizon. She looked deep in thought.

"Nobody is waiting on me," she replied. "I have...difficulty with relationships."

Maybe she didn't mean those words as a passive-aggressive dig at me, but I felt it as one all the same.

"I don't think it's wrong for you to be wary, considering all the loss you've been through."

"It's ridiculous," she scoffed. "People deal with so much more in their lives than I have. Who am I to operate off a little trauma?"

I shook my head. "Don't minimize your experiences. Your parents abandoned you, then you lost the only parent you had when you were still a teen, and to top it off, you got in a car accident with—"

"I don't regret that," she blurted, "I got in the truck with you willingly that night."

My insides froze. How could she not?

"I regret that night enough for us both, then," I said, my voice barely a whisper.

"I would rather not talk about any of that."

The finality in her tone caused a nervous lump in my throat. Merely a few minutes into our journey, and everything was going wrong quickly. I had to change the subject. "Okay," I said. "Tell me about yourself. What have you been doing these days?"

This seemed to interest her, and she sat up a little in her seat.

"I ran social media marketing for a publishing company for the past ten years. But I lost my job the week before last."

"Fuck. I'm sorry. I can confidently say they had no idea what they were losing."

"That's sweet of you to say," she replied. "But how do you know? I could have been crap at it."

I grinned, keeping my eyes on the road ahead. "No one keeps a job for ten years if they suck, especially a high-stakes one like that. Did you like doing that type of work?"

She sighed. "Yes, I loved it, and I think I was good at it."

"I'm sure you were. It sounds like a them-problem, not a you-problem."

"Maybe." She looked down at her lap. "I won't say I'm not upset about it, but the news about my back has overshadowed the grief of it."

"Understandable. How did you end up here?" I already knew this part of the story, but I absorbed her voice as she told me the things Whit already had.

She cast a prolonged look straight at me when she was done, but I pretended not to notice and stared out the windshield. "Whit didn't tell you any of that?" she asked.

I loosened my grip on the steering wheel, letting one hand rest casually on it. My mouth curled into a sly smile. "I wanted to hear you tell it." I let myself ooze the charm I so rarely used anymore.

To my surprise, she smiled back. "You always were the biggest flirt." Of course, she had caught on immediately.

"Some things never change," I replied with a shrug.

"What about you?" she asked. "What do you do these days?"

I shifted in my seat, uncomfortably trying to conjure the

right words. "Work. Volunteer." *Think of you.* "I'm a supervisor for the US Forest Service."

"Ooh, that's fancy. Sounds important."

"I've worked for the Forest Service for a while." I didn't elaborate because I longed for her to know me as someone seasoned by life, not as the Bram Winchester of our teens. I briefly considered telling her about my work with Mill Creek Aid, but it felt like bragging, which I did not want to do. I wasn't always the purest of heart, but MCA was too important for me to use it to score "good guy" points.

From my periphery, I noticed that she was still clasping and flexing her hands in her lap.

"Are you cold?" I asked.

"No." Then she startled, as if remembering what she was doing. "Oh, my hands? It's a nervous thing..."

I should have considered how nervous she was, just as I was. I felt like I was forging a river without a raft. So much tension remained between us.

I needed to get a grip on myself. There would be an opportunity to apologize for the wreck and tell the whole truth about what happened if I were patient. Until then, I could stay close as the friend she needed. Part of that meant not pushing her to talk about our tragic past when she had drawn a clear line.

"I'm sorry this is anxiety-inducing, too. What can I do to make it better? I want you to be comfortable."

I imagined it was on the tip of her tongue to tell me I could go back and erase that December night from her memory. But we both knew that was impossible, and she would never say something so blatantly unkind.

"I'll be fine," she said, and she looked out the passenger window where I couldn't see her expression anymore.

After a few minutes of silence, I turned the radio back on at a low volume. We were nearing the turnoff. When we arrived at it and I slowed, she turned towards me and said, "You live here? Down this road?" The dashboard lights illuminated her curious face.

"Yeah," I replied, turning the steering wheel with one hand. "It's the old Wheeler farmstead. Do you know it?"

I could hear my pulse in my ears and feel anticipation tightening my insides.

"Yes! I used to come here with Grams when I was little to see old Mrs. Wheeler. They were friends. Even after she died, Grams would bring Whit and me here sometimes for a quiet day out. I bet Whit told you about that."

"Maybe." I didn't want her to know that I bought it solely because of her affinity for it. It hadn't been an easy property to procure. It sat abandoned for years with the forest slowly creeping down the hill to reclaim the barn and house. When I visited ten years ago, the porch had caved in, and weeds and vines covered the old clapboard siding.

But I saw the vision of what I wanted the house to be. I often pictured Julianna as I restored it. Many days, it felt like I was sharing the experience with a ghost.

But now she was here, and she would see what I'd made of it.

"It's going to be obvious I had no intentions of you coming out here today," I said. "Let's just say, I am a bachelor in the most stereotypical sense. And I have a dog. Probably should have mentioned that."

"Oh? What breed? What's their name?" She sounded excited, and I was relieved. Grams never let Whit and Julianna have pets, so I wasn't sure where she stood.

"I'm not sure of her exact breed. I got her from the shelter a couple of years ago as a pup. They thought she was a beagle and golden retriever mix. Her name is Lakey."

"Lakey." She tried the name on for size, a broad smile flooding her face. "That's cute."

We turned onto the long driveway to the main house, gravel

crunching underneath the wheels. It wasn't until we turned the bend that we could see the porch lights shining in the pitch-black of the hollow.

Julianna said nothing when the truck stopped in front of the three-car garage fifty yards from the house. I knew what my home looked like with my eyes closed. I'd touched every inch of it with my bare hands. But she seemed unsure, squinting to make out the details in the dark before she slipped out of the truck. I watched as she better took in the white siding and black tin roof of the house. She could see the long, covered porch on the front lit up, showcasing a double swing and rocking chairs. I tried to keep everything well-maintained and clean, and I was glad my efforts were finally paying off. She moved around to my side of the vehicle, still staring at the façade.

Her expression melted into one of awe and appreciation.

"How did you do all this?" she asked.

I ran a hand through my hair. "Well, after the football injury, I took a construction job for a couple of years. I learned a lot doing that, and I was good at it."

"So you have a big boy job, and you can also do this? Color me impressed." She turned to face me. The faraway porch light reflected in her eyes, making them sparkle in the dark. "It is breathtaking, Bram."

I held out the key to her. "Go check it out. I'll get your stuff."

I grabbed her small suitcase from the back bench seat of the truck. She hadn't brought much with her since she was planning to stay only one night. I wanted to turn her single night into two, three, maybe four, or perhaps a week, or even the whole time she needed to be in Roanoke.

When I opened the screen door and walked in, I saw Julianna standing stock-still in the middle of the living room, her deep-brown eyes lit with curiosity as she scanned her surroundings. I set her bags down and flipped on the light.

Stuff was everywhere: a random flashlight, dog toys, papers, and a few empty beer cans.

"Bram," she whispered, her eyes finally resting on mine. "It is perfect. The original woodwork restored—and this fireplace..." She skimmed her fingertips over the refinished mantle as her voice trailed off.

Then she floated across the room to the forest green velvet cushion of the built-in picture window seat. Her graze against the fabric was slow and reverent. It made me smile and tingle with awareness of her. I would give the world to have that touch turned on me.

As if hearing my inner thoughts, Julianna quickly walked over and threw her arms around me.

It had been a long time since I had been pleasantly surprised by anything, but the feel of her pressed against me...

This was what should have happened that night on the road.

This was what should have occurred when I went to see her in the hospital on that sad, snowy day of Grams' funeral.

This is how it should have been.

I wrapped her in my arms tightly, unable to resist what was given to me, even if I couldn't keep it. She put her cheek against my shoulder, and I had to fight to keep the smile off my face as I slowly rubbed her back.

Incessant barking came from the utility room where Lakey waited in her kennel.

Julianna untangled herself, and I let her pull away.

Cockblock dog.

She pulled a few loose strands of hair behind her ears and averted her eyes as a blush spread along her cheekbones.

"Come on, let me introduce you to my girl," I said, shoving my hands in my pockets to keep from touching her again.

I led the way through the dining room and the kitchen and walked into the back utility room. Lakey's whines ceased when she sensed my presence, but when I flipped on the light and she saw Julianna, she went into guard dog mode and her barking became shrill.

"Lakey, come on now," I scolded.

But Julianna was unaffected. She walked around me confidently.

"Hi, darling," she cooed, softly and sweetly. She knelt before the kennel door and stuck her hand through the grate so Lakey could smell her. Julianna petted her with her fingertips. Lakey took to her immediately, nuzzling against Julianna's hand.

"She likes me!" Julianna exclaimed, then she looked up at me and smiled.

The most vile, dirty thought possible ran through my mind of Julianna on her knees in front of me, her eyes fixed on mine with sparks of unmatched excitement.

I knelt beside her to quell my quickly rising situation. I unlatched the door to the kennel, and Lakey bounded out with the force of a thousand elephants. She ran directly at Julianna, knocking her back with untethered excitement.

"Whoa!" I grabbed for Lakey's collar, but Julianna was giggling as Lakey licked her face. I let go and watched the scene unfold.

Julianna's dark-painted fingernails dug into Lakey's spotted fur as she gave the deep scratches Lakey loved so much. I was unable to keep the smile off my face. It was as if they were long-lost friends reunited after an eternity apart—happy, joyous, and enamored. What I wouldn't give to have that sort of affection between us.

Was I jealous of my dog?

"You didn't tell me how sweet she was!" A hug around Lakey's neck punctuated Julianna's words. "How in the world did someone like you come across a dog like this?" She asked it teasingly, but something within me couldn't help but feel a little sting of truth. Even Lakey was too good for me.

I shrugged.

She didn't seem to notice my demeanor shift as she gave Lakey one last scratch on the neck before she got to her feet and wiped dog hair off her lap.

"Let's go," I said, gesturing with a tilt of my head, "I'll show you upstairs."

I first led her through the rest of the downstairs area, which consisted of a half bath, another bedroom, and a small room I had turned into an office. Lakey walked behind us, her tongue wagging, happy to fall into step.

I led Julianna up the stairs in the entryway. "This"—I gestured to the first room on the right at the top of the stairs—"is my bedroom."

She peeked in. I hadn't made the bed. Clothes, random shoes, and more dog toys were strewn about. I would have been embarrassed, but there was something about letting Julianna see my life like this that felt right.

"I'm so happy you didn't paint everything man colors," she said and stepped through the threshold into the bedroom. "I love all the soft white against the farmhouse fixtures. And these floors?"

"Original," I replied, toeing a little at the dark-stained, wide-wood planks under our feet. "One of my favorite things, I think. They're still rough, but it reminds me of the house's history. They were a labor of love, for sure."

She looked at me over her shoulder. "They're my favorite, too." One hand rested on her waist as she turned to face me. "I can't believe you own this place and all you've done. It's amazing."

She was considered in every refinished floorboard and paint swipe. She just didn't know it. I leaned against the doorframe as she talked.

"I dreamed about this house sometimes. Some of my best memories of Grams, Whit, and me are here."

"I hope this place isn't as hard for you as where we were." I held my breath, waiting for her reply. I didn't want her to leave, but I didn't want her to be uncomfortable either.

She smiled. "It's not. That house feels like an alien planet, but this place feels like a warm fire on a cold winter night. Like..."

Please say it feels like home.

Instead of finishing her thought, the words died on her lips.

I wanted to take her face in my hands and press my lips to hers. Instead, I did nothing and kept my longing locked inside myself.

"I'm exhausted," she said, breaking me out of my thoughts. "I know it's still early, but I would love to lie down. Do you prefer which bedroom I stay in?"

Yes, actually, I do. You should be staying in my room with me.

I cleared my throat. "That one is ready for guests, and it's by the bathroom," I said, pointing to the other end of the hallway.

"Then that is the one I pick." I moved out of her way, and she walked down the small hall and opened the door of the bedroom, looking in briefly. "It's perfect."

"I'll bring up your overnight bag. Is that all you need?"

She nodded. I ran to do her bidding. Lakey followed me down the stairs, then back up, excited about whatever was happening. Julianna took the bag from my hands at the threshold of her room.

"I put your snack box in the kitchen. I'm pretty low on food. There's some bottled water down there in the fridge. Would you like me to get one for you? I mean, the spring water from the tap is pretty good, and there's a filter, of course, but, you know."

My cheeks heated. I was never flustered, but the impromptu situation had me out of my element. She shook her head, trying to hide her snicker behind her hand. "No, I'm okay. But if I need one later...?"

"Be my guest. You're welcome to anything I have," I said, gesturing to the stairs.

She held the doorknob. "Thank you for taking me in. Although it was absolutely under duress." Her tired eyes crinkled with a smile. I wondered if she was thinking about when she said those words to me about Whit the night of the wreck.

"I hope it's the best kidnapping you've ever had," I replied cheekily.

She dipped her head and giggled, and my heart soared.

Even though I knew it was dangerous, I couldn't help but think, *"How does she feel about me, really?"*

But Whit's words echoed in my head as I headed back downstairs.

"Don't even think about it, Bram."

CHAPTER SIX

Julianna | *September 29, 2024*

The bedside lamp cast soft shadows over the walls. According to the antique wall clock, I'd lain awake for three hours. Distractions were not working. My mind was on an endless loop, a barrage of emotions threatening to choke the tiny bit of peace I'd attained since entering Bram's house.

As much as I didn't want to be indebted to Bram for taking me in, I was thankful I wasn't staying at what was left of Gram's house. The home I knew no longer existed. It would never again have the smell of cinnamon pinecones and wood smoke in the winter or sun tea and freshly cut grass in the summer. All those memories were remnants of the past. I should have known I couldn't go back, but I hadn't been prepared.

I couldn't believe I was staying in this farmhouse that had only existed in the recesses of my childhood memories. Bram had restored it beautifully with his bare hands and sharp skills. The man had more capabilities than I ever thought possible.

He left you alone, injured on the side of the road.

He broke your heart into a million pieces.

He didn't come for you.

My mind kept pinging between past occurrences and present truth.

It wasn't loneliness that made my brain work overtime. I was used to being alone. The only person I'd shared personal space with as an adult was Kallie. None of the short-term boyfriends of my past ever so much as stayed overnight. I couldn't do casual cohabitation. I was a hopeless romantic in a world of instant gratification and cool indifference. I had not even had sex yet. My sexual resume wasn't empty, but intercourse was a line I had yet to cross. No one ever seemed worth that type of closeness.

My thoughts were interrupted by a slight cough. Bram's footsteps echoed as he padded up the stairs, followed by the click of Lakey's nails on the wood. My insides tensed, including my back, which protested over my muscles flexing. I didn't relax until I heard his bedroom door creak twice, indicating that it opened and closed.

I was in a strange, yet familiar, house with a strange, yet familiar, man, wrestling with a mattress that wasn't supporting my back.

I had to be very picky about what I slept on, and the guest bed wasn't cutting it. Pinching and burning pains tore through my body, sensations that had become more frequent as the days passed, punctuating my lack of time. Surgery was no longer a maybe. It was a must. And I refused to bother Bram about moving rooms. I didn't want him to know how badly I suffered. I got up and removed the heating pad and naproxen from my overnight bag, which made me realize I had no water to take the pills. There was no choice for me but to make a quick expedition down the stairs.

I tried to be quiet on my socked feet, but the old house made it impossible. The floor and doors creaked. I cringed at the noises but decided I was being ridiculous. Bram told me I could go downstairs if I were thirsty. I still slinked down the little hall, pausing at Bram's bedroom door when I noticed it was slightly ajar.

I stood there for a moment in the semi-dark. A light from the foyer below illuminated the space, but it wasn't enough for me to see into his room. I took the tiniest sliding step toward the open door.

I didn't notice the deep knot in the old wooden floorboard, and my toe caught in it. My heart stopped as I pitched forward into the bedroom door, unable to find anything to grab to stabilize myself. It flung open, and I fell onto the floor inside the bedroom face-first, right in time for me to glance over and see a completely naked Bram Winchester walk out of his ensuite bathroom.

Eyes wide, I stared up at him. Lakey jumped off the bed and leapt to get to me. Her wet tongue on my face blocked my vision of Bram.

"Whoa!" was all I'd heard Bram exclaim. He ran back into the bathroom and slammed the door shut. I gently pushed Lakey away, and before I could gather my wits to flee, Bram was already on his knees beside me with a white towel wrapped around his waist.

"My God, are you okay?"

I looked up at his dripping wet form, trying to take him in fully, but it was impossible.

No trace of boyishness remained in his broad shoulders, roughened skin, or the chest hair that haunted my dreams. He no longer had defined abs, but his stomach and chest were solid, and his arms were well-defined without flexing. I hadn't noticed the veins in his forearms earlier. I hadn't even known forearms could be so attractive.

I tried, and failed, not to think about his dick.

He was so perfect. And I'd crashed into his bedroom in the middle of the night like a fucking creep.

I groaned, the thoughts of his handsomeness eclipsed by the sharp pains in my back.

"Can you move?" His deep voice felt like velvet against my skin.

I tried to move and gritted my teeth as my muscles protested."My back," I said in a small voice, then I exhaled a groan.

Before I could react further, Bram bent over and scooped my large body up like I was nothing more than a feather. I gasped, struggling against him in pain and embarrassment. I was entirely too heavy for him to lift. "No! You can't—"

"But I am," he interrupted, committed to his act. It wasn't an easy transition, but he walked me to his bed and gently placed me on the worn quilt and rumpled sheets.

The mattress enveloped me like a cloud. Of course, his mattress was perfect, while my borrowed one across the hall was a torture device.

"Tell me if you're seriously hurt." His words were harsh, but his voice was trembling, and I blushed under his concern and attention.

"No, it's...I was already hurting." I rubbed my back a little, near the middle part, where the damage was. "And I'm embarrassed. I'd evaporate into thin air if I had the power."

He chuckled. "I could ask what you were doing, but let me guess, you were going down the stairs, saw my door ajar, and decided you'd go full Peeping Tom like you used to when we were in high school."

My eyes snapped to his. His amber irises shone with teasing warmth.

"You knew I watched you?" I shrieked and sat up clumsily, ignoring the shooting pains from my sudden movement.

It was true. I'd watched him change more than once when he'd stayed at our house growing up. I was a creeper from way back. I thought I'd been discreet, but obviously not.

His eyes shone bright with mischief. "Oh, I knew. I could see wisps of your hair from around the door."

I dropped my face into my hands, and my cheeks burned with mortification.

"But you never said anything?" I peeked through my fingers and saw the intense smolder he was giving me.

"Why would I? I liked having the attention of a hot girl on me." He winked, and I had to pretend he didn't, lest I giggle like a schoolgirl with a crush.

Which I was *not*.

"Come on, it was years ago. Fun memories," he said it with ease, trying to absolve my shock.

I dropped my hands in surrender. There was a pause, and his eyebrows furrowed a bit. "Tell me how I can help you, Jules."

He squatted beside the bed, and I turned to face him. We were only a foot apart from each other. I took a deep breath.

"I really need some of my naproxen and water to take it with. And maybe you can let Lakey sleep with me tonight?"

"Hmmm..." He acted like he was thinking it over, rubbing a hand along his shaped, scruffy jaw. "Well, let me put on some pants, then I'll get you a drink downstairs, and some naproxen from my bathroom." He nodded toward the open doorway a few feet away, "And considering Lakey's already curled up behind you..." Lakey's warm, furry body was lightly tucked against my back.

"I meant, can she sleep with me in the bed down the hall?" I corrected, even though I would do anything to sleep in this perfect bed with Lakey and Bram.

I shoved the wayward thought aside.

"Lakey likes to sleep in here," he said.

My heart fell—no Lakey, no bed, no Bram, just me and my humiliation. I swallowed and began to get up, but Bram stood and reached out, grabbing my upper arm to steady me.

"Don't move! I mean, you stay here. We can switch back rooms tomorrow."

I tilted my head.

"But, t-this is your room..." My voice cracked with emotion.

Your bed. Your sheets. You are everywhere here, and I can't stand it.

He smiled broadly. "It's still my room. It's not a big deal. Let's get some sleep."

"I won't be here tomorrow night," I replied matter-of-factly. "So you'll have your bed back, promise."

"Mhm. We'll see."

Before I could open my mouth to protest, he walked into the bathroom, closing the door behind him. As if to cement the decision, Lakey spread out her body whole against mine, settling in for her night's rest.

My back was screaming, my head was pounding, and my shoulder throbbed where it hit the floor when I fell into the room, yet I was comfortable. The sheets felt and looked clean, and knowing they held him at some point was overwhelming.

I intended to wait for him to emerge from the bathroom to get my water and pills, but somehow, sleep found me first.

THE SECOND I WOKE UP, I WAS ACUTELY AWARE THAT I WAS IN Bram's bed in his bedroom in his beautiful house. My back felt rested, and my body was warm and cozy, snuggled under his soft, colorful quilt. Bram must have covered me with it.

I could only imagine the snoring mess I was when he came back with my water. I was probably drooling, too.

I peered through the glass of the nearest window. Seeing the Appalachian Mountains covered in autumnal colors made it one of the most breathtaking sights. The slightest bit of morning sun peeked over the ridge, the first few beams of light spilling onto the hardwood, soft and beautiful.

Back in Charlotte, I often yearned to see the thick forests and the rounded tops in the distance. Those geographical markers were home to me.

Lakey had abandoned her post, and I was alone. I looked around leisurely from my spot in the bed, taking the room in more thoroughly than I had the night before. Clothes were strewn about the floor, and shoes were in a pile beside a closed door that I assumed was the closet. A worn, navy robe hung on a single hook on the mystery door.

In the far-right corner of the room was a small bookshelf with history and nature books. I didn't see any recognizable fiction, except for one worn novel near the bottom. It was a copy of Bram Stoker's *Dracula*, which made me smile.

A brown leather belt and shiny badge caught my eye on the dresser. I assumed these items were part of his work uniform. Thinking of Bram in a uniform made my heart flutter, but I pushed that feeling away.

There weren't any pictures on the walls, but some photos in wooden frames were on top of his dresser as well. One of them was from a weekend trip Grams had taken us on, not long after Bram had entered our lives. We had visited a Wild West-themed amusement park located somewhere in North Carolina. I couldn't believe Bram had a picture of me in his bedroom. It was a young, twelve-year-old me, but me, all the same.

He'd kept it in plain sight, even though I had no idea all these years later that I ever crossed his mind. It made me feel thrilled and angry. He'd been seeing me all this time, every day on his dresser, and never thought to track me down? What had kept him from getting my phone number from Whit? It was enough to make tears form in my eyes.

The other picture was of Bram and an unknown woman standing in a tilled field, wearing sunglasses. His arm was around her shoulders. She was tall, like me, but slim. Her long, highlighted hair was pulled back into a high ponytail at the top of her head. They were both wearing outdoor clothing with bright smiles. The picture didn't look very old.

Is she Bram's girlfriend?

He had said he was unattached, but what if that was a lie? Something to make me feel more at ease about being around him? Was I sleeping in his room, behind the mystery woman's back?

I felt like bugs were crawling over the surface of my skin at the thought. I tossed off the covers and pulled my pajama shorts into place. Cold air hit my legs, and I shivered, wanting immediately back under the quilt. But I had sobered up at the pictures and needed to leave the room immediately. I had to find out who the woman was.

I could ask him outright, but would he be upset I was snooping in his room? Was it snooping if the picture was on display?

No, of course, it isn't. It's fair game. Now, I was asking and answering my questions. *Awesome.*

I sprinted to the en-suite bathroom.

Every wall and tile was white, and the fixtures were matte black. It was a pristine space. I closed the door, used the toilet, and washed my hands. I looked at my reflection in the large mirror over the sink.

For once in my life, I wanted to wake up and not look like a bridge troll.

"Jules?" Bram's deep voice reverberated from downstairs. I ignored his call. I scurried across the hall to the spare bedroom and looked around for my bag. It wasn't where I'd left it by the guest bed.

"Crap," I muttered, looking behind the door and finding nothing. I heard Bram moving up the stairs. I froze.

I don't know why it felt like I was being caught. I only wanted my overnight bag. Yet I panicked and slammed the bedroom door shut before he could reach me.

"Julianna?" he asked, bewildered. I let out a big breath, my heart racing.

"I'm not decent!" I lied, trying to sound pleasant.

"What? Why? I put your bag in my room beside the bed. Did you not see it?"

I gasped. I didn't think I was loud about it, but I heard him chuckle.

"It's okay. Open the door."

"No," I squeaked out. "I told you I'm indecent."

"It's nothing I haven't seen before."

Humiliation crawled up my neck, and a hot tingle of something between my legs appeared that was most unwelcome.

"That doesn't mean you get to see my...my parts," I replied, frustrated at my body's betrayal. Bram and I were only old friends, and my libido needed to get the memo. "Brothers don't see their sisters naked."

"I'm not your fucking brother," he spat in disgust, and it was my turn to laugh.

"That's not what I heard," I muttered, thinking about that day at the hospital.

There was silence for a moment, and I was worried I had upset him. Quickly, before I could talk myself out of it, I swung open the door.

Bram put one arm up over the doorframe, and my eyes immediately latched onto the defined muscles of his biceps and forearms. The fitted gray tee he wore hugged every part of him perfectly. His attention was fixed directly on my face. It was unfair how hot he was.

"Damn it. You're clothed," he said with a smirk.

I rolled my eyes.

"Great observation skills." I pushed his chest with open palms, and the solidness under my hands was melting my resolve to forget how attractive he was. We both knew that if he'd wanted to keep me trapped, it wouldn't have been an issue for him. But after a couple of non-aggressive shoves, he moved back. I headed toward his bedroom.

"You could have just told me you didn't see the bag instead of running from me," he called out behind me. Lakey circled my legs as I entered Bram's room again, and sure enough, my blue weekend bag was on the floor near the bathroom. I'd walked right by it.

"I assumed it was in the other bedroom, and I closed the door because I was going to change. Simple as that." I would not admit to him that I'd been acting ridiculous. I looked back at him down the hallway.

"I won't argue." He sauntered toward me. He was not guarded, not like he used to be. It made me want to know all the things that had changed to make him seem more confidently open.

"Come downstairs," he coaxed, doing the same doorframe lean as earlier. I couldn't look at him and remain indifferent to his presence when he stood like that. All I could picture was his bare chest and strong body doing that same move over me.

"I need to dress first," I said, looking down at my ratty tee and pajama shorts. Usually, I would have been self-conscious about flaunting my leg cellulite in front of anyone, but I refused to let him affect me that way. We were just old friends. I did not need to try to impress him in any way.

Maybe if I kept repeating it, my mind would get the memo.

"After," he said, slapping the doorframe like his words were final. "Lakey and I made you breakfast."

I rolled my eyes once again, but I followed his command.

In the kitchen, Bram explained that he'd called out of work. I felt guilty for keeping him from his life, but he assured me it was fine. I hadn't thought about him going to work. My life had been turned so upside down that I had momentarily forgotten working was a thing. I would soon have to look for employment. It wasn't something I could put off.

He presented me with a plate of fried eggs and toast.

"It smells wonderful," I said.

"Thanks. Fixings are there." He pointed to the table. "Just waiting on my toast."

I took the plate, walked to the small, rustic kitchen table, and sat. Like upstairs, sunlight spilled through the windows and onto the kitchen floor, casting shadows unique to the time of day. The house was drafty downstairs from the morning air, a product of its age. I forgot how cool fall mornings were in the mountains. Lakey sat at my feet as I spread butter on my toast, and Bram took his place across from me.

"The bread looks homemade," I noted, picking up a glob of berry jam with a butter knife. "And the jam. Domestic much?"

He shrugged. "It's elderberry jam." He took a big bite of his piece, chewed, and continued. "It was given to me."

"Given? Who makes such things?" I poured a splash of half-and-half into my coffee from the small carton he'd set on the table.

I thought it was a harmless question, but I was surprised when he squirmed a little, looking unsure.

"Just some people in town. I volunteer sometimes, and some of the ladies like to pay for the help." He winked.

"Help? Are you carrying old women's groceries to their cars?"

I watched as he ran a hand through his hair.

"Something like that," he said. "That butter is local from Elson's farm, and that elderberry jam is elderberry. It is from—"

"Let me guess. The elders?" I laughed. Corny jokes were my specialty. The more nervous I was, the worse they became.

"Weak," he chuckled, spreading butter on his toast, "but also cute."

Silently pleased with myself, I took another bite.

I studied the integrity of my eggs, unable to think of one thing to say. I wanted to ask about his volunteer work on a serious level, but would that make him uncomfortable, too? While I was still deciding what to say, he spoke. "Are we gonna skirt around the elephant in the room, or are we gonna talk this through?"

I sobered, slowing the chewing of my toast.

"Which elephant?" I whispered, unable to grasp which string he wanted to pull.

He chuckled. "Fair question." He downed a gulp of hot coffee, despite the steam rising off the liquid. I had no idea how he managed to do it without burning his tongue. He continued, "Let's take it one elephant at a time. What are you doing in Roanoke for your back? Why here? And what's the plan? Whit only told me bits and pieces."

I licked jelly and crumbs off my fingertips. "Long story short, I have to have surgery because of what I told you last night. Cutting off my spinal nerves could leave me paralyzed."

He stared at me but said nothing.

I could tell from the context clues over the past half day that he still blamed himself for everything that happened with the wreck and my back. But the deer running out in front of us hadn't been his fault. I remembered the desperation in his voice and the pain in his face as he begged to stay with me on the side of the road. I'd pushed him away. I made him leave me. I'd even threatened him.

And I owned my decisions. I loved him beyond myself.

I softened my expression, letting my guard slip ever so slightly. "The situation will only worsen. My normal orthopedic surgeon is retiring this month, and he referred me to the best specialist he knows. She is here in Roanoke. Things should move quickly. Then, in a couple of months, I should be all healed up and back to Charlotte I'll go. If everything goes well."

"It will, I'm sure of it. I'm glad they're moving fast." He looked down into his coffee.

"And the day before I found out about the herniated disc, is when my company let me go. They said that it wasn't personal, just a change in structure. But you can't tell Whit, okay?"

His gaze whipped up to meet mine. "What? Why?"

I shrugged. "I don't want him or anyone to know. I'm sorry, I shouldn't have saddled you with that information."

His lips twitched slightly.

"Secret is safe, if that's what you want. Did you know it was coming?"

I nodded. "I ignored the inevitable. The worst part is that it's left me without health insurance for the surgery. I could probably qualify for some government assistance, but how long would it take? I thought about waiting for the new doctor in Charlotte, but my doctor was insistent that I have the procedure as soon as possible. So, I guess I'll worry about medical payments like every other American."

He drank his coffee, bent over with his elbows on the table, homed in on my every word.

"Whit could pay for it." His words were matter-of-fact.

I shook my head. "No. That's why I don't want him to know I lost my job."

"That doesn't make sense. You have to tell him. He'll pay for it in a heartbeat," Bram insisted.

I held my mug. "It's not that easy for me. I don't want my brother's money. I don't want that feeling of owing him hanging over me. I love him, of course, but things got so weird between us after Grams died. When I found out he'd kept buying Grams' house from me, I was disappointed. It cemented how far apart we are. And then I saw what he'd done to the house yesterday—"

"It wasn't what you thought," he finished for me. I looked down at the wood grain on the breakfast table. I could hear the heaviness in his deep voice. "I didn't know it would affect you so much, or I would have refused to do the work."

"It needed updating. It's not a museum. It's just me being silly…"

"Julianna." His voice sounded like a reprimand.

My eyes met his again, ready to defend myself at his tone. But what I saw in his face unraveled my anger. He wasn't reprimanding me. His face showed a tangle of more complicated emotions, raw and exposed, like a nerve left to the open air.

"It's never silly to chase what makes you feel safe and comfortable."

I tried to let his words sink in before speaking. "Do you ever feel like you want things to be like they used to be?"

His jaw worked for a minute.

"In some ways. My life was never great unless it was with Whit and Grams and you. I don't talk to my parents anymore."

"Not at all?" Vince and Elsie Winchester were terrible people, but they were still his parents. I'd hoped they had gotten better over the years, and that their relationship had gotten better, too, for his sake.

"Nope. The why of it isn't very easy, and maybe I'll explain it someday. But I get what you're saying about Whit's money because I don't want my parents' money either. They've tried to throw it at me, but I don't want anything to do with inheritances or gifts, none of it. Everything my father has gained has come at the expense of so many people. I have a million-dollar trust fund from my grandfather, my Dad's father, who was a good man and made his money honestly. That will be released when and if I get married. But all that's going straight to Mill Creek Aid."

"Mill Creek Aid?" I asked.

"It's the foundation the community started after Dad sold the plant, and it closed down. They helped people get back on their feet after the closure, and they still do a lot of relief work in the county now. Every bit of my grandfather's money will go to help the people it should, the lives my father ruined."

I'd never heard of Mill Creek Aid. Had they helped us after Grams lost her job at the plant? She had never said.

"No one would begrudge you for keeping that money for yourself, for your future, or your own family."

He shook his head. "I would never be able to live with myself. I don't need it anyway."

"What I meant—"

He cut me off. "Let's get back to the original conversation here. Whit is your brother, a good man, and not my parents. He loves you. He didn't know how to work through his grief when Grams died. Neither of you were old enough to know how to keep yourselves together."

But I didn't want to switch subjects.

"What did they do to you?" I whispered. We both knew, with just one look into each other's faces, that I was speaking of his parents. He hadn't expected me to ask because his eyes widened, then softened as he took in my expression.

I'd heard what he said about Whit, and what he said meant a lot. But my heart was breaking for whatever caused Bram to cut off his parents. How bad had they been to him? Grams knew, but she never said a word. She would only say that everyone had problems and would leave it at that.

Had they still been harming him as an adult, too?

"They aren't good people, sweets," he said, his timbre low. I was caught off guard by the nickname. Where had that come from?

"You think you can distract me with a cute nickname, but you are mistaken," I lied. "I won't beg you to tell me, but hopefully, one day, you'll trust me enough to want to."

He cast his eyes down, and my insides flip-flopped.

"It's not that. I trust you," he said. His hand covered mine on the tabletop. Electricity flowed from his skin to mine, and it was my turn to look stunned. "Now, how should we tackle today? Do you have a plan? If not, let's make one."

I tried to gather myself, but I couldn't think. He squeezed my hand and removed his.

"You have too much to do. I can take care of everything myself," I insisted. "Go to work. They need you there, I'm sure."

"I think the forest will stay standing for one day," he replied, getting to his feet and looking down at me with his charming smile. "I'm all yours."

I did not want to admit it, but my heart was becoming entangled in knots that wouldn't be easily undone. Although years had passed, we were still us—two souls with a connection that defied common sense.

CHAPTER SEVEN

Bram | *September 30, 2024*

Julianna returned from upstairs carrying her overnight bag, declaring she would stay at Grams' house. I watched her hug Lakey's neck, and a weird ache radiated in my chest.

I had no say in where she stayed or what she did, but I wanted her with me. It felt essential to keep an eye on her and her condition. Isn't that what Whit would do?

Yeah, but Whit doesn't want to stick his tongue down her throat.

We were miles down the road when she remarked on the color of the trees and how they were so much brighter in the mountains than in Charlotte. The scarlet leaves were her favorite, and when I told her the red color came from a specific pigment that was difficult for many trees to produce in bulk, she laughed.

"Of course, I love the most complicated color. You know a lot about trees, huh?"

"It's my job," I replied with a shrug, having to work to keep my eyes on the road and not on her. "I majored in forestry. I loved it. I got to be outside a lot. Well, until the football injury, at least."

"That must have been so disappointing." I heard the hesitancy in her voice. I wasn't sure if I wanted to talk about it, but I wouldn't cut her off. "Whit texted me when it happened. I was floored. It didn't feel right reaching out to you, but I'm sorry. I probably should have."

"There is nothing to be sorry for. You weren't under any obligation to contact me."

I reached over and turned the heat down as the truck cabin became stuffy.

"What did you do after it happened? Did you stay at college?" Her words were hesitant.

"No. I went to my Mom and Dad's."

"Oh." Her tone told me she wouldn't say anything further, so I continued, "I had to have surgery, and Elsie somehow morphed into a parent for five seconds. She stayed with me through the surgery and brought me home, even when Dad told her not to.

"Of course, she didn't care for me herself. She hired a nurse for that. But she handled the logistics, which was much more than she did when I was younger. Dad was so angry. 'How dare I make a stupid mistake,' that kind of thing..."

"Why would he be angry at an accident? It's not like you wanted to be hurt." She looked indignant.

"It's who he is," I replied. "Failure of any kind was never an option for me. He didn't look at me for weeks after the surgery. I moved out the second I was back on my feet. I finished college online and never went back to Alabama."

"But you kept up with Whit?"

I nodded. "He was becoming more stable by then, more like his old self. He visited me here in Mill Creek a few times."

The trees swayed as we drove through a canopied part of the mountain road.

"I want to ask about Whit," she whispered. "I have so many questions."

"And I would love to answer, but don't you think it might be better for you to ask him?" I hoped my words weren't too sharp. To deflect, I brought the conversation back to myself. "I never told him, you know. About that night. You asked me not to, so I never did."

I glanced over at her then. Her attention was fixed on the road, her face neutral to my admission. "Good," was all she replied.

"I wanted to tell him," I said. "But what you want is more important to me. I need you to know that."

"Hmmm."

I couldn't bear to look at her as my heart pounded loudly in my chest. Instead, I kept my hands firmly on the wheel and my eyes on the road.

"It's funny how we all three came unglued without Grams. She kept us together," she mused softly.

What she said was technically correct. Grams had been significant to us, individually and together. And we'd all made poor choices in the aftermath of her death, but she didn't have anything to do with those choices. Grams had taught us better.

I didn't reply. I couldn't. Instead, I tried to lighten the mood. "How did you meet your best friend? The one with the bakery?"

It was the right move. Julianna pivoted and gushed about Kallie, her bakery, their long friendship, and their lives in Charlotte. "I've been alone a lot since her fiancé Brandon entered the picture," she tacked on at the end of her welcomed sharing. "I've got other friends, but none as close as Kallie. When she moved out of the townhouse, I didn't know what to do with myself. I'm happy for her, and I like being alone most of the time. Nothing is better than curling up with a good book, a piece of pie, and some mood lighting after a long day."

"Still a pie gal after all this time?" I smiled, thinking of the Christmas party where she said Whit had lured her out of the house with the promise of pie.

"Of course. Pie isn't something you get over or grow out of." She pulled on her seat belt a little. "Not that I need to be eating so much pie, but—"

"I think you should eat all the pie you want," I interrupted, unwilling to let her go down that path. I'd never let her think I felt anything but appreciation and yearning for her body exactly as she was. "What is your favorite pie?"

"Blueberry," she replied without hesitation. "Maybe cherry? I also enjoy a nice peach pie in the summer and apple pie on the Fourth of July."

"So, you like fruit pies?" She was beautiful, with her long, dark hair cascading around her shoulders and full lips pursing into a thoughtful pose. I loathed missing one second of her expressions. I hadn't paid enough attention years ago when my crush hadn't fully bloomed. I regretted the time I'd squandered. Now, all I wanted to do was watch her.

"Well, yes. But also chocolate pie, butterscotch, and peanut butter. Pecan, on the holidays. Kallie made me one a few months ago called a shoo-fly pie. It was a warm vanilla custard made with buttermilk and sugar. It was sinfully good. She said the recipe came from her great-grandmother and..." She continued on and on, nervously rambling, and I wanted to chuckle. Not to poke fun, but because she was trying to remain calm about pie, and failing.

Watching her passion was both endearing and inspiring. I loved it when she lit up. I didn't want to offend her with teasing, so I remained neutral and listened to her soothing voice, tinged with an Appalachian drawl.

"I could listen to you talk all day," I admired when she

wrapped up her pie talk. A fierce blush streaked across her porcelain cheeks, but I saw her smile reflected in the passenger window. I'm sure she thought I couldn't see her, but I looked for her everywhere.

"Don't try to butter me up, Bram Winchester."

"You should consider my attentions a privilege, sweets. They're not given to just anyone." It was a lie born of sarcasm. There wasn't anything special about my attentions, but I wanted to egg her on.

Her blush deepened.

"The only privilege I want is you agreeing to let Lakey come and stay with me at Grams' house."

I laughed. "Which, if you remember, might actually be your house."

"I'll be having a little talk with my brother about that."

"You know what would really stick it to your brother? If you come and stay with Lakey and me while you're in town. You'd have your own room. We can move you to the one downstairs after the surgery. Plus, it's thirty minutes closer to Roanoke for the appointments and the surgery."

"You've been thinking about this all morning, haven't you?" she replied, reading me like a book.

"That doesn't sound like me."

She gave me a sly expression. "I can't believe you're trying to get us to cohabitate. What would Grams say?" Her feigned offense was endearing.

"I know exactly what she'd say. 'Don't give up the pig for a little bit of sausage.'"

She laughed, and I drank it greedily like ice-cold lemonade on a hot summer's day. "I didn't say a thing about your sausage, Dracula."

"My bacon, then?"

She laughed even louder.

"You make it difficult to ignore you when you turn on the charm."

"Good to know. Wonder how charming I could get?"

A few seconds ticked by unfilled, and then, slowly, I put my hand on top of hers on the center console. She glanced at our hands, her face shaping into an adorable mix of nervous shock and pleasant acceptance. I lowered my voice as I squeezed her fingers. "I will take care of your every need, Julianna."

She rolled her eyes. "You're putting it on thick," she murmured.

"Hell, I'll even let you see the sausage. Or bacon. Whatever meat you prefer."

"You're insufferable!" she squealed indignantly, then threw her head back with the biggest, most beautiful laugh yet.

I chuckled with her. She still didn't push my hand away from hers on the console, and I felt like I'd won the lottery. Why hadn't it ever been this easy with any other woman? I tried to file back through the years I'd had dates and short-term girl-friends. All those conversations had been pleasant. But none of them made me feel as alive as when I talked with Julianna.

"I thought of you every day." I ran my thumb over the top of her soft hand.

She stilled then, and the smile that spread across her face sobered. My heart dropped slightly, and my mind raced. Was she thinking about the night of the wreck? Or when I came to her in the hospital, and all the pain and heartache I'd caused? Would I have to live the rest of my life wondering if she was thinking about my terrible choices, fearing the day she realized I wasn't worth her time or effort?

"I never thought I'd be here again," she whispered.

I tightened my grip on the steering wheel. My voice was sincere. "I'm sad and sorry for why, but I can't tell you how glad I am that you are here."

CHAPTER EIGHT

Julianna | *September 30, 2024*

He held my hand. He called me "sweets," which was a new nickname. He said he missed me. Now, he wanted me to stay with him. I didn't know what to make of it all. My heart was a mess. Part of me thought he was being too forward, the other part thought it felt so natural, so…right.

When we pulled into the driveway of Grams' house, a wave of melancholy hit me and tears sprang to my eyes. This place would never be the same, and it wasn't easy to accept. Before I could remove my seatbelt and reach for the door, Bram was already outside, opening it for me.

"That's not necessary," I said before climbing down, ignoring the hand he held out. "I'm not going to break." That wasn't precisely true, but the minor twinges of pain made me feel invincible compared to the usual mid-morning stiffness.

"I'm not taking any chances with you." He placed his hand on the small of my back and guided me to the side so he could shut the truck door behind me. His fingers against me were intimate and calming, though I had no business being soothed by them. We were friends. Sometimes friends touched, and it wasn't anything to wax poetic about.

"So, you drove here in that truck?" He nodded toward the U-Haul.

"Yes. I left my car with Brandon, Kallie's boyfriend. He's going to sell it for me." I omitted the part where I didn't think it could make the four-hour drive. "I plan to rent a cheap car until I find something else. I won't drive much anyway. Obviously, I've got to find a job to afford something else. I'm hoping to find a remote position. A lot of marketing and social media jobs are done that way these days."

His brow furrowed. "I'm not sure you should be working right now."

"But *I'm* sure I should be working," I replied firmly. "I *need* to make money. I *need* health insurance."

He stared at me intently.

"You look like you have a lot to say," I said.

"You didn't ask my opinion."

I made a sweeping gesture with my hands. "Let's hear it."

"I think you're being stubborn. Maybe someday, you'll see reason and let your brother help you. It would be easier for you if you gave in now."

My eyes narrowed on him.

"I'm not asking my brother for money."

"Hmmm."

"It's my decision."

He turned and walked toward the front door. There was nothing worse to me than being dismissed. My hands balled at my sides.

"Why are you giving me grief?" I shuffled to join him on the porch, where he entered the code on the front door. He knew the house's code and could access me whenever he wanted. That would need to be changed as soon as possible.

"To get you riled up, why else?" He looked over his shoulder and winked at me. My face burned. "I respect everything you say, sweets. I only want you to take care of yourself."

"How many ways can I explain it? I am *fine*." The door unlocked, and we walked into the sterile living area.

"Says the woman who is having back surgery."

There wasn't much I could say to refute that, so I did what I did best: I avoided it. "I've gotta run to the restroom, and then we'll unload the truck, okay? Would you mind following me to the U-Haul drop off and then driving me over to the car rental place?"

He ran a hand down the dark stubble on his face. He hummed, as if thinking over our options. "Or... I'll unload the truck. You gather up some more things you need, and then we'll be back at the farmhouse with Lakey by lunchtime."

I frowned. "The only part I approve of in that plan is Lakey," I said.

Bram shrugged. "We'll talk about it." Then he went into the garage without another word.

Exasperated with his refusal of my requests, I huffed and went into the hall bathroom. I had just sat on the cold toilet seat when my phone buzzed in my jeans pocket on the ground. I fished it out and checked the screen.

Kallie: Calling in five.

Talking to her wasn't something I could do in front of Bram. I could call her now, but I couldn't hide in the bathroom forever. What if he came in to check on me?

I finished and walked out to the garage, where Bram was carrying a stack of boxes that was taller than he was. I had only been gone for a few minutes, and he had unloaded half my things.

"Let me help you." I rushed toward him. He drew back when my hands went around a box at the top.

"Absolutely not. Get your little ass back in that house."

"This is my problem, not yours. And my ass is larger than average, thank you very much."

"I'm very aware of your ass size."

I froze, then slowly removed my hands from the box I was trying to poach. The boxes blocked my view of his face.

Afraid my ears were deceiving me, I went and picked up another box from the truck. I turned and saw Bram standing in his green flannel, worn jeans, and brown work boots, hands loosely resting on his narrow hips. He was giving me a smoldering look under his ball cap. It made me simultaneously hot, cold, angry, and excited.

"What did I say?" The intensity of his tone and his directness touched me in places that had no business being disturbed —*again*. I must have liked being bossed around more than I thought...

"My back is fine," I squeaked, still clutching the box.

"And we want it to stay that way." He stalked toward me with predatory focus. He took the box out of my hands and pinned me with his eyes. "This is why you need to stay with me during this ordeal. You're so stubborn. You're going to make your demise quick and sudden."

I laughed. "All I can see are those commercials for call buttons, you know, where you wear it around your neck? I probably need one of those things." I was amused, but he wasn't smiling. His teeth clenched as he carried the box into the garage.

"Don't make me install cameras to keep an eye on you, sweets."

"That could be interesting..."

He looked over his shoulder, and I became more flustered. "I mean—"

"We both know what you meant." He grinned, interrupting. "It doesn't matter anyway because you're coming back to the farm with me."

"I can't do that, Bram. It's too much."

His eyebrow did a sexy cock thing, like he didn't believe a word I was saying.

Whatever armor I'd built over years of noncontact, he was disassembling it within twenty-four hours with his words, actions, and demeanor.

"Listen," I said, "I have a phone call to make, and I—"

"Perfect. I'll finish this up. Then we can finish the conversation you're trying to avoid." He gave me another grin.

I had to talk to Kallie. I had to have some objection to everything my heart—and my body—wanted to give in to. She would provide that levity.

"I'll be back in a minute." I fled to the other end of the house, where I promptly closed and locked the bedroom door. It was my old bedroom, which no longer looked like the sanctuary of my youth. I dropped into a new, fluffy blue chair in the corner just in time for Kallie's name and photo to pop up on my phone screen.

"Hey," I answered with the speaker on low volume.

"Hey, girl. You'll never guess what happened. Brandon's grandma fell down the stairs at his parents' house last night! It was a whole thing. We were with her in the ER forever, but she's home now. I wanted to call you last night, and I forgot to text you back after you told me you'd made it. I am so, so sorry! Did you settle in? How's everything?"

Her barrage of words made my mind spin, but a single sobering thought of Bram brought me back to square one. "It's...going. I'm sorry about Brandon's grandma."

"It's okay, she's just bruised up, she'll heal," she said. "What do you mean by 'it's going'? You sound weird. What's up?"

I swallowed hard. "I've got to talk to you about something. Well, someone."

"Okay." Her voice was now full of hesitancy. "Did you run into someone?"

"I ran into Bram. And before you make a joke, no, he doesn't have Dracula teeth."

"Quit acting like you know me," she scolded. "Bram, Bram? Your crush from high school? Your brother's old best friend? Kissed you on the night of your grandma's death, Bram? Broke your freaking back, Bram?"

"I've told you repeatedly it wasn't his fault. It was more complicated than that."

She ignored me. "The Bram you were hopelessly in love with, even though he ruined your life and broke your heart while you were in the fucking hospital? Same dude?"

I shut my eyes tightly. "Stop, please. We've already talked through this a million times. It was my choice. I'm the one who told him to—"

"Is he the same one?"

"How many other Brams do you know?" I snapped.

"I only want to ensure I'm working with the right information. What's he doing crawling out of the woodwork? Please tell me he looks like an old high school gym teacher." I could hear the eagerness in her vitriol.

"No. He's even hotter than before."

"Of course he is! The bastard." I rolled my eyes, even though she couldn't see them.

"Whit sent him to help me move in. But we've...been together."

I waited for her to respond for at least thirty seconds. "What do you mean by ' been together?"

I took a deep breath and exhaled slowly, then spoke. "I got

to Grams' house, and Whit had completely remodeled the whole thing. Bram did the remodel work. They are still best friends. I wasn't expecting everything to be so different, and I had a panic attack. All of this was more emotional than I thought it would be."

"Oh no, I'm so sorry. I know how much that place meant to you."

My heart sank. "Thanks. Then Bram showed up to help me unload my things from the truck and caught me losing it. Before I knew it, I was on my way to his house, which just so happens to be my childhood dream house. Then I fell in love with his dog. Her name is Lakey. Anyway, we got deep—"

"Julianna Joy East, did you sleep with him?"

My mouth flew open. "Of course not! Let me finish my story."

She scoffed. "Blah, fine. This is weird, but finish."

I picked invisible lint off my lap to keep nerves at bay. "There's not much more to it. I accidentally fell into his bedroom and saw him naked."

Silence sliced deep from the other end of the phone.

"Kallie? You there?"

"You let him fuck you, didn't you?" Her words were accusatory and made me roll my eyes again. She was dramatic, and I loved her for it sometimes, but this was not the moment.

"No. I swear on my life. I slept in his bed with the dog—"

"I don't even know what to say to all this right now."

"Well, you better get to dishing out that bestie wisdom because I have two more minutes, tops." My voice was a hiss.

I listened for any signs that Bram had returned inside, but didn't hear anything. Kallie was uncharacteristically quiet, and I drummed my fingers on my thigh.

"Please, tell me—"

"Let me get this straight," she interrupted. "You stayed at his house? You slept in his bed?"

"And he wants me to come back and stay with him." I bit my lip. "He's worried about my well-being."

"Are you worried about being alone?"

I thought about it for a moment. "Not really. If I ever did go down, I could call him, and he would rush over. Or I'd call 911. I always keep my phone on me for that purpose anyway."

"Do you think he's asking you because of the guilt he feels over the accident and the whole crushing your heart thing? Like he's trying to make himself feel better about the past?"

"Maybe? Probably. We didn't discuss it in depth, but he said last night he regretted everything, so he obviously still thinks about it."

"As he should," she muttered. "He should be on his hands and knees, licking your feet clean. I hate him, Julianna. I hate what he did to you. You need to get away from him as soon as possible."

I sighed audibly, already tired of the conversation. I don't know what I expected from Kallie, but she provided me with no clarity.

"Bram and I have a history," I replied. "We made mistakes. Both of us. I need you to let go of your anger and give me actual advice."

"I'll always forgive your mistakes because I know your motives were pure. You have a heart of gold. But Bram? I don't know him. I don't know his inner workings or his motives. He could jump off the side of a mountain, and it's not going to affect me."

I sat up in the plush seat. "I can't dismiss him because you hate him, and I don't want to be cruel. If I tell him I'm not going back to his house, I need a solid reason."

"Just admit you want to go with him, then. I know you want to. If you didn't, you'd have told him no, and we wouldn't be having this conversation."

I wasn't doing well at appearing objective, and it was time

to come clean. "I think I still have feelings for him." Kallie was an empathetic person, but I wasn't sure I could get her to understand the pull I felt toward Bram.

I had been in love with him for years. Granted, it was during my teenage years when I didn't fully understand the intricacies of the choices that come with loving someone. But had I ever stopped?

Kallie let out a very breath. "Fine. Go home with him. Let him watch over you until I can take over. He owes you that much at least."

That was not what I had expected her to say.

"He doesn't owe me anything."

"Bullshit. He told you he wanted you, that he cared for you, and then changed his mind. He told you he changed his mind on *the day of your grandmother's funeral* while you were in the hospital. Then he never came back around. Until now... It all makes no sense. You deserve answers."

"I don't need the rehash," I scolded, standing to my feet. "He removed himself from my equation—no more, no less."

Kallie sighed. "He should have stayed, Julianna. He could have at least been there for you in the aftermath, when you were grieving. Quit making excuses for him. Why are you defending him so much?"

I wanted to say I didn't know, but that wasn't true because the truth was written in my mind in bold letters: I still care for him. I'm still attracted to him, and I'm going back to his house like he wants.

What I needed was for Kallie to tell me it was fine. But how she judged him and our situation made it clear I wouldn't get that from her.

"I can't explain to you how complicated our situation was."

"So complicated that you couldn't even explain it to your brother?"

My breath hitched. Her words were like a cold splash of

water on my burning defiance. She must have sensed my shock when I didn't respond with words.

"That was a low blow. I'm sorry," she said, regret laced in her tone. "I know why you didn't tell him Bram was with you that night. I love you so much, but I can't say what you want me to. But are *you* happy being around him? Do *you* want him around? That's really all that matters. I will be most happy if you are happy."

I let myself speak before censoring my words. "It's better than being here alone. Coming here has been harder than I thought it would be."

"So this has nothing to do with the fact that you've been pining over Bram for fifteen years."

"I have not been pining!" I cried, indignant. But my brain whispered, *Liar.*

Kallie's voice became clear. "If it were up to me, you'd send him back to his stupid house and dog, call your brother and tell him about losing your job, and he'd give you the money to cover the surgery. Then I would take care of you when it's surgery time, and we'd come back to Charlotte after you healed. Here, you would work part-time at the bakery until you found your footing again. And the vampire would be toast."

She snapped her fingers for emphasis.

"Kallie—"

"I worry about your hopelessly romantic heart. You are the smartest woman I know, but emotions play a number on everyone, even smart women."

"I like being close to him," I admitted, my voice lower than it had been, more subdued. "He feels like home, something I've missed so much."

"I know, babe," she replied. "I support you no matter what. Just make sure your heart can handle him back in your life. And you might as well use his dick while you're at it."

"Kallie!" I scolded her, but couldn't keep the smile off my face.

"What? You might as well get all you can out of your trip." She laughed. "Listen to your gut about him. You deserve happiness, whether it makes you happy to let him look after you or if you decide to break his heart."

"I can't break something that's not mine." The words made a lump form in my throat, but I needed to make that my new mantra.

"That sounds like famous last words."

"He's my friend. He's still close with my brother, and I want to get to know Whit again. Maybe being around Bram will help."

"Perhaps." She hummed. "Maybe you'll understand Bram better, too, and then I can understand him, because I don't get this at all."

"Kallie! Seriously?"

"Okay, okay, fine, fine. I will stop. I had to get one more jab in. I hate him."

"I know," I replied. "So you've told me, more than once. I'll send you pictures of his house later. It's a dream."

She laughed. "You're so getting boned."

Chapter Nine

Bram | *September 30, 2024*

Julianna had closed the bedroom door, so I knew the conversation was meant to be private. But the house was small and quiet, and the room echoed, which made her voice reverberate down the hall like a loudspeaker.

At first, I busied myself with moving things in the kitchen that didn't need to be moved. I contemplated turning on the TV. I even walked toward the front door to go outside and escape the temptation to eavesdrop. But in the end, I stood at the front of the hallway, taking every word in.

I wasn't proud of it, but I had to know what she was thinking.

Hearing how much Kallie despised me was a punch to the face, but I understood. As Julianna's best friend, Kallie needed to be the protector and truth-teller, and I had been a terrible asshole. There was no denying that.

I saw myself as reformed, but I fought every day to erase

the barrage of insults my father had placed upon me in my youth: a coward, a user, inadequate in every way. Parts of me wondered if deep down I was like him, ruining everything I touched and always wanting more of everything, no matter the cost. I could very well hurt her, even if it weren't on purpose.

I couldn't help but smile to myself when I heard her say she thought she still had feelings for me and intended to take my offer to stay at the farm. I wasn't surprised. The pull between us was undeniable. When she hadn't moved her hand in the car, I knew I was burned into her like she was me.

Julianna ended the call and opened the door, and I adjusted my baseball hat slightly so I could see her whole face from under the brim. She froze halfway out the door when she saw me.

"How much of that did you hear?"

I leaned against the wall, arms crossed against my chest in feigned neutrality.

"The important parts," I drawled. "Like you'll come stay in the farmhouse and let me watch after you. And who I assume is Kallie, loathes me. Understandably."

Her cheeks flushed so hard I could see their color in the dim lighting.

"Those are Kallie's feelings, not mine." She crossed her arms, but her mouth twitched slightly. She was nervous. It meant on some level, I affected her.

I pushed off the wall and approached her, my steps purposeful but slow.

"And I heard you stick up for me. Which I don't deserve," I said. Her eyes tracked up to meet mine when I reached her. I leaned against the wall. The heat that radiated off her body singed the resolve I'd made not to pursue her. She was the sole woman who made me feel like a thousand torches had been lit under my skin, and I would burn down everything for her. I looked into her brown eyes, rich like soil, reminding me of all the good things I appreciated and revered in nature.

I studied her and took in her beauty. The fine lines on her face enhanced the maturity of her features, and I couldn't believe I'd forgotten the freckle just below her left eye. I first noticed it the night I kissed her on the road.

"I wasn't lying in the truck, sweets," I said, my voice low. "I never forgot you. I never stopped regretting what I said and what I did." I regretted what I *didn't* do or say, but I kept that part to myself.

"It's in the past." Her words were stern, but her voice shook.

"I truly hope so." I pushed off the wall and away from her, letting the invisible string that pulled us together fall to the ground. "Let's return the U-Haul first, and then I'll pack up what you want to take to the farmhouse."

"Wait a minute. I didn't tell you for sure that I was going with you," she said defiantly, her folded arms falling to her sides.

"You, me, and your best friend all know what is happening here," I replied with unwavering authority. "I remind you of the past. Maybe the bad parts, but the good parts, too. And I'm here. Not Kallie. Not Whit. They can't be here right now, but I am, and I want to support you. I would count it a privilege if you would allow me to."

She bit her lip. My heart raced in my chest as I waited for her reply.

"Lakey sleeps with me," she finally said.

"Done," I replied immediately, holding my hand out for her to shake. She looked up at me, mouth slightly agape, then down at my hand. She shook it but pulled away quickly.

I wanted her, but I couldn't have her. Not yet. Perhaps not ever. I needed to keep her at arm's length until everything became clearer.

I had a couple of missed work calls to return, so I stayed inside while Julianna and Lakey explored outside. I watched them explore the yard and small field behind the house from the window over the kitchen sink. Somehow, the sun always seemed to be shining on her. Her brown hair moved freely against her figure, which was hugged by those black leggings, and she smiled even when she thought no one was looking.

"Bram?" Melanie said on the other end of the phone.

I snapped back to reality. "I'm here," I replied.

"Did you hear anything I said?"

"Um, yeah. That's fine."

"It's fine that Doug ran the government truck into the ditch, and Junior tried to use the winch on the UTV to pull it out, causing them both to be in the ditch, and I had to call Lucky's Towing?"

"What?" I slammed the beer I was casually drinking onto the countertop. "Why the hell would they do that? My God."

"That's what I thought," she reprimanded. "You're not listening to me at all. What are you doing? Are you at home? I thought you were sick?"

"Are Doug and Junior okay?"

She sighed. "They are fine. You're deflecting."

Julianna threw a stick for Lakey, who happily ran to retrieve it.

"Can I ask you something? Not as a supervisor, but as a brother."

Melanie was not only a park ranger, but also my half-sister. Ten years younger than me, she had sought me out after finding that we shared paternity. She said my dad knew about her but denied the DNA results. It was no surprise to me that he had another child. I'd even tried to bring it up to my mother once. She cried when I started asking questions, so we didn't discuss it further. My father refused to listen to my questions. Despite all that, Melanie and I formed a friendship over time, especially after we started working together. We got along well, both as siblings and coworkers.

"What's going on for real?" she asked. "You're not sick, are you?"

"No," I admitted. "I didn't call in sick anyway. I'm using personal leave, if you must know. Because...things are personal."

"Noted. Lips are sealed." I heard a door shut, and I knew Melanie had entered her tiny office. "What's up?"

"Do you remember when you and I got tipsy at that Blue Ridge winery a few years ago? And I told you about Whit's sister, Julianna?"

"I remember. She was the reason you bought that house. Have you seen her or something?"

I rubbed the back of my neck, trying to de-stress. "Something like that." I looked out at the yard where Julianna was poking around at something under the giant oak tree off to the right by the field gate. Lakey sniffed around her. "She's here at the house."

Melanie's gasp and excited squeal made me pull the phone back from my ear.

"Oh my God, are you serious? Is she staying with you? Did you profess your undying love? Did you at least tell her how big of a crush you've had on her for years? Did you kiss her? Have sex with her? Anything?"

"No to those last few questions, and don't ever say the word 'sex' to me again," I replied sternly. "But I think...I think there's still something between us."

There was silence.

"As in, she could feel the same way you do?"

"I doubt it since I don't even know how I feel. But from the moment we saw each other yesterday, we've had something. And I can't tell Whit, so I just thought..."

"This is so exciting!" Melanie's exclamation and hand claps made me roll my eyes and wonder why I'd ever called her. "Why is she in town? I thought they didn't have any family here anymore?"

"She's having back surgery. She was supposed to stay at her grandma's old house, but she wasn't expecting it to be remodeled, and I think everything hit her at once. Anyway, I invited her to stay here with me. Thought I could look after her."

"Of course." Melanie laughed, seeing through my ruse. "What does her brother think?"

"He doesn't know yet," I replied. "I have to tell him. Soon." I took a sip of my beer. "But it's weird between them. I think they get along, but they aren't close. She doesn't want to ask him to help her with the surgery expenses."

"Why? Isn't Whit loaded?"

I chuckled. "Loaded doesn't begin to describe it. He's a starting NFL quarterback."

"I don't know the first thing about football or Whit. I've never even seen the man. So, Julianna's an independent sort?"

"Trying to be," I replied. "I've encouraged her to tell Whit, but damn, she is stubborn. Anyway, she's getting ready to go through some serious stuff. I don't want anything to be too messy between us."

"I hate to be the one to break this to you, but I think it's already messy," she replied softly. "She's always been it for you. You won't even entertain the thought of committing to anyone else. Is she single?"

"Yes," I replied. "I don't know how or why, but she's single."

"Then it's easy. Be together. Be happy. Make little happy Dracula babies. I always wanted to be an aunt."

I downed the rest of my beer and tossed the bottle in the

trash. This was hard for me to explain. She didn't know anything about the night of the wreck. I hadn't wanted my sister to see the level of callousness her father could attain. She knew he was terrible because of the paternity denial, but that was all the evidence she had. I hadn't been a true brother long, but Whit has taught me how to be a good one, and I'd do anything to save Melanie one ounce of unnecessary hurt. Another part of me didn't want her to know how badly I'd messed up with my decisions, afraid she might look at me differently, too. Mel looked up to me, and I wanted to keep it that way.

"It's not that easy. Her best friend hates me, and personally, there's a lot of regret on my end. It's a lot to consider."

"You're the best man I know, Bram. If this woman is worth her salt, she knows it too."

The compliment made me smile.

"Thanks, that's kind of you. I gotta go. Tell Doug and Junior I want to see them in my office first thing tomorrow morning."

She laughed. "That'll scare the shit out of them."

"That's the goal. Talk to you later."

I pressed the end button, and my phone immediately began to buzz again.

"Hey, Gladys," I answered. Gladys Bell was Mill Creek Aid's president of operations. Five years ago, she took on the role after retiring from city government. The job didn't pay anything—no one who helped MCA took a salary—but she treated it like the career of a lifetime. And she was efficient.

"Oh, Bram, it's bad." Gladys was the most uplifting and optimistic person I knew, so this instantly captured my full attention.

"What's going on?"

She took a deep breath and let it out. "It has to do with the secret project." I froze.

"What's happened?" I asked, gripping the edge of the counter.

"I had some extra time today, so Allie and I came to the storage container. We were sorting through some things and taking inventory for Friday's dinner when some man showed up and handed us a plain white envelope. It was addressed to MCA on the front, so I opened it. But inside, it was addressed to you.

"It said that the mobilization of heavy equipment was spotted on the property off the park, and it reminded you that buildings within so many yards of public recreation spaces are prohibited under some ordinances. It said to cease all construction immediately or face hefty fines from the town. It's on Mill Creek Township letterhead."

I frowned. "That's not right. I have all the required permits. They said it wouldn't be an issue, even if it were a little close," I quickly remembered Gladys didn't know anything more than I did. "Something is up. Can you send me a picture of the letter? I'll get it on Friday."

"Yes, of course," she replied.

I hung up, and a few moments later, a picture of the letter came through. I opened it, zoomed in, and my blood boiled. The letter with the zoning board president's signature was on the town stationery. Yet, the first paragraph referenced my father's lawyer in Roanoke.

I was building a new community center for MCA. I had wanted to do the project for a long while and finally pulled the trigger a few months ago. The Senior Citizens' Community Building, where we had most of our events, was aging and too small. The wealthy nearby who funded significant upgrades to the local schools didn't care much about MCA out of solidarity with my wealthy father. So, I'd taken the burden to find more space upon my shoulders.

All my assets, including my home, were tied up in building

this center. But somehow, my bastard of a father found out, and he had found a way to hold the town accountable for shutting me down.

Part of me wanted to jump in a vehicle, drive straight to my parents' mansion, and deck the man right in the face. But that's precisely what he was doing—baiting me. Not only was he denying solutions for problems he created, but he was also sticking it to me personally. He knew I'd be angry and wanted me to lose my cool. He wanted me to confront him to fit his narrative that I was just like him, to make me out to be his protégé, if it was the last thing he accomplished. He thought that the town would believe I had abandoned the project, making me more like my father in their eyes.

No one knew I was building the center, except the contractor and crew I'd hired with NDAs. Gladys and Allie were involved, but I wanted my contributions to remain confidential. I didn't like the attention and the wariness of the older community members who only saw me as an extension of my father.

The land we were building on had come from my maternal grandfather. His father had once owned half our little town, and my grandfather inherited it at a young age. He'd sold much of it off. When he eventually passed away, four years ago, I inherited five acres of land on the main road of Mill Creek, adjacent to the small city park, along with a tidy sum of $500,000.

Over the years, I'd used the $500,000 to pay for MCA operations, the house I was standing in, and the surrounding land of the adjacent valley. My last $100,000 had secured the massive loan I needed to build the community center.

Who did my father have in his pocket to make the officials change their minds after I'd been issued verbal reassurances and official permits? I knew he had the police force in his back pocket, but was the town government as well?

The back door opened with a creak. Lakey bounded through the mud room and into the kitchen, tongue and tail wagging.

"Getting kind of brisk out there." Julianna's voice echoed into the kitchen before I saw her, and her presence changed everything. It was as if the sun had pierced through the fog that had clouded my mind. I drank her in as she walked over to the breakfast table.

Would I ever not be stunned by her unyielding beauty?

"I saw you outside," I admitted, reaching down to pet Lakey, who panted happily.

She looked up at me from where she sat at the table and paused from unzipping her boot. "What's wrong?"

"What do you mean?" I was a terrible liar. I ran my hand through my hair. "I'm upset about some stuff going on." I mulled over the facts and tried to decipher which ones I could share and which ones I needed to keep secret.

"What happened?" Her furrowed brow showed her worry. Meanwhile, I stood there, arms crossed, leaning against the counter and deciding what to lie about.

Don't be an asshole.

"You can tell me. I'm a vault. Anything I can help with?"

I shook my head. "No. It's my dad. He approached some people in town, and they called to tell me he was making mischief. Not even sure what he was doing in Mill Creek."

You are a lying asshole.

"Does he make 'mischief' often?" She put the word in air quotes.

"He's a professional at it," I murmured. "Just set me off."

"I know you're not telling me the whole truth, for the record."

I sighed. "I'm sorry. I don't want to weigh you down with my problems. You're going through so much." It wasn't that I didn't want to share my issues with her, but I didn't want her to feel like she needed to be concerned with me and my problems.

I didn't want her to scheme ways to help me when I was supposed to be helping her.

"It'll feel better if you spill your guts. Misery loves company." She smiled up at me.

I mulled it over. If I wanted to support this woman, I needed to be transparent. I knew the saying: to have a friend, you have to be a friend.

I sighed. "I was building a community center for MCA, the nonprofit I told you about. It's something I've dreamed of for a while. My grandfather left me some land in town, and it's the perfect spot. Ground broke this week. Now, I've been told I can't build there because it's too close to Mill Creek Park. So, unless I can change someone's mind, I'll have to back out of the build. I'll still owe partial payments to the contractor for the dirt removal they did and the materials they've bought. Then I'll have to find other land and buy it, which is much more money than I can afford. The project will be dead."

I watched her absorb my words, chewing her lip.

"So what are your choices? What if you could find another spot to build? Maybe someone else would be willing to donate land?"

"Unlikely, seeing as this roadblock is my father's doing. And he has his hands in everyone's pockets." I got a glass from the cupboard, unable to look at her lest my face give away more than I was willing to tell.

"Why would he want to stop it?" I turned around just in time to see her brows lift. "Oh, I see. Because this whole foundation had to start because of him, and so now he's pissed you're a part of it at all."

"Exactly." I reached into the fridge, pulled out a soda can, popped it open, and poured the contents into the glass.

"Money talks. Where can we find more money?"

"We?" I said, handing the glass to her. "*We* will not be finding anything. This isn't your problem, sweets."

She looked into the glass.

"How did you remember I prefer a Coke in a glass with no ice?"

I remember everything about you.

I shrugged and winked. "Lucky guess."

Her cheeks pinked, and she took the glass from my hands, our fingers touching for half a second—enough to make the hair on my arms stand on end.

"It may not be my problem, but I want to help," she said.

My chest tightened as I watched her openly. I tracked her every movement as she gathered her long, dark hair and secured it with a tie from around her wrist. As she let go of her hair, she looked up at me, our eyes meeting.

"Are you watching me?" She laughed. I smiled, not at all embarrassed about being caught. I wanted her to know I loved watching her every move.

"I like seeing you be comfortable here," I admitted. "And I like seeing the smile on your face. I think I just like you in my general vicinity."

Her blush deepened. "I think you already said that today. You need some new lines. You're losing your touch." She stood, holding on to the table for balance as she readjusted her socks. "And quit getting me off track. Surely you have other donors in the organization?"

Everyone pitched in as much as possible with their families and bills to attend to, but I was the principal patron. I wasn't prepared for her to have that information, at least not yet.

"No one of note. No one with those kinds of funds hanging about," I replied.

She bit her bottom lip. "Local businesses? Maybe you could pool some money for land? Seems like it would be in their best interest, maybe even a tax write off?"

I shook my head. "I already tried to get a few bigger factories to donate materials, and I was declined every time." Looking back, that was probably my father's doing, too.

"Hmm. Didn't you say you get more estate money once you marry?"

I didn't think anything could stop me from watching her, but with that, I froze.

"It doesn't have to be legit, does it?" Her voice echoed in my ears.

How in the hell had I not thought of that?

Probably because I never want to marry anyone.

I'd have to be in love to do that, and I had never been in love with anyone that deeply, except for maybe the woman who was in front of me. "I-I mean, this isn't a movie. I'm sure there isn't a romance clause in the terms," I stammered. "But who would I marry? And what would be in it for them?"

I watched her begin to pick at her cuticles. Julianna East was nervous.

"I could do it," she whispered.

The words made me exhale deeply, and I closed my eyes. When I opened them, I was shaken to find her face was beet-red and her eyes wide.

"I'm sorry!" she exclaimed, her voice frantic. "I didn't mean—"

Did she think I was reacting unfavorably to her? Without hesitating, I did what my instincts told me to do. I took the four strides to where she stood, gathered her up, and pressed her to me. It would have been a hug between ordinary friends, but it set my body ablaze.

I relaxed visibly, relieved.

I wanted it to be her.

I backed away to avoid asserting myself. She must have felt it because she stepped back and sat in the chair, her lips parted and her dark eyes entreating.

"That's the nicest thing anyone has ever offered me," I said, running a hand over my short hair. "But you know I can't do that."

Her brow furrowed. "Because of my surgery? Will that delay things too much?"

I'd forgotten about her surgery for a moment. Now that she'd reminded me, a brilliant thought leapt to the front of my mind.

"I should have been thinking of you and your surgery. And I shouldn't have said no because if we get married, I think I can help you, too."

Her eyebrows shot up. "Really? How? I won't let you or Whit pay for my surgery if that's what you're—"

"No," I interrupted. "That's not what I'm saying. I'm also not saying you shouldn't use Whit's money because you should. But if we marry, you'll have my health insurance. I'll have to check on the specifics for surgery, but my insurance is pretty damn good. You could end up paying much less for all this."

Her mouth dropped open in shock, but she didn't miss a beat. "Best idea you've ever had, Dracula!"

I rolled my eyes at her use of my nickname, but I was smiling. Lakey, tongue wagging and sensing the joy, came right up to Julianna. Julianna took long strokes down her fur and spoke without looking at me. "So, it's a deal. We get married in name only. A civil, quickie service at the courthouse..." Those words conjured up images of having Julianna in a dark corner, all to myself, able to touch her velvet skin and hear her intake of breath. "I'll benefit from using your health insurance, and you'll get money for Mill Creek Aid?"

"1.1 million dollars, to be exact," I said. Her eyes popped wide.

"Do you think you'll have problems getting the money? There won't be any delays once we're legally married?"

"I'll make a call." I was acquainted with a lawyer in town whom I trusted to do some reconnaissance work.

"That's very mob-esque of you," she said, teasingly.

What did a man say who planned to marry a woman for money and insurance purposes?

"Seriously, you don't have to do this."

She smiled. "Cold feet already?"

"No, not that. I'm not sure if having me on your record is a good idea. To have to tell someone you were married before. You know, when we eventually…" My voice trailed off. I didn't want to say it. But if we were going to do this, we needed to establish that it was temporary. It was the safe and responsible thing to do.

Yet I didn't want to be safe or responsible. I wanted to pull her to me, tell her all my wayward thoughts, and decimate any chance of us being merely friends.

"On my record?" She laughed. "Is there someone keeping tabs on me? I don't think there's a more noble reason to fake marry someone than to help them inherit a million dollars to build a community center. If someone later can't understand that it sounds like I'd be hitching my horse to the wrong cart."

I smiled at the metaphor that Grams used to use sometimes. Her Appalachian sayings were ingrained in our minds and hearts. "Okay. But if you change your mind anytime, you can tell me. Don't feel obligated because of the money."

She pivoted to me and put her soft hand on my rough face. My heart raced. "I'm not a child. This was my idea, don't forget that," she said, her features soft. "We can talk particulars later. Now, do you have anything here that I can fix for supper?"

I ran a hand over my jaw. I hadn't thought of food. There was nothing much in the way of groceries in the house. I was a bachelor, and I lived like one.

She looked up at me with searching eyes. "Oh no. I have my

appointment in Roanoke tomorrow. With all this, I didn't even think about it. And I don't have a vehicle."

Of course, she didn't remember. With me bursting into her life, the accommodation change, and now agreeing to get married, I was surprised that either of us remembered our own names.

"Use my truck. I've got a Jeep in the garage," I cut in, shrugging, letting her know it wasn't a big deal. She looked relieved, but her lips pursed.

"Why am I not surprised you have two vehicles? I can't do that, though."

"Can't do what?"

"Take your vehicle." She crossed her arms.

"I don't think I asked." I ignored the look on her face that told me she didn't appreciate what I was saying. I continued, "It makes sense. Pick your battles, sweets. We'll be married soon. We have to learn these things."

She rolled her eyes. "Fine. But since we're handing out vehicles, can I drive the Jeep?"

I quirked my eyebrow. "It's not that I mind, but the top is off, and I don't think you're going to want to drive around like that. It might mess up your hair and all that."

"Au contraire," she replied brightly, turning around from the empty fridge. "If the weather is okay, I'd love to take it."

"Imagine the attention you'll get," I warned. "You want everyone driving around the city staring at you?"

Did I want everyone staring at her? The answer was a resounding 'hell no'. But as I watched the smile on her face dim a little, I heard myself blurting before I could stop, "It'll be sunny tomorrow. The key fob is hanging by the door. It's got a full tank of gas. I'm curious to see how you like it."

"Really?" She brightened once again.

"Sure. But I can put the roof on if you want me to."

"No way! I want to try it as is."

"Okay, then." I chuckled. "Maybe it'll take your mind off the appointment."

I tried to look disinterested. Did she want to go alone? Or was she hoping I'd ask to go with her? My mind was full of questions I usually didn't have to deal with.

I wouldn't ask. I couldn't give her any more stress. She was already going through a hard time with her pain, her job loss, and whatever demons she was fighting with Whit, not to mention the anxiety of an upcoming surgery. And now, the added complication of a marriage? She didn't even have a car. There was no one else in town to watch after her.

If I hadn't come along, she would have been alone.

I looked at her. It was the first time since we'd met again that I'd ticked off everything she was going through. How much strength did one possess to maintain kindness and beauty under such rotten luck? I stepped toward her. Her eyes widened slightly, and her mouth parted, but I ignored any sense of shock. If she pushed me away, I would let her go.

I pulled her toward me firmly until our bodies touched. I wanted her to warm up to my touch. I could be a patient man. She looked back at me with wide eyes. I didn't allow my eyes to break from hers, and I watched as her gaze went from surprise to soft acceptance. It was all the permission I needed. I pressed my lips to hers.

It was a sweet kiss, something quick and without extensive lingering. Yet, the impact was profound.

She pulled back slightly. "Oh," she said.

I wanted to go in for a deeper kiss, but refrained.

Patience.

I gently wrapped my arms around her, bringing her to me again like before. I couldn't hold back the satisfied smile that crept onto my face as her chin instinctively rested on my shoulder.

"What's all this for?" Her whisper tickled my ear. I hugged her a little tighter, my fingers slightly digging into her softness.

I put my mouth near her ear. "Marry me, Julianna Joy East."

She stiffened a little, but as I rubbed her back lightly, her body melted into mine. Her heart beat in time with my own.

"Okay, let's do it."

I pulled her back from me a little so she wouldn't feel the arousal she'd caused once again. That was going to continue to be a problem.

"When should we?" I asked.

"Any day you want," she replied. "Not like I have a job or responsibilities on my schedule, although I am working on my resume and found a few things I can apply for online, so hopefully not long."

I tucked a loose strand of hair behind her ear, and her eyes never left mine.

I was going to marry the girl I used to watch dance outside to her iPod with abandon, and who read in quiet corners of rooms. The girl who used to spy on me while I changed clothes in her brother's room. The girl who haunted my dreams for so many years.

A chilling thought doused the flames that ignited.

This is not a real relationship. You're getting too close.

I stepped back. "I've got a frozen pizza in the deep freeze in the garage for supper." I headed toward the doorway, separating myself.

"Sounds great," she replied with the sweetest smile, and I wished I could read her thoughts to tell if she could feel the tether between us that seemed so apparent to me.

Chapter Ten

Julianna | *October 1, 2024*

I buckled myself into the sleek, black leather seats of Bram's Jeep Wrangler. It was the cleanest, most pristine vehicle I'd ever driven.

I'd bundled up in a Blue Devils hoodie and skinny jeans and wrapped my hair into a bun. The moment my foot hit the pedal, my suspicions were confirmed: I loved the vehicle's openness. I drove down curvy backroads, watching the beautiful autumn colors shift in the distance, with the wind whipping around me and the road following beautiful, flowing creeks. The experience was a balm for my fragile soul.

I thought about Bram as I drove. I couldn't deny that adult Bram was superior to the younger version I'd known and loved. When we were teens, he had been flirty, adventurous, and a little cocky. Now, he maintained the best parts of his past self but mixed them with humility and maturity. How was I supposed to keep myself from falling back into him?

Kallie didn't want me to get my heart involved, and I was fighting hard. Yet there was no easy way for me to separate my heart and brain when it came to Bram. There had never been.

I stopped by a Roanoke eatery and grabbed a fancy biscuit sandwich and a coffee. An idea crossed my mind. Bram and I had awkwardly traded phone numbers the night before. This could be an opening to make things casual. I took a snapshot of my breakfast and sent it to him.

> Me: Trying not to get grease all over your leather seats.

Five seconds later, a reply bubble appeared.

> Bram: The seats can take it. Enjoy every bite. Wish I were with you.

My breath hitched. What could I say to that? My fingers hovered over the keyboard of my phone screen for a couple of minutes before I settled on "same". I hit send and then cringed.

A one-word response?

Ugh.

I was a little worried when he didn't write back immediately. Was he expecting more from me? Should I have waxed poetic or maybe made a joke? That chaste kiss we'd shared the day before—did it change anything?

You're overanalyzing this.

I had something else to attend to before the appointment. Still parked, I polished off the end of my breakfast sandwich and grabbed my phone, dialing the number before I got too nervous.

Kallie answered on the third ring. "What's up, mountain hottie?" I heard the chime of the bakery door and the muffled sounds of diverse voices in the background.

"Morning rush?" I asked.

"Yeah, kinda busy. Everything okay?"

"Everything is great. I won't keep you. I'm on my way to my appointment. And oh, um, Bram kissed me. And we're getting married."

Proverbial crickets sounded down the phone line.

"Kallie?" I asked, wondering if she was still there.

"Did you say you are getting married because of a kiss?"

"No, not because of the kiss," I said steadily, although I was smiling. "That was separate. Marriage is in name only, not a real marriage."

"Will there be a license? Because that seems legit."

"Yes. It's a long story. I'll explain everything later, but it's for a good cause."

"I-I don't know what to say to what you're telling me, except, have you lost your fucking mind?!"

I cringed. "No, it's all good, I promise. It's for a million dollars."

The sounds of shuffling paper and the woosh of the bakery case opening and closing echoed. "I have to go, we're backed up. I don't know what you're pulling here with this joke of a phone call, but you will explain later. You better have something good lined up too, or so help me, I will drive my ass there tonight."

"I'll explain it all, I promise," I replied. "Have a great day. Talk to you later."

Hanging up, I wondered if I'd ever be able to adequately explain to my best friend how this was a good thing—the marriage part, at least. I wasn't sure how to describe the kiss that could have lit a thousand torches with its spark. Kallie didn't trust Bram, and no amount of charity work or fire was going to make her change her mind.

But there was no time to dwell on it. I had no idea what to

expect from this appointment and didn't want to be preoccupied. I put the Jeep in drive.

I walked into Dr. Kaveh's office in Roanoke's medical complex with minimal nerves. The friendly nurse excused herself after taking my vitals, and I waited patiently for Dr. Kaveh's physician's assistant, since that's who the nurse indicated I would be seeing.

A knock sounded at the door, and I let out a small, "Come in." I'd seen my fair share of medical professionals over the years, but nothing could have prepared me for the man who walked through the door of that sterile room that reeked of alcohol and plastic.

The physician assistant's smile was the first thing that struck me, followed by his height (at least six feet), broad shoulders, and angular jawline. He had to be around my age, given the attractively deep grooves and fine lines in his features. Shoulder length, blonde hair was neatly gathered at his nape in a tie. Stormy gray eyes rested on me. Warmth radiated from him, and my heart beat a little harder. I felt out of my element with his considerable presence.

My eyes did a quick sweep of his form, and Kallie's voice popped up in my mind unbidden, "*Probably not the only thing that's big.*"

"Miss East?" he asked, his voice low and smooth.

I could only nod.

"I'm Hunter Kearsley, the physician's assistant here. How are you today?"

He shook my very sweaty hand with a firm grip, and I tried not to cringe at the moisture in my palm. He then went over my prognosis and what they'd been informed of from Dr. Billingsly's office. He stood ridiculously close to me, making the windowless room seem boiling for an autumn day.

"So, we'll get some blood drawn for labs today and try to

get your scans scheduled for Thursday. Does that work? I want to try and get you in as soon as possible, but I have to pull some strings." He winked, and something inside me fluttered. "Dr. Kaveh will bring you in for a proper consultation on the scans next week, and if she sees no issues, we'll schedule you for surgery within the next few weeks."

I couldn't manage to do anything but stare at Hunter Kearsley. I hadn't spoken one coherent word since he'd entered. He continued talking about the excellent facilities and asked about my pain. I barely heard what he said.

"Are...are you okay, Miss East?"

You're staring at him and not responding, you idiot!

"Y-yes," I recovered, my voice too shrill for the occasion.

"Are you sure?" He waited.

I sighed, closing my eyes for a second. "Yes. I'm so sorry. I wasn't paying attention. It's just been a couple of hard weeks, you know? I'm still adjusting to the surgery news. And I lost my job in Charlotte. Then I came here alone to have surgery, and now I'm crashing with my brother's best friend, which feels like an inconvenience even though he insists it's not." The words came out faster than vomit. Thankfully, I caught myself before I started confessing about the soon-to-be fraudulent marriage.

I glanced up at him, expecting to find a firm grimace or at least a look full of puzzlement. Instead, he was smiling broadly.

"And here I was, wondering how I could ethically ask you about yourself, and you just volunteered so much I was curious about."

My heart stuttered.

Was he...flirting with me?

He was so attractive. Why would he want to know more about me? That couldn't have been what he meant.

"You could have asked," I replied, not knowing what else to say, and my nerves amplified at warp speed.

"Tell you what." He smiled and handed me a small business card. "I can't think of anything better than giving you this card and you deciding if you want to text or call that cell number at the bottom."

I bit my lip, trying not to appear as stunned as I was. I reached out and took the card.

"I mean, maybe—"

"Think it over. A friendly conversation is all I request." He motioned toward the badge, which was attached to his shirt, displaying his credentials. "I'm sure I'm not supposed to ask patients out. I've never done it before, so I don't know."

My cheeks burned. He *was* hitting on me!

I nodded profusely. "Got it." I tucked the card into my pocket.

"It was nice to meet you, Miss East." With a parting smile, he pivoted to leave.

"Julianna," I replied, sitting up a little straighter. "Call me Julianna."

Hunter Kearsley's card burned a hole in my pocket as I went to get my blood work. I could feel it while I shopped in the discount food store to pick up some off-brand snacks and ingredients to make chili and cornbread for Bram.

As I drove back from Roanoke to the farmhouse, the mountain wind in my hair and the feelings of pure freedom mingled with the heady awareness that I, Julianna Joy East, had been noticed by an attractive and successful guy who wasn't Bram. Contacting Hunter Kearsley was out of the question, though. The thought of it made me ill with nerves. Plus, how would Bram feel about it?

It shouldn't matter what he thought. Sure, he and I were going to be married, but for convenience. Then I imagined trying to explain the situation to Hunter, and I shook my head at what my life had become for health insurance and an inheritance. I pulled the Jeep into the garage, and my phone alerted with a text.

> Bram: How'd it go?"

It was a simple enough question, and given the one-word answer I'd come back with earlier, I shouldn't start analyzing his one-dimensional question too hard.

Before I could stop myself, I typed out what the truth was, but also held a bit of an agenda.

> Me: It was great. Got some blood work as well as the hot physician assistant's phone number.

Nerves ignited in my stomach as I pressed send. How would he react? What if he wasn't concerned in the least?

Three dots popped up on the screen as if he were typing, but then they disappeared.

I watched it happen again.

And again.

Unable to watch anymore, I grabbed my belongings and ran to the back door to release Lakey from her kennel.

She was excited to see me. Then, as I stroked her spotted fur, a notification came through on my phone. But it wasn't from Bram, it was from Whit.

> Whit: How's it going? You like the house?

He had no clue I was at Bram's, and he had no idea how I had reacted when I saw what he'd done to Grams' house. He definitely didn't know about the marriage yet, or I would have already heard from him.

Yet, I felt unprepared to face everything and masked the truth.

> Me: It's nice. Thanks for letting me stay there.

> Whit: There? Where are you now?

I didn't realize I'd typed *there* instead of *here*. Of course, he would latch on immediately to that. I sighed as I typed.

> Me: What happens in Mill Creek, stays in Mill Creek.

He had no idea how close to the truth that was.

> Whit: Cryptic. Have you seen Bram? He was supposed to come and help you.

My fingers hovered over the keyboard, my heart beating out of my chest. I started typing, knowing what I was doing was a risk. I didn't owe my brother an explanation for my actions. Yet, for the sake of transparency and growth, I let the truth fly.

> Me: I'm actually at Bram's house right now. I'm staying here.

Just like Bram had done a bit ago, I saw the typing dots appear and disappear on the screen repeatedly, until finally a message appeared.

> Whit: What are you doing at Bram's? Why are you staying there?

I needed to play it cool. I took a deep breath.

> Me: A lot to explain. But nothing is wrong. I couldn't stay at Grams'. It was too different.

> Me: It was like she was erased.

The bubbles bounced around once more, and I held my breath.

> Whit: I should have told you. Didn't think you'd have big feelings about it, or I'd have warned you.

> Whit: I'd never hurt you like that.

I exhaled in a loud whoosh.

> Me: I had no idea I'd react like that. Bram invited me here, and I'm staying for now.

> Whit: Stay where you need to. The house will be there when you need to go back.

> Whit: You should ask Bram why you staying there is dangerous for him.

Fear ran through my body, and I sat up straighter. *Dangerous?*

> Me: What do you mean? Can I call you?

> Whit: Can't talk this second. But ask him. I'll text you later.

My heart thrummed inside my chest. Lakey began to jump on me, panting. I sat at the breakfast nook in the kitchen and bent down to hug her neck. The mysterious nature of the conversation intrigued and worried me. How could my staying there be dangerous for Bram?

My mind flitted back to that picture on his dresser of the mystery girl, but I pushed the thought away. He couldn't be with someone, not if he were going to marry me. But that was an agreement just for show, wasn't it?

I'd offend him if I started asking questions when he'd plainly stated he was unattached. All I could do was hope that eventually the truth of everything would spill out into the open, and that this perceived "danger" was Whit's imagination.

CHAPTER ELEVEN

Bram | *October 1, 2024*

> Julianna: It was great. Got some blood work as well as the hot physician assistant's phone number.

I read Jules' last text repeatedly, trying not to let my emotions get the best of me in front of my coworkers. The forest service staff was gathered for our monthly safety meeting, and as the supervisor, I should have been paying attention. Instead, all I could think of was some douchebag in a white coat inappropriately soliciting Julianna at her doctor appointment. I shook the thoughts away for the twentieth time, trying to listen to my employees as they dutifully discussed chainsaw safety.

"Chaps are required for all operation of the chainsaw," Doug droned in front of the large screen that projected his rudimentary PowerPoint slides. "Always operate the chainsaw within your skill level—"

"I'm pretty sure that means you shouldn't be using one, squirt," Tom, an older forest ranger, joked. The staff around the table snickered, and Doug scoffed. Junior rangers always received a hard time from the staff—it was a rite of passage.

"Ha-ha," Doug replied. He continued to read aloud more OSHA rules, and my phone rang. I'd forgotten to turn the ringer off. Whit's name appeared on the screen. Melanie's eyebrows raised when she glanced over and saw the name on the phone, which lay on the table.

"Guys, I'll be right back." It wasn't my finest leadership moment, but I felt it could be significant if Whit called midday. I retreated to my office, shutting the door behind me. "Hello?"

"All I'm going to say before I blow my stack is, don't you dare fucking lie to me. Did you talk my sister into staying with you?"

I didn't think Julianna would talk to Whit before I did, but I was wrong. I ran a hand through my hair and sat behind my desk, the chair squeaking under my weight.

"How did you find out?"

I heard the echo of voices in Whit's background, but he pressed on at full speed. "She told me, how else would I find out? What the hell, dude? Did you touch her? That's your sister."

I grit my teeth together. "She's *not* my sister. We don't share one drop of blood." I put a clear emphasis on my words.

"Semantics. What happened to 'I won't touch her, Whit?'"

I closed my eyes. "I haven't touched her, not like that. What did she say?" I needed to know if she'd told Whit about the fake marriage, too.

"That she didn't want to stay at Grams' because of the remodel. That it hurt, she didn't know what I'd done, maybe? I'm confused…"

I bit my lip. "I can't speak for her. Things are complicated. She's going through a lot."

He huffed. "Listen to you, talking like you know her better than me. You've been with her for less than seventy-two hours."

I shook my head, even though I knew what he was getting at. I didn't know her, not really, even if I wanted to.

"There's no reason to be a dick," I snapped. "You know how I feel about her."

"Yeah. That's why I'm telling you, do not touch her. Don't make any moves on her."

He must not know about the fake marriage, then. I shoved that aside as anger swept through me. Who did Whit think he was? He was Julianna's brother, but he wasn't her keeper. Nor mine.

"I won't promise that. It's not your decision to make."

"Listen to me closely," Whit countered, his voice steely. "I know how you are, Bram. You'll get Jules in your system, then you'll get bored, and then you'll break her heart. It's what you always do in every relationship you've ever had. I've watched it happen over and over. I can't watch it happen to my sister."

"How do you know she wouldn't be different?"

"How do you know that she would be?"

I let the words sink in, and my anger cooled into doubt.

I had already hurt Julianna in so many ways. I was trying to show her how sorry I was for the mistakes of my youth and the truths I had yet to admit to her, but nothing would ever be enough. I could never make up for how I'd failed her.

What if I admitted to her that I still had feelings for her after all these years, and she accepted me, then I messed up again? I couldn't imagine doing it in a million years. But still…what if I did? Even if it wasn't on purpose?

"You're right," I conceded. "I don't want to hurt her. That's the last thing I want."

He let out a long breath. "I didn't mean to be harsh. But she's my sister. You know she is not going to stay in Mill Creek.

She's going back to her life in Charlotte once this is over. That's always been her plan."

I could hear the nails being driven into my coffin of hope with every word he spoke.

How could I tell him about the fake marriage now? He'd see it as another manipulation. I bent over in my seat. "I hear you. You're right. I'll stay away from her like that."

"I wish I could come out there. It would make all this easier. Life's really teaching me that I need family. I miss her, and being around you, too, man."

"Yeah." My heart wasn't in the conversation anymore. My friend could not support me in what I wanted most, and I couldn't find the false optimism to be there for him either. "I gotta go. We're in a meeting."

"Sure thing. I'll holler at you."

I ended the call.

Julianna: When are you coming home?

The text came through about four-thirty pm. It was simple, yet it made my insides twist with so many stupid emotions. She'd called it her home, and she cared what time I would be with her. Knowing those two things was enough to make my chest puff with pride. Fuck that physician's assistant.

"Got a hot date?" I typed out the teasing, somewhat flirty remark I would typically make. But then I erased it.

Me: Soon. I'll pick up some burgers.

I put my phone down and started the truck. An immediate reply appeared.

Julianna: No need. I've got something here for us. I was hoping you were on your way.

I ran a frustrated hand through my hair. She had taken the time to fix supper for us.

> Me: Go ahead and eat. I've got some errands. Your back feeling okay?

I had to ask. It wouldn't matter if I pulled away. I would always care.

> Julianna: Not too bad. See you in a bit.

I wish I could read between the lines in those words and gauge her level of disappointment, but I couldn't. I knew better than to make assumptions. Maybe she cared, perhaps she didn't, and whatever the answer, this could only end one way.

I had to think of random things to kill time so I wouldn't go home and make terrible choices. I went to the pet store in South Roanoke and bought a few things for Lakey. Realizing I'd only wasted an hour, I stopped for some food and a beer at Lady Jane's, the only bar in Mill Creek.

The place was empty. No game was on to draw crowds, and there were no weekend tourists. All that suited me fine. The last thing I needed was to be among people wanting to initiate conversations. I'd just bitten into the first couple of fries I'd ordered when I felt a friendly slap on my back and a hand clutching my shoulder.

"Well, if it isn't the best tight end to ever play in North Carolina!"

The immediate groan that wanted to climb out of me could barely be contained. I turned to face the pleasant yet rugged face of my old high school football coach, Jim Mayfield.

"Hey, Coach," I said casually, turning and shaking the man's hand.

I had no ill will toward Coach Mayfield. He'd been a great

example of a good man for many years when I needed it most. We had been close then. But Coach was the embodiment of football in my mind. Seeing him now made me think of things I wanted to forget, like where my father claimed he paid the University of Alabama to accept me on a football scholarship, something he'd held onto until the night of the wreck.

I didn't want to remember any of it. Not the wreck. Not the betrayal. And certainly not the satisfied look on my father's face as he threw my world into a tailspin.

I often wondered if Coach Mayfield knew I was recruited falsely, but I would never ask him. I had an image of him that I didn't want tarnished.

"How you been doing, son?" Coach Mayfield asked.

"I'm holding up." I took a bite of a fry, wanting to groan once again as he sat beside me. "How's Betty doing?"

The older man's eyes glistened as they met mine. "She's fair to middlin'. We're moving to Florida, in case no one's said anything to you yet."

I internally recalled my conversation with Josiah in the parking lot after the MCA dinner. It had only been last Friday, but it felt like a million years ago.

"You know damn well Josiah already told me."

"Never could get one over on you." He laughed good-naturedly. "I had to sic someone on you. You never called to take me up on the offer. You ought to see what I'm working with this season." He whistled for punctuation, then he nodded toward the bartender, who came over and took his order. The third unspoken groan echoed within me as he ordered the same thing I had. Food meant I was in for the long haul.

"Good talent this year?" I asked.

"Oh yeah. Got a couple of freshmen with promise, and you ought to see the quarterback. He's a good leader, and that's on top of a mean throwing arm. Good eye, too."

"That's great."

I couldn't focus as he talked about his team. My thoughts swam to my father, Whit, and Julianna.

"What's eatin' you? You look miles away."

"Sorry," I replied. "Not personal. It's been a long day. Weekend can't come soon enough."

"Hmm," he said, his eyes narrowing in thought. "Wouldn't have anything to do with the talk I heard about Whitaker East's sister being back in town?"

My eyebrows shot up. "Word travels fast around here," I said, then downed a swig of my beer. "How would that affect me?"

A smile played on the older man's lips. "Wouldn't have meant a thing if old widow Erma hadn't seen you two moving boxes at Leota's old house."

I groaned aloud this time. "I should have known someone was watching. Whit can't be here. I'm stepping in for him. Simple as that."

"I see." Coach Mayfield nodded. "She always was a sweet gal. I remember her coming to practice sometimes, waiting for Whit to take her home. How is she?"

"She's okay," I replied. "Came home to have surgery on her back in Roanoke, though."

"Oof. From that wreck she had when you guys were teens? It was bad. Does she have anyone to tend to her?"

I sat straighter. "Yeah. I'll be helping her as much as she'll let me." I'd self-nominated, but Coach Mayfield didn't have to know that.

"Mmm...Isn't it funny how sometimes the past collides with the present? I'm sure Whit is grateful you're here for her when he can't be. His stats this season are impressive, especially since he's been at this a while."

I tipped my beer to him in agreement. "Yeah, he's doing great." I took my last drink. The small talk was beginning to be too much, and after a moment of silence, I threw my wrappers and used napkins back into my burger basket, unwilling to finish the few bites I had left. I stood, primed to escape quickly with a goodbye, when I felt the old man's hand on my arm, steadying me.

"I know you feel some way about what happened way back when, Bram. Your injury in college and all that. Just know that when the scouts came to see you and Whit during your senior year in high school, they told me you had what it took to make it. Life throws us some awful punches. You've dealt with them better than anyone I've ever met."

I looked my old coach in the eye, searching for any sign of lies on his face. But I saw nothing. Coach Mayfield was an honest man, and I trusted him. If his words were true, I might have earned that scholarship. Maybe it wasn't given to me because of money. It wouldn't be the first time my father had manipulated a situation to his advantage.

I shook myself out of my daze.

"Thanks, Coach," I replied. "That helps to hear." I stuck my hand out, and he shook it.

"I'm not pressuring you, but think about the head coach position. There is no one I would trust more than you to take over the program. Those boys could use you." A small smile appeared on his lips. "Stop by the field one day and watch them in action. It's always open to you. And take care of Whit's sister, son. And maybe let her take care of you. You deserve that."

I DROVE AROUND A LITTLE LONGER, THINKING AND REFLECTING ON the few things Coach Mayfield said and my relationship with the sport that had defined my life. What would it feel like if I had made it to the pros like Whit? How would that have changed me? Would I be less bitter? Or would I be much less humble?

No matter what, one thing remained true: I would still think about the woman waiting for me.

I was used to dealing with everything on my own, but I should have trusted her and shared my thoughts with her. I wanted to talk everything over with her. My father's deceit, my mother's alcoholism, Melanie's presence in my life. What football meant to me, how I felt when it was ripped away. How I let that passion die.

Yet I couldn't dump my worries on her. She didn't deserve my problems. She needed to worry about herself, and I would do everything to ensure she was taken care of. She was already doing me a huge favor with the fake marriage. For both our sakes, I would stay as emotionally distant as possible. I couldn't afford to hurt her again.

With that in mind, I turned the truck toward the house with a new resolve in my heart to keep my distance. I was sure I could switch off the longing and the anxiety I had with every moment in her presence.

Think of Whit. Think of Whit…

I walked in the back door to an eager Lakey, her tail swinging and tongue wagging. "Hey, my girl," I said, petting her. I set my things on her kennel, just as I did daily, and pulled out a bone I'd bought for her. She took it with a whine and scampered off, making me smile.

Something delicious had been cooked by the smell of it. Maybe soup? My stomach growled. I'd only eaten half my meal at the bar. I turned the corner into the kitchen and stopped in my tracks.

The breakfast table had been set for two. A tall taper candle had burned halfway down, but the flame was extinguished. Where had she even found a candle? A glance at the kitchen counter revealed a cast-iron skillet covered with a cloth, and beside it, a frosted cake with vanilla icing.

She'd wanted to do something special, and I had taken the opportunity from her.

"Julianna?" I called from the middle of the kitchen, hands at my sides.

She entered in a few moments.

"Hey," she said, leaning slightly against the wide wooden doorframe. There was no smile on her face, but she wasn't scowling either. Neutral. Unaffected.

But I knew her better than that. Julianna could do many things, but neutral emotions weren't one of them.

"You did all this?" I asked, not clarifying or indicating what *it* was. We both knew.

"Yes," she whispered.

"Julianna..."

"It's okay." She crossed her arms across her chest. "I wanted to do something to thank you for letting me stay here. I didn't realize you had plans already. But the chili is in the pot in the oven, if you still want some."

"Grams' chili?" I asked, knowing the answer was yes. That's why the aroma felt like a warm hug.

She nodded affirmatively, looking me in the eye without flinching.

"That is...that's so thoughtful of you," I stuttered. "I'd love some. Have you eaten?"

"I ate a bit ago in the living room." She pointed with her thumb over her shoulder toward said room. "It's early, but I think I'm going upstairs to shower and sleep. It's been a long day."

"Of course," I said, though my heart dropped into my stomach.

She nodded, as if reaffirming her choice to herself, and turned to leave. Every fiber of me yearned to run after her. If she'd let me touch her, I could try to fix this. But all the reminders of who I was, how I told Whit I'd behave, and what I needed to avoid stopped me.

I took a bowl of chili to the living room. It transported me back to Grams' small kitchen table. A younger Julianna sat across from me, reading her book until Grams made her put it down and finish her food. I remember baiting her by hitting her leg with my foot. Her head would shoot up, and she'd glare daggers at me. Then I'd wink, and she'd smile and blush. Whit would not notice, and Grams pretended not to. The memory ached in my bones.

The shower was running upstairs, and when it stopped and the door creaked open, I jumped to my feet. I ran to the edge of the stairs, heart racing.

"Julianna," I called. I couldn't see her in the hall, but I heard her footsteps stop.

"Yes?" Her voice was small.

"Take my bed again, for your back. Please."

Her feet shuffled, the hardwood creaking. "Bram, the guest room is fine."

"Take my bed, or I'll come up there and throw you into it."

My pulse beat in my ears, and I realized what I'd said and how it sounded. Yet I let the innuendo hang in the air between us.

"Okay, okay. No need for violence," she replied sarcastically, although her usual banter tone was subdued.

Satisfied, I went to wash my dishes and let Lakey out in the yard for a minute before deciding it was best for me to go to sleep as well. I turned off all the lights and made sure the doors were locked.

At the top of the stairs, my bedroom door was wide open. Julianna was sitting cross-legged on the bed, looking through some papers with an open laptop next to her.

"Hey," I said, opening the door wider.

Her surprised face looked up, and then her eyes narrowed.

I saw what she was holding—her little black box.

"Why do you have these?" she whispered, trembling.

My stomach churned, embarrassment washing over me. I knew why she was angry. I had no right to own what she held. Heat crept up my neck for the first time in a long time.

"Julianna, I can explain—"

"These were my private thoughts," she interrupted, her voice cracking. "Things I wrote in my bedroom, alone." She waved the papers in the air. "Why do you have these? How?"

Part of me wanted to ask why she was going through my bedroom drawers, but I refrained. I didn't care if she went through every drawer I owned or how many mementos she found of hers in my space.

"I found that box when I was remodeling Grams' house. I had to take up the old flooring, and it was under the floorboards in the closet. The pages were in the box."

"I don't even remember putting the box in the closet. I thought I'd destroyed all of it at some point. I'm sure you read them," she snipped, her face flushed.

"Yes, I did," I replied honestly, keeping my tone somber.

She closed her eyes.

I sat on the edge of the bed. I reached over and removed the papers from her hands. Folding them over, I put them in the box and shut the lid. She put her head in her hands.

"This is way worse than me watching you change in high school," she said from behind her fingers. "These were my most private thoughts about you. I even talked about— "

"How we were perfect soulmates?" I interrupted, smiling, trying to catch her eye between her trembling fingers. "How you watched my ass as I played ball out in the driveway with Whit? You did write about wearing my football jersey while I took your virginity and how you wanted me to—"

"Oh my God! Please stop!" She scrambled over and jerked the box out of my hands.

I tried hard not to chuckle. "Julianna. That's from fifteen years ago. We were kids. We're adults now. It doesn't bother me that you felt those things about me then, not at all." I didn't take my eyes off her face, even though she wouldn't look at me. She clenched the black box to her chest.

"But it was wrong for me to keep them and not destroy them or send them to you, so I'm sorry for that," I continued. "Forgive me, please." I placed my hand on her bent knee. She looked down at it. My heart skipped a beat as her eyes lifted to meet mine.

"I was fanciful back then," she whispered. "I'm still in love with the idea of love, but I'm not as naïve now."

You're perfect now. The thought ran through my head unbidden. And not saying it to her was one of the hardest things I'd ever done.

"No one is," I said. "I am sorry, sweets." I gestured toward the box with my head. "I thought about giving them to Whit. That was the alternative I was working with here."

"Oh my Godddd!" She fell over onto the bed. "If that was the alternative, then thank you a million times over. You should have destroyed them."

I would have lit myself on fire before I destroyed those words, but I kept that thought to myself, as well.

"That was a huge ego boost for me, you know. There's no way I was getting rid of them," I teased. I noticed her open laptop and some paragraphs on the screen.

"What's that?" I asked, pointing to it. She snapped the lid closed quickly.

"Nothing."

"It didn't look like nothing. Do you still write? Like you did in high school?"

She bit her lip. She was still flushed, so much so that I could feel the heat radiating from her.

"Yes. Sort of. Sometimes."

"That's amazing. You were always so good at it."

"It...it calms me. Redirects my thoughts when things get overwhelming."

"Today was overwhelming for you, I'm sure." I thought about the appointment, the PA. I had missed the chili and the dinner setup. Then she'd found the letters.

I stood. "I'd love to hear about it. Maybe read some to me, someday?"

She flashed a half smile. "No way. It'll be in a fully published form if you ever see it."

"Oh, come on. You were going to let me take your virginity, but you won't let me read your stories?"

She gasped and threw a pillow at my head. I caught it before it hit me.

"Uncalled for!" She was laughing with me, her rich tone echoing off the walls.

"I couldn't help it," I chuckled, tossing the pillow back to her.

"I'll try to find it in me to forgive you." She clutched the pillow to her chest. Lakey jumped up on the bed. "I'll keep your dog as repayment."

"She's a bed hog anyway, take her. I'm heading out. Can I use this bathroom in the morning to get ready? I'll keep it proper."

She tucked the box behind her back.

"Yeah, of course. Just wake me up, and I'll leave you to it."

"No, you can sleep. As long as you're comfortable with me coming in here."

She smiled sweetly then, her cheeks still bright pink. "Of course, it's fine," she said, her grin more playful than before.

"Sleep well, sweets." I left quickly before I made a move on her that I could not take back. I'd wanted to kiss her all day, and I knew any further reflection on what I had memorized in those pages would be my undoing.

Diverse, innumerable mixed signals bounced in my mind. We had kissed but never spoken of it again. We hadn't declared feelings of any kind, but we were getting married.

We were a complicated puzzle of contradictions, and I wondered how this could possibly play out without one or both of us getting hurt.

CHAPTER TWELVE

Julianna | *October 4, 2024*

I smiled as I set down my phone on Bram's kitchen table, satisfied. I'd just finished speaking with a small independent publishing company in Charlotte. The job listing for a Social Media Marketer had seemed to appear out of nowhere a couple of days before, and I'd jumped at the chance to apply the second I saw the start date was three months out. The callback came quickly after I turned in my resume. The phone interview went well, and the publisher set up a virtual interview in a week.

Hope was blooming in my chest as a plan came together in my mind. I would fake marry Bram, have this surgery, heal as needed, and let Bram collect his trust fund. Then I would go back to Charlotte, back to Kallie, and our shared acquaintances and haunts. I needed to return to familiarity as soon as possible. Being in Mill Creek was a thing of the past, and it was best left there.

Living with Bram the last few days had been uneventful. We'd had some casual conversation about our lives when our paths crossed, which hadn't been often. He seemed to stay gone until late at night, and I couldn't figure out whether or not it was on purpose.

There'd been no more heated moments, not after the night of the journal, and no more attempts to kiss me. Not even a slight brush in passing. There was no talking about Whit or our past. No more talk of the marriage we'd agreed to. We left so much unspoken, and I hated it. The one time I'd tried to mention the marriage, he'd changed the subject.

It didn't help that every day a text came through from Kallie that read: Have you texted the hot doctor yet?

Even without Kallie's reminders, I hadn't forgotten about the card with Hunter's cell phone number on it and the open invitation I had to contact him. The temptation was strong. Bram was pulling away and distancing himself from me; that much was obvious. So what did I have to lose?

Before I could stop myself, I grabbed the card from my purse and my phone from the table.

> Me: Hey, Hunter. It's Julianna East.

Nerves ate at my stomach as I pressed "send". Lakey looked up at me from the dining room carpet, her knowing eyes watching me. I couldn't decide whether I was imagining how sad she looked or if she knew how much I regretted what I just did. Before I could unsend the message, the phone buzzed in my hand.

> Hunter: Hey there! Glad you decided to get a hold of me. How are you?

Something warm settled into my chest.

> Me: Fine. How are you?

> Hunter: I'm good. Want to get dinner tonight?
> 7 pm? So sorry to be forward, it's a busy day.
> Not much time.

My mouth dropped open. He wanted to take me to dinner in five hours?

It was the night of Mill Creek Aid's community supper, and I had told Bram I wanted to go with him. I wanted to meet the key players of the new center that would be built and see the charity organization in action. Could I reschedule with Bram to see Hunter instead?

Maybe I wouldn't have to cancel at all. The dinner started at six. I could have Hunter pick me up at the supper, and then we could go out. I sent a text to Bram:

> Me: Do you mind calling me when you get a minute?

Not even a minute later, a phone call came through from him, and I answered.

"Hey, what's up, sweets? Feeling okay?" I found myself smiling at the sound of Bram's voice.

"Yes, I'm fine. I had a question. Would you be upset if I left the MCA dinner a little early tonight?" I tried to stem the nervous energy that was creeping into my voice.

"You need my permission?" he replied, puzzlement in his tone. "Got a hot date?"

"Actually...I do have a date, maybe. With that physician's assistant, Hunter."

I was met with silence.

"Bram?"

"Okay." Bram's voice was deeper, but...off.

"I can explain to him about the fake marriage later on, if I need to, right?" I asked hurriedly. "Since he and I are not together, it's not pertinent for him to know right now. This is just a date. " I was stumbling over my words, disappointed I hadn't thought this through more thoroughly, already regretting my impulsivity.

"It's fine." He cleared his throat. "Will he pick you up at the senior citizens' building?"

"I'm sure, but it's not set in stone yet. I wanted to check with you first before I made further plans."

"Again, you don't need my permission. Set your date. I'll pick you up in a bit."

I picked at my cuticles. "No, that's okay, don't backtrack from the other side of town," I insisted. "I'll drive the Jeep out, and then Hunter can bring me back to it so I can drive myself back to your house tonight." I bit my tongue as the word *home* nearly slipped from my lips.

"No, you're not driving anywhere," he replied steadfastly. "I'm coming to get you now, and he can drive you home later."

"Again, I'm not made of glass."

"I will treat you like porcelain if I want to." I heard a smile behind his words, and I was sad at how relieved it made me. "Be ready about four. I'll be there."

"Okay."

I hung up the phone and texted Hunter.

> Me: It's a date! Can you pick me up at the Mill Creek senior citizen building at 7?

> Hunter: Hmm. Strange meeting spot, but I'll be there :)

Later, Bram pulled into the farmhouse driveway as I was talking to Kallie.

"Do I still need to come up and help after the surgery, or is your husband caring for you?" I'd explained to her a couple of days ago why I was marrying Bram, but she hadn't quit with the sarcasm.

"Be nice," I scolded. "Of course, you're coming. I'll go back to Grams' house, and we can stay there in peace."

"What will Bram think about that?"

I knew from context clues that Bram was assuming I would stay with him after the surgery. He'd even said I could have a bedroom downstairs. All afternoon, I'd mulled over how to tell him that Kallie was still coming to look after me. I didn't want him to watch me struggle in the aftermath. There were some things an attractive man was not meant to see, and potentially soiling herself or having to be sponge-bathed were two of them.

"I don't know, but he's going to have to accept it," I snapped in reply to my best friend. "I gotta go. I'll text you later."

Bram walked in through the back door, boots hard against the utility room floor. Lakey ran to meet him, and I stood from the couch, heart pounding as he neared. He rounded the corner, wearing a ball cap and his forest-green ranger uniform. It fit every inch of him to perfection.

Damn, he is so hot.

"I'm ready," I sheepishly said.

"You look so beautiful." He looked me up and down with a subdued, genuine smile.

"Thank you, it's an old sundress I had," I said, smoothing down the crisp blue fabric. I reached down and grabbed my jean jacket from the sofa.

He walked up to me then, stopping an arm's length away.

"It's not about the dress. It's about you." His hand brushed my slightly curled hair off my shoulder, and goose bumps erupted on my arms.

"Oh. Thanks."

I couldn't stop staring into Bram's eyes. They were so warm and intense with emotion.

"It'll be a good night, sweets."

"I think so."

His smile fell, and although I had no way of knowing for sure, I sensed a negative wave of energy coming from him. He recovered quickly, and his eyes softened. "Okay, let's go do some behind-the-scenes good."

We pulled into the worn, paved parking lot of the Senior Citizens' Community Building, which was already full of vehicles. Old, young, well-dressed, and work-worn people milled about outside the door. Kids of all ages played around the basketball hoop behind the building.

"This is a big production," I remarked.

Bram smiled wryly.

"It's a great achievement. Mountain people are proud and don't take kindly to handouts. When I started volunteering with MCA, several people told me behind closed doors that so-and-so's family didn't have any food and that the kids were going hungry. That's why we created a community dinner. Everyone comes, people of all kinds. Those who need to pick up necessities and get a hot meal are more likely to do so because the scrutiny is low and there is diversity. There are still holdouts, but one family stocked and fed is better than none, you know?"

I couldn't keep the grin off my face. "What a great idea. Do you feed lots of kids?"

"Oh yeah," he replied, turning into an empty parking spot in the back. "We have about 250 people total every Friday night, and lots of them are kids."

"That's amazing," I said on a breath, taken aback. "Who cooks?"

"Volunteers. Generally, it's older ladies who used to work in the school cafeteria," he said, putting the truck in park. "They spend all day cooking. We also give out canned and dry goods, toiletries, and bottled water every Friday. Some of these people I've found only have the spring or well water at their homes, and sometimes it doesn't run clear, so drinking water is a hot commodity."

I was speechless. I looked at the man beside me and studied him quietly for a moment. His ball cap framed his angular jaw and the slight stubble on his face. The long-sleeved black tee hugged his muscular arms and broad shoulders just right. His hands, worn by hard work and time, gripped the steering wheel. He looked like a regular guy, although ruggedly handsome. No one would suspect he had come from money. No one would think he had a heart that beat to help others.

I wished Kallie could have seen Bram through my eyes and not through his mistakes. Despite all that may have happened between us in the past, this was who I knew Bram was. This was who I'd fallen in love with so many years ago.

"All this has to take a lot of money," I said.

Bram shrugged, and I noticed he didn't comment as he opened his truck door.

"Don't you dare," he said when he saw me reach for the interior door handle. "I'm coming around."

I rolled my eyes but obeyed.

Three or four teenage boys hanging out with a football across the lot noticed Bram and ran toward him, all shouting their greetings simultaneously.

"Wanna throw around with us?" The tall, skinny boy with the football asked.

"Not right now, guys." Bram looked back at me through the

semi-tinted window. Then the guys noticed me, too. I sent up a little wave.

"Ohhh," one of them said in a sing-song voice. "Bram's got a girrrllfriend." Bram did not correct him. It was not true, but since we'd be married soon, it was probably best to let it happen. I smiled back at him.

"Maybe later," Bram remarked to them, and they took it as their cue to leave. Bram jogged over to my side of the truck and opened the door.

"You should throw with them," I insisted as I took his offered hand and hopped down to the graveled pavement. "It's probably not often they get to toss a ball with a college football legend."

He hmphed. "That's hardly what anyone would call me. Come on."

I thought he would reach for my hand. *I want him to reach for my hand.*

But he didn't. Instead, he placed a hand on the small of my back. Many men and women milled about in front of the building. No one made any move to talk to us, but they eyed us curiously as we entered the back door.

We walked into a bustling kitchen where three lovely, elderly ladies with tight gray buns and worn aprons were at work. A couple stirred pots of steaming food, and another took hot baked goods out of an industrial oven in the corner. It was easy to see that the amount of food being prepared required a lot of people to consume it. My heart warmed when I thought about what the money from Bram's inheritance would do.

"You're late," a woman snapped at Bram. I reared back in surprise and ducked behind Bram slightly. She was short and plump, with graying-brown hair that cascaded in ringlets around her shoulders. She wore a pink paisley scarf over a white turtleneck and black slacks. The other three women in the room still hadn't stopped to acknowledge our presence.

"Hello to you, too, Gladys." Bram appeared unaffected by her abruptness. "I've brought a guest." His large hand reached once again to splay across my lower back, lightly nudging me back around him. "Julianna East, this is Gladys Bell. She's the director of operations here."

"Hello," I said, and held out my hand for her to shake.

Her eyes widened, and her dour expression turned bright.

"I remember you," she replied fondly. "You wouldn't remember me, but I knew your grandmother. Leota was one of a kind."

"She was." I swallowed the lump in my throat. "How did you know her?"

It was a silly question. Mill Creek was small. Everyone knew everybody.

"I got to know her after the plant closed down."

She didn't say anything else, and I read between the lines. Grams was a single woman raising two young kids. She'd probably needed all kinds of help after she lost her job, and being a pre-teen, I hadn't known it.

"I should have been here earlier, but it was a busy day," Bram broke in, alleviating my need to formulate words. "What is left to do?"

"You know there's nothing." She touched his arm fondly, her tone much more pleasant. "The nephews helped a lot, so I've not been without hands to carry things. Just stick around and do the running for the ladies here."

"I'm glad you had help. I apologize again." He turned to me and nodded toward a small hall, where echoes of voices, clinking spoons, and laughter bounced off the walls. "Come on. I don't go out there much, but you'll want to see this."

I followed Bram toward the noises. The room opened, and we entered behind a large serving station with volunteers doling out steaming hot food onto Styrofoam plates. Kids were laughing, and people were smiling. It was wholesome and warm.

Several people in line at the serving area saw us and stopped to stare.

"Don't bring girls here much, do you?" I whispered, leaning my head close to him. He grinned back at me.

"Here's a little secret, sweets. I've been doing this for nearly seven years, and I've *never* brought anyone with me," he said in a low tone, and I felt his warm breath on my ear. A shiver ran up my spine. "The level of exposure I've given you to my world is more than I've ever given anyone."

Goosebumps swept over my body, all the way to my feet.

"Probably a good thing you're putting a ring on it then," I whispered back. Our faces were close. One move forward, and our lips would touch.

I stayed still.

"Why are they staring at you?" I asked, wondering if he could feel my breath on his lips.

"Honestly? They don't care much for me."

I reared back a little. "What? Why?'

His eyes met mine, subdued and full of resignation. "They don't understand me."

His fingers lightly trailed down my lower arm. It was the slightest caress but packed full of meaning.

I understood him. I always had.

"Some think I'm my father," he whispered. "It's why I work behind the scenes."

I nodded a little, understanding what he was saying, although everything within me wanted to protest. We both knew he wasn't his father, and there was no need to say it.

"Hello there, Bram," a man with a long white beard greeted from the line, throwing up his hand. Both of our gazes went to him, and I stepped back like we'd been caught.

"Hey, Charles," Bram returned and walked closer to the

man. Charles's gaze cut to me, and a smile spread across his hair-covered lip, revealing his bare gums.

The man looked at me, offering a slight wave. "Who's the beauty?"

"Charles, this is Julianna East. Julianna, Charles Beacon."

"East? You that football player's kin?" Charles asked, gums whistling.

"I'm his sister," I answered, nodding. "It's nice to meet you."

"Well, now. You're practically royalty around these parts!"

"Get on through the line, Charles," someone down the row hollered, and Charles moved as if he'd been burned while Bram laughed. He told the man he'd talk to him in a bit and then turned back toward me.

"Why don't we go help the best cooks in Mill Creek?"

CHAPTER THIRTEEN

Julianna | *October 4, 2024*

An hour later, I had frosted cupcakes until my fingers were puckered from the buttercream that leaked from the piping bag. "Thanks for the apron," I said, looking down at the white smudges across the front of the red fabric. Euetta, one of the cooks, had draped it around me when they'd given me the task.

"You're welcome, dear," she said from behind me. "I'm awfully glad Bram brought you along to help. You are so much faster than Mary."

"Hey!" Mary's shrill yell sounded from across the kitchen, and we both laughed.

"My best friend owns a bakery, but that's my closest claim to fame," I replied. I set the last cupcake on a serving tray and turned around.

Bram was alone in the doorway of the kitchen, leaning

against it. His eyes smoldered as he stared at me with his handsome grin. He had clearly been watching me.

"He's been watching you for five minutes," Euetta teased, elbowing me, as if she'd read my mind.

"That's enough," Bram replied playfully and kicked off the doorframe, walking toward us. "I think it's almost time, sweets, isn't it?"

I had been so immersed in the conversation with the ladies that I'd forgotten Hunter was coming to pick me up.

"Oh. Right. That." I stuck my hand in my dress pocket and pulled out my phone, checking the screen with my sticky fingers. Sure enough, there was a text from my date.

> Hunter: Hey, Julianna. I'll come in and get you, I guess? I'm 10 minutes out.

The text was from twenty minutes ago!

I scrambled to throw the apron off, realizing too late that I hadn't properly cleaned my hands. In my haste, prominent white sugared smudges swept the front of my blue sundress.

"I gotta—oh no—" My hands went up and out to the side as if I was being robbed. I looked around, but Bram was already on it. He grabbed a clean cloth from the side table and ran it under water. I reached for it, but he had no intention of giving it to me. I watched, stunned, as he softly cleaned the dried frosting off my fingers.

Our eyes met briefly, and I tried hard to show him my appreciation for what he was doing through a look. He averted his attention back to his task. Euetta had stopped whatever she'd been doing and was watching us intently.

"Take a picture. It'll last longer," Bram laughed at the older woman, who did not look the least bit chagrined.

"If I knew the first thing about those new phones, I'd do it,"

she replied with a shrug. "Far be it from me to look away from
a moment of sparkin' happening right before my eyes."

Sparking?!

"He's just helping. I'm going on a date," I blurted, my blunt
words startling both Bram and Euetta. Bram's soft ministrations
stopped, and regret flooded my chest.

"Yeah. A date," Bram reiterated, and with only slight hesitation, put the wet cloth into my hand, leaving me to grab it.
Dejection was written all over his face, and for the first time, I
realized he honestly didn't want me to go.

I stared at the rag in my hands, not able to watch Bram walk
away from me. He went toward the serving area.

"Well, can't say I'm not disappointed," Euetta said, slicing
through the uncomfortable moment. "Hope this other fellow is
a good man because you won't find any better than Bram. His
father is a piece of cow manure, but Bram is the best of 'em."

"He is," I confirmed, swallowing the lump in my throat.

"Let me tell you a thing or two you may not know then,"
Euetta said, taking the cloth from my hands. She went straight
in for my dress, so close I could smell the talcum powder on her
tender skin. "I don't know what a quarter of those people
would do out there if it weren't for Bram."

My brow furrowed. "What do you mean? I know he volunteers, but—" I was afraid for a moment that she was privy to
the information about the new community center. If she was,
and the secret was out, Bram needed to know.

Her wrinkled hands stopped wiping, and her squinting eyes
met mine.

"He's not told you," she said, her mouth quirked. She
lowered her voice. "He pays people's electric and water bills.
Buys groceries for people every other week. Gets Christmas
gifts for so many kids, coats in the winter, lawn mowers in the
summer. All kinds of little things that are a big deal to so many
out there."

"Oh," I replied. It was the only thing I could think to say. It wasn't surprising to me that he did this, but why hadn't he told me?

"He does it on his own?" I asked.

Euetta nodded. "Lots of those people never signed up for all the government programs when the plant shut down, so they've struggled, even so many years later. But Bram has his ways of finding out who needs things, usually through Gladys. He thinks no one knows, but people talk. Don't keep some from disliking him because of his daddy, but that number dwindles all the time."

My heart swelled with pride. It was never plainer to me that the boy I knew fifteen years ago wasn't the same man I was going to marry.

Fake marry. Get a hold of yourself.

"He is pretty special," was all I could think of to say.

At that moment, Bram walked back into the room, followed by Hunter.

With my heart racing, I watched the two men stand next to each other. Bram was taller, broader, and more rugged. Hunter was suave, sleek, and classically handsome.

Hunter's piercing blue eyes met mine. Nervous energy spread throughout every cell in my body as I drank in the sight of him. He was so handsome.

But Bram was, too. And he was familiar and warm.

"Julianna," Hunter said on a breath as if I was a sight to behold. Euetta stepped back and smiled at Hunter.

"Isn't she a sight?" Euetta preened, and my cheeks heated.

"Beautiful," Hunter said in his clear voice, charming.

Bram's eyes met mine over Hunter's shoulder, but his expression was blank. No smile. No frown. Just consideration.

I had the wherewithal to smile politely at Hunter, introduce Euetta, and grab my small crossbody purse from the counter.

"Well, I guess we're off?" I said, my hands shaking. Hunter

was waiting patiently, eyes still on me, but Bram was leaning against the doorway, dividing his attention between me and the back of Hunter's head. I wanted so badly to read his thoughts at that moment, but I still couldn't tell anything from his face.

I knew somehow that he did not want me to go on this date. But I'd initiated the contact with Hunter, and I'd agreed to go. I couldn't back out due to an errant thought that held little to no weight. I stared at Bram, trying to let him know with my gaze that all he had to do was say the word, and I'd call the whole thing off.

His dark eyes intensely assessed my own. But then he shook his head slightly and turned away from me.

That was how I left my first Mill Creek Aid community dinner—analyzing Bram's last movements and my hand looped through Hunter's awaiting arm.

BEING OUT WITH HUNTER IN DOWNTOWN ROANOKE WAS THE equivalent of being on a date with a celebrity. Everywhere we went, people spoke to him without reservation. He was always friendly, but I could tell by the time we'd made it through dinner and had moved on to the local soda fountain for some ice cream, he was growing weary of the attention.

"Does this happen everywhere you go?" I'd asked before sipping my chocolate malt.

He'd nodded. "How has your back been lately?" The switch in subject was a clear indicator that he didn't want to discuss my observation any further.

"It's been okay," I replied. "Not a lot to do during the days, considering I'm out of work at the moment. I do have a virtual interview in Charlotte, where I'm from. But of course, the surgery is a priority." I was rambling, but he said nothing to show he was put off.

"That's good to hear," he said, and then pivoted the conversation again to my old life in Charlotte.

Hunter was a deep thinker and insightful. His answers were concise, and his gray eyes mesmerizing. He had everything I could have ever wanted in a man, and he (a handsome medical professional) had asked me out without significant prompting.

I should have been soaking up every moment, yet the night felt very much like a friend date, and I knew why. Bram's face when he left the kitchen at the aid dinner would not leave my mind, no matter how hard I tried to push the image away. When I went to use the restroom before we left the soda fountain, I checked the muted texts on my phone.

Kallie: How's the doctor date?

Me: Again, not a doctor. And good. I think. Can't stop thinking about a certain vampire.

Kallie: That's not how this is supposed to go.

Me: The heart is a fickle organ.

Kallie: Focus on what is in front of you. Bram Winchester doesn't deserve your headspace.

Me: I think he was jealous. I can't stop thinking about it.

Kallie: Of course, he had to go and fuck this up for you.

Me: *eye roll emoji*

I went back to a visibly tired Hunter. He was in the tiny red-leather booth, wiping at his eyes.

"Hey, it's a long drive out to my friend's house. Maybe we

should go?" I felt the words slip from my lips, slithering out like I was lying even though I wasn't. It was a long drive. But the whole night felt off. Off, in an unexplainable way. Hunter must have thought it as well, because he offered no protest and got up from the booth.

Driving to the farm in the dark countryside was quiet, interrupted only by the occasional landmark comment and random question. It was comfortable, even in silence, but not anything like a drive with Bram.

In the driveway of Bram's house, Hunter opened my door, and I climbed out of his SUV. He didn't try to take my hand as he walked me toward the front door. The porch light had been left on for me, though, and for the first time since the night had begun, I was nervous.

Was Bram watching? I didn't want to be standing outside with Hunter, as handsome, kind, and smart as he was. I wanted to be inside, comfortable with Bram on the couch, Lakey at our feet.

I let out a deep breath, and Hunter smiled.

"Your mind is here, isn't it?"

"Am I that easy to read?" I laughed. "It isn't personal, Hunter. I just—"

Hunter took a step back from me. "It's fine. I enjoyed our time together. I apologize if I was too tired; it was a harder work day than anticipated."

"Oh, it's perfectly fine." I bit my tongue to keep from rambling.

I could already feel that he wasn't going to go in for a kiss, and I didn't blame him. Our surface-level conversations hadn't even warranted a hug, but that is what he went in for, quick and incomplete. His arms went around me in a loose, friendly fashion. I felt...nothing.

It was disappointing and telling.

When I walked into the unlocked front door, Lakey greeted

me, her tail swishing around my legs. The television was on in the living room, but Bram wasn't there.

"Bram?" I called out, setting my purse on the couch.

"Hey! Hold on, I'm coming." His deep voice called from the kitchen, and I heard his footsteps on the creaky floor.

He entered the living room, beer bottle in hand. He wore loose black sweatpants and a green T-shirt, barefoot. He leaned casually against the open doorway of the dining room and looked at me.

"This seems like a thing with you," I said, pointing at him up and down.

"What?" His face looked far from innocent.

"This doorway leaning you've been doing all day."

"I don't know what you mean." His smirk said otherwise, and at the first sign of it, my heart raced.

"Oh, you know what you're doing." I rolled my eyes and took a seat on the couch.

"How was the date?" He emphasized the 'T' in date.

"Great," I lied, then looked at the TV, absently watching a commercial for a car. "How did the dinner wrap up?"

"Fine. The ladies told me to tell you they hope you come back next week."

"Of course I will," I replied, feeling a warm kinship with the women. But I shoved the emotion away. The last thing I needed was to get attached to Mill Creek residents and their world. I was going back to Charlotte in a couple of months.

"No more dates, then?" He tried to keep any pleasure out of his voice, but I felt it radiating off him. He already knew.

I sighed. "I don't think so." I settled back in my seat, and my gaze swung to meet his. "You and I need to talk."

His brow furrowed as he took a sip of his beer.

"Okay..." he said, after he swallowed. "Shoot."

"I know what you're doing." The words tumbled from my lips in a rush.

"Is that so?"

"You are paying people's bills, buying groceries, gifts, and other things. Euetta told me. You're paying for all that on your own, separate from the organization."

He shrugged nonchalantly. "It's not a big deal. Feels good to help."

"It's incredible. I wish you'd told me how involved you were."

He didn't seem pleased by my praise. He ran a hand through his hair. "It didn't seem important. And I didn't want you to think I had become altruistic, not fully," he admitted. "I still think about how much I owe on behalf of my father. He ruined so many lives. It's what drives me. I want to erase the hurt he caused. And maybe turn some opinions around in the process. My work is not entirely unselfish."

I shook my head. "You don't get it. You don't just throw money at things. You give your time and energy, too. Even if it's misplaced guilt, it's a huge sacrifice on your part."

"I don't like making a big deal of it." His eyes locked with mine, and electricity passed between us as it had earlier at the dinner.

"So I won't," I replied. "But I admire you more than words can say."

He seemed speechless by my admission, but I noticed the moment he took control of the conversation. He grinned and tipped his beer bottle toward me. "You like being engaged to the secret big man about town, don't you?"

I rolled my eyes, feigning annoyance.

"I'm engaged to a vampire. Don't think I have forgotten that," I jested, and he chuckled.

Something shifted, and I was ready to admit it to myself.

I wanted Bram.

And I wanted him to want me, too.

The weekend was full of casual conversation, FaceTimes with Kallie, and writing on the porch with Lakey. Come Monday morning, I was ready to resume my search for a place to live when I returned to Charlotte. It was never too early to start looking.

I'd sat down with a cup of coffee in the empty living room when the phone buzzed with an unknown number. I recognized the Virginia area code and answered it.

"Hello?"

"Hello, is this Julianna East?"

"Yes, this is her." Lakey lay down at my feet.

"This is Dr. Kaveh. I'm sorry we have to meet over the phone for the first time."

I sat up fully. "Oh, it's okay. It's nice to meet you."

"And I apologize for bothering you so early. However, something came through on your scans, and we might need to address it quickly, hence the personal call."

My palms began to sweat as anxiety flooded through me. "Oh. What was found?"

"I will cut to the chase. The discs are significantly more bulged than they were in your previous scan, just a couple of weeks ago. All this degeneration has done a number on you. I, honestly, cannot believe it's not affecting you every day. Are you having any numbness or tingling?"

My mouth dropped open. "A little tingling down the back of my legs sometimes and the normal pinched nerve feeling in my back, but I haven't had any numbness," I replied, acutely aware the call wasn't going anywhere well.

"Hmm. That's curious. I'm looking at your MRI, and according to the radiology report, the bulge is sitting directly on the nerves," she said, careful thought in her voice. "I fear you might be a walking landmine. Any wrong move could cause the herniation to press further into the spinal cord. It could immobilize you instantly. I would like us to proceed with this as quickly as possible. What do you think about having surgery scheduled for this Friday, October 11th?"

I gasped. "So soon?" I began to shake, but I couldn't lose it with her on the phone. I steeled my emotions. "If you think that's necessary."

"I assure you, it is," she replied. "I have had a cancellation, and I want you to have it. Time is of the essence here."

"If you believe that's what needs to happen, then I'll do it. I-I can't thank you enough. I don't want to lose movement or control."

"I'm more than happy to help you. Dr. Billingsly spoke highly of you, and my PA told me he'd taken a particular interest in your case, so you've got a lot of people pulling for you, Ms. East." The mention of Hunter made my cheeks heat on top of the anxiety that permeated under my skin.

Dr. Kaveh continued, "I'll send this to our scheduler, and they'll be calling you with official word of the date and intake information. Meanwhile, I suggest taking it easy. No strenuous activity and avoid sudden movements, anything that could pull or tug."

"Thank you so much for calling me. I know you didn't have to do that," I said. My mind was reeling, but I was grateful.

"It's no problem. Take care."

I hung up, and my hands began to shake. My plans for the day had consisted of online house hunting, laundry, trying my hand at baking a pie, and polishing my interview skills. In an instant, everything changed.

Surgery was scary, but so was being immobile. I couldn't win either way. I needed to tell somebody. Bram popped into my head instantly, as did Kallie. My best friend deserved first place. She'd be in the morning rush at the bakery, though. I couldn't bother her.

I picked up the phone, typed out a message, and pressed send before I second-guessed myself.

> Me: MRI came back. Discs are bulging more than in the last scans.

> Me: Surgery is scheduled for Friday. Do you think we can get married before then? Legally? Insurance?

The read receipt appeared on the text string with Bram. I wiped away stray tears as the phone rang and his name popped up.

"Hey, sweets."

"Hey," I said, hiding a sniffle. "So, things are moving quickly. I'm sorry if that's inconvenient for the whole married thing, but insurance..."

"I'm calling the courthouse when we hang up. I'll get all the paperwork, license, all of it," he assured me. "Don't worry about all that, I've got it. How are you feeling?"

The concern in his voice made me break down in earnest, and I knew he could hear my despair through the phone.

"I-I can't believe this is happening. I...I wasn't prepared. I don't know how I couldn't be prepared. I knew something was wrong. I knew there was no stopping the surgery, but I thought—"

"I'm not sure you could have prepared for this," he cut in, his voice smooth and low. "It's scary, plain and simple. But you're so strong. God, if I could do this for you, I would. I'm sure you wish I could, too."

I sniffled and wiped away more tears that had fallen down my cheeks. "Yes, but no. I wouldn't wish this on you."

"But I would take it, if it would spare you," he replied, reso-lutely. "What did the doctor say, word for word?"

I explained it in more detail, and he exhaled a large breath.

"You shouldn't be alone right now. I'm coming home," he declared.

"No," I insisted. "I'm fine. I will be fine. I will call Kallie in a bit and text Whit to let him know what's happening. You work. Tonight, we'll do something to distract me." Visions of us tangled up on the couch together, not sitting apart as we had been, ran through my mind.

"It'll be okay, sweets." He sounded so sure. "Deep breaths, okay?"

I took one in and out, letting him hear me. "It's going to be okay."

"Distract yourself today, but take it easy. Promise?"

"Promise."

"I'll check on you in a bit."

We hung up, and I looked at Lakey, who stared up at me. She moved her head to where it sat on my foot, and tears sprang to my eyes anew.

"How will I leave you?" I whispered. I would have the surgery, then I would recover at Grams' old house and go back to Charlotte. Lakey, the farmhouse, and Bram would all become a memory.

My phone buzzed in my hand.

Bram: I'm right here. It's going to be okay.

CHAPTER FOURTEEN

Bram | *October 9, 2024*

I t was our wedding day. I'd set my alarm to wake early to make Julianna breakfast. My feet hit the cold hardwood floor, and I threw on the black sweatpants I'd worn the night before. When I emerged from my room, the lights in the house were still off, and the main bedroom door was only cracked, which had become our new routine. Neither of us fully closed our bedroom doors. It felt like an unspoken dare. I'd almost gone to her more than once in the night, but held back, thinking about how infinitely more complicated things could get if she rejected me. I wouldn't survive it. Watching her go on a casual outing with that physician's assistant had been fucking torture enough.

Being casually around each other the last few days had been so easy. We were old friends who reminisced and laughed at the silliest memories. Flirting was minimal, but a continuous undercurrent of electricity flowed between us. I knew she felt it too.

She was as much of a part of me as anyone could ever be.

You don't deserve her.

I shook the thought away. It popped up more than I cared to admit. But I couldn't dwell on it. I needed to focus on the task at hand.

I was cracking eggs into a hot iron skillet when Julianna shuffled into the kitchen, wearing only a worn t-shirt that was two sizes too big for her. Her bare legs thoroughly stirred my blood, and I tried not to let my gaze linger on her for too long, but I was failing. Her dark hair flowed around her seductively, and even though her face wore the vestiges of a night's sleep, she had a slight smile.

"Sleep well?" I asked her.

She bit her lip but didn't take her eyes off me. I leaned against the white stone countertop and gripped the edge behind me while the eggs sizzled.

"I woke up a few times, but my back feels good today," she replied. "I can't tell you how glad I am you're letting me sleep in your bed. It's just the right firmness for me. So a million times, thank you."

"My bed is your bed until the end, sweets. Case closed."

She opened her mouth to speak, but I didn't give her a chance to argue. I turned around from her and grabbed the coffee pot. "Ready to get married today?" I tried not to sound too eager, but I failed.

"I think so. I don't have anything nice to wear. Is that okay?"

"Is it an option for you to go unclothed? Because that's what I'm rooting for." I turned around with full mugs of coffee and winked at her. She tilted her head, and she watched my face—and my naked chest—as I handed her the coffee I'd doctored up with cream.

"I'm serious." But she was smiling, and a blush rosied her cheeks. It was everything for me to watch her melt under my truths.

"I'm serious, too," I replied with a chuckle. "But southerners don't take well to public nudity, so I think anything you've got will be fine unless you want to dress up fancy. If that's the case, I'll take you wherever you want to go and buy you whatever you want."

She shook her head. "No, I don't want to do that. I have never considered what I'd wear to a fake marriage. Feels anticlimactic to go in my regular clothing, but I guess anticlimactic is kind of the point." She looked at the floor.

She was trying to separate the intensity between us and what was happening today.

Keeping those thoughts separate was wise. But for me, I was marrying Julianna East, and whether it lasted one month or the rest of my life, I would greedily take what I could get, no matter how fake it was.

She was worth every piece of my heart that I would lose and never regain.

"Let's color coordinate," I suggested, flipping the eggs with a spatula. "Your favorite color is olive green, right? Let's wear that."

She looked up quickly, her eyes sparkling and bright.

I'd do everything I could to keep that look right at that moment on her face.

"That's perfect," she beamed and sipped her coffee.

WE WERE MARRIED IN OUR JEANS AND MATCHING OLIVE SHIRTS. Mine was a plaid flannel, hers a soft knit sweater that hugged her curves perfectly. We hadn't spoken much on the way to the courthouse. During the two-minute ceremony, I'd done what I could to soothe her, caressing her hands with my thumbs as I held them during our vows. She didn't look at me much while we recited sacred words, but I couldn't take my eyes off her. The only time they did was when I saw my sister, Melanie, dressed in her green ranger uniform, slide into the back seat of the courthouse.

Julianna noticed as well. Her eyes went wide.

"The girl from the picture," she whispered forcefully.

"What picture?" I frowned. "That's my sister, Melanie."

"Sister?" She'd exclaimed, and the judge stopped speaking whatever nonsense he was reading out of a small book.

"Sorry," Julianna said to him when he looked bothered. Then he continued. She didn't say anything else, but I caressed her hands more thoroughly and whispered, "You'll meet her. I'll explain everything."

Sliding a thin, hammered gold band on her finger near the end was my favorite part. I'd picked it up over the weekend, and it was a little snug, but the gamble had been worth it when her face transformed from apprehension to delight. At the end, when a kiss was expected, I looked at Julianna's hesitant face, leaned over, and quickly pressed my lips to her warm cheek. She exhaled and whispered a faint, "thank you" under her breath for only me to hear.

The judge who married us looked vaguely familiar, but I couldn't place him. Regardless, I shook his hand and said thank you. Mel ran up to us the second we were done, her ponytail swishing with every hurried step.

"Eeek! I am so happy!" She hugged me first, her slight arms tightly wrapping around me, before moving onto a shaken, wide-eyed Julianna.

"Julianna, this is my half-sister, Melanie Richardson," I said. "Mel, this is Julianna."

"Ma'am, we need you to sign this," the clerk interrupted, holding out a pen and the marriage certificate to Melanie. She signed on the adjacent desk and gave it back to the awaiting clerk before swinging back to us.

"We share a father, unfortunately," Melanie announced without preamble. "Bram will have to tell you all about it because I have to get back to work." Her eyes swung to meet mine. "Do you know how lucky you are, Bram? She's beautiful."

"The most beautiful woman in the world," I replied without hesitation.

"Thank you," Julianna said with a slight smile, wary. I should have told her that Mel was coming, but I wasn't sure if Mel would be able to get away from the office, and I didn't want to make Julianna extra nervous. It was unclear whether I'd made the right call.

As quickly as Mel had come, she was gone.

"Sorry, I didn't tell you," I blurted.

Julianna shook her head. "It's okay. I, um...I saw a picture in your room, and I thought she might have been an old flame. I never thought about her being your sister."

"It's quite a story. I can tell you about it over lunch," I said, ignoring the old flame comment, ushering her toward the door. The next couple waiting on the officiant was coming in as we walked out.

"Congratulations!" the woman cooed jovially.

"Thank you." A blush had spread across Julianna's face. It took so little to make her shy. It was something I loved about her.

"I can't believe we did that," Julianna said when we emerged into the sunlight. She twisted the small ring I'd given her on her finger. I picked up her hand as we walked out of the justice building and intertwined our fingers. It was a risk, but she didn't pull away.

I brought her hand to my lips for a quick kiss. I heard her

breath catch, but I pretended I was doing the most natural, normal thing in the world.

"Julianna Winchester has the best sound to it."

She reared back. "Not sure I want your Dad's name. Umm…what about Bram East? I like it much better."

I laughed. "Me too, honestly. Nothing would be better than if I had the same last name as Grams and not Vince Winchester."

Her face scrunched. "I understand the sentiment, but it sounds gross. Please don't repeat it. You'll get Whit fired up a million miles away, and he won't even know why."

I laughed. "I don't know why he's not answering our phone calls or texts yet. It's been two days." I opened the Jeep door for her. "If I hadn't seen the fucker on TV yesterday, I'd request proof of life."

She sat in the bucket seat, adjusted her clothes, and then reached for the seatbelt. "I don't know, either, but he hasn't even checked my messages about the surgery from Monday. Hopefully, he'll respond to one of us soon. What are we going to tell him?"

I shut the door and leaned into the window area. The top was off, and the windows were down, leaving hardly any barrier between us. The light breeze blew through her hair as the sun kissed her skin. Would I ever stop being mesmerized by her?

"Not sure, to be honest. He'll have his opinions, but you're getting insurance, and Mill Creek Aid will be $1.1 million richer. That's what matters."

"I guess so," she replied.

"What do you think about lunch? And I'll tell you all about Melanie."

We drove into Roanoke for food, away from the prying eyes and questions in Mill Creek.

"I want today to be comfortable," she'd said, looking down at her ring. I knew that she would take it off once we were back in Mill Creek. I obliged her location request, as hard as it was. I wanted her to wear that ring in Mill Creek. I wanted everyone to know she was my wife.

The only people I did not want to know were my parents. I was going to have the entirety of my trust fund—a sum my father no doubt coveted—but I had used the one woman he told me not to touch to do it. He would be livid. I wasn't sure how my Mom would react exactly, but she always sided with him.

Retaliation against my father wasn't why I'd married Julianna at all, but it was a perk.

We ordered our pulled pork dishes, and I explained how Melanie came into my life.

"That is insane," Julianna exclaimed, playing with the straw in her glass. "And your father still says she's not his, even with the DNA test?"

"Yup," I nodded. "Denies all of it. It isn't surprising, since it's Vince we're speaking of."

"Wow," she mused. "That has to be hard for Melanie."

"She takes it in stride. She never knew him, so she doesn't have much to go on."

Our food arrived, and Julianna doctored up her sandwich with various barbecue sauces that sat on the table. I smiled, remembering her doing that same thing when we were young.

"Are you going into work after this?" she asked, putting down a bottle of sauce.

"No, I thought I might spend some time with my wife instead." I nudged my leg against hers. She smiled, and I popped a couple of fries in my mouth through my smile before continuing, "How is your back? On a scale from one to ten, one being the worst?"

She thought a moment. "I'm probably at a five right now," she said, dabbing at her mouth with a napkin.

"Do you think you feel like going for a little walk in the woods?"

"In the woods? Trees, Lakey, all that?"

I swallowed hard. "Yeah. I thought it would be nice to be outside."

She bit her lip. "Is it uphill?"

I shook my head. "No. We'll drive the side-by-side up and walk around at the top of the ridge. I'm not taking any chances with your back."

She thought for a moment. "I'm not opposed. I've never been outdoorsy, so it could be annoying if I'm clumsy or slow—"

"You could never be annoying," I reassured her, rubbing her arm lightly for a few seconds. "If you want to go, we will. If you don't, or you're hesitant, we won't."

"I do like the fall weather," she mused, tapping her finger against her lips as if in careful thought.

"And the temperature and sun are perfect. We can go as slow and careful as you want."

"Okay. You've got me. I'm convinced." She laughed, her reaction making me smile. "You're going to make me an outdoors girl if it kills me, aren't you?"

"An outdoors *wife*." I winked at her. "Words matter, sweets."

Still grinning, she averted her gaze, her token blush spreading again across her cheeks.

I would never get tired of that blush.

An hour later, leaves crunched under my boots and her sneakers as we walked through the woods. We'd driven up the mountain on the all-terrain vehicle and then taken the path in the flatter areas. I'd cleared out a lot of undergrowth a few months prior, so the way through the area was easy to explore. After spending so much time wandering the woods, I was familiar with them. I didn't need the marks on the trees I'd painted anymore, but I pointed them out to Julianna anyway so she would be aware.

"How resourceful," she said, letting her fingers run over the marks on the tree bark. "It's like you know a thing or two about traversing a forest." The sarcasm in her voice was not lost on me.

"Yeah. A thing or two."

"What made you want to be a forest ranger?" she asked. "You and Whit used to do a lot of outdoorsy stuff, but I thought it was mostly getting drunk by the lake and driving around in the mud."

I chuckled. "That's fair. But after my football dreams died, I knew I wanted to do something outside. Being in an office sounded like hell, and nature has always felt worthy of my respect. It's amazing how it's always changing but still stays present. It's always there." I looked up into the tops of the trees, and her gaze followed. "And there's a freedom out here you can't experience anywhere else. A type of peace."

"I'm glad you found something you loved to make a career of," she replied, petting Lakey's head as we walked along. "There are so many paths we can take in life, and I'm glad you didn't settle for something you didn't care for."

"My dad wanted me to be his protégé, and I would rather set myself on fire."

She laughed for a moment, then fell silent. We were moving more slowly than usual, but I didn't mind. I would stay outside with her all day at any pace she set.

"Do you ever think about football? Those old dreams?"

I looked at her, slightly puzzled, but she continued, "I thought maybe you would coach or something? You were so good at playing. And you were always teaching Whit things. Without you, I don't think he'd be as good as he is."

I stumbled a smidge over a thick stick on the ground. I hadn't expected her to say that, but I grasped the opportunity to share with her.

"You remember Coach Mayfield?" I asked, and she nodded. "He's still at the high school, but he's been on me for years to help him coach, and I never would. I didn't feel like I could. Now, he's retiring at the end of this year and wants me to take over. I don't know how I feel about it. Sometimes, secretly, I think I'd like it."

I'd never said those words aloud to anyone.

Her brow creased. "Why secretly? Football was a huge part of your life. Do you think you're not allowed to love it anymore?"

I sighed. "It seems like something that should be in the past. And it reminds me of a lot I don't want to remember. Things I think I'm over sometimes, but maybe I never will be. Stuff like the injury, our wreck, my parents, losing Grams, leaving you behind..." I trailed off. "I've never said that to anyone. I think about football a lot, but I never mention it. Not even with Whit."

She reached over and took my hand into hers. As our fingers intertwined, she said soothingly, "I think there is a lot in life we can't forget, no matter how hard we try. Feelings imprint on us. Those feelings, those times—they become a part of us, and forgetting the past would be denying who we are. I think it's good enough to keep moving forward and realizing that the present and future are as important as the past."

I let her words settle into my bones.

This was not the light-hearted afternoon walk I thought it

would be. But I realized that Julianna was a magnet for emotion. Nothing was surface-level with her. She dug under my skin before I knew what was happening, drawing out the depth within me. She might enjoy reality television and pretend worlds, but she was more intense and thoughtful than anyone I'd ever known.

"I know I should embrace getting close with Whit again," she whispered. I thought maybe I hadn't heard her at all until I looked over at her and saw her eyes glistening with unshed tears. "I think about it all the time. But admitting I want that after he pulled away from me so many years ago so easily...it's always been more than I can handle. I've had to protect myself, and it's hard to trust anyone. I've never told anyone that either."

I squeezed her hand.

"Julianna...I should tell Whit," I said, letting the words slip from my lips, knowing that bringing this up could change everything.

"About the marriage? Of course, we should—"

"No, not about that. I should tell Whit about what happened the night of the wreck."

She stopped, her smile dissolving.

"No."

She didn't want me to say it, but I did anyway.

"I have to," I countered. "He needs to know I was driving drunk that night. It weighs on me. And I want a clean slate between us, now that we're all reconnecting."

Our shared secret had never been spoken, and the words felt dry on my tongue. She dropped my hand like it burned her and turned to face me.

"You can't do that." She breathed out the words, her brow furrowed. "You promised you wouldn't tell him."

"And I didn't," I replied quickly, running a hand through my short hair, feeling the anxiety building in my chest. "I've kept the secret for fifteen years, and I've been grateful many times over that you made me do it." I knew she'd asked me to keep it to myself to preserve my relationship with Whit in the wake of Grams' death. Julianna was always looking out for everyone except herself.

"It's still important," she snapped. "Whit will never forgive you. I'm the one who begged you to drive, anyway, remember? You didn't even wreck because of the whiskey. It was because of the deer."

I swallowed hard. My mind was filled every day with memories of that night. I replayed our passionate first kisses and the way it felt for my fingertips to skim across her soft skin. I had repressed my feelings for her for so long, and it felt like the most significant release to let her know how I wanted her.

"I haven't forgotten one second of that night," I said, low and steady. Her lip quivered, and I reached for her hand again, but she pulled it away.

You're ruining everything.

"You don't need to remind me." I continued, "But the facts are, I had been drinking. I was driving. You were riding. I swerved. I couldn't control the truck down the mountain. You had nothing to do with any of that. You were innocent. I'm the reason your back is fucked up."

She closed her eyes and shook her head slightly. "No, it's not. You didn't do anything, Bram. You didn't—"

"Yes. I did."

I annunciated the words so she'd understand I knew my role and no denial would change the truth. She stared at me, her gaze hard. The tension between us was right on the precipice of snapping.

"I told everyone I took your truck, and it was me driving it. If you refute that, you'll make me look like a liar." Her tone frayed something inside of me.

"I'm not taking out a full-page ad in the local paper. I'm just telling Whit. He is the only one who would care. He deserves to know what I did."

She shook her head. "That's idiotic. Why confess to him when we both know he'll never forgive you? Maybe even never forgive me for not telling him the truth. Do you want to be responsible for that? For tearing Whit and me further apart when we've just agreed to work on our relationship?"

Her words were like claws sinking against my heart.

"It weighs on me," I said, more somber. "What I did and then hiding it from him, it eats at me. Leaving you on the side of the road with all your injuries, I—"

"I begged you to leave me!" Her interrupted cry echoed through the trees, and tears fell onto her flushed cheeks. "I made you leave me. You didn't want to, and I threatened you."

"I was an adult. I should have stayed no matter what you said. I was scared. I was a coward."

"You were a child!" Her booming voice echoed through the trees. "How can you say that?"

I let out a long breath. She had her demons as I did, and I knew in this situation, those demons outweighed the empathy she usually so easily employed. She would never understand my perspective.

I ached to tell her the rest of the story —what had happened after I left her, how I had come back.

But it wasn't time, not yet. *One confession at a time.*

I needed to wait. I'd tell her when it felt right.

"I don't want to argue with you about this, especially not today." I said the words calmly and stepped back from Julianna. Lakey watched us and whimpered when we went silent. Julianna's attention went to the pup, and she walked over and began to soothe her.

"Julianna."

She would not look up at me.

"I just want everyone to get along," she whispered, scratching Lakey's head. "I want to move on."

"I do, too," I said. "That's why I want everyone to be on an even playing field. I want everyone to have all the facts so that we can move on."

"No, you don't. You don't want to move on. You want someone to affirm your belief that you're the piece of shit you think you are."

It was my turn to freeze. Was that true?

It didn't matter if it was. I would win this argument.

"I don't need anyone to tell me what I already know," I scoffed. "I might be a man worth knowing now, but when it comes to you, I'll never be good enough. I don't need Whit to tell me that. I don't need you to tell me that."

"I'm not a fucking saint, Bram."

"I'll only hurt you in the end. It's who I am. It's what I do."

She looked up at me, her lip wobbling, tears pooling in her dark eyes. But as if the night switched directly to daylight, I watched her demeanor morph before my eyes. She steeled her spine and swallowed her emotion.

The tears stopped. So did the trembling.

She was stoic. Determined. Unaffected.

"We're mutually benefiting from this arrangement," she said. "Let's not forget that. We can agree to disagree." Lakey stood beside her, tail wagging. "I think I'm ready to go back to the house."

CHAPTER FIFTEEN

Bram | *October 10, 2024*

Julianna was still in the bedroom when I left for work the next morning. The door was fully shut. It was the first time that had happened in days, and my heart sank when I noticed it. The invitation was most definitely closed for me. I left her a note on the kitchen table telling her she should use the Jeep to go anywhere she wanted.

I thought she might text me during the day.

She didn't.

When she'd retreated to her room with her laptop last night, I'd stayed outside alone on the porch most of the late afternoon and evening with Lakey. I'd casually drank beer on an empty stomach until I was pretty drunk, which left me disgruntled at work with a pounding headache. I kept playing through my mind the past, my failures, and how much I wished more than anything we had spent our wedding night together.

And not as friends. I was so tired of being merely her friend.

I CAUGHT MELANIE IN THE PARKING LOT AFTER WORK AND ASKED her to go out for dinner in downtown Roanoke. Her brow furrowed, then she turned away, dismissing me with her hand and her long ponytail swinging in my face.

"No way! Take your wife out, not me," she replied, checking something on her phone.

I looked down at my feet and took a deep breath. "We...we fought yesterday, and...we aren't speaking."

Melanie turned around. Her blue eyes were wide when I looked her in the face. "Are you kidding? You've barely been married twenty-four hours!"

I shrugged. Her hand went to her hips.

"What did you do, you idiot?"

I frowned. "Hey, I'm still your boss."

"Not outside those doors." She pointed toward the forest ranger office building. "Out here, you're an idiot. That girl has always meant so much to you. Why did you fight with her?"

"I love how you assume I'm the idiot," I grumbled.

"Are you?"

I thought about it for a moment. "Probably."

She rolled her eyes and paused. She seemed to be debating something internal. She let out a large sigh.

"Fine. We'll go eat and talk about it."

We met up at The Red Plate Diner. If there were two things Melanie and I had in common, it was the love of the outdoors and breakfast food for supper.

"Lordy. These eggs are perfect," she praised before taking a huge bite. She was the tiniest woman I knew, and she always ate like a burly man. "Okay. Let's talk about it."

I knew she was asking about Julianna, and I huffed.

"Nothing to talk about."

"I swear, if you make me roll my eyes again, I will pluck off your fingernails." She leaned over the table. "What happened?"

I took a deep breath. "The day was going great. I took her for a walk in the hollow. But then we started discussing the past, and things went wrong. I need to tell Whit something Julianna doesn't want him to know."

"Something recent?"

I shook my head.

Melanie's brow furrowed. "Does it involve you?"

"Heavily," I replied, taking another bite of my remaining food. "I don't want to talk specifics. It doesn't affect anything right now, but it was something Whit should have known a long time ago."

"Did you sleep with her in high school?" Mel was on a fact-finding mission, but I wasn't ready.

"No, I haven't slept with her," I replied. "Anyway, we disagreed, we argued, and then she just sort of went...silent."

"Oh," Melanie said, sitting back in her seat again. "Oh, that's bad."

"Yeah." I couldn't have agreed more. "She went to the bedroom last night, and I heard her come downstairs once, but I didn't see her. We haven't talked since."

"Do you think she was waiting for you to come to her?"

It was a fair question and one I'd asked myself all day. "I don't know," I answered. "I don't know if she wanted to talk or not. I should have done it, but I didn't know how. I did something in the past that I regret toward her, and I don't want to hurt her again."

"I'm gonna need more context."

"Not right now. Listen, I know I'll have to approach her and make this okay again, and I need to know how to do it. How can I tell her I'm sorry without showing my full hand? I keep trying to create distance between what's happening and what I want."

"Do you really want to know what I think? Good, because I'm going to tell you," she said without pause. "This whole thing is ridiculous. You should just fuck each other already and—"

"Don't you dare say another word." I closed my eyes briefly.

Her lips pursed. "Fine. I think you guys should get together and quit denying what's happening. You need to realize she wouldn't be at your house if she didn't want to be. She has a perfectly awesome house to stay in while she's here. I'm assuming she has some sort of support system wherever she lived before. She doesn't need you. She wants you. Can you not see that?"

I blew out a breath. "It makes sense, in theory, but she also wants to use my insurance."

"Considering she came to your house before your insurance was even a question, I'm confident that's not playing into her decision-making right now." My sister scooped up the last of her eggs and let the fork fall with a clatter on the ceramic plate. "The history between you all is thick, but perhaps it's time to make some new memories. You should go for it."

"I can't do that."

"Why not?"

"Because it's complicated."

"You think you're not good enough."

Her quick words were like an ice pick to my brain. But then again, she had our father in her, which meant she was cunning and perceptive. I should have known she'd read me.

"I *know* I'm not good enough for her," I replied.

"You're exasperating, you know that? You're handsome, well-off, smart, capable, and selfless. How could you possibly believe Julianna doesn't want that?"

I shrugged. "I'm not terrible. But Julianna is different. All these years, I thought of her, and I told myself I was idolizing her. But this last week, I've seen her flaws, and they pale in comparison to her beauty, warmth, and talent."

"Talent?"

I took a drink of my sweet tea. "Yeah, she's a writer. She carries her laptop all around the house. She's not let me read anything yet, but I remember she was so good at it when we were in school. She was great at her social media marketing job, too, and that company let her go, the idiots." Melanie smiled, and I kept going. "She gets nervous around crowds, but she's so friendly, always smiling at everyone. It takes a level of comfort to bring it out, but she's witty and interesting. And best of all, she and Lakey have bonded from the second they met, and I trust my dog."

"Over any person, of course." Melanie laughed. "She sounds amazing. You should bone her."

"I swear to God, Mel—"

"At least tell her how you feel. Make it clear you care for her and that you'll always be there for her, even if she doesn't want you the same way. And that you want to bone her."

My sister was killing me.

But maybe…just maybe…she was right.

"I should never have agreed to this," she continued. "I should have insisted you go home and climb into bed with your wife." Her smile was wide and bright.

"Nobody is climbing into anything with anyone," I muttered, leaning back as the waitress delivered our pumpkin pies, along with the piece I'd ordered to take back to Julianna. It would be part of my peace offering. "Whit is going to be so mad about the marriage. He hasn't responded to our calls and texts yet. I don't know if they have him on lockdown or what, but he called last week and warned me off her."

She scoffed, waving a hand in dismissal. "Whit is all hot air and fancy pants. He has no control over his sister or you."

I knocked my fork casually against the table. "Yeah. Well. You don't know him."

"Yeah, well," she mocked, "I have a feeling he's just a man and that means he's not very smart and shouldn't be trusted." She took a bite of pie and then moaned much too loudly.

"Jesus, that was disgusting," I grumbled. She pointed her fork at me.

"It's too good not to make noises," she replied, swallowing, then going in for bite two. But she stopped midway and pointed her fork at me again. "Listen, we don't have to talk about it. And I can't make you do what I want. But be happy, Bram. You might have grown up rich, but you were dealt a shitty hand in the ways that mattered. You deserve to have happiness now."

My throat was too tight with emotion, and I loathed the feelings. I shook my head. "I've done many things you don't know about, Mel."

She smiled. "We all have. Quit thinking you're special because you've been through some stuff."

She was goading me a little, but shame crept in. Mel had been through more in her life than I could fathom. While I was growing up in the most prominent house in the county, she was living on a backwoods compound with her abusive cousin and religious nutjob of an aunt. She was scarred emotionally and physically. I couldn't see them, but she'd told me about them the same night I'd first told her about Julianna, the night at the winery.

"I'm sorry, I shouldn't have insinuated you haven't felt pain."

She waved her hand. "Come off it. You're changing the subject. Whit's problems are his problems. He'll come around, or he won't."

"He's like a brother to me. The things he says about me, to me, they matter."

She snorted. "Yeah, if you were like a brother to him, he'd be thinking about you a little more and about himself a lot less."

There wasn't much I could say to that.

"Just don't push away the opportunity that's right in front of your face," she begged. "It might never come back around. *She* might not come back around. Be open. That's all I ask."

She eyed the Styrofoam container on the tabletop and giggled. "That's for her, right?"

"Quit it," I said, and threw a ball of straw paper at her.

It was nearly nine pm before I returned to the farm. I was so nervous on the drive home that I had to keep both hands on the wheel to steady my shaking. I had no idea what to say to her. What was too much? What was too little? I hadn't decided by the time I pulled into the driveway.

It was pitch black outside, and the air was cool and crisp. The familiar night sounds were few and far between. The seasons were changing, much like my life was, like Julianna's life was.

I'd pulled up to a dark house. Only the TV illuminated the living room through the window. I opened the back door gingerly, thinking she might be asleep. Lakey didn't rush to greet me as usual. I found them both in the living room, Lakey asleep on her dog bed on the floor, and Julianna curled up on the couch, eyes closed.

I looked down at her form. She was serene and achingly beautiful.

"Hey." Her eyes opened, and she peered up at me.

I froze.

She wasn't smiling, but she wasn't frowning either.

"Hey," I said back.

She moved to sit up a little, and I didn't miss the wince she gave as she scooted. I wanted to take all that pain away from her.

"I...I waited for you for a while and was going to text, but I didn't want to disturb you," she said. Her eyes flashed toward the TV and the wall, anything to keep from looking me in the face.

"I didn't mean to worry you."

"Who were you out with?"

I stared at her, puzzled. I tried hard to read her expression in the dim lighting, but I only saw what I didn't want to.

Sadness.

Apprehension.

Part of me should have been elated that she cared who I was and wasn't with. Instead, it reminded me how much I'd kept from her and how badly I'd failed her. She wasn't confident in what she meant to me. She didn't know the extent of my desire for her, the secrets I kept inside about her for an absurd amount of time.

She didn't understand that I lived to drown in her over and over.

I took a step forward. I was tired of fearing what wrongs I might do to her. Even if the most dreadful circumstances had brought her back into my sphere, I couldn't run away from how happy and peaceful I felt when she was near me, so close I could touch her.

And she was my wife.

My *wife*.

Fuck it.

I leaned over her and brought my face down until I could smell the sweetness of her breath and feel the heat radiating off her soft body. Her eyes widened, but she wiped the shock away and let her gaze concentrate on me fully in the dimness—a perfect, unaffected mask.

"You didn't answer my question," she whispered.

"Melanie," I whispered back.

My eyes flitted between her lips and eyes, drawn to her like a moth to a flame.

"Oh." Her gaze drilled into me. "Melanie, the sister? Or a girlfriend with the same name? If it was, you could tell me, you know. I can handle your preferences."

My heart skipped a beat. "My preferences?"

She squirmed and averted her gaze. Uncomfortable feelings stirred in the tiny space between us.

"Yeah. I mean, if you have a girlfriend, she's probably petite, blonde, skinny—all the things you liked when we were young. She probably loves the outdoors as much as you. Maybe even goes fishing with you on the weekends. She shops at outfitter stores, for sure. She can probably make a delicious deer roast. She raises free-range chickens. She drinks beers with you in the evenings..." She still wouldn't look at me.

"That's my girlfriend?" I chuckled softly.

My smile quickly fell away as I watched tears pool in the corners of her eyes.

"Hey." I soothed, reaching over with my free hand and gently cradling it against her flushed face. I used my thumb to smooth over her cheek in a loving stroke, infusing everything I had into my touch. She didn't pull away. "Why are you so worried, sweets?"

She considered me for a moment before replying. "I don't want you to lie to me," she whispered. The first tear fell, and I caught it with my thumb, wiping it into her skin.

"I haven't lied to you," I replied as softly as possible, framing her heart-shaped face with my hand. "I would never lie to you, especially about another woman. I went to dinner with Melanie, my sister. I told you I am unattached, and I am. And as for my preferences..." Adrenaline pumped through my body as I slid my hand down her jaw to her neck, letting my fingers rest on her collarbone peeking through the top of her distressed T-shirt. I let my rough fingertips slip over her soft skin. I felt her shiver, yet her body gave off heat unlike anything I'd ever felt.

There would be no one else after I had her.

"You're my preference," I whispered. Her breathing stopped.

Giving pleasure through words and touches turned me on the most. But this gesture of want, this tiny admission of my true desires, gave me more satisfaction than I'd ever had in any previous encounter with another person. Unmatched.

Julianna East wasn't just any woman. I leaned into her fully before I could stop myself, and I kissed her. Firmly. Fervently.

On the inside, my heart was racing, beating loudly in my ears. The heat built between us as our mouths met passionately, lips moving over each other in sensual perfection; I lost all conscious thought.

She had to know how I felt.

Actions spoke louder than words. Why did it take me fifteen years to realize it?

CHAPTER SIXTEEN

Julianna | *October 10, 2024*

A dream.
It had to be a dream.

Yet these weren't phantom images that I conjured in the darkest recesses of my imagination late at night. His warm lips were moving over mine, and I had never felt more in a kiss than at that moment. It was raw, surprising, and so very real.

With each meeting of our mouths, he was branding himself on me. This was how our wedding night was supposed to be. Even if our marriage wasn't legitimate, it belonged to us.

I couldn't steady myself at first, shaking and trembling. But soon, our lips found a rhythm, and the anxiety melted away into something fulfilling.

I had the most attractive person I'd ever encountered making out with me—again.

Though Bram was so much more to me than a pretty face, I

couldn't deny it felt good to be wanted at that moment by someone so unattainable.

I let the sensations of desire carry away my defenses. I was weaponless when he was being so bold. His tongue swept over my own, and I let out a small, involuntary moan.

That seemed to invigorate him further, and his weight pressed against me. He was careful, but he devoured me until I was fully on my back. He was patient and skilled with his movements. There wasn't an ounce of hesitancy on his part, and I tried to match his confidence.

He was heavy, grounding, and solid. I wound my arms around his shoulders, my hands moving up behind his back and through his close-cropped hair. He used his elbows for balance and seemed to be fighting to keep his body weight from pressing on me fully, but I wanted him to let me feel his weight. Pain be damned.

It took me tugging on his shirt collar before he acquiesced.

"I'll hurt you," he protested huskily through our kissing.

I shook my head vehemently, not wanting to part with the sensations I was feeling. I would die before asking him to move.

His lips roamed my cheeks, my temple, back down to my neck, and licked my skin reverently. Sometimes he'd simply breathe me in.

"Bram," I exhaled his name, slipping my hands down to rest on his sides, then sliding along his clothed back, feeling every delicious muscle and dip. "We don't have to do this. It's okay."

I couldn't shake the feeling that he felt bad for me. He pitied that my body betrayed me, for losing my job, and being alone. He was only kissing me because I'd cried again, like a jealous and petty wife, when I was nothing. I was simply a business arrangement so he could get his inheritance. Or his best friend's sad sister.

His pelvis ground into me, and I gasped.

He smoothly dipped his body against mine, then looked straight into my eyes. "Does it feel like I don't want to, sweets?" His voice dripped with lust.

I felt so singular to him when he called me that. Did he give nicknames to other women? I almost asked, but I was interrupted by his hands making their way under my shirt. My breath caught as his coarse fingertips slid up my sides, caressing the soft padding that was me.

I was realistic about how I was shaped and how most men perceived me. I wasn't insecure in my reality, but I was insecure about what he might think. He'd probably never touched any other woman like me, one with a thicker stomach and thighs. In high school, he only dated girls who were skinny. Did men ever stray from those preferences of their youth? What if I had sex with him and then he decided he wasn't truly attracted to me physically? I wanted so badly to give in to what he was offering, but I had to keep my wits about me. He wasn't just some man. He was Bram Winchester.

He touched my stomach softly, kneading my skin under his skilled fingers before I could voice my wary thoughts. It was the part of my body I thought he would ignore, like every other man who'd gotten that far.

I flinched.

He stilled. "Are you okay?" He leaned back, the look of lusty intoxication still heavy in his eyes.

"Sorry, I was surprised. I've never...and I-I...listen, Bram, I..."

I'd said enough with my word vomit, which was an ailment I could not seem to shake.

What did I think I was going to say to him?

'Oh, by the way, I'm a virgin.'

His brows furrowed. He must have seen the hesitancy in my gaze. He eased off me and got on his knees, staring over me as I lay still in the light of the television. He let out a long, heavy breath as he ran his hand over his head.

"Okay." He seemed to have decided something.

I wanted to reach for him, but I was paralyzed. He swung his legs over and stood quickly. He held out a hand to help me sit up, which I took, my eyes never leaving his face.

"I'm going to go to bed." His voice was quiet. "I'll see you in the morning. We can talk then, if that's okay? I don't want to go another day not speaking."

"Oh." I didn't know what to say, think, or feel. "Oh...okay. Sure."

I wrapped my arms around my midsection defensively. He watched the movement, and I saw his jaw tic. I was so stupid. Confused, horny, and foolish.

Then he was gone, his steps hard and quick up the stairs, Lakey on his heels with her little paw taps on the wood. He clung to me like cigarette smoke in the winter, lingering and unmistakable. I could still feel and smell his presence all over me.

I was desperate for a resolution, but I was too much of a coward and a cautious soul to chase it. Like always, I'd made assumptions about people's feelings and intentions.

I picked up my phone and clicked on Kallie's name.

> Me: I can't call because he might hear, but I royally screwed up. Bram kissed me. We started making out on the couch, but I got inside my head. I froze, and he ran off. Do you think he did it because of what happened yesterday?

> Me: I am not his type. I am confused. I'm supposed to be cautious. I'm supposed to not care about him. I need perspective.

> Me: Help.

Kallie, ever the best friend, was quick to respond.

> Kallie: I disapprove of this. But let's pretend for a minute I did approve…

> Kallie: Damn straight, he was trying to make you feel good! That's what real men do! What do you mean by "not his type"? Is he so shallow that he only sticks to one idea of a woman, and that's it? Didn't he make out with you a million years ago?

I was letting her words sink in when another message came through from her.

> Kallie: I'm gonna go out on a limb and say you're doing that thing again where you're assigning people feelings they might not be having. I have a hard time believing he'd give you a pity kiss. But he owes you a conversation about his intentions. Ask him why he did that.

I bit my lip.

> Me: What if I can't handle his honesty?

> Kallie: What would you be losing? You never had him to begin with, right? Which I hope you understand is laughable.

> Me: Then what do I do?

Kallie: This isn't Victorian England. Go up there and make him talk to you. And if he tries to play tonsil hockey again, don't treat him like he's poison. Use. Him.

Me: I can't just use him. I'm trying here. I really am.

Kallie: Try harder. I know what he means to you, even if you won't say it. Whatever happens, you deserve nothing less than perfection.

Kallie: And you should have touched his penis.

I chuckled softly.

Me: He ground it into me on the couch.

Kallie: OMFG! Are you kidding me? Why are you still texting me? Get up there!

I took a deep breath.

Me: I love you.

Kallie: Quit stalling.

The walk up the stairway felt like I was going to my death. Not because Bram was a sentence that couldn't be undone, but because I knew we'd never be the same once I learned the truth about how he felt about me. Either way, this would change us.

He was in his bedroom, where I'd been staying. The door at the top of the stairs was slightly ajar. I heard him shuffling around inside the room, but I didn't pull a first-night mishap again. Instead, I knocked on the door.

My heart was beating so hard I thought it might fly out of my chest. I couldn't wait one more second, and even though it wasn't proper, I slowly pushed open the door.

Bram was standing by the bed, gloriously shirtless and still wearing his belted jeans. His hands rested low on his hips, and his face was blank as he looked straight at me. I read nothing there—no regret, sadness, delight, or relief.

It reminded me of a colder, less adjusted Bram from fifteen years ago, and I hated it.

"I'm getting a few things and then I'll be gone," he said, voice clipped.

My heart sank. He had put up a wall because I wouldn't let mine fall.

"I'm sorry," I said, my hand still on the door. "I might have given off some wrong vibes down there."

He shrugged. "It's fine." He looked away. "You don't have to let me down easy. You've always had more control, more poise about you, while I was a bullshitter. And now it seems all I do is wear my heart on my fucking sleeve." He ran his head over his head and down his neck.

"Let you down easy?" I took a couple of steps into the room.

"Yeah, and I bolted. I'm sorry. I should have had a little bit more understanding."

My heart sank.

"It wasn't like that," I insisted. I looked away as I said the next words, "I just can't let you have sex with me out of pity."

He scoffed, then glanced toward the ceiling before he looked back into my eyes.

"You can't seriously think that. First, I don't pity fuck. Ever. I'm a man with a healthy appetite, but I damn sure want everyone I've ever had sex with."

He took two steps toward me, and I took two steps back.

"Second," he continued, "I told you; you are different than any other woman. You've always been different."

I scoffed. "You called me your sister. You said kissing me was a mistake. I even said that you thought I wasn't good enough for you, and you didn't refute it. Did you think I'd ever forget that day in the hospital?"

"I was lying, Jules. I blamed myself for how hurt you were. I still do. But how I feel about you…" He shook his head. "How I want you? It's not from guilt or pity. It never was."

I should have pivoted, but I couldn't stop.

"Why did you kiss me, then? What was your goal? Was it because of what had just happened, the adrenaline? Or was it because—"

"Dammit, it was because I *wanted* to!" His hands flew up, and I jerked back. "I've wanted to be with you for so long. Even before I left for college, I wanted to make a move on you. But I was a douchey kid with a fucked-up family, who had to fight every day to feel like I was worth something, and you were so…*so* fucking high above me. I valued you so much that I couldn't taint you with who I was. I was scared of hurting you. And scared of you."

Intensity swirled from every word he spat, but all those words only fed my frustration.

"Scared of me? A chubby orphaned girl who was so insecure she had to hide behind books and be terrified of making a wrong move, so that no one would leave her. Yeah, that sounds like someone *soooo* high above you. I was a big, goody-two-shoes girl in love with a handsome, popular star football player. Who was the bigger fool?"

I rolled my eyes but continued forward, the truth scathing yet freeing, "For fifteen years, you didn't call me. Not once. You never came to visit. And never checked on me after you broke my heart. You completely abandoned me. What was I supposed to think? I wanted you to change your mind, but you never came. I left town. And it bothered me that you didn't try to find me. But I mended because I didn't have any other choice but to go on, or die. Trying to forget you was the hardest thing I did after losing Grams. I had so much to grieve."

His face fell.

"I was alone!" I screamed, weeping and clenching my fists. I could not stem the feelings I'd held back for so long, no matter how foolish I sounded, letting the words tumble from my lips. "I was alone, and you didn't care."

Silence fell between us. I wiped my eyes with my hand, looked up at him, and saw that he had closed his eyes.

"I am such a jackass," he whispered. "I might not be exactly like Vince Winchester, but fate made sure the apple didn't fall far from the tree."

I took a deep breath to gain control of myself. "Don't say that," I snapped. "You're not him. You never were. Grams was determined you wouldn't be, and you aren't."

"Whit says I am," he said, his words small and unsure.

"Whit only thinks of himself," I spat angrily. "And someday, I'll find the courage to tell him that, too."

We glanced at the picture of all of us with Grams on his dresser. I was trembling. I put my hands on my hips, mirroring him.

"You've seen me through rose-colored glasses since we met," he said, shaking his head. "I can't blame Whit for feeling like he does. He doesn't even know I am the one who wrecked the truck, and he still sees me as a guy who screws around, a man who will just hurt you."

"Is that who you want to be?" He was quiet for a moment, but I pressed on with a firm voice. "Is that your goal? To hurt me?"

His jaw ticked as he stared at a point on the opposite wall.

"I have my own list. First, what makes you or my brother think I would *let* you hurt me? I'm not some damsel in distress who needs protection. I've taken care of myself for quite a while now." He absolutely could break me, but he didn't have to know that.

I took a couple of steps nearer to him, and even though he still wouldn't look me in the eye, I didn't look away, determined to see this through. "Second, we're adults. There's no shame in what we want."

I took two more steps, and his breath hitched. "And we're married." Two more steps. "Even if it's just right here, right now, for this one time—I'll let go of my fear, if you'll let go of yours."

He let out a long exhale, closing and re-opening his beautiful, dark eyes before they collided with my own. My resolve to resist him ended before it began. I moved toward Bram, not stopping until we were toe to toe.

"So, do you want me, Bram Winchester?"

He swallowed, his Adam's apple bobbing. I studied the curve of his dark, stubbled square jaw and let my eyes wander up his face until they met his own.

"Yes," he whispered. The heat pulsing off his body beckoned me.

"Then take me." My fingers came up to lightly touch his delicious chest, which was dusted with dark hair. "Make me your—"

He grabbed my arms and pulled me into him. His lips crashed into mine, a punishing kiss that I felt all the way into my fingertips and toes. Lips and teeth collided, the desire to devour one another unable to be contained. Hard and heavy, our tongues danced, and I savored every stroke.

His grip on me tightened as our mouths fused. He wrapped me in an embrace that pulled me almost impossibly closer to him. Yet he was slowing his movements and kisses, and I wasn't sure I was ready for that. I liked the passion and his displays of strength. So, I did what any inexperienced girl, with no idea what to do with herself, would do. I put my hand flush against his crotch, finding the evidence of his desire for me hard against my palm.

"That's right, sweets." He put his forehead to mine. "Do you see what you do to me?"

Goosebumps broke out all over my skin.

"Is this real?" I whispered, my words filled with wonder and delight.

He smiled. "I can assure you, what you're feeling right now is completely, one hundred percent real."

As I laughed, his lips caught mine again. I dropped my hand, but he ground his pelvis into my own, his hands roving along my sides. My head tipped back to allow him greater access to lick and kiss across my neck and down farther...farther...

"I need this off," he growled, grabbing the ends of my shirt and pulling it up. I put my hands up to let him drag the shirt off, which he promptly threw across the room.

My breasts were encased in a full-coverage black bra. I wasn't planning on this, so it wasn't fancy, but from the look on his face, he didn't mind. But I became increasingly nervous as he stared at me. Even my stomach, nowhere near flat or hard, was on full display. Yet, I saw nothing in his eyes except desire.

He bent and kissed the tops of my breasts where they spilled slightly over my bra. I languished in his touch as his hands roved up and peeled the material down, his mouth pressing open, wet kisses down my chest, until he took my breast into his mouth and sucked hard.

My mind separated from my body as an ungodly moan poured from my lips.

"So damn responsive," he muttered with a smile as he used his tongue to tease my nipple—first one, then the other. Nothing had ever felt so good.

I'd experienced quick fondling and kisses on my breasts

before, but I'd never had a man spend so much time savoring them.

"Lie down," he commanded, and a thrill ran through me straight from my brain down to my crotch.

"Yes, sir," I replied submissively, my words serious, and I watched his eyes light up with new interest. I scooted back on the bed, never losing eye contact with him while gently lying down. I was adept at adjusting my mindset to work around discomfort in my back, and this situation was no different. Wild horses couldn't have stopped me.

The quiet was comfortable, our eyes and movements talking more than our words ever could. He pulled at my leggings, working them down my legs until I was able to gently kick them off and onto the floor.

He stood and looked down at me, lying only in my black cotton underwear. I felt vulnerable and imperfect, but so very alive.

"Look at you," he said, his deep voice gravely, creating a path of want from my ears to my core. Usually, I would have felt fear or embarrassment at that type of praise, but I felt safe and free with him.

Not thinking twice, I lifted a little and reached up to unspool my hair from its messy bun. My dark tresses, one of my favorite assets, spilled onto the bed and around my shoulders. He ran his hand over his hair, that nervous gesture, like what I had just done was too much. But the bulge in his sweatpants seemed to get even harder, tenting them.

"You're gonna kill me," he muttered, and he took one of my legs and lifted it like it was nothing as he stepped up to the bed. He kissed down my leg, and I tried to push all thoughts of insecurity away from my brain.

"Quit thinking," he commanded, looking at me from where his lips pressed against my knee.

"I can't help it," I whispered, but I let my arms fall open on the bed, allowing myself to be completely open to his gaze.

"Enjoy what I'm doing to you," he whispered back, between the hot, wet kisses. "This means everything to me." More kisses pressed against my leg, moving up and up. "If you knew the number of times I've wanted to do this..."

"Do what?" I asked, my voice sounding slightly embarrassed and strained.

"This." He dropped to his knees, grabbed my hips, and pulled me down the bed, my legs on his broad shoulders. I was unable to gather any wits before his hot breath was between my legs, right up against the damp fabric of my underwear.

He stayed there, so close to my center, yet far enough away that there was no skin-to-skin contact. "Tell me what you want, Julianna." It took a moment for me to register that he'd spoken as his exhales drifted over my sensitive areas.

"W-what do you mean?"

"Tell me what you want me to do to you right now."

I dared to look down my body, and there he was, between my legs, dealing me a predatory, audacious look.

"Lick me?" My voice was so soft and hesitant.

"You can do better than that," he replied in a soft cajole. "You're the smartest girl I've ever met. Use your words."

I took a deep breath and smiled.

"I want you to devour my pussy, Dracula."

Bram laughed, and so did I. I watched as he then pulled aside the crotch of my underwear. His soft lips met those between my legs. It was perfect and decadent, the gentle suck of his mouth, the sounds that echoed in the small bedroom as he licked and savored me. He flicked his tongue around my clit so gently and expertly that I was already building up and falling apart at record speed.

"I don't think I can come this way," I squeaked between moans. "It's not personal. I just never have before, and I..."

He disengaged a little, and his rough hands reached up. He backed up slightly and began to peel down my underwear, but not without gently swatting my butt to indicate I needed to move so he could slide them all the way off.

"I don't care if I have to stay here in this heaven all fucking night. You will come for me. Let me know if you need a rest."

And he went back to work.

It took a few minutes for my mind to accept that he enjoyed what he was doing. He wasn't bothered at all, and the little varied things he was doing were to see what I liked. This made me think about how many others he'd done this very thing to.

Suddenly, I was insanely jealous and supremely insecure.

"You're in your head again," he muttered against my pussy, and the vibrations made me moan.

"Don't act like you know me," I chided, my hand going up to caress his head and gently holding him down against me.

"I can feel it from here," he said, his voice muffled. "You're pulling away."

I bit my lip. Now was not the time for an internal crisis.

"I'm trying to make sure this is still real," I murmured. He moved, and it pulled a stronger moan from me.

He looked up at me then, fully, his chin and mouth glistening with my wetness, a feral grin across his face.

"Nothing, and no one, has ever tasted as good as you do."

"I bet you say that to everyone." I rolled my eyes.

"I don't talk during sex," he replied matter-of-factly. "Ever." My heart stopped.

"Oh, so it's like I'm your...first?" I gulped. I still hadn't told him about my technically virgin status.

"You could say that." He was pleased with what I'd said, and without further preamble, he dropped between my knees again. But this time, he slowly inserted a finger into my very wet entrance.

"Yes," I hissed, and as he massaged inside my walls. I died a little in the best, torturous way.

It was mere minutes before I felt the familiar tug of something building deep inside my belly. It grew as he worked, inserting another finger, and I began to lose control as he kept hitting one spot repeatedly.

"That's it," I hissed, grabbing for anything I could, finally settling on a pillow. "Oh God, I'm almost there. Bram, it's too much."

Yet he kept going, not acknowledging my pleas for mercy.

When the dam broke and I tumbled into ecstasy, he grabbed my hips and rode the breaking waves with me until I settled on the bed, barely hanging on.

He removed his finger and licked my sex one final time with vigor, from center to front, and then withdrew. I watched with wonder and shock as he put his finger into his mouth and licked it clean.

"So fucking delicious," he mumbled.

Completely spent, I removed my legs from his shoulders, letting them fall gently to the floor on either side of him. He got to his feet and reached out his hand to help me up, where I hung precariously on the edge of the bed.

And that's when I felt it.

My back gave way.

CHAPTER SEVENTEEN

Bram | *October 10, 2024*

My cock throbbed and my adrenaline pumped as I got to my feet. I could still taste Julianna on my tongue and lips, the velvet feel of her skin under my fingertips. Then all my lust dissipated as I looked down at her. Her expression was somewhere between a grimace and regret.

"What's wrong?" I asked, but I knew what it was instantly. I squatted and reached out to push some hair that had fallen in her face. She gritted her teeth, closed her eyes, and shook her head. I didn't know anything about what she was feeling. I'd pulled muscles in my back while in football or when I'd pushed a little too hard while hiking. But her pain wasn't something I could understand.

I cupped her cheek in my palm.

"Please tell me what to do. Do we need to go to the hospital?"

"No," she replied quickly, her word clipped.

"I'm so fucking sorry, Jules," I whispered.

The weight of the pain I had caused made me want to run. I wanted to remove myself from her presence—her life—before I ruined it any further. I was the reason she was like this. I caused this.

You can't leave her to suffer alone again.

She had let me see her intense fear of abandonment. She allowed me to know how it made her feel. So, no matter what it cost me, I would never leave her again. She breathed deeply, exhaling in full breaths through pursed lips. "I need a minute," she ground out, eyes still closed.

I waited, wanting to bundle her into my arms but afraid I'd only make the pain worse. I cradled her face, lightly running my thumbs over her flushed cheeks.

"Please don't say sorry," she whispered with tears in her eyes. She let the tiny droplets fall. "This happens sometimes. That's why the surgery—" She froze.

Panic rose in my chest. "Can you move?"

She waited, then nodded. "Can you get my shirt?"

I wanted to grab my t-shirt and throw it on her, but I thought it might be tight, and I wanted her to be comfortable. Instead, I retrieved her shirt and gingerly placed it over her head. I slowly helped guide her arms through the holes.

Note to self: buy more oversized shirts. I needed to see her in something of mine.

"Is it okay if I lie down here?" she asked. "And do you mind getting—"

"This is your house, too. You exist anywhere you want, at any time. And I'll get whatever you need. Tell me what to do." I took her hand and helped her bear her weight as she got comfortable. One lone whimper slipped from her lips, and I grimaced. She settled on her side, tears continuing to roll down her cheeks. My insides ached watching her suffer.

Julianna directed me toward what she needed: medicine

from her bag, water, and a heating pad. When I returned to her, I fed her the pills and pressed the heating pad to the middle of her back. The pad was worn and small, and I knew my first order of business was to get her a new, king-sized, plush one.

"I'm sorry," she mumbled, sniffing. "I'm so sorry. Of all the times—"

"I should have been more careful." I scolded myself aloud, realizing that those words encompassed everything about me with her, not just this time.

"Will you lay down with me?" She glanced up where I stood, looking down at her beside the bed, and a lump formed in my throat.

"I don't want to hurt you," I replied.

"Please," she whispered, her eyes filled with fresh tears.

I knew I'd give her anything she asked. I carefully lay down behind her. Her body nestled into mine with my chest to her back, and her soft hair against my cheek. I finally felt a moment of relief from the heap of guilt and terror that had taken me over.

"I'm okay, don't worry," she said into the silence as if she sensed my inner struggle. "This happens sometimes."

"A lot?" I asked, like a masochist, knowing she'd say yes and knowing it would hurt me all over again.

"More often lately, considering," she replied, instead. "I'm sorry I can't make you feel as good as you made me feel."

"Shhhh," I soothed, running my hand over her side, then moving her hair off her neck, kissing her soft skin. "It was the greatest privilege of my life. I shouldn't have pulled you across the bed, I'm such a fucking idiot."

"Don't treat me like I'm breakable." Her voice was still soft, but firm. "None of this is your fault. I'm the one who should feel bad, and believe me, I do. I completely killed the mood."

"There'll be more moods," I replied. She didn't confirm or deny what I said, but rather snuggled into my body. The room was quiet, save for Lakey trying to situate herself at the end of the king-sized bed.

Julianna relaxed quickly, but I was floundering, losing the battle of my mind against my body. I could still recall the noises she made when she came. That, combined with the way my fingers held onto her plump curves, was killing me. I tried to keep my cock from growing hard between her ass cheeks, but it was impossible. I snuck my hand under her shirt, lightly running my fingers over her side. The luscious feel of her and the way she curled into me was heaven.

Slowly, she began moving her ass against my groin. I growled in frustration.

"What?" she asked, her voice feigning innocence.

"You know what you're doing. Quit being devious."

She giggled. "I couldn't resist."

I draped my arm over her middle. I was burning up from the heating pad between us, but it was touching her that was making my blood boil the most.

"It's okay. There'll be punishment later."

"Mmm," she hummed. "Can't wait."

I tried to think of anything I could to keep myself from combusting while I held her. I thought about how much pain she was in, which only made me feel more protective and terri-torial. I would never hurt her, never compromise her health for my selfish needs, but her vulnerability made me want to fight some invisible force to avenge her pain. She nestled into me further, and I snapped back to thinking about the things I wanted to do to her in the future.

We were friends. But after tasting her, knowing she wanted me as badly as I wanted her, I could not turn back even if I wanted to. She was my wife. And if she'd allow me, I wanted to be her husband outside of name only, for however long she'd have me.

To calm myself down, I thought about Whit and the fight

between Julianna and me. That was the best cockblock. The heat in my veins cooled, chilled by the guilt I didn't want to feel.

"Bram?" Her voice pierced the silence.

"Yes?"

"This has been the best thing that's happened to me in a long time."

I smiled. "I pride myself on being a giver, sweets."

She laughed like I hoped she would.

"No, not just *that*." She reached around and grasped my hand where it lay on her side. "Coming here, seeing you, being together. I could never gather the courage to ask my brother if you were taken or married. I have been stuck in that hospital room for fifteen years, watching you leave. I just...I never expected..."

"This was never a choice," I whispered, smoothing her hair, understanding what she was saying because I felt it, too.

"Any guesses on why Whit hasn't contacted us?"

"No idea. I'll try to reach him again in the morning. I didn't try at all today."

"Neither did I. There's so much weighing on me right now, I didn't think about it. My life feels so unsettled. No definite job news yet. Remote jobs seem harder to come by, even though I have the experience and the education. It is brutal out there."

"I'm so sorry. It has to be scary, but you have to allow yourself this time to focus on your health. Jobs will be there later."

"I don't even have a place to live anymore." Her voice was small, almost frightened. I hugged her closer.

"You have a place to live. You can stay here for as long as you want."

"This is temporary, I think we both know that." But before I could go into a monologue about how wrong she was, she continued, "I missed you. Is that weird of me to say?"

I swallowed my retort instantly.

"I missed you, too. I'm sorry we fought."

"Our first fight as a married couple. It wasn't that bad," she replied. "And I understand what you were saying about Whit yesterday. I was being selfish. I know we have to tell him the truth. I didn't want…"

"Shhhh," I soothed as her voice trailed, softly running my fingers through her hair. "As much as I want to gloat that I was right, I want you to rest. We can talk about this when you feel better."

"You make everything better."

Her whispered words were all I ever wanted to hear, and as my body sank into deep sleep, I repeated them over and over, drowning out the voice that made me feel unworthy of holding her.

THE FOLLOWING DAY, I STAYED HOME FROM WORK FOR A FEW hours to ensure Julianna was well. She'd seemed to bounce back and wasn't even hobbling when she came into the kitchen, holding out her phone.

"Whit's calling."

Before I could respond, she answered and put the phone on speaker.

"Hello? Whit?"

"Hey! Sorry it's taken me so long to get back to you. There was a media blitz, and we were on the road. It's no excuse, though. Surgery is tomorrow? That is so quick."

"Yes," she replied. "It is. But there's something else I need to tell you." Julianna's eyes met mine, and I nodded. "Bram and I came to an arrangement of sorts. We got married, so Bram's trust fund can be released."

Silence filled the line.

"Did you say you married Bram?"

"In name only, but yes." Julianna's eye shifted from mine. The night before didn't seem like "name only," but I said nothing.

"No. No, you couldn't have. That's insane."

Julianna did not skip a beat. "I'll have Bram tell you the details when you have time."

There were a few agonizing moments of silence, and Julianna made a face at me that showed apprehension. "What? This is crazy. Am I too late?" Whit asked, "I can't stop you from marrying that asshole?"

"That asshole is on the phone," I announced, leaning over the receiver, and Julianna slapped her hand across her mouth, silencing a laugh. "It's already done. We were married the day before yesterday."

"Fucking figures," Whit grumbled. "So, you guys having fun ruining your lives?"

"You're so dramatic," Julianna said, rolling her eyes, clutching the phone. "It's not a big deal."

My brow furrowed, but she didn't look at me, staring at Lakey at our feet. What did she mean by that?

"Call me crazy, but getting legally married for money seems like a big fucking deal," Whit replied, his voice hard. "I could have given you whatever money either of you needed."

"But it wasn't about you," Julianna said, not waiting for me to comment. "Bram has plans for his money, and what he's doing will be so good for Mill Creek."

Whit sighed. "I've got too much going on. I'm just going to pretend like I didn't hear this. But I am happy for Bram to be able to stick it to his Dad with the inheritance."

"I'm not sure Dad knows yet," I interjected, and Julianna looked up at me, her expression a little shocked. "I sure as hell didn't tell him. Time will tell."

"He won't come for you, will he? He wouldn't do anything bad?" Julianna's question was meant only for me. I looked at her and shook my head. But in truth, I wasn't sure.

Whit coughed a little, breaking up our conversation. "Well, congrats, I guess—something like that? I don't know. This is weird. I need to talk about something else. How are you feeling about the surgery, Jules?"

"I'm dealing," she replied, looking me in the eye again as she spoke to her brother. "I'll be glad to have it over with." I softened so she wouldn't see the worry on my face. We hadn't discussed her feelings about the surgery much, but I knew she was nervous by the way she fidgeted every time it was mentioned. I would rather be sliced open with a rusty knife than watch her go through what was coming.

"I'm sure you will," Whit replied, concern in his tone. "You know I'd be there if I could, right?"

There was no denying that, despite Whit sometimes acting like an ass and his relationship with Julianna being strained, he still loved his sister deeply.

"I know you would, but I'm fine," Julianna said. "My best friend is coming to help, and we'll probably stay at Grams' house once I'm released from the hospital."

My eyes snapped to hers.

"Sounds like a plan," Whit replied to Julianna. "I can't believe you're not asking your husband to care for you."

"Well, actually..." she said, "I haven't talked to Bram about it yet, but Kallie needs to wait for a few days before coming, since everything was so last-minute. I was hoping he would be able and willing to—"

"Yes," I interrupted her, my mood soaring. She smiled softly at my enthusiasm. "Yes, I'll take off the rest of the week. I'll drive you, I'll be there at the hospital, I'll—"

"Keep it in your pants, Dracula." Whit's rude interruption couldn't keep the smile from overtaking my face. She needed me. I didn't have to try to worm my way into her sphere. I could be there for her and help her.

I knew then that the feeling in my heart, which had been there since I was a teenager, remained.

I knew I loved her.

Chapter Eighteen

Julianna | *October 11, 2024*

"Bram, for the last time, I don't need a wheelchair." My breath came out in large white puffs all around me. The frigid early morning air cut through my layers of clothing and into my bones as I stood outside the parked Jeep in the hospital parking lot.

Bram grabbed my floral overnight bag from the back seat. "I didn't ask. Stay right here." Bram's commanding voice sent shivers of something warm down my spine as he pivoted toward the entry.

I pulled him back to me. His arms went around me, and I sank my face into his shoulder.

He dropped my bag on the damp pavement and gently but firmly pulled me into his embrace.

I was still nervous about touching him, yet being in his arms felt so *right*.

"Hey," he whispered, and his hand smoothed my hair. "Everything is going to be okay."

I took a deep breath and released it.

"Do you remember the last time we were in this hospital together?" I asked.

His eyebrows shot up, his skin turned pale, and understanding dawned. I was calling him out.

"I do remember it, every single day of my life," he replied, searching my gaze, his hand touching my face gently. "It's the worst memory I have. And I have so many that I want to forget."

"Did you really think kissing me after the wreck was a mistake?" I was embarrassed when tears sprang to my eyes as I repeated his words from long ago.

"No. Never." He breathed heavily, the white air billowing outward around his mouth. "I lied. Pursuing you then would have been selfish. I was scared of hurting you further. I wasn't good enough for you. I'm not good enough for you now—"

"Stop," I said firmly. "You keep saying that, but you're wrong. And you don't have to explain. I just wanted to hear you say you wanted me then as badly as you act like you want me now."

"None of this is an act." He took my hand and planted it palm down on his chest, over his heart. My heartbeat stuttered with nerves that had nothing to do with the surgery awaiting me. "You're all I ever wanted. I never forgot about you. Nothing has felt right since that day I walked away from you."

My mouth parted in surprise. "That's so sweet."

I didn't know what else to say. I could tell him I had carried a torch for him all my life, too, but that wasn't true. Yes, I'd wanted him badly during my teen years. Yes, I had continued my adult life, wishing for things that hadn't happened. But I'd compartmentalized his existence. I didn't honestly think he'd ever be a part of my life again.

Now, we were married, if only by name. He was caring for me. I was relying on him. We were making our hometown better. I loved his dog. I loved his smile. I loved...him.

What would he do if I told him?

"I'm not trying to be sweet," he replied. "I'm trying to be real."

There wasn't anything left for me to do but press my lip to his, and he welcomed my kiss, eagerly returning the sentiments. I pulled back before we got carried away in the hospital parking lot.

"I don't need a wheelchair, husband," I said. I put my hand in his. "Let's go get this over with."

Mission Hospital was a bleak place for me, filled with terrible memories. Yet everyone inside was friendly and helpful as they checked me in and prepared me for surgery. Bram followed me everywhere. He left me alone to change into my surgical gown, but that was the only moment he left my side. He put the socks on my feet. He even placed the surgical cap on my head, carefully tucking my hair into it.

A little while later, Hunter's familiar face appeared in the doorway of the curtained waiting area. I was stunned to see him.

"Hello there, Julianna," he said, holding the curtain. He was dressed in non-descript blue scrubs, his hair neatly tied in the back. He looked as attractive as he ever had. "I heard today was the day, so I wanted to stop by and see you beforehand."

"You shouldn't have come if you didn't have to be here," Bram said from his seat beside my hospital bed.

I looked over at Bram, mouth agape at his rudeness. He sat back against the small chair, his muscular arms across his chest, his expression flat.

"Hi, Hunter," I replied amiably. Hunter had paled slightly at Bram's comment. "It's so nice of you to come by. I really appreciate it."

"It's not a big deal. I'm sure Doctor Kaveh will be here in a little bit. I think your surgery is scheduled for ten?"

"Yes," I confirmed, smiling at him.

Bram, however, had not warmed. He put an arm over the bed and picked up my hand. Hunter tracked his movement, and I could see he got the hint. My cheeks were on fire.

Hunter flashed his award-winning smile. "You're Julianna's friend, right? From the community dinner?" he asked Bram. Hunter took several long steps forward and held his hand out for a shake. Bram hesitated, but I let go of his hand and prodded him to return the gesture, which he did.

"Yes. Bram Winchester. Except now I'm her husband, not just her friend."

Hunter's eyes clouded with confusion. "Hunter Kearsley. I'm the physician's assistant for Dr. Kaveh." He looked once, then twice, at the name on the whiteboard beside my hospital bed: *Julianna East Winchester.*

"It was a spur-of-the-moment thing," I blurted. Bram's brow furrowed as he watched between my response and Hunter's surprise.

"Well then," Hunter replied. "Seems congratulations are in order. That was...super fast."

Bram reached back over and retook my hand. "Couldn't for everyone to know she's mine."

Did his voice get lower?

"I don't think she'll be calling you again, if that's what you've been waiting on," Bram finished.

"Oh my God," I muttered, hand flying to cover my face, wanting to crawl under my hospital bed.

Hunter chuckled. "It's okay, Julianna. You're good with this one. He's nervous for you."

"That's why he's acting like an ass," I snapped. I was addressing Hunter, but giving Bram a dark look. He completely ignored me, his eyes not leaving Hunter.

This was too much.

Hunter was handsome, but Bram was devastatingly so.

Hunter was kind, but Bram was selfless.

Hunter would have been a catch, but he wasn't Bram.

"But I think I'll keep him, anyway," I tacked on.

Hunter looked at me and winked. "You're in the best hands."

"Thank you again for stopping by."

When Hunter left the little room, I peered over at Bram.

"Was that necessary?"

Bram shrugged and pointed to where Hunter had been. "Was *that* necessary?"

I rolled my eyes. "He was just saying hi, Dracula. Don't get your cape in a wad."

"I'd love to take a fucking bite out of him."

"Stop." I laughed.

After a brief meeting with a very confident Dr. Kaveh, they were ready to wheel me back to the operating room.

"I'll give you a moment," the young nurse said as she closed the curtain and stepped out.

Bram stood and reached for my hand. He tenderly kissed the thin gold band on my ring finger, his lips warm on my cold skin.

"It's a pretty routine surgery," I reminded him.

Based on the look on his face, he was more upside down than I was.

That is love. I heard the words in Grams' voice, and my eyes misted.

"I know. I'll be here when you get out, sweets," he whispered as he reached down and hugged me and pressed his lips to my own, just for a moment. "You're the strongest woman I've ever known."

"You said she'd be awake thirty minutes ago. Are you sure she's okay?" Bram's deep voice sounded like he was attempting to whisper, but he failed. As my eyes peeled open, I saw him facing a white coat-clad intern.

"S-she's fine, Mr. Winchester," the poor young woman stammered. "Her vitals are good. It's just a matter of time—"

"But you said—"

"Bram," I croaked. His eyes snapped to me instantly.

"Julianna," he whispered as if I were returning from a long journey, and he hadn't seen me in years. He hurried to my bedside. "Thank God. Are you okay?" His hand went to my head, smoothing back my hair. Comforted, I smiled.

"I'm as well as I can be," I said, my voice scratchy.

"Mrs. Winchester, how are you feeling? Any pain?" The junior physician walked over to the side of the bed, checking my IV line and bags carefully.

"No pain, I don't think. I'm just groggy and weak," I whispered. "And thirsty."

"Here." Bram all but threw a small cup of ice water at my mouth. I sipped it, reaching up and using my hand to steady his shaky grip.

"Thank you," I croaked, looking up and meeting his eyes, letting him know as much as I could with a gaze that I appreciated him.

"Groggy and weak is to be expected," the woman continued. "We will keep you on the morphine pump overnight, and we'll get you moved into a regular patient room within the hour. The doctor will come in and let you know what was accomplished. I can tell you that everything went exactly as planned."

"That's great," I replied. I heard her clearly, but the information was not sinking in, and my eyes were closing slowly.

"I'm going to be staying with her tonight," Bram said, holding my hand in his. He spoke to the intern, but he looked at me.

"Mr. Winchester, we do recommend you go home overnight," she said, looking hesitant as she spoke. Bram's brow was furrowed, and his eyes narrowed on her slightly. "She'll have two nurses in the hall, and—"

"Thank you, but I'll stay the night with my wife." Shivers ran down my arms and legs at his possessiveness. At least I knew I wasn't numb.

"I think he's staying with me." I laughed, trying to lighten the mood even in my weakened state. "And I want him to stay, please." It at least made the young woman smile, and she continued to look at me while she spoke, ignoring Bram's pointed glance at her.

"Don't try to get up on your own. Please let your husband," —she glanced over at Bram, then back to me—"or a nurse help you. We'll keep your catheter in overnight. I'll let you know when your room is ready, and then we'll transfer you. Then Dr. Kaveh will be by later."

"Thank you so much," I said. I watched Bram's eyes track her retreat through the curtain.

"Will you ease up?" I muttered, suddenly feeling a little nauseous. Bram took a seat beside my hospital bed. His hand hadn't left mine, holding it firmly but not too hard, like I was the most precious piece of crystal.

"I just want to know you're okay. Are you okay? You still feel all your parts?"

I wiggled my toes enough that he could see them under the blanket. "All good."

He smiled and squeezed my hand gently. I noticed large, dark circles under his eyes and the wrinkles in his clothing. Had he grown more stubble within the few hours I was out?

"You look worse than I do," I commented.

His million-dollar smile spread across his handsome features. "You have to be fine, leading with insults like that."

I nodded. "For the millionth time, I am okay. I pulled through."

He leaned over the bed. "Yeah, well, if you go, I go. I need you to know that."

I scoffed. "That is the craziest thing I've ever heard, and not how it works."

"It is, sweets. If you jump, I jump." He brought my hand to his mouth, moving his pillow-soft lips across the back of my hand. It was a sensual moment, one meant to be comforting, but instead sent my scrambled mind reeling. All he had to do was touch me, and I was listless without a life raft. I wanted to find purchase and stability. What was this? What were we?

He'd made it clear he wanted me. I'd made it clear I wanted him. But under the haze of morphine and post-anesthetic, nothing seemed confident.

"I'm exhausted," I whispered. He reached for the light-blue hospital blanket and stood, spreading it over the sheet that already covered me.

"Get some sleep, my love. Who knows when they'll be back to move you."

My love. Another nickname I could get used to.

"I will," I relented and snuggled into the blanket. "One more thing. I think you should go home."

He shook his head emphatically. "Not up for a debate."

"Lakey?"

"Mel is watching her tonight."

"But it's Friday and the MCA supper is tonight. You have things to do. I'm well looked after here."

"Gladys has it all handled at the dinner. There are plenty of boys to help her with the supplies."

I pursed my lips. "You've thought of everything, haven't you?"

He shook his head. "No. If I had, I would have brought your fuzzy plaid house slippers."

My cheeks heated. "How did you know my feet are icicles?"

"I notice things. And your feet are always cold if they touch me while we're on the couch together." He laughed.

"So, you knew when you brought me here that you were staying?" The medicine was making me emotional.

"Why is it so shocking that I want to watch out for you?"

"Because you...you forgot about me for so long."

His eyes glazed over with unshed tears, and my heart swelled. He kissed my forehead, my cheek, and then my lips gently. "I never forgot you. In some form or fashion, I thought of you every day. My life has been full of the memory of you, and I wanted it that way."

"That's so sweet," I said weakly, holding his hand, feeling my eyes closing. He kissed my forehead again before I slipped into blissful slumber, thinking of what he said and how much I wanted to believe it.

Chapter Nineteen

Julianna | *October 14, 2024*

I turned off my true crime podcast and rearranged my wet hair on top of my head. Standing in front of the bathroom mirror, I played with the thin ring on my left finger and fell into thought.

I'd not had one moment to myself since coming home from the hospital on Saturday night. Bram had been right beside me every moment. He'd even taken off work more to watch over me, despite my protests. He'd finally taken a couple of hours to go into town to do MCA business.

I was grateful for his help. Yet the facts always brought me back to reality. We were married, but not in a relationship. We were friends again, and something more, but the past still lingered and probably always would. He'd made no definitive claim of keeping me, and I'd not clearly indicated that I wanted him to. I couldn't forget that I needed a job and that I had to get back to my life in Charlotte. I needed to begin concentrating on myself and my next steps. I couldn't use Bram as a deterrent from worrying about the future.

Just say you want him.

I pushed away the thought.

When Lakey and I settled into the couch, I turned on reruns of *Project Runway.* It wasn't long until I heard a vehicle coming down the gravel lane toward the house. Excitement erupted inside of me as I realized my husband was home. I sat up and looked out the picture window, and my face fell. An unfamiliar, sleek black car with bright chrome wheels was speeding down the gravel road. I gingerly got off the couch and moved over just enough to peek around the window sash to see who it was. The Jeep was in the garage, and Bram's truck was gone, so I could pretend no one was home.

I watched as a man exited the car in a navy three-piece suit and brown leather shoes, his expensive watch glinting in the afternoon sun. He was tall and broad, and his gray hair was slicked back effortlessly. He appeared to be looking for something in the car, and I gasped as he straightened and turned towards the house. I'd know him anywhere.

He was Vince Winchester—Bram's father.

Vince walked under the weeping willows and up to the front porch. He wore an apathetic expression, but I wasn't fooled. Vince had always been a snake. Only my grandmother had been able to reach him. She'd seen through his masks, called him out, and kept him straight while he was CEO of the factory. He respected her for her bluntness and kept her close for her loyalty, until he'd stabbed her and the entire town in the back.

I watched as this terrible man I hadn't seen in years strode onto the porch and knocked forcefully on the front door of his estranged son's home. Lakey growled and barked, bound and determined to protect me from whoever was trying to invade. I had stared at Mr. Winchester for too long from the window and couldn't run away without him noticing me. I tried to soothe Lakey as best I could without making too much movement or sound.

The crunch of gravel from another vehicle caught my ear. I didn't have to look to know it was Bram this time. Vince stopped slamming his palm against the door. I didn't dare glance out the window again, not until I heard Vince's footsteps moving away from the porch.

"What are you doing here?" Bram's booming, deep voice reverberated through the yard. He had jumped out of his truck without closing its door and strode right into his father's path.

"Hello to you, too. Is that any way to greet your father? You haven't talked to me in months." Vince's hands went out to his sides as he sauntered toward his son. "Besides, it's not you I'm here to see. It's your new *wife*."

Chills ran down my spine. I watched with rapt attention, Lakey growled quietly beside me. I held on to her neck, comforting us both.

Bram scoffed. "Like I would let you anywhere near her." He stared directly at his father.

"Imagine my surprise when Judge Rhodes called me up while I was out of town and told me he'd married my only son to that East girl. The same one I warned you to stay away from years ago."

Vince had warned Bram not to come around me?

"Shut up while you're ahead," Bram warned. "She's not here anyway, so you can go back to whatever hole you crawled out of."

"You're mad at *me*?" I could hear the smile in Vince's voice, and it made me shiver.

"I have no feelings about you at all. I want you off my property."

"You married to cash out your trust fund. Did you think I wouldn't put it together?"

"I try to never think of you." Bram's voice was stern and definitive. "I married Julianna East because I wanted to. And I'll get my inheritance as a perk. According to the lawyer this morning, it's due to be transferred into my account by next week. End of story."

Vince's hands hit low on his hips, his comfortable stance a farce to what was happening before me. "What do you think you're doing, Son? Big man like you could have any woman he wants, and you shack up with your more successful friend's sister?"

Bram's voice was firm. "She's not just Whit's sister, she's my wife now." The words made something warm flow in my veins. "And don't call me 'son' again," he spat. "You lost that privilege a long time ago. Get off my property and do not come back."

Vince waved his hand in dismissal. "You can't get rid of me, and you know it."

"Oh yes, I forgot," Bram scoffed. "You've got every law enforcement office in Virginia in your back pocket."

Vince took a step forward. "I do. And that privilege got you out of a heap of trouble when it mattered. Or have you forgotten?"

My mind scrambled to make meaning of what he was saying, but it came up empty.

Bram's eyes narrowed. "All you did was prove to me how low you'd go to fuck me over."

Vince chuckled. "They would have had your ass in jail for a DUI, and you'd have lost that little scholarship I secured for you. You almost got yourself in so much shit over that twit—"

"And none of it fucking mattered. I lost the scholarship, anyway. I lost her. I never even had you as a father. You've ruined Mom's life, cheating on her every chance you get and beating her when things don't go your way. And you refuse to acknowledge your daughter—"

"That bitch is not my daughter!" Spit flew from Vince's mouth.

"Yeah, DNA means nothing to you since you've swapped it around so often," Bram replied. "When will anything be enough? When will you be satisfied?"

I was shocked. Pieces fell into place like a puzzle, but I couldn't know the whole picture without some context. Bram had held back something from me about that night of the wreck. Had he come back to the scene? Was he almost arrested? I couldn't decipher the extent of it.

"Quit being so dramatic."

I watched helplessly as Bram's face reddened to an unnatural shade. "Get. Off. My. Property."

Vince let out a taunting laugh. "Or what? You'll hurt me? Kill me? You're too chicken shit for any of that. Always have been. And you want that money so bad, there's no way you'll risk an assault charge."

"You're right, but I only want that money to heal the things *you* destroyed."

Vince continued like Bram hadn't spoken. "You could have been something huge in this town. Instead, you're playing in the woods all day like a child and fucking a fat chick at night."

I winced and strained to see Bram's reaction.

Bram stepped toe to toe with the man he loathed the most. I had to concentrate to hear their voices through the window glass. "Is this why you've come here?" Bram asked. "To tell me how much you hate me and insult Julianna? You're pathetic."

"I've told you before, I made you, Bram," Vince growled. "You came from me. I gave you everything when you were a kid: all those trips, professional ball games, even that truck you wrecked. Plus, don't forget that future you wanted so badly in football. None of that would have been possible if it weren't for me. And a long time ago, you chose all of those things over that woman you're calling a wife now. Remember that."

The warmth that had engulfed me was replaced by a chill that ran through my veins. I let go of Lakey's neck. I stood to full height, no longer caring if they could see me. Bram's attention cut to the window, and they both stared at me.

I met Bram's gaze, and his expression morphed into tragic worry. Bram made to move around Vince, coming toward me. But I shook my head, and his eyes returned to his father. Yet Vince held my gaze. I wasn't sure what face I was giving him, but it must have pleased him. He smiled, his menacing grin mocking me.

"Punch me, Son. You know you want to." He was still staring at me.

Bram shook his head. "I'm not you. You've had your fun. Now go."

Vince's eyes shifted to Bram. "When I die, you won't get another fucking penny, you hear me?" He was yelling forcefully, pointing at Bram in accusation, his voice full of evil spite.

"I don't want one fucking thing from you," Bram seethed through gritted teeth. "And the day you're gone can't come soon enough." And like the bigger man he was, Bram walked around his father and started toward the house, coming for me.

Vince left in his fancy car, squealing tires as he retreated. Bram was shaking out his hands, which had been fisted, as he strode toward the front door, his face grim.

I was rooted in my spot by the window, unable to decide what to do or how to react. He'd confessed to the police about driving the night of the wreck at some point and hadn't told me. His father rigged his football scholarship. And his father had warned him off me. And he'd listened and broken my heart. Like bones breaking, my feelings were morphing into something I hated with each realization. All I held were small pieces of the truth. I wanted the entire story.

Bram stopped in the large doorway to the living area.

"Are you okay?" I asked, ashamed of how shaky my voice sounded.

"Yeah," he murmured, flexing his hands again. His eyes met mine. "How much of that did you hear?"

"All of it," I whispered, staring back at him. "I have questions."

He exhaled long.

"I know you do, and I'll answer them all. But I want you to know, before you ask them, I wasn't trying to keep anything from you on purpose. I just—"

"You just never thought it was important that I know? Because if you chose me, you'd have lost your football scholarship, right?"

That was as far as my mind had gotten in solving the highly complex puzzle. Saying the words out loud made my heart drop into my stomach. Sadness and truth flashed across Bram's features.

"It's not as simple as it sounds, sweets."

My eyes filled with tears. "Do not call me that."

His expression fell. "I went back that night."

I froze, my heart racing. He stayed rooted in his spot in the doorway. "I came back for you. I was a coward to leave you. No matter what you threatened, I never should have done it. But when I got back to the scene, the ambulance had come and gone. I was turning myself in to the cops when my father showed up. He paid them not to arrest me, and then he dropped the bomb that I only had a football scholarship to lose because he bought one for me."

I mulled that over for a minute before responding, the air thick with tension.

"You came back for me. Knowing you'd get in trouble..."

He nodded. "Yeah. I did. But I'm not proud of what I did. I never should have left."

"You earned that scholarship; it was all you. Vince is lying."

He sighed. "He told me—"

"I watched you play," I interrupted. "You were magnificent. Even Whit knew that."

"Yeah, well…" Bram replied, shrugging, "I heard that unprompted from my old high school coach, too, not long ago. But I don't know the truth. And I've had to live with the fact that the future I thought I created by myself was a lie bought by my sperm donor."

The gravity of his words weighed on me like a thick blanket.

"And he warned you off me? Why? What was I to him?"

Bram's eyes again met mine, and extreme sadness swarmed in his dark irises.

"He did tell me to stay away from you," he replied, unflinching. "He hated the link I had to Grams, and to you and Whit. Hated that I had another family and a parent who was so much better than he could ever be. He told me you couldn't be a part of my future, or he'd revoke the scholarship." His eyes fell to the floor.

Of course, I understood, but I'd suffered so much.

If only you had told me.

I had no idea what to say or think. My heart was wholly conflicted, my thoughts erratically organized. He walked toward me.

"No," I said and held my hand up. He stopped in his tracks, his face paling. "I don't want you near me right now. I'm absorbing."

"But I can't be apart from you, not like this. I love you. I always have, and I think you know that."

Something that should have been shrouded in joy and celebration felt lackluster under the circumstances. I'd waited so long to hear those words from Bram, and I had to listen to them right after realizing he hadn't chosen me. Anger flared deep inside me.

"I can't believe you'd say that right now."

"Why? It's true." He was genuinely confused, but I was livid.

"When will you get it through your thick skull that you could have been with me *this whole time*, but chose not to? You *chose* that. It's been fifteen years, Bram." I let my emotions flow out. "Why are you acting like you saved me from some terrible demise by not telling me all this? Like you were helping me by lying and leaving me to think you didn't care at all?"

"You want to know why? Look at this, Julianna," he shouted passionately, his hands gesturing between us. "This is what I do. I hurt. I ruin. I am defective. My dad knows it. My mom knows it. Whit knows it. Even Grams knew it, and she tried to fix me."

"She wasn't trying to fix you, dumbass. She loved you! She was trying to give you a family and show you what that meant. My only solace is that she died not knowing she failed so miserably."

I regretted the words as soon as they left my lips, but there was no taking them back. Bram put his head in his hands, but it didn't deter me from continuing, "You were all I wanted for so long. Despite the good and bad, I knew what you kept out of sight." I pointed at myself forcefully. "You think it's easier to hate yourself now than to accept that you're not perfect, that you can still be loved and forgiven. We could have fixed it together if you'd explained it to me. But you didn't, so now all that's left is forgiveness. We can't go back in time and change our choices. Am I hurt that you didn't choose me? Yes, obviously, how can I not be? But I want to forgive you."

"I'll never forgive myself for what I did to you that night," he said firmly, his gaze coming back up to meet mine. My heart twisted. "I've tried, but I can't. And right here, you crying like this, again, because of me...it's too much."

"Quit thinking about yourself for five seconds."

"I've never thought about myself. I've only ever thought about you."

I could see confusion burning in his gaze. He couldn't figure out why I was becoming so upset. Maybe I didn't either. But I was determined to try to explain it in a way he could understand.

"Have you loved anyone else?" I asked him. "You say you loved me all this time and only thought of me. Has there been anyone else?"

My heart was beating so hard that it was hard to breathe.

"Not anyone I've loved," he said, his response definite and immediate. "I slept around, started a few relationships, but everything always fizzled."

"Then why didn't you come for me?" I was breaking my own heart, and I didn't care.

"I told you why." His voice boomed. "What are you looking for? What do you want to hear? That I wasn't man enough? That I didn't really want you? I always wanted you. It was the guilt and the shame that overtook me, that held me back. That holds me back now." He took a step towards me. "Something else you don't know. All those women I was with, I never saw them. I only ever saw you. It was you I heard, you I pictured. Every *single* time."

"But you could have had me, Bram. Not just someone you liked and could pretend was me. I would have taken you, flaws and all. After the football dreams had to end, I was still out there. And you're telling me you were giving someone else what you wanted me to have. You chose yourself." I spat the last few words, unable to hold back my vitriol.

"Julianna, please—"

"Your reasoning is the most idiotic thing I've ever heard. I don't know how to feel right now." I took off the thin band on my finger and calmly set it on the arm of the chair beside me. "I want to forgive you and tell you how much I've always loved you, too. But I can't do that. Not when you won't accept what I'm saying."

He gritted his teeth and set his jaw as he watched my movements.

"Taking off the ring doesn't make us unmarried, Julianna."

"And me putting it on never made us married, Bram. It was a contract—a business transaction. Kallie was right. I should have left my stupid, fucking romantic heart locked away. This was my mistake." Before he could speak, I walked past him and up the stairs as quickly as my back would allow me.

I collapsed on Bram's bed with Lakey and shut the door. If I could have locked it, I would have. Yet I knew he wouldn't confront me again right away, anyway. It wasn't his style. My body was stressed, and thankfully, Bram's mattress allowed things to settle. I cried intermittently in the darkness and the quiet until the daylight disappeared. At some point, Lakey and I fell asleep.

When I woke, the clock on Bram's nightstand read seven pm. I had a text from Kallie:

> Kallie: Running late. Should I meet you at your Grams' house in town, or do I need to pick you up in the country?

I wasn't sure. I texted her back that I would find out. Lakey was whining at the door, so I stood carefully, opened it, and moved toward the top of the staircase. The only light on was in the front hall downstairs. Slowly but surely, I made my way to the living room, where I realized all the other house lights were off. A sweep of the rooms showed no signs of Bram.

Maybe he was upstairs in the other bedroom? I was hurting too badly to go back to check, so I went to the kitchen for a drink, taking a pain-reliever. I walked over to the kitchen window, expecting to see Bram's truck in the driveway outside the single-car garage, illuminated by the outside pole light. But it wasn't there.

Maybe he had left the truck where it was when Vince had come. I moved to the living room, clutching my cup of water. I went out the front door onto the porch. Bram's truck was gone. He'd left me.

Fresh tears tracked down my face as I wrapped my arms around myself and retreated into the house. I grabbed my phone and carefully climbed the stairs to pack my bags.

CHAPTER TWENTY

Bram | *October 14, 2024*

The cup of coffee slid a small distance across the small kitchen island and into my awaiting hands. I let the hot liquid burn my tongue and down my throat.

"Geez. At least sip it," Melanie admonished, bringing her steaming cup to her lips. "One of the great things about being young is that I can enjoy coffee late at night. Now you, on the other hand…"

"I don't think I'll be sleeping anytime soon, anyway," I murmured, looking down into my cup.

"Tell me what happened, but start from the beginning this time. 'Julianna and I got into it' isn't going to cut it."

With my head pounding and my tongue burned, I spilled out everything. The night of the party, the wreck and its aftermath, the words I'd said to Julianna in the hospital when I told her I didn't feel anything for her. She didn't interrupt, but I watched her face morph into a thousand diverse expressions.

Then I recounted the moments earlier in the day, after I'd come home from the MCA runs. I told her about our father's appearance and what he'd said about our marriage. And how Julianna had heard everything, including the insult about her weight.

"Holy crap. Why didn't you punch him?" she mused.

"I wanted to," I admitted. "But I watched him use his fists my whole life to inflict pain, even on me. And I don't want to be that person. It wasn't easy to hold back."

Then I told her what Julianna and I had shouted in the parlor, the back and forth between us, and the way my insides twisted as I watched her fall apart. I told Melanie as much as I could remember, anyway. The moments were a blur.

"I'd wanted to hold her. But I'd lost that privilege again." I rapped on the counter in frustration. Then I ran my thumb and forefinger against my closed, misty eyes a few times while recounting events.

There was silence for a moment after I finished, which I appreciated.

"That was all...a lot," she said.

"I know," I replied.

She took a deep breath. "I'm going to say this with all the love in my heart, okay?"

I nodded but recoiled as she leaned over me and swatted at my arms. "Are you crazy?!" she cried. "Do you have at least one self-destruct button you haven't pushed yet? Substance abuse, maybe?"

"Ow! That's not funny," I grumbled, holding my arm where a particular slap had stung.

"No, it's not," she agreed, standing behind the counter again. She adjusted her shirt, which had ridden up slightly with her attack. "You've built yourself a prison, locked yourself inside it, and mourned your existence for years. When the whole time you could have been free.

"Even now, you could be there in that house with her, waiting for her to calm down, trying to have a constructive conversation. But you aren't. Instead, you're here with your sister, bemoaning your life. You have no idea how frustrating it is to watch this happen to someone you love. To see them be their own worst enemy. Especially someone like you, who gives so much of themselves away for the greater good."

Did she have a point? I shook my head. "Our dad made my prison."

"That's bullshit. It was all you. You took the easiest road in your grief and disappointment instead of fighting for what you wanted. Our dad is a psychopath and a cheater. You can't change him. He can't be trusted, so quit giving him power. Own your mistakes. Apologize. Move on and get out of the damn prison. Julianna doesn't hate you. She's confused and hurt because you never truly claimed her. You made her feel disposable, first by leaving her on the fucking side of the road, and then in the hospital, and then never coming for her after that. No woman wants that."

"My concern was for her, not myself."

"You should have told her you came back for her that night immediately. You should have told her our father forbade you to be with her, Bram. You should have told her all that, instead of letting her think you didn't care."

I sighed. "I know."

Melanie made sense, but I couldn't grasp the hope that came with what she said.

"It's too late now," I mumbled, sipping the coffee this time. "I waited too long."

"She held out her heart to you a long time ago, and you crushed it." Melanie reached over and put her hand over mine on the cool granite. "And now she's back in your life so many years later, living in your house, *married* to you, and you're still holding back. How many chances do you need?"

I shook my head.

"Julianna's back problems were my fault. She says it was the deer that made us wreck, that it was unavoidable. And she says repetitively that she was no worse off because I left her that night. But the facts remain—I put her at risk and then I ran away in fear, and those two things are beyond forgiveness."

Melanie shook her head, pain etched in her features. "You were a kid, Bram. And you came back for her. And, you just said the most important part. She knew you didn't mean to hurt her. She's taken responsibility for her end of that night, too."

I swallowed the lump that had formed in my throat. "But I can't forgive myself."

Mel's eyes narrowed on me. "So, what's more important to you? Your misery or Julianna's? Because every time you say you can't forgive yourself, even though she's forgiven you, you diminish her worth. You tell her that your opinion of yourself is more important than her opinion of you. Are you okay with that?"

"But that's not true." A protective gruffness wove into my words, and Melanie smiled slightly.

"Then act like it. Quit holding back. She's put it all on the line more than once. Now, it's your turn."

THE COFFEE WAS COLD BY THE TIME MEL AND I FINISHED TALKING. Looking down at my phone, I panicked and saw it was nearing nine pm.

"Shit. Her best friend was coming in tonight," I explained while grabbing my keys. "I was supposed to drive her to Grams' house before eight."

"Seriously?" She rolled her eyes. "Men."

My sister followed me to the front door of her apartment. "If you decide to take another day off work tomorrow, I can do whatever needs to be done."

I shook my head. "I have to come back to the office. It'll be too lonely without Julianna around."

"Is she coming back to stay with you when her friend leaves?" Melanie leaned against the doorframe, and I paused.

"I'm not sure," I replied, running a hand down my face. "I didn't think she would ever come back, but now I don't know about anything. Not until I get to talk to her about everything calmly."

"Just stay home tomorrow."

"I have meetings."

"You're always late anyway."

"Smartass."

"I'm learning from the best."

Without overthinking it, I walked back to her and wrapped my strong arms around her petite frame in a chaste embrace. "I appreciate you," I said.

"I always wanted a big brother, and now I have one. And a boss. Not sure which role I like you in more."

"Good answer," I muttered into her hair. I left her standing in the doorway with a wave, grateful anew that she was in my life.

THE DRIVE BACK TO THE FARM WAS A BLUR. I PARKED THE TRUCK outside the garage and killed the engine. I planned to go in, spill my guts, beg Julianna for forgiveness, and convince her I wanted to change because I did want to change. If it came down to choosing to wallow in pity or to be with her every day, I'd pick her every time. Forgiving myself and moving on from my past mistakes was the best way to honor Julianna's commitment to me, paving a path forward for us to be together.

If that's what she wanted.

What if I was too late?

I remained as stealthy as possible as I moved through the house. Lakey met me in the living room with a wagging tail, and I petted her before making my way up the creaking stairs. My bedroom door was half open, and I pushed it open gently, thinking she was probably in there.

Empty.

The bed was made with not one wrinkle on the sheets. I raced to the bathroom and flipped on the light. It was empty. The vanity was cleared of her things. Frantic, I looked around for her bag. It was nowhere to be found. I checked the other two bedrooms, and they were undisturbed.

I ran down the stairs and grabbed my phone, which I'd deposited on the dining room table, pulling up her number. It rang as I searched the downstairs rooms. I even stuck my head in the cellar. I trembled as her phone continued to go to voicemail.

I switched to text and received a notification that her phone was set to *Do Not Disturb*.

Wherever she was, whoever she was with, whatever she was doing, she was icing me out. Kallie must have picked her up. I let Lakey outside to do her business before putting her back in her kennel. I wouldn't be okay until I knew Julianna was safe and until she would listen to all the apologies I needed to make. I headed towards Grams' house.

CHAPTER TWENTY-ONE

Julianna | *October 14, 2024*

"I'm so sorry. I didn't know who else to call."

Kallie had been delayed with a bakery emergency and wouldn't be in Mill Creek until almost midnight. I was so far removed from Uber or taxi services out in the country that it was laughable. So, I called the only number I had of someone in the area, and someone I knew would make Bram angriest.

Hunter Kearsley leaned against his vehicle, arms crossed loosely, amusement playing across his face as he spied me walking toward him.

Was I losing it? Yes. I acknowledged and accepted that I had lost my mind.

I could have taken Bram's Jeep, but how could I stay away from him if I stole his vehicle? I also wasn't yet cleared to drive after the surgery.

I'd left Lakey out of her kennel. It felt wrong to cage her since she usually spent nights free in the house, and Bram would be back eventually. I wanted to take the pup with me, but she wasn't mine to keep. None of it was mine: the house, the bed, the Jeep, the precious fur baby who whined when I closed the front door behind me. Even my title as Bram's wife wasn't mine to keep. Bram had invited me in and told me to make myself comfortable, and in less than a few weeks, I had staked a strange claim over his space.

You love him.

I pushed the feelings down. I locked them away so deep inside that I couldn't feel them, not as Hunter stared at me with those gray eyes.

When he saw me carrying a bag, he jogged over and took it from my grasp.

"Thank you for coming to get me," I said sheepishly. "Everything is still kind of tender."

"You shouldn't be carrying anything," he admonished. "I am not past doing favors for beautiful women or patients who just had surgery." He laughed then, blushing a smidge. "But this is not something I've done before."

I was in crisis mode and didn't care about my state of dress. And for once, I didn't worry about what he may or may not have been thinking. He didn't seem to mind my unglamorous looks, my aloof demeanor, or the fact that I had asked such a huge favor.

However, his time and fuel were worth something, and I resolved I would pay him for the Uber service. But I didn't say anything about it yet as I settled into the passenger seat. Hunter broke through all those thoughts as he put the vehicle into reverse.

"So, back to Mill Creek proper?" he asked, confirming where I needed to go.

I nodded. "Yes, a house in one of the cul-de-sacs over by the high school. I'll direct you."

"I'm still trying to figure out why you called me of all

people. You're a mystery, Julianna East," he mused. "Or what is it now? Winchester?"

I picked invisible lint off my sweatshirt, feigning disinterest. "Yes."

His face made a quiet "oh" in the dash lights as we traveled the twisting highway in the dark.

"You're the only other person I know well in this area," I continued, letting my hands fall to my lap. "I'm sorry if I put you out. I'll pay you—"

"Absolutely not," Hunter replied, cutting me off. "More than happy to shuttle you. I'm just confused. Why are you leaving? Did something happen you need to tell me about?"

I swallowed, hearing something in this voice that indicated a fear for me. "No, nothing violent happened," I clarified, and I watched him ease a little in his seat. "It's just been a hard time for me lately."

"I know," he sympathized. "Did you not want to be alone so bad that you married him?" I wasn't sure whether to be impressed or appalled by his bluntness.

"Did you not want to be alone so bad tonight that you drove an hour to pick up a married woman and drop her off at a house that isn't yours?"

A smile, pleasant and coy, played across his features. "Touche."

He kept his eyes on the road. He was a cautious driver, and I was thankful.

"I'm glad it was nothing too bad, but I have to ask for some context. What are you running from?" he asked. "Are you playing a game with him of some sort?"

I huffed. "That's presumptuous, but astute. It's a long story. Let's just say it started with a teenage girl in love with her brother's best friend, and now we're married, in name only. Between here and there, there are braids of lies all tied together so tightly I can't unknot them."

"In name only? So, it isn't a real marriage?"

I stiffened, realizing I'd dropped a significant secret.

"It's okay," Hunter chuckled. "People do these things. I guess it makes a little more sense now."

"Health insurance," I said, my cheeks on fire. I was glad he couldn't see me fully in the dark.

"Now it makes even more sense."

I didn't reply, not wanting to elaborate any further. I lay my head back against the leather headrest of the seat. It had been an emotional afternoon, and I was sore and developing a headache.

"Are you okay physically?" Hunter asked.

"Yes, just tired. Today has been a lot."

"So, what happened today that would make you leave like you have?"

I shifted. "The initial back surgery I had years ago was an injury from a car wreck where Bram was driving. I learned today that after the wreck, Bram's father told him he had to stay away from me. So, Bram came to the hospital while I was recovering and told me he didn't want me. It broke my heart. It was a lie, but he made the choice. He stayed away from me, so his 'daddy' wouldn't be upset with him." I glanced at Hunter, but he wasn't mocking or smiling at my dramatic words. Instead, he stared out at the illuminated road pensively.

"How old were you guys when this happened?"

"I was eighteen. He was nineteen."

"I see," Hunter mused. "Honestly, and I don't mean to be rude, it sounds a little petty to be upset about that now."

My mouth dropped open. "I'm not petty. I have a right to be hurt."

But Hunter's opinion didn't budge. "Maybe," he shrugged. "But, maybe you should remember you guys were kids, and his whole life was in front of him at nineteen. It's not like it is now. He's got life experience under his belt."

"Then you think he'd have started sharing with me immedi-ately instead of leaving me in the dark. For instance, he could have led with the information that he had a long-lost half-sister. I had to find that out the day of the wedding."

"Mmm."

"What about telling me that his father forbade him from having contact with me? And I still can't understand why he never tried to find me after it was clear his father's threats no longer mattered."

Hunter tapped the steering wheel with his fingers. "I'm sure he regrets those things."

I shrugged noncommittally. "Maybe."

"And you're in love with him?"

I shut my eyes. "Don't make me say it out loud."

He made a couple of turns before he asked, "Does he know you are?"

I shook my head. "No. He said it to me earlier today, but I didn't say it back." I looked over at him. "You're asking a lot of questions. How do I know I can trust you with my feelings?"

He laughed. "I'm already an accomplice to your fake marriage."

"Wow, ok. I guess you are," I replied, laughing a little myself. "I saw him a few weeks ago for the first time in fifteen years. It's been a lifetime. I couldn't just come out and say, 'I love you'. He would think I was crazy."

"Oh yes, but it's perfectly sane to marry someone when you've never said, 'I love you'." The look on Hunter's face was pure amusement as he poked fun at my circumstances. I sat back more firmly in my seat.

"I think I've lost my mind."

"Look, I have no dog in this fight," he said in his smooth voice, "But having a history like you and him doesn't seem insignificant. You feel how you feel. You should tell him you love him, too, and let it happen."

"But how can he feel like that when he's rejected me repeatedly?"

He seemed to mull this over for a moment before responding.

"Why do you think he rejected you?"

"Bram was never one to follow rules that didn't suit him, so I don't think his staying away from me was just pure obedience to his father. And he said that he broke my heart and left me alone for so many years because I didn't deserve someone as flawed as him. He was terrified of hurting me, not understanding that his avoidance already devastated me. But how is that not a stupid excuse? I am firmly of the belief that if you want to, you will."

"That's true, to an extent. But he probably can't forgive himself, so he doesn't understand how you can. And it's my guess he's been through some traumatic rejection himself. Probably from the father he hates? Maybe his mother? You've not mentioned her."

My cheeks reddened further as my nervous energy climbed.

"I was a minor in psychology in college, if you can't tell," Hunter added smugly.

"Figures," I murmured. "I should have told you he was abused and neglected as a child. We could have saved ourselves a whole conversation. Tell me, Mr. Psychology, how am I supposed to know this isn't one long cat-and-mouse game to him?"

"Well, if it was, even if it's subconscious or overt, it's probably because he fears intimacy."

"Of course he does. He was an only child, neglected by his parents. He doesn't want me to see him as flawed because he doesn't want me to leave or hurt him."

"You're very intuitive. That's sexy in a woman." I snorted in derision, but he continued, "You could divorce his ass and go out with me."

"Did you seriously go there?" I laughed. "After I said all that, and after I look like I do right now?"

It was his turn to shrug.

"I like you like this, Julianna. Not artifice. Honesty looks good on you. I do not doubt that your fake marriage partner feels the same. You should ask him."

THE SECOND WE PULLED INTO THE DRIVEWAY, I WAS ALREADY dreaming of a hot shower to ease my aching back. Hunter refused to take gas money, as I expected.

"Promise me you'll call if this all goes south between you and him. That's all I ask."

I tried not to overthink what I'd done by calling him. He was a good man, and I hoped maybe even a friend.

"I will," I promised.

As I entered the dark house with my bag and began flipping on the lights, I was met with a wave of exhaustion. I texted Kallie and told her I needed to lie down, but that she should call me when she arrived. Then I shed my clothing and went straight into the shower, contemplating my pseudo-husband and what Hunter and I had discussed in the car.

It wasn't my job to fix Bram Winchester. However, I wasn't naïve enough to hand him my heart on a silver platter to take a bite and spit it out again. We'd nearly met with the ends of the bargain we'd made, anyway. He almost had his fortune for the Mill Creek Aid charity, and I had used the insurance I'd needed. We might never be together like I'd always dreamed of, but I couldn't regret what had happened between us.

So much in my life was healing, and I needed to be grateful for that.

The new, pristine beds Whit had put in the house were inferior to Bram's. Regardless, I slept like the dead until my phone woke me up.

"Hey," I said in a groggy tone.

"Hey! Come open the door, you whore," Kallie's voice demanded.

I moved as fast as possible. When I opened the front door, she was standing with a smile, holding on to a small, lime green suitcase in one hand and balancing a wrapped pie in the other. I burst into tears at the sight of her.

"It's just cherry. Don't get too emotional," she cooed, waltzing in the door. She was like a burst of fresh air into a stale space, even at a late hour.

I was glad she and I didn't have much to catch up on, since we kept in touch every day. Instead, I could tell her about what had happened earlier with Bram while I dug into the pie with a fork straight from the tin.

"Are you kidding me? His daddy told him not to date you, and he listened? What a bitch move." She picked up a pillow off the couch and pressed it to her chest. She rubbed the fabric. "Ooh, what is this made of? Cashmere?"

"Probably, since this was all Whit's doing. But focus." I sighed. "Yes, his dad threatened to take away his football college scholarship if he messed with me. It had to be because he was jealous of Grams' relationship with Bram."

"Hmm," Kallie mused. "That family sounds like a real piece of work. And now you've gone and married into it. How does that feel?"

I ruefully snickered. "Not so good. The me from a month ago wouldn't have a clue how to handle everything that's happened in such a short amount of time."

Kallie clicked her tongue. "See what happens when you leave the safety of your mundane life?"

"Exactly," I replied.

"I was being facetious." I shot her a confused look, and she continued. "Julianna Joy, love of mine, you and I both know you weren't thriving in Charlotte. You were existing. I am your only close friend, and you've been sad since I've known you."

"Well, tell me how you really feel," I sarcastically scoffed. "I've just been...in a rut."

"In a rut is when you can't pick what book to read next."

"Actually, that's a slump."

She threw the cashmere pillow at me. "Shut up. Listen, I am not on Bram's side here. I'm on Jules's side. I want you to thrive. You rarely leave the house. Besides your writing and pie, you weren't excited about anything or anyone until Bram waltzed in again. It's been infuriating as a Bram-hater for me to hear you giggle over that turd every night on the phone, but I've listened and absorbed it because we're best friends. You've been happier since you've been here, which is saying a lot, considering your back was sliced open and sawed off with a laser."

"Weird way to put all that, but I see what you're saying," I admitted, biting my lip. "I can't help how he makes me feel. But now everything is upside down. When I came here, I thought it was cut and dry. I never thought that he wanted me. And now that he adamantly says he wanted me the whole time, and I'm confused and dubious."

"People do weird things, babe," Kallie replied. "Like you calling your physician assistant to come pick you up off a mountain and drive you into town."

"That was a necessity. I don't know anyone else's number. I offered him gas."

She pursed her lips toward me before continuing, "My point is, people do weird things when feelings are involved. And I don't want you to miss out on what could be because of the past."

I thought of what I'd said to Bram the day we were married, when we were out for the walk: "I think it's good enough to keep moving forward and realizing the present and future are as important as the past."

Well, shit.

"But I'm here now, and you don't have to be around him anytime soon if you don't want to be." She waved a hand in dismissal. "I hate his guts anyway."

"Yeah, I think some time apart is good," I confirmed with a small smile. "I wonder why he hasn't..." I pressed the messaging app on my phone and gasped with a hand to my mouth as his name lit up. There was a string of unread texts. I hadn't taken my phone off *Do Not Disturb*.

"He's texted a million times! I've had the *DND* setting on."

"How did you get my call then?" Kallie asked.

"I had you set up as an exception, of course. He's on his way here!"

"Do you want to see him?"

As if on cue, an engine roared into the driveway.

"I don't want to talk to him," I gasped. "I'm going to hide in the hallway to hear what he has to say, but don't let him get to me. Can you handle him?"

"Oh, I've been waiting for this," Kallie said with a grin, rubbing her hands together, looking like a cross between the Grinch and Mr. Burns from *The Simpsons*. "Go on. I've got this."

I pressed myself up against the wall where I couldn't see the door. My heart was pounding, my palms were sweating, and I felt dizzy and hot. I hoped I didn't pass out.

The knock on the door was explosive, and I startled. Kallie wasted no time and threw it open. I couldn't see their expressions, but their conversation echoed throughout the house.

"I'm looking for Julianna. You must be Kallie. Nice to meet you. Is she here?"

My best friend dramatically scoffed. "You could start by introducing yourself. And like I'd tell you if she were here, Bram Winchester."

A few moments of complete silence between them made my racing heart skip a few beats.

"Kallie, look, I know you don't know me, but—"

"Oh, I know you. I know everything I need to know. From the moment I learned about your existence, I have been waiting to tell you what I think about you. What kind of coward do you have to be to leave a girl alone on a mountain road in the cold with a broken back? And then what kind of man comes to a girl's hospital room on the day of her grandmother's funeral and tells her he doesn't want her, after you *told* her how much you cared for her? I'll tell you what kind of man does that—"

"Calm down. I was a bastard. I own it. I live with the guilt every fucking day." There was a desperation in his voice that twisted my heart. I almost stepped out from around the corner to go to him, but stopped myself. "She's too good for me. You don't have to convince me of that. Is she safe?"

My heart had dropped to my feet.

"She's safe," Kallie replied, her voice calmer. "She needs some time. It'll be good for her, and for you, I think. At least be apart for this next week until I'm gone."

"I want to talk to her first, for a moment."

"Not possible."

"She's *my* wife."

I heard Kallie's footsteps shift. "And she's *my* best friend. You decided to be without her for fifteen years. I'm pretty sure you can do another week." The snark in her voice could not be mistaken. "Give her space. She needs it. This has all been a lot on her, and she's still healing."

I heard his feet move, and I thought he had retreated until I heard his voice again.

"I've been living half alive for so many years. But now I've had a glimpse of how it could be, how *I* could be if she chose me. I might not deserve her, but I want her. And I won't give her up."

Without a response, Kallie shut the door. I knew it was over, yet I didn't come out from around the corner until I heard his truck start up in the driveway.

I met the eyes of my best friend, and they were wide, staring at me in shock. "Julianna Joy East. Why didn't you tell me he was so hot?"

I deflated, moving toward her with loose arms, and rolled my eyes. "Are you serious? That's the first thing you're going to say to me after all that?"

"I'm observant! My God, the guns on that man... and his hands...Damn. Fire emojis everywhere."

I put my head in my hands, shaking it profusely. "I'm married to that."

"Yes. Yes, you are."

I groaned. "I should call him now and hear him out."

"I'd hear him out, too," Kallie said with a smirk, and I rolled my eyes again.

"I didn't mean it like that. I...I think I love him, Kallie."

She didn't say anything to that, just stared at me in thought.

"I want to spend time with you this week," she said, finally. "We can figure things out as we go. It doesn't have to be all figured out tonight. Let's get some sleep."

I fell asleep with Kallie in Grams' old room and dreamt of a past I couldn't erase.

CHAPTER TWENTY-TWO

Julianna | *October 18, 2024*

Time moved quickly after Kallie arrived in Mill Creek. I didn't feel like doing too much, and we spent lots of time indoors. Whit texted often, and even though I desperately wanted to, I wasn't sure whether to mention what had happened the day Vince showed up. Whit never mentioned it to me, so I assume Bram didn't talk to him about it.

It was Friday morning when I realized I couldn't take it anymore.

> **Me: I need to talk to you soon.**

I texted my brother's number and bit my lip, waiting for him to respond. While it usually took quite a while, this time it was immediate.

> **Whit: What did Bram do?**

> Me: Bram did nothing. Why do you always assume it's him?

> Whit: Because it seems like his goal in life is to hurt you.

> Me: We got in a little tift. I'm with Kallie at Grams' house.

> Whit: I figured it was something like that. You can always tell me, even if it has to do with Bram. I can't guarantee I won't smash his face in, though.

I smiled. Was this what it was like to have a big brother as an adult? It's how I remembered it from when I was a teen. He would have burned down the world for me. And now?

Some hope flared within me.

> Me: I don't want you to, but it's sweet of you to offer.

> Whit: I know I've been a shitty brother to you, but I want to be better.

I sighed aloud. I had wanted to have this conversation with him in person. I hadn't seen my brother in so long. But Whit was in season with football, and there was no such thing as time that belonged to him.

> Me: Call me when you have time.

Much to my surprise, my phone rang immediately.

"Hey," I said.

"Hey, sis," he replied, his voice tired. "How are you feeling?"

I could lie. I was so good at it. But I chose not to. If I were to clean my slate and let the past be the past, I would have to take the necessary steps.

"Physically? I'm great. Everything is healing nicely with minimal pain if I take my meds." I took a deep breath and exhaled audibly. "Emotionally? I'm not so great."

"What's wrong?" Concern filled his voice. "Is it about Bram?"

"Mostly. But I do need to apologize to you." I wasn't about to tell the wreck secret to him, but it was past time for us to discuss our relationship.

"Okay…that sounds cryptic and unnecessary. For what?"

"For avoiding you over the years," I said, my voice shaky.

"Stop," he commanded. "Stop it right there. Us drifting apart was not your fault. I'm not sure you know how messed up I was after Grams died. There's no excuse, but there's so much I never told you."

"I think you hated taking care of me."

He sighed loudly. "You're right, I did. But it was only that I was young and frustrated. I was failing in school because I couldn't grasp anything online. I tried to dull the pain of losing Grams with any substance I could get by with. Amazing that I didn't get caught. Bram and I only stayed friends because he wouldn't give up on me.

"I wanted to run right after Grams' funeral, but I couldn't because I knew you were counting on me. But then I couldn't look you in the face, so I stayed gone from the house all the time. I felt pressure because of my scholarship. I felt pressure because of the responsibility I had for you and the regret of leaving you alone the night you wrecked the truck. I was depressed. I wanted to lie down and die, get rid of the pain. It was horrible."

I continued to listen, unable to hold back tears.

"And when you stopped talking to me, and Bram got hurt

and left college, it all became so much worse. Football was my only saving grace." I heard him swallow hard. "We changed head coaches the year before I went into the NFL draft. That man changed my life. He got me back where I needed to be. I still carry a lot of it around with me, though. I know I hurt you, and I'm so fucking sorry."

"We've all made mistakes, Whit," I soothed, hearing the panic in his voice. "I should have told you how I felt long ago. I miss you. I've always missed being close to you."

I heard him sniffle. "I've missed you, too," he said, and then chuckled a little. "I can't remember the last time I cried. I've got to get it together before someone walks in here and catches me. Not a good look."

"I wish I could hug you right now," I replied, a smile on my face.

"Me too. But I'm kinda glad we talked like this, so it won't be so awkward when I get into town to see you in a couple of weeks. I've got to leave for a charity auction in a few minutes, but I'll be free after that. Can I text you?"

"Anytime," I said. "I'll reply."

"And I don't know what happened with you and Bram, but if you want to talk later, we can. He's in love with you, you know."

My heart flipped in my chest. "How do you know that?"

"He's been carrying a torch for you for a long time, Jules. That's why I said it was dangerous for him. No offense, but it's been ridiculous. The number of times I've had to drag his drunken ass home with him mumbling your name...I'd be embarrassed if I were him."

So what Bram had been saying was true? He missed me for years? Some small flame of hope lit inside of me.

"So he didn't forget me? I mean, he never got in touch with me. And he still dated around all these years."

"Yeah. On and off. Nothing became serious, though. There was always an issue."

"What's that?" My heart hammered in my chest.

"None of them were you."

My face lit up as tears sprang to my eyes. Whit was oblivious to my roller coaster of emotions as he continued, "You guys will get it straightened out, I'm sure. Do you still not like Grams' house? If you're uncomfortable there, I can put you and your friend up somewhere else. It won't be an issue. I can arrange for someone to move your things for you. Someone who isn't Bram."

I looked around. Inside the house was different from our childhood, but I noticed a few things that were the same as in the past: the arch of the doorways, the beam across the ceiling above me, and the picture window where Grams' enormous Christmas tree was set up every year.

Things were different, but the bones of the home remained. This was still *our* house. Just because it had been upgraded and rearranged didn't mean it wasn't still her at the core.

I smiled. "No, I like it here," I said quietly. "I was wrong before, Whit. She's still here."

KALLIE FORCED ME TO WEAR ACCEPTABLE CLOTHES AND WASH MY hair. She had never been to Mill Creek, and so she pushed me into the car with her and made me show her around town, including all the places from my childhood. As we passed the high school, I pointed out all the little spaces and small memories I had of my teenage years. We drove around the corner of the school, and the new stadium-like football field came into view.

"Whoa," she breathed out. "Are they professional here?"

"You would think. It was built with funds from many

wealthy donors a few years ago. Football is a big deal at this school. It always has been."

"Does Bram coach or anything?"

I debated for half a second whether or not to tell details of Bram's life, but I knew my best friend was a steel trap.

"No. He's been asked to take over for the retiring head coach. I don't know if he will take on that responsibility since he already has a pretty important day job. But who knows? I think he wants to. But don't tell anyone that."

She smiled. "Who would I tell? But why doesn't he coach if he wants to? Does he have bad feelings about football since the injury and the stuff with his Dad?"

"A little. I think it's complicated."

I didn't want to talk about it. Not because of Kallie, but because that subject was one of the leading confessions up to our first fight that day in the woods. Which led to how we made up.

I squirmed in my seat uncomfortably.

"Are you feeling okay?" Kallie asked, referring to my back.

"Yeah, I'm fine. But I'd love to head back soon. Maybe we could pick up—"

I was interrupted by my phone buzzing in my hand. I looked down and saw an unknown number with the Roanoke area code.

"Answer it. What if it's the doctor?" Kallie urged, sensing my hesitancy. I put the phone to my ear.

"Hello?"

"Hi! Is this Julianna?" The woman's voice was bright and warm.

"Yes, it is. Who is this?"

"It's Melanie. Bram's sister."

Panic invaded my system.

"Is Bram okay?" I asked, my gaze meeting Kallie's wide eyes.

"Oh! Oh, yes. Sorry. I didn't mean to worry you. I just wanted to chat a moment."

"Okay…" I pressed the speaker button. Kallie silently mimed, clapping like a seal that I'd let her into the conversation.

"First, Bram has no idea I'm calling you. I was able to steal your number from his phone because he leaves it lying everywhere. Men are so weird. Anyway, second, you must come home and fix him. He's pathetic. And by pathetic, I mean he's a nightmare. None of us can handle him at work. I even tried to sister him, and he cried. *Cried*, Julianna. My brother. Bram Winchester cried. I'd never seen him like that before."

"Oh." It was the only thing I could say.

"I had to move in with him temporarily because of some housing issues, and he's so, so sad."

"I'm sorry, I really am. But what does this have to do with me?" I asked innocently.

"Please don't act like you don't know. I don't have time," she begged, her little moment of laughter letting me know she was half-teasing. "He's crazy about you. Do you not know that? He's been happier since you came into town. Not the superficial happy he shows everyone, like at the MCA things. But truly happy. I can tell."

I bit my lip. "I…I'm spending time with my friend this week while she's in town. She's waiting on me hand and foot, and I—"

"I know a few more days shouldn't hurt, but he's a mess. He's masking it, but he's desperate to make up with you. I know he has a lot to say to you that he hasn't yet—"

"I appreciate you calling me, and I'm so happy to talk to you again," I said, interrupting her, "but things moved quickly between Bram and me. I am only just starting to take it all in fully. I will end my week with my best friend. Then I'll reevaluate. This time apart is good for us."

I didn't believe a damn word coming out of my mouth. I was desperate to talk to Bram. The time apart was torture, and I wanted to forget the past. I wanted to speak to him about what we meant. How real was our marriage? How would we decide when to part?

"It was always meant to be temporary," I tacked on, and Kallie went still beside me. It felt like the air was sucked out of the car for a moment.

There was silence on the other end of the phone.

"Melanie?" I inquired.

"Okay. Just...please don't make any decisions about the future until you talk to him," she replied more timidly than before.

"I promise," I vowed.

As we said our goodbyes, the call disconnected.

"That was brave of her," Kallie remarked. "I like her."

"Me too. But I had no idea what to say," I replied, placing the phone on the car's middle console.

"We haven't talked about it in a few days. What is the plan here? When are you going to talk to him?" Kallie tried to act nonchalant, but I could see the eagerness in her eyes for me to spill my inner thoughts.

I sighed. "I don't know. Does he even want to talk to me?"

"Well, his hot ass came over the night I arrived and growled at me to get to you."

"I remember. I was there."

"And, you said you love him."

"I did say that, didn't I? But he's not perfect. He has a few quirks, things I should consider. He leaves his dirty shoes sitting all over the house, which drives me insane. He wakes up way too early."

"Is this what we're calling quirks these days? He sounds positively beastly." Her sarcasm was palatable.

"He's also stubborn, possessive, and overdoes everything.

He can't give the minimum. He has to give 110% to everything. It's off-putting."

"I can't get Brandon to do shit. These sound like good qualities, not bad ones. You should talk to him."

"I know, I'm going to," I said with a sigh, "after you leave town." I cocked an eyebrow at her. "I thought you didn't like Bram."

She shrugged. "He's growing on me. And if you're going to be married forever, I must learn to love him. And I guess your brother, too."

I sent her a pointed look. "You don't know Whit, don't judge him too harshly."

"I call them as I see them. And he was a terrible brother to shrug you off and make you fend for yourself after your grandmother died. Not a fan."

"I appreciate your undying devotion, but if I have to forgive them both, you have to, too."

"Was that not what I said?" She smirked and then began cackling enthusiastically. "You're so gonna get boned."

My mouth fell open. "Kallie!"

"Boned with a capital B. Actually, it'll probably be all sweet and shit. Which is what you deserve for your first time." Her eyebrows wiggled.

I rolled my eyes. "You're insufferable."

"Sometimes I can be. But listen, if his sister says he's pining for you, then the man is pining," Kallie shrugged, turning the car off the school's street. "She would know."

"I'm still looking for a sign," I hummed. "He hasn't texted my phone once."

"Oh. It'll come," she replied with a grin. "That's what she said."

Our laughter echoed off the small interior, and I was grateful anew to have a few days with my best friend in the chaos my life has become.

I was exhausted by the time we returned home. Clenching the bag of tacos that Kallie and I had picked up for lunch, I nearly tripped over a small box in front of the door, sitting alone on the porch.

"Shit!" I cried out as I stumbled. Kallie shut the car door loudly, the click of her boots hitting the pavement as she hurried toward me.

"Are you okay? Did you hurt yourself? What is that? Is it a bomb?"

I looked down at the box and back at her. "Seriously? A bomb? Here?"

She shrugged and bent before me, retrieving the box, unfastening the lid, and peering down into the cardboard. "It's...a pie."

I investigated the open flaps and took in the creation. It was made by someone who knew nothing about pie-making. The crust edges were extra crispy brown, but it wasn't a run-of-the-mill frozen pie crust. It had been hand-rolled and poorly shaped within the tin.

"Blueberry, maybe?" I said, grabbing the note that was slipped into the side of the cardboard.

Julianna,

After fifteen years without you, your absence has been torture. I hope you think of me as often as I think of you.

Happy 9-day anniversary. Enjoy this pie. It was the least burnt of the batch. Lakey enjoyed the other ones.

With Love,
Bram

I ran my fingers over the smudged black ink of his scratchy handwriting and felt my heart squeeze.

He'd made me a pie.

"He made you a pie," Kallie said as if reading my thoughts. "I guess he knows how much you like pie?"

"Yes," I simply replied. I met Kallie's understanding gaze. "I have to text him."

"Do it. And if you want to go over there, or if you want me to go home—"

"No," I said, grabbing her arm. "Not yet. Please stay until Sunday. I...I will text him, but I don't want to see him until next week." I needed time to gather courage.

She nodded, although the facial expression she gave me didn't match her nod.

After going inside, I grabbed my phone and gingerly sat in the comfortable living room recliner. I typed, then erased it all. And retyped again. Erased again.

"Are you kidding me? You've been at this for ten minutes! Send something!" I looked up to see Kallie watching me from the kitchen island, knife in hand.

I shifted uncomfortably in the recliner. "I am being cautious. I want it to be perfect."

She went back to cutting her lime. "Tell him you want to suck his dick."

"Kallie!"

"What?"

I pursed my lips and looked back at the blank screen again. I was spiraling, worried I would say too much or not enough. What was he expecting? Did he want me to apologize for leaving?

You miss him. Tell him that.

I swiped the words "Thanks for the pie" on the keyboard and pressed send before I could double- and triple-think it over.

The phone dinged with an immediate response.

"That was quick. What did he say?" Kallie walked toward me with a plate of tacos.

I opened the text.

"It says, 'You're welcome.'"

She paused. "That's it? What did you say?"

"I said, 'Thanks for the pie,'" I whispered, watching as my best friend's face went slack.

"What?! You didn't say, 'Come over here right now and take me?'"

"No!" I exclaimed, taking the plate she offered me. "Ugh. Things were so kismet between us. And now it feels like everything has shifted. It's all wrong. It's..."

"Tainted?" Kallie offered, walking in with her tacos and settling on the couch. "Talk to him. Like a real person, not like a robot."

I didn't answer her. I curled up my legs into the recliner, feeling my back stretch uncomfortably, and I winced.

"We did too much today," Kallie said, mouth full of taco.

"It's fine, really," I replied. The ache subsided once I settled. "It's time for my next round of pills, that's all. I hope the doctor tells me tomorrow it's okay for me to drive."

We ate in silence, and my thoughts ran in circles until I thought I might combust. Clenching my plate of tacos, I'd only picked over, I carefully stood up from my seat.

"I think it's time to write," I declared.

I would process and pour every emotion I had into my fantasy world, where the girl accepts the past and looks toward the future. And the guy gets the girl.

Chapter Twenty-Three

Bram | *October 21, 2024*

"For the last time, get up!"

My eyes were still closed when Mel's shrill voice reached my doorway, penetrating my solace. Lakey was somewhere close, panting. I'd been without my wife for one week.

A miserable, soul-sucking seven days.

Melanie had moved in temporarily while Julianna was away. Her townhouse complex was sold, and all the tenants were given thirty days to get out. We moved most of her items to storage since I needed something to do to keep my mind off Julianna, and although she was on the hunt for somewhere new to live, I was grateful she was with me, so I didn't have to be alone.

I had been morphing into a vampire-like state, staying up until the wee hours of the morning and clocking only a few hours of sleep. If Mel hadn't been there to get me up in the mornings, I would have slept all day until I lost my job.

But I did everything I could to keep my mind off the fact that Julianna was so close, yet so far. I hadn't attended the MCA dinner on Friday, feigning illness, but mostly, I couldn't go and face the elderly ladies asking me where she was.

I thrived off the memories of the one night we'd spent together in my bed, the way she tasted on my tongue, the way her soft moans and whispers filled my ears, the pleasure of the moment imprinted deep into my very being. Her plush lips on my own. Her laugh, smile, and the way she was shy and kind with everyone she met. She was perfection. She always had been.

Her missing clothes and toiletries in the bedroom and bathroom were reminders of the harshest reality: she was gone.

She wants space.

She doesn't want you.

Fifteen years of desire had been fulfilled, and I didn't know how to deal with it being torn from me so suddenly. I dealt with her dismissal of me by reminding myself that we were still legally married. She couldn't get away from me without severing that union, and I wouldn't let her go anywhere without a fight.

I showered and dressed in my uniform, complete with badge and hat. I had a political pony show to attend, and I had to look official. If only the uniform would hide the dark circles under my eyes. I honestly did look like my nickname.

"You clean up nice, bro." Melanie whistled as I entered the kitchen. She handed me an insulated travel mug of hot coffee, and I tipped my hat to her.

"Thank you. It's an important day."

She moved things around the kitchen, packing her lunch, dressed in her clean, pressed uniform. "You don't have to pretend with me. I know how you feel about these photo opportunities for the senator." The sarcasm echoed in her voice.

"Quit acting like you know me," I grumbled, grabbing my jacket. "See you at work."

I ushered Lakey into her kennel, ensured she had water, and added a treat for her. I gave her generous pats and heartfelt goodbyes before walking out into the shockingly cold October air.

I'd tried to bake a blueberry pie for Julianna five times. After so many failures, Melanie swooped in to help, and we created something decent enough that I could take it to her. I had so much I wanted to tell her, but I settled for a simple note. Her "thank you for the pie" text was everything and nothing at the same time.

As I did every day, I thought about her while answering emails and preparing the team for the day. We were unveiling a new accessibility ramp at Pelham Falls Picnic Area. It was a popular spot in the national forest and presented a great publicity opportunity for our senator, who had helped secure significant federal funding for the area. I'd done these events many times and knew it came with the position. I went through the pomp and circumstances of the ceremony, giving all the charm I could muster in my diminished state.

It was a successful unveiling. Pictures were taken, hands were shaken, and it was over quickly. My team and I were loading up the last of the chairs to return to the office when Melanie walked over and stood directly beside me. "Head over to Julianna's house, now," she whispered near my ear. "I think she needs you."

My blood ran cold. "Is she okay? Did she call? Wait, how did she call you?"

She didn't answer but smiled brightly and winked.

"Tell me what she said." I tried to make my voice stern, but Mel was having none of my tactics.

She just shook her head. "Nope, no info. She called. Go. Now. She's waiting."

I felt hesitant about abandoning the employees to complete the grunt work, but I didn't have to be told twice when it came to Julianna. If she wanted to speak to me, she wouldn't wait one extra moment. I left Paul, the oldest ranger, in charge of the group and sped off toward Grams' house in my ranger vehicle. Some part of me thought something might be wrong, an accident or injury, and Mel didn't know the whole story. Why else would Julianna have had a sudden urge to see me?

I ran to the front door of Grams' house and rang the doorbell instead of pounding on it like a baboon. If she didn't answer within ten seconds, I was going to use my code and go in, propriety be damned. I had to know she was okay. The door swung open when I was pushing the numbers on the keypad above the doorknob. My wife stood in the tall doorway, whole and seemingly unharmed.

My jaw dropped.

Julianna had always been the sexiest woman I'd ever seen. Yet this time, she'd taken careful steps to showcase it. Black jeans and a black, long-sleeved bodysuit highlighted every curve and bump of her tall and full figure. Her hair was down, slightly curled at the ends, and lying across one shoulder. Her makeup was light, but impeccable, her lips a cherry red that sent a jolt straight to my cock.

"Julianna," I said on an exhale. The scramble in my brain due to fear had switched to another, more primal feeling.

She grinned, her smile enough to set my cock at full attention. Her gaze was tantalizing and sweet, and I wanted to fall to my knees and worship her.

"Hello, Ranger," she replied coyly, ogling me openly up and down as she held onto the door frame.

My face flushed, my desire rising higher. Many ladies I'd met during my career liked uniforms, and I guess Jules wasn't much different.

"Mel told me to come over, that you needed me?" I mused. I

wanted to grab her and hold her to me. I wanted to smear her lipstick all over my lips as I took her mouth to mine.

Then, later, smear that red lipstick all over my cock...

But I wouldn't make a move until she told me she was okay with it.

"I do need you. Come on."

I followed her into the living room, where a candle was lit on the coffee table and a book she was reading was open beside it. Everything was cozy and warm, like she had settled into the space. I didn't like it, not one bit. She belonged at the farmhouse.

She gestured toward the couch, and I took a seat. She remained standing, looking down at me, her face less pleased and more pensive.

"There's so much I want to say," I started.

"I want to speak, please," she replied. "I will ask you a few things, and I need your honest answers with no elaboration. You can't deviate from my question with your answer. When I'm done, you can say what you want. And don't get up from your seat."

I cocked an eyebrow at her assertiveness. "I'll tell you whatever you want to know. As long as you're where I can see you and talking to me, I'm happy."

She crossed her arms, showcasing her ample breasts. It was everything I could do to meet her eyes as she spoke. I grinned at her interrogative pacing. She was on a mission.

It was hot.

"That day in the hospital, when you said you didn't want me, did you love me then?"

She went straight to the point, no pretenses.

I took a deep breath. "Yes," I said, not taking my eyes from hers, willing everything I had into that one word. "I'm not sure I had the correct word for what I felt since I'd never loved someone before, but yes, I did. I loved you. I wanted only you. That was the worst day of my life."

She nodded, accepting my answer. It took everything I had not to get up when tears started to flow down her perfect face.

"Why did you come back the night of the wreck?"

"You meant more to me than myself. But I acted too late. I constantly think about how things could have been so different if I'd stayed. I'll never really be over it, Julianna. But I want to forgive myself now, if you'll forgive me too."

"Hmmm," she said, her gaze narrowed. "You deviated, but I'll allow it."

A smile played on my lips.

"Why haven't you had a serious girlfriend? Or gotten married? It's been so many years."

"Because I've only wanted one woman—you. No one ever measured up. No one was as beautiful, smart, creative, sweet—"

"You're deviating..." she warned, eyes narrowing and her voice trailing. She paced for a few moments before standing still, facing me, her gaze directly on mine.

"Do you still love me today? Right now?"

"Yes." I didn't need one single second to think about it.

The flush on her neck and the nervous pick of her finger-nails told me I had rattled her with my simplistic reply.

"Why didn't you tell me everything sooner?" she asked, her voice softer.

I scooted to the edge of my seat, thinking she would come toward me, but she didn't. I remembered her rule, and I stayed seated.

"I know I've hurt you throughout your life in so many ways, and I can't say I'm sorry enough. I'll spend the rest of my life being sorry. But I want happiness, and I'll never be happy until I have you. And if you allow me to be with you, I'll do whatever it takes, whatever you want…I can't let you slip through my fingers again.

"I should have told you every day, shown you so many years ago, how much you mean to me. I don't deserve your time, much less your affection. But my God, do I want it. I crave it more than breathing, more than—"

She straddled my lap, leaning us against the couch. Her arms rested on my shoulders. Her lips met mine softly, tentatively. Without hesitation, I curled my arms around her and let my tongue push between the seam of her lips. She was soft and pliable as I pulled her body closer into mine. She moved atop me, the friction quickly becoming unbearable. Our mouths clashed repeatedly, a dance we didn't have to practice. There was nothing to learn, instinct driving every move. Passion dripped from her kiss, and I poured my love into each press of our lips.

I was fully erect when she pulled back, gasping for air. I kept my arms around her, sliding my hands up and down her back. "Bram," she whimpered, and I lost control.

My hands came up to cup her breasts over her bodysuit, kneading them in my hands. Their weight in my palms was perfect. "Stop me now if you don't want this," I murmured clearly, but didn't give her any warning before I jerked down her bodysuit and bra. Her lush breasts spilled out in front of my eyes.

She said nothing, but let her mouth fall open, and her head tilted backward, thrusting her tits closer to my mouth. I was unable to resist them, and I groaned with her as I wrapped my mouth around one of her tight, pinkish-brown nipples. I was a man possessed. I took her into my mouth over and over, licking, sucking, and tugging with my teeth and fingers until she was pressing down harder against my erection.

"That feels so fucking good." She exhaled, and I smirked, letting her breast pop out of my mouth.

"I'm gonna make you feel even better, sweets."

I hadn't called her that in so long, and the endearment seemed to embolden her further. Her hand came between us, resting on the crotch of my pants. She rubbed her palm gently against the impossibly hard bulge, and I looked down in time to see her hand undoing the belt of my uniform.

"Can we move to the bedroom?" I asked, unable to think about our first time together being on a living room couch.

She stopped and stood, fondling her breasts, enjoying every track of my eyes against her movements.

Fuck. Me.

I pressed her along toward Grams' old bedroom, but at the last second, she pulled me into the back bedroom—her old bedroom—the one where she'd written those journal pages that I'd memorized.

The thing I loved most about what she'd written wasn't that she'd elaborated about wanting me to deflower her. I was flattered by that. But my favorite part was the section where she talked about how much she loved my laugh. How she knew I was quiet, but that all the best thinkers were. And how she hated when I made jokes about myself, or when she overheard the girls at school saying I played too hard to get. She'd preferred to believe I wanted quality, not just a nice piece of ass.

She'd been right. It was true then, and it was true now.

I stared at my Julianna, her tits bared to me, her face and neck flushed with our frenzied emotions. "I have to see all of you again," I whispered, letting rough fingers slide over her smooth skin. She shivered a little and nodded her consent as I peeled her jeans down. She was so fucking delectable. I wanted to crawl inside of her and never leave. My hands roved over her waist and trailed down her hips, something I could easily do without awkwardly bending down because she was so tall.

She was my equal, my match, the one worthy of the world

—I'd spend however long I needed to give her everything she ever wanted from me.

CHAPTER TWENTY-FOUR

Julianna | *October 21, 2024*

When I thought about how our reconciliation would go, I hadn't envisioned so much of what happened in the first ten minutes. I'd hoped and prayed he would admit he loved me again, but what guarantee did I have?

Yet I felt the truth of what he said when he touched me. He loved me, and I loved him.

I also hadn't expected to lose control and climb him like a tree. Or expect him to be ready and waiting to receive my affections. I had wanted to drag out our reconciliation as long as I could, making him work for it. That did not happen.

I was a live wire, my senses sharp. I caught the faint pine scent of his cologne, mingling with his sweat. It made me feel feral. I absorbed the sound of our kisses and the exhale of our breaths. The scruff of his beard built friction everywhere his lips touched, and the rough pads of his fingers gripped onto my soft hips, waist, and back.

His muscles flexed as he pulled his uniform shirt and undershirt over his head in a fluid motion, his hands back on me instantly. I began to kiss his chest, tasting the salt of his skin.

"Are you sure about this, Julianna? Your back—"

"I'm fine," I panted. "The doctor said Friday, and as long as I was careful, that sexual activity would be fine."

"I'll be gentle," he assured me, his hand sliding down my side and grabbing my thick buttocks. I'd already unbuckled his belt in the living room, and it took nothing for me to help him out of his pants and boxers.

His cock was pointing out and upwards, thick and proud. There was a bead of precum already, and I watched as he stroked himself in his large, veined hand—once, then twice—sending a wave of want through my body.

He pulled me toward him once again, and I felt his hardness against my softness. It was intoxicating, the dichotomy between our two bodies. This was the part of my sexual experience where, in the past, I freaked out. The expectation of what would occur, what I looked like, and what it would feel like usually began to eclipse the pleasure I sought.

But not now. Not with Bram.

I wanted him more than I'd ever wanted anything else. I wanted him more than I breathed, more than I lived. Our coming together was essential. It couldn't be any other way.

"I wanted to go slow with you, but obviously, I can't," I said, the truth spilling from my lips so he wouldn't have to admit it first. I knew he was following my lead, taking the back seat, and trying to be cautious about how this played out.

That wasn't what I wanted. I needed him to take charge. I wanted him to command me. I needed him to know it was okay.

He sighed a little and smiled, his ridiculously handsome face making my heart flutter. "Thank God, because there is no way for me to slow down now."

He gently laid me on my back and climbed over me so carefully and sensually. I had forgotten how delicious it was to have him on top of me, and even though he was careful not to put his full weight against my still-healing body, the feel of our skin against each other was satisfying.

His hand crept down my side and curled toward the front of us, until it came to the apex of my thighs. He felt around in the slightly trimmed curls until he found what he sought, his skilled fingers touching me reverently.

I arched my back as much as I could comfortably, as a low whimper escaped my lips. I knew he could feel the evidence of my want.

"So slick and ready for me, aren't you?" His voice was husky, dripping with want.

I nodded profusely, unable to speak. He then let out a gravelly laugh. "I'm going to give you what you want. Don't worry, sweets."

I let my hand trail down his chest and squeezed one of his nipples, which elicited a low, enticing growl from his chest.

"Condom?" he breathed out, and I closed my eyes and moaned as his fingers slipped in and out of my tightness, barely penetrating. He knew exactly what to do.

I didn't know whether to be upset or impressed.

"No," I replied between heavy breaths. "I'm on the pill. Are you—"

"I was tested long ago, and I was cleared. I used a condom every time. And I haven't had sex in three years."

I paused, trying to comprehend what he said. It wasn't easy with his talented ministrations. My brain was mush, but still, it rapidly fired questions internally.

Why hadn't he had sex in three years? Who was the last person he had sex with? But this wasn't the time to ask. I had bigger declarations to admit to. I took a deep, shuddering breath. "I've got to tell you something. I've fooled around, but I've never had full intercourse," I said in a small, unsteady voice. "It almost happened once, but I'd started thinking about how this guy didn't care about me, not really, and I freaked out and left."

He froze.

I wanted to cry when his fingers fell away from between my legs, and he sat up on his knees beside my body, looking down at my face. His eyebrows were raised in surprise, his lips slightly open. I was embarrassed, but I resisted the urge to hide my face. I was tired of hiding. And if he were going to make me feel like shit about being a thirty-three-year-old virgin, I would never let it show.

"No one has ever been inside you before?" he asked with such surprise that all I could think about was him bolting, wanting to escape the weight of the confession. I was internally panicking. I sat up slightly and grabbed his forearm as he continued talking. "Are you sure you want it to be me?"

"I want this. I want you. I've always wanted you."

He ran his hand through his hair, blowing a long breath as I held mine.

"I know virginity is a social concept used to advance the patriarchy or whatever, but damn, Julianna. Do you know how possessive I feel right now? To know I'll be the first to be inside your perfect pussy?" He shook his head, a sudden smile playing across his lips, eyes shining.

Something inside me flipped, and I reached up and pulled him down to me again.

"Please, Bram, be my first," I whispered, my tone teasing, and his hooded eyes and his solid cock between my legs gave me all the confirmation I needed that my feigned innocence was a turn-on for him.

He lined up against me, his hard dick meeting my clit. He slid once, twice, and three times over the sensitive spot, making himself wet. My heart raced even faster as his hand went down, exploring me.

I trusted Bram. I wasn't scared he'd do anything I didn't want. But I would be lying if I said the unknown wasn't affecting me. I hid my thoughts as I felt the tip of him breach my opening. He was so thick and hard, but I was drenched and ready to take him. I could feel the stretch and pinch as he began to slip inside.

"We've gotta loosen you up," he encouraged, using his low voice near my ear as a soothing balm. "You've got to relax for me."

I shook my head slightly, panicking a little. "It's too much."

But Bram, who cherished my heart, moved his lips along my face and down my collarbone, leaving a trail of hot kisses in his wake. I was beginning to fall into the sensations when he moved inside me another inch. "Do not worry. You can take me. You were made for me, sweets."

I felt a stronger pinch between my legs, but I gave in to his ministrations, encouraged by his words. I realized this first time wasn't going so bad, but other fears crowded my mind.

"How can I help? Am I doing this right? Do I feel good for you? I just—"

"The first time I wanted you, I was sixteen," he interrupted, looking down into my eyes. "You were wearing white jean shorts and one of those tie-dyed T-shirts, carrying a stack of textbooks." He made a little progress inside me, ever so slightly, and I didn't fight it, letting his words and voice soothe me into submission. "I'd never noticed your body like I did that day. It was the way your thighs moved when you walked, the way your breasts filled out that t-shirt. I got hard right there in the living room, just watching you move." He pushed in a little more, and it hurt a little, so I squeezed my eyes shut. He smoothed my dampening hair away from my face, putting his forehead to mine, his hips thrusting slightly. "You were so fucking beautiful with your long, dark hair and perfect smile." I opened my eyes to see him watching my face like I was a treasure. "You were like some ethereal being I couldn't touch, but I wanted to so much. Like forbidden fruit."

He moved in a little more. I clung to him, urging him on.

"When I read how much you wanted me in those journal pages, I knew I would never be the same. I would never be satisfied until I had you." Bram suddenly thrust inside me to the hilt. He kissed me hard, silencing my gasp, and I melted into him.

He pulled back slightly and looked down at me, a bit of worry etched in his features.

"I'm fine," I breathed out, reassuring him with a little grin.

He nodded, his teeth gritting together. Was this painful for him? I watched as sweat beaded on his forehead.

"Are you okay?" I whispered.

He waited a few seconds before speaking. "I'm trying to let you acclimate to me," he explained, his words clipped.

I bit my lip. "Do I feel…"

"Amazing. So fucking incredible. I can't…I'm so sorry. I've got to move, love."

I nodded, the initial, uncomfortable pinch subsiding, and I watched with awe as he slowly slid in and out of me. Each movement was slicker and more manageable, and the friction between us increased, creating a delicious wave of need inside my body. I homed in on how my muscles were taking him in so effortlessly, until everything felt like it wasn't working against us anymore.

The satisfaction on his face made me feel empowered. His movements were still steady, but were growing increasingly desperate. "Julianna, you're so tight. You feel so fucking good," he moaned.

I preened under his praise. Something sparked inside me, and he must have caught on to what his words did to me because he didn't stop. "You're perfect." He kissed my neck, then buried his head in my shoulder. "I knew it would be perfect. To know I almost missed you…"

Tears gathered in my eyes.

We'd almost missed this.

I didn't want anyone else to have this part of me. I had wanted it to be him, and I wanted it only ever to be him.

"Only ever you, I promise," I whispered, even if the words didn't make sense to him. He didn't question, but kissed my neck as his movements picked up speed.

I moved right along with him. I lifted my hips slightly, digging my fingers into his back and feeling his muscles tighten as he worked harder. His face moved to meet mine, and our heavy breaths mingled, our lips millimeters away from each other. I could hear the obscene sounds our bodies made with every thrust, and I drowned in the view I had of watching this beautiful man unravel above me.

"Holy—" I gasped, unable to finish my expression, feeling something new running through my body. I'd had many self-induced orgasms in my life, so I knew this was the beginning of my body building up for it.

Yet he was so far ahead of me, his movements erratic.

"Julianna, I can't—" he pleaded.

"Don't stop, please don't stop," I insisted, clinging to him, my nails digging into his shoulders and his back. "I want you to come. I love you, Bram."

When I saw the pure joy spark in his eyes, I remembered I hadn't said the words aloud yet. He moved with renewed vigor, and as a specific spot within my walls was repeatedly pressed, I threw my head back in ecstasy.

His fingers came between our bodies, circling and pressing my clit precisely how I needed it. He kept moving in and out despite his desperation, so determined for me to have my pleasure.

"I'm coming," I whimpered, unable to stop the cresting

wave that suddenly overtook me. I felt so full, and his hand came up to rest reverently on the side of my neck as I went over the edge. A thousand sensations flowed through me. Music, like magical, glorious beings, rang in my ears until his deep voice cut through.

"I love you. I love you," he whispered, bending down to my ear and repeating the words over and over. He was pushing into me with renewed vigor. My whole world narrowed to him as he fell over the edge. It was the most beautiful sight I'd ever seen, more intense than I'd ever imagined. His muscles strained, and I felt his cum pump deep into me.

I enjoyed every second of his release. He stayed inside of me, looking down into my eyes. I could not keep the smile off my face, and Bram looked happier than I'd ever seen him.

"That was amazing," I declared after we'd caught our breaths, and he chuckled softly.

"*You're* amazing," he replied in his deep voice. "I want to live here, I don't want to pull out."

"Then don't." I moved my hips, caging him in with my legs.

"If only my refractory time matched my desire." He laughed.

I released him and watched as he removed himself. I felt the stickiness of his release drip onto my inner thighs. I went to move, but his hand on my pelvis steadied me. I watched in surprise as he took his fingers and gently gathered up his release and slid those same fingers back into my tightness. I groaned.

"Are you okay? Your back?" he asked.

I nodded.

"And your pussy?"

I nodded again, smiling, but unable to speak. He smiled back. "I want a part of me inside you, even when I can't be. I can't get over how perfect this is." My heart melted at his possessive honesty. I'd never felt more seen. More wanted.

He gently turned us over so we could face each other.

"Are you sure your back is okay? Did I—"

I interrupted. "I am perfect."

"I can't believe I'm the one who got to be inside you for the first time." He nestled my body into him, and I melted into his bare skin. "I never thought that would be the case in all my fantasies about us."

"You had fantasies about us?"

He caressed my arm. "Oh yeah. I couldn't forget these thighs." He put his hand down to caress my thigh and then moved to my exposed cheek. "Or your ass. The number of times I've thought about taking you from the back is criminal. There's so much I will show you if you let me." I felt a blush creep up my face.

"It's quite embarrassing, really," I replied, burying my face into his shoulder. "What thirty-three-year-old has never had intercourse before?"

"One who knew what she wanted," he said, kissing my head. "I love you. To think we could have had this for so many years—"

I put my finger against his lips. "Please stop. I don't need you to keep saying that. I need you to show me that you won't—"

"Never again," he interrupted, running a hand through my hair. He cradled my head in his large hand and looked directly into my eyes. "Never, ever again, Julianna Joy."

CHAPTER TWENTY-FIVE

Bram | *October 21, 2024*

W e stayed in bed for three more hours, naked and talking—well, talking sometimes...

I discovered that one of Julianna's many talents was giving a killer blow job. It made me want to murder anyone who'd ever touched her to know she had the practice to be that good, but unashamedly, I was more than willing to reap the benefits. I watched her work as I pressed into her mouth, her lips stretched over most of me, her red lips smudged. I'd feared my decreased libido over the last couple of years had been a byproduct of aging, but with Julianna, I was insatiable. Just the sight of her sucking my cock and the feel of her fingers on my balls was enough to bring me to the edge.

I told her I was about to come in case she didn't want to swallow my release. But she looked up at me, and the desire I saw in her eyes was intoxicating. Her hands tightened around the base of my cock. It took nothing but a suck and a slight gag from her to make me explode.

When we were both collected, I pulled her up toward me, nestling her into my shoulder again. "Do you need a drink?" I asked, and she shook her head.

"No, it went down perfectly." She laughed. "Maybe in a bit. Hold me first."

I did as she asked.

"I wonder who gives oral better? You or me?" she teased, resting her hand on my chest. I took her hand in my own and squeezed it. I wished for a world where we could measure that and take bets. I considered myself a confident, skilled lover, but Julianna was the dark horse in that race. I would bet on her every single time.

"I think we should practice until we figure it out," I said with a smirk and a wink. She laughed.

"I think before we do that, I will have to have that drink," she replied. "And probably a shower."

I stroked her soft skin near her collarbone. "Is it strange that I like the thought of my cum still between your legs?"

"I didn't know you were so possessive," she replied, shivering with my gentle caress.

"I am when it comes to you. Is that a turn-off for you?" I'd always played a little dominant in the bedroom, but I knew I would do whatever she was comfortable with and be content.

"Quite the opposite," she replied, a blush coloring her cheeks. She was so easily turned upside down. "I like it. I like being taken care of and wanted. Regardless, I already knew this about you anyway."

"What? How?"

"You ooze confidence, Dracula." She giggled.

I couldn't keep the smile off my face at her gentle teasing.

"Has your dad contacted you again?" she asked, steering the subject toward more serious topics.

With anyone else, this would have been the point where I deflected, where I did anything to stop from exposing my true feelings. She might have hated to make herself physically vulnerable, but for me, it was the emotional vulnerability that did not come naturally.

But it was different with Julianna and slightly different with Mel. I trusted them both explicitly.

"No, he's not contacted me, and I don't expect him to. I don't want him to. The money is a done deal. I made all the necessary phone calls. I sent in the marriage documents, and the money is set for transfer in installments. He knew he couldn't stop it. He just wanted to come and try to hurt me," I replied in one breath. "It's what he does. Everyone always says that your kin is your kin, and no matter what they do, you have to respect your blood, but that's bullshit. I can't function with my dad. It took me a long time with professional help to realize I didn't have to put up with him, that I could separate myself, and it wasn't shameful."

She seemed to mull this over. "I'm so happy you got help, Bram. It says so much about you. What about your mom?"

I shrugged. "I don't know how to feel. I tried to get her to leave so many times, but she refused. She always said I was overreacting. She was never there for me growing up, either, with all the drinking. What do you do when someone wants to stay in that life?"

"I'm sorry it's like this with them," she whispered, now caressing my upper arm with her soft fingertips. "Grams never wanted you to hate them. But she wanted to make sure you were loved like you deserved."

"And she did. She showed me what family was. You all did."

"Too close to the sister thing…" She scrunched her face, and I chuckled.

"Believe me, the last thing I thought when looking at you

was that I wanted to be your brother," I assured her, kissing her forehead, unable to stop the frequency with which I was doing it. "I won't keep saying it, but it kills me how different our lives would have been if I'd been honest with everyone from the beginning, including you. I'm sorry for all the wasted years, Jules." I meant it with everything I had.

She sat up and put one hand on the other side of me to steady herself, and gently stroked my trimmed beard. "They weren't wasted," she said, looking into my eyes, and I fell into her deep irises. "I've been looking at it all wrong. We were waiting. Because this, right here, is perfection."

"There's the romantic I knew back in high school." I caught her hand and kissed it reverently.

She pushed some of her hair out of her face. It was wild and beautiful, and I suddenly wanted to be inside her again.

I'll never have enough of her.

"I haven't talked to Whit since you left the house," I said. "It's not unusual during the season, but he'd been checking up every day until you left. I haven't heard from him and don't know what happened."

"About that," she said sheepishly. "I talked to him. We discussed things. I confronted him about his behavior after Grams died."

I sat up and scooted back against the headboard, unable to do anything more than pull her into me, where she snuggled.

"How did it go? What did he say?"

She became misty-eyed as she recounted their conversation.

"I love that for you, sweets," I replied, kissing her twice. "New beginnings all around for us. I think Grams would be proud."

"I think so, too."

"Whit is going to hate me once I tell him about the wreck."

As strongly as I felt about protecting the woman in my arms, Whit felt the same. When he found out what I'd kept from him, it would be hard to get him to understand that Julianna had done it for him and that I had, too. I had a hunch he would only hear the part about me lying to him for fifteen years.

"Even if he forgets himself in the moment, he will forgive you eventually, Bram. I'll make sure of it. We have to get the band back together, as Grams would say, and I will make it happen."

I pulled her down to me and kissed her deeply.

"How will we pass the time tonight, wife?" I asked in a low voice. Her breathing hitched at my words, her eyes glazed over, and she leaned toward me.

"Take me home, Bram."

I froze.

"Shit. Melanie is staying with me. Her apartment sold, so she's moved in for a while."

"She told me when she called," Jules said. "I'd forgotten. That's okay. If you don't want me to see her right now, it's okay."

"How did you talk to her anyway? How'd she have your number?"

She shrugged, but with a coy look that made me laugh.

I grabbed her, gently pulling her directly onto me until her head rested on my shoulder, where I settled my arm around her.

"I can't think of anything better than having my three favorite girls under one roof." I smiled, meaning it with my whole heart. "You will love Mel once you know her better. She's opinionated, but she means well."

"She and Whit would get along famously." She laughed. "Do they know each other?"

"No," I replied, thinking about it a moment. "They've never met."

"Hmm. Maybe a good idea?" She smiled slyly.

I shook my head. "Whit and Mel in the same room? Not a good idea. I'm not sure the world could contain it."

"We'll come back for everything else later," I said definitively, closing the front door.

"We'll see," Julianna replied, echoing how I treated her the last time I insisted she was coming home with me. I swatted her butt as she walked toward the truck.

The drive to the farmhouse was smooth. The weather was still lovely in the early evening, and the sun was setting right behind the mountain tops.

"We've seen so many sunsets together," she remarked, and I reached over and squeezed her thigh, resting my hand across the console. I was holding onto her like I'd always wanted to, satisfaction engulfing me.

"I won't be happy until we've seen as many sunsets together as we have apart."

She didn't reply, but I didn't miss the smile that blossomed across her face.

"So, should I call your sister Mel or Melanie? Any topics I should avoid?"

"Just be yourself, you're perfect. I didn't mean to make her sound intimidating earlier. Besides, I've hyped you up so much. She already loves you."

"Does she know about everything? The marriage and all that?"

I nodded. "Yeah. She knows it all, including the wreck. I've been pretty open with her."

"Okay. I didn't want to slip up and say something that would surprise anyone."

That didn't sit right with me. It was true that I married her for her convenience and as a form of penance, but it was so much more than that. It always was.

We were so much more than that.

"You can say and do whatever you want. Always." I squeezed her thigh again. "Mel is not a bullshitter. I like that about her."

"Like Grams?" Julianna asked, and I nodded.

"Mel had a hard upbringing. She was pretty much without family until she found me."

"Does it bother you that she existed for so long and you didn't know?"

I took a deep breath. "Yeah. I try not to feel guilty that I lived luxuriously while she was in a shack in the woods."

Julianna's face fell. "You shouldn't, you didn't know. Your life was bad enough and the only one you experienced. You've got to find a way to quit bearing the burdens of other people's circumstances."

I knew what she was saying was true, but I found it hard to accept.

"I never asked you how you got to Grams' house the night we split. You didn't take the Jeep."

She blanched a little, and I narrowed my eyes, going back and forth between her expression and the road.

"I...called Hunter to come get me."

Jealousy swept over me, my muscles stiffening in protest.

"Julianna Joy. You did not."

She flinched a little but then cracked a wide, teasing smile.

"You could have gotten yourself fucking killed," I grumbled, deciding to embrace the anger for a moment.

She squeezed my hand. "You'd have found my body," she soothed, her voice as sweet as honey, shoving off my admonishment. "I'd already been out with him before. He was a perfect gentleman. I thrived under his tutelage."

I raised my eyebrow and watched as her smile widened. She

was toying with me, and I could play this game all night for the rest of my life if it kept her smiling like that.

"I feel like you might need to be punished for a decision like that, sweets."

"Mmm. Make it a good one, please. Don't bore me." She flipped her long hair over her shoulder.

"Deal," I replied.

Lakey met us in the lane leading to the house, which meant Mel was outside. I'd texted her before we left Grams' house, letting her know we were on our way together. She said she'd make herself scarce, but I explained it was time for them to get to know each other and asked her to stay.

Lakey jumped on Julianna, and their love reunion was more heart-tugging than expected. They'd grown so close in just a few weeks.

"My girl," Julianna cooed, scratching Lakey with vigor. Lakey soaked up every stroke, raining kisses down on Julianna at every turn.

Mel exited the garage side door, wiping her hands on a cloth, her clothes covered in spray paint.

"Hey, bro," she said. She stepped into the floodlight from the garage so we could see each other. She looked out at Lakey and Julianna. "Looks like that discussion went well."

I arched an eyebrow at her. "We discussed...a lot."

"I'm sure you did," she replied, rolling her eyes. She stepped forward, and Mel and Julianna exchanged bright greetings.

"I can't hug you because I have paint—"

Julianna pulled my sister into a tight embrace anyway. I stood back, watching Lakey circling them.

"I can't wait to hear all your stories about young Bram,"

Mel said, finally looking my way. "And I'll tell you all the stories about this love-lorn fool. He's been pining for you since I met him."

Julianna blushed, looking back at me, and I shook my head with a smile I could not contain.

This was happiness. This was bliss. How could life ever get any better?

Chapter Twenty-Six

Julianna | *October 21, 2024*

Melanie had taken it upon herself to fix dinner before we arrived, and I was beyond grateful. She roasted a chicken with a pan of vegetables and made an excellent chopped salad that I could not stop gushing over.

"You're amazing," I praised, putting my napkin on the table.

She smiled, picking up a piece of chicken with her fork and putting it in her mouth.

"I love cooking," she replied after chewing. "And it's the least I can do with Bram letting me bunk here. But now that you two are back together, I will be moving out quickly."

"You can stay as long as you want," Bram and I said simultaneously.

Melanie laughed. "I don't think anyone in their right mind wants to share a house with newlyweds. So excuse me if I make myself scarce."

I blushed and felt Bram's hand slide over mine on the table.

Did our declaration of love make our marriage legitimate? Neither of us had said the words out loud.

"You should stay in Whit's house," I said, the thought popping up suddenly in my mind and out of my mouth just as fast. "It's fully furnished, and it's closer to work."

Melanie startled. "I don't want to put anyone out."

"You won't," Bram assured her. "Julianna doesn't need it now."

"Is this your official offer for us to live together, Bram Winchester?" I feigned shock.

He frowned at my theatrics. "We're fucking married."

I put an arm around my stomach. "So presumptuous."

He rolled his eyes, which made Melanie laugh.

"Yeah, be respectful, Dracula," Melanie guffawed, her loose, long mane of straw colored hair swishing behind her.

"I don't like all this teaming up against me. This needs to stop."

His ire made Mel and me laugh even harder.

The conversation and alcohol flowed easily. Bram opted for beer while Mel and I tackled a bottle of wine. It was our little celebration of our new family coming together.

I appreciated the ease with which Melanie accepted me, especially when I was prone to being quieter and more self-protective. Her confidence didn't make me feel stifled, and she wasn't pushy in her questions about my back or the story of Bram's and my shared past. She listened well, and there were many moments in conversation when she reminded me so much of her brother. Before I knew it, our bottle of wine was gone.

Melanie stood and gave a large stretch. "I'll put my earbuds in, so I don't have to listen to a symphony of copulating," she said with an eyebrow wiggle to Bram, who threw a pillow on the couch at her.

"Are you sure you don't want to listen?" I joked, taking her wineglass from her as she got to her feet.

"Now that you mention it—"

"Stop!" Bram yelled, and Mel and I fell into exuberant fits of wine-tinged laughter.

"Goodnight!" She made her way up the stairs, Lakey on her heels.

"I think I lost my dog," I whined, lifting my wineglass off the side table and taking it with Melanie's into the kitchen. Bram came up behind me with his empty beer cans.

"She'll come back around. Her three favorite people are all under one roof. She's probably confused about where to land." He chuckled, stretching after throwing the cans in the trash. "I'm so damn tired." He yawned, full and deep, as I put the glasses into the dishwasher and closed the door.

"Oh, I forgot to tell you," Bram said, leaning against the counter. "I put in an offer on a few acres of land right outside the city limits. The realtor called this morning and said it's been accepted. We'll break ground in a month for the community center. Once I can get everything back into place."

"That's great news!" I exclaimed, grabbing onto his arm. "I can't wait to see it."

"I'll take you out there tomorrow," he replied, and put his hand over mine.

I had Bram. He loved me. We were married, and I was home.

I turned around and let my hand fall as tears spilled onto my cheeks. His face fell when he saw them, and he rushed to pull me into his embrace.

"Hey. What's wrong, sweets?"

"It's the wine." I sniffled into his solid shoulder, then pulled back to meet his eyes. "It's making me sentimental. I lost my job and don't have another one yet. I no longer have a car. My best friend is three hours away. My back is still healing. All of that, yet I'm so happy that I could burst." I pointed at my face. "And I guess I did."

He kissed my forehead and gently rubbed my back, his strong arms holding me tightly and expertly.

"Have I told you how happy I am? How much I love you?" His words were low and quiet, meant only for me. I pulled back to look up into his eyes.

"I still can't believe we're married," I said. "I'm a little nervous about this whole thing. I know it's for the insurance and your inheritance, but I..."

"I want it to be real," he said, pressing his forehead to mine, his hands dropping to grip my hips. His lips lined up with mine, and he spoke sensually against them, "Say it's real, Julianna."

"This is real," I whispered, letting the tears fall from my eyes without wiping them. "But my life isn't easy. I don't know what the future looks like yet. And with my back, I don't know what it means for kids, for my abilities..."

"It means we'll have each other and weather every problem and decision together. I can live without many things, but I will never trade you for anything." He ran his hand lovingly through my loose hair.

"I feel the same." I sniffled.

He kissed me, slow and deep, so sensually that I felt the tingling of want in every nerve of my body. Finally, he stepped back and took my hand.

"Come on. Let me show you how a husband makes love to his wife."

We walked up the stairs, and instead of leaving the door open as he had every other time, he shut it. I was surprised to find myself nervous as we faced each other in the dimly lit room. Although I was comfortable with Bram and his space, I hadn't fully been integrated into his bedroom yet. It still felt like *his*, but I was sure that would change with time.

"What's going on in that head of yours?" Bram asked. He read me so easily.

"I was thinking that it still feels like I'm sleeping over at a boyfriend's house." I giggled but sobered before speaking again. "Are you sure you want me moving into your space, Bram? I—"

"I bought this house because of you."

I froze and stared blankly at him.

"What?"

"Whit told me you loved it, so I bought it. I didn't care if the house was falling apart or if I had to fly out of state to get the papers signed. I wanted it, and fell for it, because you loved it."

"That's crazy," I said, trying to be practical, but my heart raced. He'd bought all this and fixed up this whole place because of me?

He shrugged, rubbing the back of his neck nervously. "In my mind, I couldn't be with you, so I got closer to you in any way I could. It was half-grown up with weeds and seed trees, but I kept every notch of character I could. Every paint color, the floor stain, the restored interior doors, that vintage wood-work on the banister of the stairs...all of it was for you. It kept me going. It kept you close. Knowing I was bringing something you cherished to life. I didn't know if you'd ever see it, but I hoped. Somewhere deep down inside me, I always hoped."

He took two steps toward me.

"I know it's a little weird, but I held onto the memory of you so tight. I vowed to move on so many times. I dated, I tried, but every time, I came home at night alone. I realized I could never have another woman in this house. She would be taking your place, and that would be wrong."

He looked around the room. "I thought I might sell it after a year or two of living here. I don't know. Maybe I would have. Maybe if I'd found out you'd moved on. But here we are now. This is your home, as much as it ever was mine."

Our lips met again, and the spark between us ignited into an inferno. Clothes were shed, and I lost my ability to think when he had me lie down on the bed. Bram used his tongue and lips to devour every inch of my skin until I was a blazing fury. He looked up from his ministrations.

"Please, Bram," I gasped as he kissed so close to my center. I thought I might die if he didn't touch where I needed him to.

"Wait," he breathed, and jumped up. My mouth was agape as I watched him pick up his work trousers from the floor, which he'd worn all night. He dug around in the pocket and pulled out my wedding band. He held it up so I could see what he had.

"I've had this in my pocket every day since you left," he said.

He leaned over my body and took my hand in his. He slipped the ring back onto the proper finger, then he intertwined my hand with his own. The moment was so emotionally charged that I could feel the tears forming again in my eyes.

"Worship me," I whispered boldly.

He grinned. "Yes, ma'am," he replied, leaning down between my legs where he'd been.

Chapter Twenty-Seven

Julianna | *October 28, 2024*

I pressed send with a smile on my face.

> Me: The doctor's office called and the rescans of my back came back perfect.

> Bram: Damn. Why are you always an overachiever? ;)

> Me: The PA put in a good word for me...

> Bram: I hate him. Give me his number.

> Me: No way. I've got to keep a backup in case you aren't up to the task. Someone has to take care of me.

Bram: He can have you if he can get
through me.

Shivers ran through my body.

Me: Message received, sir.

Bram: That's my good girl.

I giggled like I was in high school at his possessive reply and looked out over the yard, watching the leaves fall from the oaks and Lakey dancing around, sniffing everything she could get her nose on.

I had my interview for the social media marketer position and was officially offered a remote work opportunity with them in December. Meanwhile, I utilized some of my skills to assist with MCA activities, including creating promotional materials for the new community center. Melanie and I were becoming fast friends. Bram and I had been learning all the little things about each other that we'd missed over the years. I even found myself closer to finishing the draft of my fantasy novel than ever before.

Most of all, I had a family again, a feeling I was afraid I'd never regain after Grams died. Whit was coming to visit during his off week from football and was due to arrive any time. My gratitude for where I was swelled into joy, and when Bram pulled up from work at four, I was a mess of tears.

"What's all this, sweets?" he asked, pointing to my face before he folded me into his arms.

"Happy tears," I replied with a laugh. I led him into the house and made him sit down at the kitchen table. I poured him a glass of apple juice, a favorite of his, and nudged the cookie jar toward him.

"Why are you trying to ruin my diet every day?" he asked, pulling the lid off the jar and grabbing a couple.

I opened the dishwasher and began placing the clean dishes in their designated spots. I could feel him checking me out, his gaze heated and intense on my body every time I stole a glance his way. I couldn't be more pleased with his reaction, but I tried to hide it.

"If you stare any longer, your eyes will dry out," I teased, turning around with plates in my hands.

He smiled. "Worth it. You shouldn't be doing so much."

I rolled my eyes. "I'm fine. And I hardly think putting up dishes will break me, Dracula."

He got up from his chair and strode to me. He took the dishes from me and set them on the open shelf in a neat stack. Then he turned and encircled his hands around me, his hands kneading my glutes through my black leggings. He brought his face to mine, our lips a hairbreadth from each other.

"Later, after I rest, I'm going to bend you over and fuck you right here in this kitchen."

His voice sent shivers down my body.

"Why wait?" I asked as sensually as possible.

Just as he kissed me, his phone began buzzing. With an eye roll of annoyance, he picked it up on speaker. "What's up, Mel?"

I expected her usual banter, but instead I only heard heavy breathing.

"You need to listen to me and listen well. What I'm getting ready to say won't make much sense, but you're going to have to trust me, okay?"

I looked at Bram, who looked just as confused as I felt.

"What's going on?" he asked.

"Whitaker East is headed to your house. He'll be there any minute..."

Gravel crunched in the distance, slinging from fast-moving

tires. Bram grabbed the phone, and we rushed out the back door and around the side of the house, standing near the garage. A dark SUV was coming full speed down the lane.

"Bram. He knows you were the one driving. The night of the wreck. He knows you were the one driving the truck."

Bram's eyes went wide.

"What? How?" he said, bewildered, and I grabbed his phone.

"Hey, Mel, it's Julianna. Whit is…making an appearance. We'll call you back."

"Julianna, he's so angry. I didn't understand. I didn't put it together in time. I can't believe I didn't put it together!"

"Wait, what?" It was all I could say. How did Mel know anything about Whit?

"I'm headed that way. I'll be there in about twenty minutes." The line went dead.

I clutched Bram's phone as he stood in front of the squealing tires of the SUV, barely avoiding being hit as Whit skidded to a halt.

"Bram! Run!" I cried as the driver's door swung open. My brother, whom I hadn't seen in person in a couple of years, jumped out of the vehicle like a wild animal.

"No," Bram said to me calmly.

I tried to protest, but my eyes locked on Whit.

"Don't!" I screamed at my brother, running toward them, but Bram grabbed my arm and moved me behind him.

"Get in the house," he said firmly. I took two steps back to escape the anger I saw on my brother's face. I couldn't stand the intensity.

"You fucker!" It was the only thing Whit got out before he punched Bram in the face.

Bram didn't retaliate, just stumbled backward and fell over into the grass.

Whit immediately jumped on top of Bram. I cried out when

the second punch cracked against Bram's face. I knew there wasn't anything I could do to stop what was happening. Besides the risk to my back, they were too strong for me to wrangle.

"Whit. Please, *please*. I'm begging you to stop!" I yelled, rushing toward them.

Whit turned suddenly and knocked his arm straight into my torso. Although I tried to catch myself, I fell and landed backward on the dirt. The impact made my teeth chatter. Pain radiated down through my legs.

Bram heard the moan that came from deep in my throat and saw me hit the ground.

A switch flipped at the sight of me, and he unleashed his fury on Whit. He punched Whit once, then twice, and fought his way to his feet. At the first opening, he dodged, leaving Whit tumbling to the ground.

Bram gathered me in his arms and set me up.

"Can you stand?" he asked frantically, his hands coming to either side of my head to hold it steady. I nodded.

"I think so. It hurts, though. I'm going to need help getting up."

Mistaking my meaning, he lifted me off the ground and into his arms, running off pure adrenaline.

Whit stood back, wiping blood from his nose, huffing for breath.

"Julianna. Oh my God, I'm so sorry—"

"What the fuck is wrong with you?" Bram boomed at his best friend. Whit didn't respond but hurried ahead to open the screen door for us to get into the house.

Bram gently deposited me on the couch, and I began trying to move my arms and legs. Everything was working still, but the shooting pain through my left leg was excruciating.

"Sweets," Bram soothed, running a hand down my head,

"tell me what you need." His face was smeared with blood and swelling and puffing up before my very eyes.

Whit had attacked him because of me.

I let out a loud breath. "Heating pad. Water. Half a muscle relaxer. That should do it. But please, take care of yourself first."

"I will clean up after you have what you need." He kissed me on the top of the head as he got up. Whit stood by the fireplace, watching us with his jaw set in a hard line. I couldn't think of one time when Bram and I had touched each other in front of him.

"I'll be right back," Bram told me in his soothing, low tone. He turned and snapped at Whit, "Do not touch her. Your problem is with me and me alone, got it?"

"I'm not going to hurt my sister, idiot."

"Funny, because you just did."

Whit's face went pale, but instead of protesting, he nodded without further comment.

Bram hurried up the stairs to get my things, and I looked at Whit and tried for a moment to compartmentalize my physical and emotional pain.

"Feel better?" I asked sarcastically.

"I did, until I hurt *you*," he replied, unable to look me in the face. "I happened upon the fact that Bram was the one who wrecked the truck the night Grams died. The asshole never told me that, and neither did you."

I rolled my eyes. "*Happened* upon it? How do you happen upon something like that? And I'm still not sure why you thought squealing your tires and beating your best friend to a pulp was going to make a fifteen-year-old decision avenged."

He sighed. "I know. I'm sorry. I lost it." He ran his hand through his hair. It was a gesture that mirrored Bram's when he was nervous, and the irony of their shared nervous twitches wasn't lost on me. "I'm so sorry—" He stepped toward me as Bram rounded the corner.

"One more step, and I will have you on your ass so fast…"

"Bram, no," I scolded. All of us stopped as another vehicle was making its way up the drive.

"Jesus, what now?" Bram muttered, but I knew it was Mel. After a few uncomfortable, quiet moments, she appeared through the front door, her expression somber and sheepish.

"Hey, guys," she said cooly, as if she hadn't just come barreling into the room. "What's going on in here?"

I tried to imagine how we looked: Whit bleeding from his nose, Bram's dirty and bloody face swelling, and me sprawled out on the couch, barely moving.

"You missed the fight of a century," I quipped.

Her mouth opened and closed like a fish, and Bram handed me water and my pill, then he looked at his sister. "Whit attacked me, and he accidentally pushed Julianna. She fell and now she's hurt."

Melanie's head whipped to Whit, who didn't look her in the eye. He was acting like she wasn't even in the room. She hauled off and started hitting him with closed fists wherever she could make contact. Her efforts were moot on his strong body, but it was entertaining to watch.

"Hey!" He made several grunts and emitted curses as he tried to dodge her hits. She stopped after a few jabs, but sharpened her eyes at him.

"You should have told me you were Julianna's brother!" Melanie exclaimed.

Bram and I looked at each other.

Before we could say a word, Melanie grabbed Whit's hand. "You're coming with me." They left, and a few moments later, the forceful slamming of a door upstairs made me jump.

"What the hell was all that?" Bram ran a hand over his beard scruff.

"I don't know, but we'll figure it out as soon as you're cleaned up." I put a hand to his blood-smeared face. "This must hurt. You need some antiseptic."

He winced like he remembered that my brother had gotten some formidable hits on him.

"I'll get myself cleaned up. It's fine. I've had my share of fights in my time, but it's been a few years. I forgot how much getting punched hurts. It will be fun to explain at MCA this week." He chuckled at that. "I'll be back in a minute. Stay right here."

My heart fell. "I wish I could help you. I've always wanted to clean up my boyfriend after he fought over me." I stuck my lip out in sadness.

He shook his head, then bent to kiss me on the bridge of my nose.

"No, stay still. I'm a grown man. I can handle it. I'll be back in a second." He plugged in the heating pad and handed it to me, then grabbed the throw from the back of the adjacent chair and spread it over me.

"Something is going on with that," he grumbled, pointing to the ceiling. We could hear mumbled voices, but they were too low to make out the words.

"We'll figure them out," I replied, unable to keep the smile off my face. "You know they've probably slept together, right?"

"Fuck me," he muttered, rolling his eyes.

Chapter Twenty-Eight

Bram | *October 28, 2024*

There were a lot of things I regretted in my life—the arrogance of my youth. I didn't tell Grams what she meant to me before she was gone. Driving buzzed with Julianna in the truck. I didn't have the bravery to break things off with my parents sooner. Hurting Julianna worse when she was already mourning and unsteady. I didn't go after her when I should have. The list went on and on.

Yet, I couldn't help but think that another one on my long list of worst regrets was never telling Whit what he meant to me.

Over our twenty years of friendship, I'd never expressed what he'd done for my life. It was past due. What was a better time than after beating each other up?

We'd talk as soon as I could get him away from my sister.

My blood boiled at the thought of them, even though I knew I had no leg to stand on. Julianna was Whit's sister, and

Mel was mine. It was ironic, and I couldn't keep the laughing scoff from coming out as I stood over the large basin sink in the downstairs bathroom, using a wet cloth to wipe the blood off my face.

I took in the damage. The knot below my left eye swelled up fiercely, but that was the worst injury. There were a couple of gashes on my forehead and one on my collarbone, but they were easily cleaned and no longer bleeding.

Worse than the damage to my face was what Whit had done to my body. I wasn't a young buck anymore. I'd felt every punch, push, and kick he administered. Welts and knots formed along my torso, and I winced as I gingerly skated fingertips over my sides.

I hadn't fought back because I deserved every punch I got. But when Julianna went down, I was blinded by rage.

I didn't regret fighting back then. No one would hurt Julianna, accidentally or otherwise, and not have to answer to me—ever.

I had a few clothes in the dryer that hadn't been retrieved yet, so I changed into clean jeans and a black t-shirt and went to the kitchen, grabbing another bottle of water for Julianna and a beer for myself. I sauntered back into the living room threshold in time to see Mel and Whit emerge from around the corner of the stairs.

"Oh, there you are," I quipped, unable to stop the passive aggressiveness from spilling over. Julianna was sitting on the couch. She reached over and gently swatted my stomach in reprimand. I took a long draw from my beer, eyeing both my best friend and my sister with piercing aggression.

The look wasn't working very well. They both stared back at me with relaxed postures and bored stares. Whit was cleaned up, yet some blood and scuffs still stained his shirt. Julianna seemed to be assessing him hard, and I wondered what they'd said to each other while I had been out of the room gathering her things earlier.

"Explain how you two know each other," I said between draws from my beer bottle.

Melanie rolled her eyes. "I'm not sure how that's any of your—"

"Picked her up on the side of the road last night," Whit said, meeting my gaze.

The implications of his statement, combined with the nonchalance of his tone, made me even more annoyed.

"You like knowing how it feels, Bram?" The smile on Whit's face made it extra punchable, and I took two steps toward him before Julianna spoke.

"Bram, no. Whit, stop." Before I could get to her, Mel was already reaching over, taking Julianna's hand and arm, and helping her stand. "Melanie, help me to the restroom."

"We're going to be back in five minutes, and don't you dare throw a single punch while we're gone. Talk like friends who love their sisters." Her voice held warning and meaning. "But also realize that those sisters are fully grown adults and make their own decisions." And with that, I watched as Melanie led the love of my life out of the room.

Whit and I stared at each other.

"That was a crazy way to see each other for the first time in six months," I remarked, my words laced with more sarcasm.

It broke the ice, and he laughed a little. "I guess so."

"How'd you get here?"

"Well, I took a car to the airport," he replied, "then I took a plane."

"Smartass," I murmured.

He smirked.

"It's our bye week," he explained. "I had to see Jules, so I came earlier than I'd said I was going to. I wanted as much time as possible."

"Trying to make up for lost time... I get it." I was the one who sounded like a smart ass now, but I couldn't help it. I'd hurt her, but so had he in his own way. I was jealous of how easily he seemed to reconcile that fact.

His feet shuffled a little. "I expected to see you. But then I got tangled up with your sister, who I didn't know was your sister. I swear it."

"You knew I had a sister, and I'm pretty sure you knew her name was Melanie..." I couldn't keep the venomous sarcasm out of my voice. Whit was a notorious player, on and off the field, and Melanie didn't roll like that. Or so I'd thought.

"She used a fake name," he explained, running his hands over his face. That didn't sound like her. "And I did too. But we eventually figured out the truth. Melanie is not the point, though. She let it slip that you were driving the truck the night of the wreck. And I don't know, Bram, I saw red." He shook his head like he was trying to dispel his thoughts. "You'd been drinking, I remember. And then you wrecked, and you left her in the woods in the dark, alone. I know it was a long time ago, but can you see where I'm pissed?"

I couldn't be sure he wouldn't attack me again, so I steeled myself. "I know I screwed up. I should have protected her for no other reason than that she was your sister, but I had a million reasons why I should have been better. I had already fallen for her by then, and still, I failed. A decent man wouldn't have done what I did."

Silence sucked up all the oxygen in the room.

"That's a beautiful speech, but I can't deny it fucking burns me up." Whit sat down on the edge of the sofa. I leaned against the fireplace mantle, facing him, standing still when all I wanted to do was run.

"Well, it gets worse..." I muttered, running my hand over my head. "She knew if the police came out—"

"They would know you'd been drinking. Damn." Whit ran

his hands down his face, his elbows on his knees. "You would've lost your scholarship, been kicked out of football, all of it."

I nodded. "But there's no doubt I should have stayed with her for help. I know that. I was a stupid, scared kid playing like a man. I should have realized she was hurt. I shouldn't have left even though she begged me to. I still think about it every day." I played through all the regrets in my mind once again. "It was too late when I came to my senses. I almost got back to the house, and I had the guy I called take me back to her. But the ambulance had already left."

"Then what?" Whit asked, but there was a light of caution in his eyes. He was listening, but he was guarded. I knew him well enough to know the thoughts behind that face.

I cleared my throat. "Well, I was turning myself in to the officer on site, and my father showed up. They'd called him since the truck was registered in his name. He paid them off, of course. And then he told me I only had a scholarship because he paid for one. And—"

"What? Ok, well that's bullshit," Whit interrupted, his lips pursed, his features hard. "You were the best tight end in the state, if not the eastern seaboard. He was blowing smoke up your ass, making you feel like shit under his shoe."

I shrugged. "He warned me off Julianna, too. He said if I pursued her and stayed around Grams, he'd have my scholarship revoked and make me come home. I knew if I went against him, he could find a way to ruin your career as well."

Whit looked to the side and blew out an angry breath. I knew the feeling. "My free ride, my career....So you let go of Julianna because of me? I'm one of the reasons?"

I didn't reply. He was right. That had sealed the deal in my mind. Losing Julianna was the worst part, but if I'd ruined Whit's future, I would have lost Julianna anyway. At least, I thought so at the time.

"I hated every second of what happened next," I continued. "I lied to Julianna and told her I wasn't interested in her romantically. I thought it was the right thing to do. I didn't feel good enough for her anyway. But when I told her this after Grams' funeral, she made me promise not to tell you I was driving because she feared you'd never forgive me. And I kept that promise, and I didn't tell you until now. And she knows now I was going to tell you. We talked about it. Actually, we fought about it. She was afraid."

"I can't lie, I wish you'd have told me way earlier," he replied sullenly, playing with the leg of his jeans. "She and I haven't been truly close since Grams died. But you and me? We have been. I can't believe you didn't tell me what happened this whole time."

"I wish I had told you, too. It was so fucking difficult to keep from bursting out with it sometimes. But Julianna's wishes meant everything to me." Whit looked up at me, bewildered. I continued, "I didn't want to make anything harder on you either. In our twisted ways, she and I were looking out for you." His brow furrowed, and I realized he was thinking through what I said, so I added, "Look, I don't have a pile of shit excuses. I have the truth. And the truth is I know I was wrong, and I'm a better man now." Aggravation melted from the furrow of his brow, and a calm acquiescence smoothed the hardness of his face.

"I guess I can accept that," he muttered. "Or I can try to. It was a long time ago. It might take a while to process, I guess. But you love Julianna?"

I nodded, unable to keep the grin off my face. "I do."

His crooked grin gave him a boyish look. "All these years, I thought you were being dramatic about her." We both chuckled deeply, and it felt good. I could feel the wall built between would dismantle, even as my body screamed in pain from the punch fest.

"I'm crazy about her," I confirmed, smiling like a fool, unable to hold my feelings back. "We're going to stay together. I'll always work to be better for her. You have my word as a brother to you."

He nodded definitively and stood. He moved toward me, but this time, he came to me with love and respect. I released my breath when his arms came around me in a brotherly embrace. We clapped each other's backs, leaning into the moment.

Now was the time, and I pivoted a little toward him as I spoke, low, in case Mel and Julianna were near. "I should have told you this long ago, but I owe you more than I could ever repay. You decided to be my friend when I never gave you a reason to, and I got to experience a real family when I didn't know that's what I was missing. And now I have a wife because of it. None of it would have happened if it weren't for you. How knows where I'd be, who I would be." I slapped my hand on his back. "So, thanks, man. You mean a great deal to me. Brothers for life."

He pulled back, and I was surprised to see tears spilling onto his cheeks. My own eyes were misting over, but I was saved from ugly crying when I heard the girls shuffling back toward the living room. By the time they came back through the threshold, Whit and I had gathered ourselves.

"Oh, thank goodness," Julianna murmured aloud when she saw Whit and me behaving amicably. I gently grabbed her arm and brought her to me for a quick kiss.

"I don't think I'll ever get used to seeing you two like this. It's so weird," Whit mused.

"You'll come around," Julianna offered. She turned toward her brother and threw her arms around him, and they hugged tightly. Whit's face was more relieved than I'd seen in a long while.

"I missed you," Whit whispered to her. I couldn't see

Julianna, but I heard her sniffling. Mel watched me from the doorway, and we exchanged a knowing look. We knew what it was like. Mel and I didn't know what we were missing until we found each other, but it had been worth the wait. And I hoped it was the same way for Whit and Julianna now.

Time had a funny way of bringing people together, and I knew that whatever came after this, all of us, in one way or another, would be family.

Epilogue

Bram | *April 19, 2025*

"I'm getting eaten alive!"

Julianna smacked her calves. It was spring, and mountain mosquitoes in the evenings were already becoming quite a nuisance. I was lucky and usually the last person to be bitten. My beautiful wife, however, was always the first to be bitten. She wore a knee-length, cerulean floral dress, accentuating her dark hair and porcelain skin. I couldn't blame the mosquitoes. All that exposed real estate made me want to bite her, too. She hadn't known we were coming here, but I was prepared.

I pulled out my pocket-sized insect repellent permanently attached to my work key ring in the center console of the Jeep and handed it to her. She saw the small bottle and smiled.

"I got you, always," I said with a wink, and a blush appeared on the apple of her cheeks. She walked away from the vehicle a few steps and sprayed her legs and arms while I reached into the back floorboard and pulled out the duffle bag I'd stashed earlier—something she hadn't noticed.

She looked down at it but said nothing.

We strolled hand in hand across the weathered, cracked pavement of the Mill Creek High School's auxiliary parking lot. The sun was setting, and the sky was lit up with every color, from burnt orange to lilac. No one else was at the football field, but that's how I wanted it.

I'd dreamed of this night since becoming head football coach for the Mill Creek Raptors a few months ago. I didn't know how or when I could make our fantasy a reality, but since Coach Mayfield handed me the key to the field gate and the coach's office, the only thing on my mind was getting my wife alone on this football field.

Admitting to others that I wanted to be a coach wasn't easy. The sport still brought back so many mixed feelings for me. But after Julianna and I discussed it at length, she made me realize my passion and talent for football was meant to be shared. I enjoyed teaching and mentoring. I'd already gotten together a day camp for the following year's football tryouts, and I'd somehow roped Whit into coming back to Mill Creek to assist.

It was a hopeful thing—a redemption.

Julianna had no setbacks from her surgery, but still, I held onto her like she was made of glass. She claimed to hate it, but whenever my grip on her would naturally relax, she'd lean into me more.

"What are we doing? Breaking and entering?" Her voice was teasing, but I saw a light spark in her eyes at the thought of mischief.

I smiled back at her, charmed.

"Not with a key." I held it up and slipped it into the padlock. I opened the heavy gate and let her walk in ahead of me. Then I closed it. She looked back at me over her shoulder, her smile wide, and it took my breath away.

How did I get so lucky?

"What's in the bag?" she asked, pointing to it.

"Things," I replied without elaboration, again taking her hand in mine. "Come on."

I walked her out onto the open field, the bleachers rising all around us. The bright lights weren't on, but the open area and dusk night sky were perfect for my purposes. Dim and shadowed, but with clear visibility.

I led her to the far end of the field, opposite the concessions, lockers, and coaches' offices.

"It's dark back here, and you're taking me away from the gate. Are you going to kill me?" She giggled, and I swung her around and pulled her into me, throwing the bag to the ground.

She relaxed in moments, and I couldn't keep my hands from roaming as our lips met and tongues danced. I moved her hair to the side and kissed her neck, and she let out a moan that sent me into a deeper frenzy. I grabbed her waist roughly and fisted the thin material of her dress. I tugged the garment upward until it reached her hips.

"Wait," she said, pulling me off her a smidge to look me in the face. "We can't. Cameras—"

"They are nowhere to be found back here," I finished for her. "They only face the buildings." I was being honest, as I wasn't about to share my wife with anyone. I'd pointed them out. She looked a little dubious, but she acquiesced. She stepped back into my reach and surprised me by taking the hem of her dress and pulling it up over her head in one smooth motion.

My breath caught. She was wearing a matching set of black lingerie, my favorite. She put her hand on her hip and let me look her up and down.

"Damn," I said on a breath, and I reached for her.

"Wait. What about your clothing, sir?" Her eyebrow quirked. She was getting quite good at imitating me.

"I'll keep them on for now. This is for you." I picked up the bag where it had fallen, unzipped it, and reached in, dramatically pulling out my college jersey. It had taken some digging, but I'd found it. I was hoping I still had my high school one, but I couldn't find it, so this one would have to do.

She threw her head back with laughter as I held it up for her to take in.

"Dracula, are you trying to take my virginity on the high school football field?" Her eyes sparkled so brightly in the dim evening that they looked like stars.

"Pretty sure I already took that." I smirked. "I've not seen those journal pages since you took them, but did you think I forgot about the rest of your fantasy?" I gathered the jersey at the neck. "Little did you know, it became mine too, the moment I read those words. Arms up."

She said nothing and did as I commanded. I slipped the jersey over her, guiding it to cover her body. It wasn't super long on her tall frame, and the sight of her bare thighs beckoned me to touch her. I put my hands on her hips and pulled her into me, crashing my lips into hers.

Kisses turned to grazes all over her soft body under the jersey. I teased her nipples through the sheer fabric of her black bra and let my fingers slip into the front of her lacy underwear. When I touched her hard clit, and felt the moisture between her thighs gathering, I lost my mind.

"I want to take you here, on this field," I said breathlessly, sucking on the delicate skin between her neck and shoulder until I knew it would leave marks. Her desperate moans confirmed she was enjoying the slight pinch of pain as much as I was inflicting it. "I want to think about what we've done every time we're here next season. I want this secret between us. How I fucked you—"

I didn't finish my sentence before my gorgeous wife tugged

me down to the soft grass of the sideline. And I wasted no time. She gasped when I removed her underwear, then kissed her upper thighs. She began to murmur my name as I feasted between her legs, doing all the things I knew she loved and all the things I loved doing.

She tugged on my head, removing my swollen lips from her. I looked up at her body until our eyes connected.

"I need you now," she whispered, her words barely audible.

Like a hungry lion bursting from his confinement, I pounced. I moved so quickly that I can't remember readying myself, but I remember the moment I entered her.

Heaven wasn't even the word. It was always different but always the same, like the exhale of coming home after a long day. A perfection made for only me.

I cradled her head as I moved steadily, the friction heating between us. Her nails dug half-moons into my upper arms, and I peppered her chest with open-mouthed kisses. I could feel the pressure building up in our bodies. Her mouth was parted in ecstasy, her hair cascading around her, and she looked so other-worldly in my old jersey under the dim light. It was more than I could take, and I realized it would all conclude quickly. I loathed and loved time in that moment, how it both gave me what I wanted more than anything, but also moved too swiftly to be a gift.

"Touch yourself," I said through labored breaths, unable to do it myself because I was supporting myself over her. She didn't hesitate. Her enjoyment turned into something more, ecstasy written on every movement of her face. I couldn't take my eyes off her.

"I know...it's in the...past," I panted, feeling the tightening of my impending release, "and our present...is amazing...but what I wouldn't give to go back in time...and do this...to you when you were eighteen, Julianna."

She shook her head. "This right here," she whispered with labored breaths, "is perfect."

We moved rhythmically, and she cried out my name as waves of pleasure ran over her. I couldn't hold back my praises as I spilled inside her at the same time, releasing as deep as I could manage. I wanted to be inside of her forever.

We remained motionless.

"That was incredible. Thank you," she whispered, and I kissed her.

"I'm the one who should be thanking you," I replied, sliding my hand to cup her face in my palm. "I have one more thing to give you. Well, two more things. If you're ready."

She nodded.

I slipped out of her warmth, unable to keep myself from watching my cum seep out of her and onto the football field. I'd never forget that sight, and I didn't want to.

"Use my underwear." She laughed, knowing what I was watching.

I used her underwear to clean her up as best as I could, loath to do so but knowing it would make things more comfortable for her. She sat up as I fastened my jeans. Then I reached over and picked up the bag. A smaller insulated bag contained what Kallie had called "the goods."

"Is this from Kallie's bakery?" She squealed as she snatched the bag from my hand.

"Wait, wait, wait," I chided, then gently reclaimed it from her. "Let me do this." I reached inside and lifted the covered pie tin. Her eyes went wide, but she didn't reach for it. Carefully, I balanced the tin and removed the lid, revealing the most beautiful and delicious-smelling apple pie I'd ever seen in my entire life. And, in the middle of the pie, on top of the latticework, lay the ring that Julianna deserved as my wife.

Was it obnoxiously large? No. Because that wasn't Julianna.

If she'd wanted, I'd have bought her a million-dollar set

from Cartier. But Julianna was unique and intentionally not flashy. She enjoyed creative yet practical things. I knew this and so much more about her. She'd shown me so much in the past months by being herself, and I'd taken care not to ignore one thing that made her special.

"Bram," she said, tears coming to her eyes, words catching in her throat.

I picked up the vintage-style ring from the crust, admiring the clear marquise diamond flanked by smaller diamonds. It was four carats altogether, but she didn't have to know that yet.

"This," I said, slipping it onto her finger, "is what you've always deserved. Well, you deserve more, if I'm being honest. But I hope you like this one—"

"I love it so, so much," she said earnestly, sniffing. It was an awkward and perfect response, something else so uniquely Julianna.

"I'm so thankful you're my wife," I said, wiping her tears. "And we can't forget the pie, can we?" She took her eyes off the diamond on her hand and looked at Kallie's pie.

"It's apple," she observed, puzzled. I nodded.

"I did some digging on the internet for this one. But in Celtic mythology, apples are the fruit of the Gods. They signify immorality and eternity. So, even though it may not be your favorite fruit, I wanted to make a point. As long as you keep me, I will be yours, Julianna Winchester."

She scrambled to me, pie and ring be damned, and pressed her lips to mine.

"You're forever to me, too," she promised.

We held onto each other tightly, our kisses passionate and heartfelt. Soon, however, she reached for something on the ground as my tongue was in her mouth.

"What are you—"

She pulled back and looked at me sheepishly. "This pie is

going to waste. Where are the forks? There's going to be bugs on it."

She was half-naked on a high school football field in the moonlight, and she still wanted the pie. I laughed, knowing that forever was no longer a thought, and the future looked deliciously decadent.

ACKNOWLEDGMENTS

I am so grateful for this journey.

Thank you...

To my author and friend Miranda Joy, for making me believe my words and ideas are worth sharing. This would never exist without her.

To my editor, Brittany at E&A Editing, for taking this broken manuscript of plot and characters and helping me shape it into something readable.

To author G.B. Bancroft and Ashley for taking the time to read through early drafts and give invaluable feedback.

To all my dear author friends who have answered my questions, given suggestions, encouraged me, and let me vent along the way.

To my mom, who instilled in me a love of the written word from birth.

To Travis, who has always been my unwavering support.

To all my lovely friends and family, those online and off—thank you for your continuous interest in my writing and your support of everything I do. You've filled me with confidence and gratitude every day. I love you all.

This book is nothing more or less than a personal dream realized. Thank you, reader, for participating in my dream.

About the Author

Charity is a creator of fictional worlds, relatable characters, and plots that reflect the impact of human emotion. She believes in stories that make people feel deeply and create capacity for new experiences. When not writing, you can find her drinking coffee, reading, baking, quilting, or absorbing history. She lives in beautiful southern Kentucky with her two dogs and one cat (who thinks he is a dog).

instagram.com/charitymassengale
goodreads.com/charitymassengale
threads.net/@charitymassengale

www.ingramcontent.com/pod-product-compliance
Lightning Source LLC
Chambersburg PA
CBHW031912120726

R18563100001B/R185631PG47903CBX00001B/1